HEARTSONG

JAMES WELCH is the author of four previous novels, including *Winter in the Blood* (1974) and *Fools Crow* (1986) which won the *Los Angeles Times* Book Award and the Pacific Northwest Booksellers Award. He attended schools on the Blackfoot and Fort Belknap reservations in Montana, and studied writing at the University of Montana. He lives in Missoula, Montana and is considered to be one of America's most gifted literary writers from the Native American tradition.

"One of the year's best works of fiction, a novel that is universal in its emotional and intellectual implications . . . By the last hundred pages I found myself in something like an altered state, reading as fast as I could while at the same time holding on to the hope that the book would never end." Chicago Tribune

"A stirring tale of a man's triumph over circumstances, a griping story of solid literary merit and surprising emotional clout." Publishers Weekly

"Welch has a natural story-telling ability, equally capable of fine focus and overview." The Independent

"Unbearably moving. Charging Elk is a magnificently imagined and understood character, and his soaring heartsong sounds, in its finest moments, much like an American Les Miserables.*"* Boston Globe

"Already acclaimed as a classic in the US, Welch's book looks set to become one here in the United Kingdom too." The Big Issue in the North

"This is a novel that Robert Louis Stevenson would have approved of." The Herald

"An amply rewarding read." Kirkus Review

"What James Welch has produced, ultimately, is a novel with an expansiveness of heart and mind, an intimate analogue of Indian estrangement worthy of any readerly voyage." Chicago Sun Times

"Utterly engrossing." The List

"An engaging, pointed, heartfelt examination of culture clash and the debilitating effects of otherness." San Fransisco Sunday Examiner and Chronicle

"I just finished reading Heartsong. I think Jim Welch has written a masterpiece." Leslie Marmon Silko, author of Ceremony

"This moving portrait of an Oglala Sioux . . . has a slow, brooding power that builds majestically . . . a brilliant representation of clashing cultures." Andrea Barrett, author of The Voyage of the Norwahl and Ship Fever

HEARTSONG

A Novel

JAMES WELCH

CANONGATE

First published in the UK in 2001 by Canongate Books Ltd,
14 High Street, Edinburgh EH1 1TE.

This edition published in 2002.

First published in the US in 2000 as *The Heartsong of Charging Elk* by
Doubleday, a division of Random House, Inc., New York.

1   3   5   7   9   10   8   6   4   2

British Library Cataloging-in-Publication Data
A catalogue record for this book is available on request
from the British Library

ISBN 1 84195 229 X

Book design by Chris Welch
Printed and bound in Great Britain by
Omnia Books Ltd, Glasgow
www.canongate.net

PROLOGUE

*I*t *was early in the Moon of the Shedding Ponies, less than a year after the* fight with the longknives on the Greasy Grass, and the people looked down in the valley and they saw the white man's fort and several of the women wept. The leaders were dressed up and rode ahead of the braves. The women and children and old ones followed, some walking, others riding on the bundles of lodge covers and furniture on the travois. He Dog, Big Road, Little Big Man, and Little Hawk wore their eagle-feather bonnets, their fringed buckskins, their beaded gloves and quillwork moccasins. Their gaunt faces were painted as if for war, but there was no fight left in them.

The leaders stopped on the brow of the hill and watched the two riders gallop up toward them. One was a soldier chief in a blue uniform, much like the ones the people had taken from the bodies on the hills above the Greasy Grass. A couple of the young men even now wore the faded wool tunics above their ragged leggings. It was a hot day and the tunics itched against their bare skin but it was all the finery they possessed.

The other rider was an Indian who had seen many winters, and the leaders recognized him at once. They had ridden with him when he led the campaign to close down the forts along the Medicine Trail. His name was Red Cloud and he had been a great war chief then. Now he was a reservation Indian and had been one for ten years. Now he took his orders from white chiefs, like the one beside him in the large white hat. Still, in his clean buckskins, with his headdress that flowed over his horse's rump, his thin hawkish face now lined with deep-cut crow's-feet, he looked as dignified and powerful as ever—a chief.

But the leaders did not register any recognition when the two riders slowed, then stopped less than ten feet before them. Both parties sat their horses for a moment, Red Cloud glancing beyond the leaders to the people behind. He recognized many of them, for they were Oglalas, as he was, and he had been their chief once.

Red Cloud looked back at the leaders and said each name with a small nod. Instead of a greeting, he seemed to be identifying them to the soldier chief. The soldier chief nodded at each leader's name but his face remained expressionless. Finally, Red Cloud looked into the eyes of a man who sat patiently on a small horse just behind the leaders. He was a slight man with light, almost sandy hair which was braided and wrapped in fur. A single golden eagle feather was his only headdress. His buckskin shirt was dirty and without decoration. The repeating rifle across his lap had no brass studs on the stock or feathers tied to the barrel. His eyes were fixed on the pale horizon beyond the valley.

When Red Cloud said his name, the soldier chief glanced quickly at the old chief to see if they were looking at the same person. "Crazy Horse," Red Cloud said again.

Then the leaders on both sides talked briefly, all but Crazy

Horse, who seemed to be impatient in a mild way. As they talked, a troop of mounted soldiers circled behind the band of Indians. They moved without words, but all the Indians watched them and heard the clanking of sabers and squeaking of leather, the hard plops of the shod hooves on the crumbly earth. The troop split in two, half of them taking up stations behind the Indians, the other half moving back to the horse herd.

A boy of eleven winters sat on the edge of a pony drag and watched the soldiers moving to the rear of the horse herd. It was a big herd, a thousand animals, and it took the soldiers some time. The boy watched them get smaller. Then he looked down at his younger brother and sister, who were huddled in the contours of the bundled-up lodge covering. "Don't cry," he said. "You are Oglalas. Don't cry."

Then the horse herd was moving down off the side of the hill toward a large cottonwood bottom. The soldiers drove them slowly, but some of the horses were nervous and shied and whinnied. They were not used to the smell of these white men.

The boy felt the pony drag jerk, then start to slide forward, the poles making a hissing sound as they gouged trails in the dirt. He slid off and trotted up to the side of the horse his mother rode. The horse was a big roan and it pulled the travois without effort. He looked up at his mother and he saw that her cheeks were wet. He had wanted her to lift him up behind her, but when he saw the tears, he stopped. Although the long journey from the Powder River country had been hard, he had not really thought about what it meant. Now, he understood. He understood that these *wasichus* had made his sister and brother and his mother cry. He understood that his father and the other men would not fight anymore. He understood that his people would not be allowed to go back to the buffalo ranges. They were prisoners. What he didn't know was what would become of them.

As he looked around him at the people moving forward, some riding, some walking, some young, some old, many horses of many colors, the dust kicked up by the hooves and the travois poles powdering the air, he felt very small and he wanted to cry too. And just as he had decided to let himself go, his ears picked up a strange, small sound. It came from the front of the band, from the leaders. And he recognized the sound. Soon the braves began to sing. And gradually the people around him began to sing.

He ran forward and caught up with his mother. He looked up and saw her lips moving and suddenly his heart jumped up. It was a peace song they were singing, but to the boy it sounded more like a victory song. As he walked down the hill he could feel every pebble, every clump of grass, through his thin moccasins and he could feel the hot sun on his bare shoulders, but now he was singing.

He looked down at the fort, at the log buildings, at the red and white and blue flag of America that hung listlessly from a pole, at the rows of soldiers with their rifles with steel knives tight against their shoulders, at the thousands of Indians who ringed the open field, and he wasn't afraid anymore. The Indians who awaited them were alive—and they were singing. The whole valley was alive with the peace song. It was a song the boy would not forget for the rest of his life.

CHAPTER ONE

Charging Elk opened his eyes and he saw nothing but darkness. He had been dreaming and he looked at the darkness and for a moment thought he hadn't come back. But from where? And where was he now?

He was lying on his back in the dark and he remembered that he had eaten soup twice during daylight. He had awoken and a pale woman in a white face covering had fed him soup. Then he awoke again and another woman with her face similarly covered gave him more soup. It was clear soup and it was good but he couldn't eat much of it. But the second time the woman gave him a glass of orange juice and he recognized it and drank it down. He liked the orange juice, but when he asked the woman for another glassful, she just looked at him above the face covering and shrugged her shoulders and said something in a language he didn't know. Then he fell back into sleep.

Now he propped himself up on his elbows and turned toward a

light that entered the side of his eye. From its distant yellow glow he could tell that he was in a long room. He blinked his eyes to try to see better. Where was he? And why did the women cover their faces here? Gradually, his eyes grew stronger and he saw, between his eyes and the distant light, several lumpy shapes on platforms. He heard a harsh cough on the other side of him and he fell back and slowed his breathing. When the coughing stopped he pushed the covering that lay over him to one side and looked again toward the light. And he began to remember.

He didn't remember much at first, just the two women who fed him soup. But now he remembered the room he was in. He hadn't seen much of the room because he had been on his back on one of the white men's sleeping beds. It was a big high-ceilinged room with a row of glass globes lit by yellow wires. There were high windows on the wall opposite his sleeping bed. Through one window he could see the bare limbs of a tree, but the others were full of gray sky.

He remembered waking up once sometime and a man in a white coat was bending over him, his face also covered with a mask. He was pushing something small and cold against Charging Elk's chest. He didn't look at Charging Elk but Charging Elk glanced at him for just a second and he saw pieces of silver metal disappear into the man's ears. He became afraid and closed his eyes and let the man touch his body with the cold object.

How long ago was that? Before the women fed him soup? As he looked toward the yellow glow at the far end of the room, he remembered burning up with heat, throwing off the covers, struggling to get up, feeling a sharp pain in his side, and the two or three white men who held him down. He remembered trying to bite the near one, the one with the hairy face who roared above him and struck him on the forehead. Once, he woke up and he was tied down. It was dark and he grew cold, so cold his teeth chattered and

violent spasms coursed up and down his back. He was freezing to
death, just as surely as if he had broken through the ice on a river.
He had seen the river for an instant, just a quick flash of silver in
the darkness, and it was lined with bare trees, and tan snowy hills
rose up on either side of it. But when he came up out of the river, it
was light and he was in the sleeping bed in the big room and his
back and side ached from the sharp spasms.

Charging Elk stared at the yellow light for a long time but he
could remember nothing more because he could not think. He
stared at the soft yellow light as though it were a fire he had looked
into before, somewhere else, far away.

W̲hen he awoke again he lifted his head and watched the gray
light of dawn filtering through the windows. A bird swooped down
with high-lifted wings and lit on a ledge of one of the windows and
Charging Elk recognized it. He had seen this kind of bird before.
Sometimes it walked, always with many others of its kind, on the
paths and cobblestones of the cities he had been in. When it walked
its head bobbed and it made strange lowing sounds deep in its
throat. He remembered a child chasing a band of these birds and
how quickly they flew up and flashed and circled in unison, only to
land a short distance away.

He had seen the big buildings of the cities—the houses that held
many people, the holy places with the tall towers where people
came to kneel and tell their beads, the big stores and small shops
full of curious things. He had been inside a king's stone house with
many beds and pictures and chairs made of gold. And once, in
Paris, he had accompanied a friend who had been injured badly to
a house full of many beds.

Charging Elk knew now that he was in a white man's healing
house. And he thought he must have been there for quite a long

time but he had no idea how long. Sometimes when he had awakened it had been light; other times, it had been dark. He had no idea how many sleeps he had passed there.

He was very weak—and hungry. He listened to his guts rumble and he wanted some meat and more of the orange juice. And some soup. He wanted sarvisberry soup, but he still didn't know where it had been that he had tasted this soup, or even that it was made of sarvisberries. He only knew that he wanted the taste of something familiar.

He heard a hollow clicking from a long way off, the only clear sound in an undercurrent of breathing, snoring, coughing, and moaning. As he listened to the clicking come nearer, he lifted himself up on his elbows and his body didn't seem as heavy as it had been in the dark.

The young woman glanced toward him, then stopped. Unlike the food women, she wore a stiff white cap with wings and an apron that came up over her shoulders. Beneath the apron, she had on a long gray dress with narrow sleeves. A flat gold cross hung from a chain around her neck. Charging Elk had seen this type of cross on other people and he almost knew where. He became interested in her.

"Bonjour, monsieur," she said, coming to stand at the side of his bed. He recognized the greeting but not the rest of the words she spoke as she reached behind him to slap his pillow. She helped him to move his body back against the pillow so he was almost sitting up. A sharp pain stabbed his side, then eased to a hard ache. She said more words to him and he saw that her eyes were blue and the hair that was swept up under the cap was the color of ocher.

She made a gesture, clenching her hand like a claw and bringing it to her face mask. She repeated it a couple of times until he understood. He nodded rapidly as he had seen the white men do. Then she went away.

From his sitting position he could see better. He could see a building out the window and its wall was golden. Above, he could see that the sky was turning from gray to blue. The bird that bobbed its head when it walked was gone. He looked around the room and he could see many beds lined up against both walls, and many bodies. Some were sitting up like him; others were sleeping under blankets on the beds. He could smell the damp, ashy odor of the bodies mixed with the sharp smell of *wasicun* medicine. They were all men, all white men. They too were in this house of sickness. But where was this house?

The woman came back, carrying a glass of orange juice on a round tray. As he drank it down, he noticed crinkles in the corners of the woman's eyes and he thought she might be smiling behind the face covering. He put the glass back on the tray, then pursed his fingers together and pointed them toward his mouth. The woman's brows came down. He repeated the gesture and the brows shot up. She leaned forward and showed him a little timepiece pinned to her apron. She pointed to the timepiece and said something and he nodded. He knew about the *wasichu's* timepiece. He pointed to his mouth again and the woman said, *"Oui, oui,"* then left.

Charging Elk leaned against his pillow and waited for his food. He watched one of the men opposite him throw back the covers, sit up, and swing his legs over the side of the bed. He sat like that for a moment. His face was stubbly, not exactly a beard, but the black stubble made his face look as white as the wall behind him. The man stood, holding himself up by the iron headboard. He reached for a robe that was hanging from a hook on the wall. Charging Elk looked behind him to the side and he saw a similar garment by his own headboard. As he watched the man slip his bare feet into a pair of soft shoes, he wondered if he had some of those too.

The man wandered off down the length of the room away from the place of the yellow light, stopping now and then to rest against a footboard. Then he pushed open a swinging door and disappeared.

Charging Elk began to have hope. He too could put on these things and walk out. He would eat something first, to give him strength, then he would leave. But as he thought this, he felt a slow, crushing fear enter his heart. Where would he go? He looked at his dark hands, which lay on the blanket on either side of his body. He was not of these people. He was a different color and he couldn't speak their tongue. He was from somewhere a long way off. And he was here, alone, in this house of sickness. He tried to fight off the panic by remembering something about himself. He remembered night and he remembered bright lights and the sound of a voice loud and clear over many voices. When the big voice spoke the other voices grew to a roar, until the lights began to swim and he was falling suddenly and violently into darkness.

⬧

"Monsieur? Monsieur?"

Charging Elk opened his eyes.

"Votre petit déjeuner, monsieur."

A young woman put a square tray on his lap. He glanced down and he saw a bowl of white mush, a piece of hard morning bread, and a glass of orange juice. The woman put a soft cloth over his chest, sat down on a stool beside the bed, then dipped a spoon into the mush. When she brought it toward his face, he moved his hand up to block it. She said something in a tone of voice that suggested she was used to this kind of behavior. Charging Elk kept his hand up but he looked at her pale hand and peculiar ice-green eyes and recognized her, in spite of her mask, as the first woman who had fed him soup. Now she held the spoon about six inches from his hand. He reached for the spoon and took it gently from her hand. He looked at the mush, smelled it, then took a taste. It tasted like nothing. It was neither sweet nor spicy. But it slid down his throat and warmed his belly. He had another spoonful and nodded to the woman. *"Café,"* he said.

"Non, non, monsieur," she said in an excited voice. She said something else, then she rubbed her own belly and shook her finger.

"Café," he said again.

She said something, then stopped. After a moment, she stood and hurried toward the end of the room where the yellow light had been the night before. Charging Elk watched her. Then he dipped the heavy iron spoon into the mush and ate. He ate half the mush and drank his orange juice. He left the hard bread—he had seen it before, a small slice curved on top and flat on the bottom, like the sign for sunrise—to dunk into his *pejuta sapa*, black medicine.

He thought of sunrise in another place. A place of long views, of pale dust and short grass, of few people and no buildings. He had seen that sunrise over the rolling simple plains, he had been a part of it and it had been a part of him. Many times he had seen it and he had been with his people.

Charging Elk suddenly moaned as he remembered the *ikce wicasa*, the natural humans, as his people called themselves. He remembered his mother and father, his brother and sister. He remembered the villages, the encampments, one place, then another. Women picking berries, men coming back with meat, the dogs and horses, the sudden laughter or tears of children, the quiet ease of lying in the sunny lodge with the skins rolled up to catch a breeze. He had been a child then too and he had spent his days riding his horse, playing games, shooting arrows at gophers, eating the sarvisberry soup that his mother made.

He remembered the big fight with the longknives on the Greasy Grass, the naked white bodies the women counted coup on with their butcher knives and axes. He and two of his friends, Liver and Strikes Plenty, had fought over a soldier's agate ring. They had cut off his finger to get it. But one of the older boys, Yellow Hand, had taken it away from them.

Charging Elk lay back on the pillow and closed his eyes. He had been proud to be an Oglala then and he thought they would never surrender. The young boys talked about Crazy Horse and how he would lead them far away from the longknives. They would grow up to be hunters and to make war on their enemies. They would kill off the soldiers when they got old enough. Meanwhile the people spent the summer and fall moving from place to place, at first high up in the Bighorns and the Wolfs, then when the weather changed and the snows capped the peaks they moved back onto the plains. Sometimes they would camp for six or seven sleeps, some- times only one or two. The scouts kept track of the longknives and they were never far away. But the game was plentiful during those warm times and the people didn't suffer. Wakan Tanka, the Great Mystery, rode with them. The Oglalas seemed almost exhilarated, as though they knew this was to be their last time together as a free people and they were determined to make the most of it. They had won a great victory and they were prepared to face the conse- quences, even if death came to live with them. Charging Elk, in spite of his youth, felt this spirit and had never been so close to his family, his people, the land. He hung on to every experience, every change of country, every night under the stars or in his father's lodge.

But when the weather changed, everything changed. The buf- falo seemed to disappear soon after the first snowfall, the deer and elk, even the rabbits and prairie hens, grew scarce, and the winds blew bitterly and constantly. Many of the people grew sick, some died, and they became frightened of what lay ahead. When the sol- diers finally caught up with Crazy Horse's band on the Powder River that winter, the people escaped into a blizzard with few ca- sualties but the sentiment around the meager fires now was more about coming in to the fort on the White Earth River rather than remaining free, which amounted to running and running. But Crazy Horse refused to listen to this talk. He began to spend more time away from the camp, riding off by himself into the surrounding hills—some said he was searching for a vision that would save the people; others thought he didn't like to be around their suffering. Charging Elk's own father said that Crazy Horse was too stubborn to be a good leader, that he put his own pride before the welfare of the people. Still, Charging Elk and his friends vowed to follow Crazy Horse, even to death if he wanted it that way. Like most of the young ones, they idolized Crazy Horse and thought he could bring forth a miracle when spring came. He would lead them somehow to a land where there were no white people, a land filled with blackhorns and berries and good water. There would be plenty of enemy horses to be taken, many enemies to be struck.

But that spring Crazy Horse led the weary, ragged people to Fort Robinson and Red Cloud Agency. They surrendered their horses and weapons, everything but their garments, cooking utensils, and lodges. The piece of paper that the leaders marked was dated May 6, 1877. Four months later, in the Moon of the Black Calf, Crazy Horse was killed by the soldiers with the help of some of his own people.

Charging Elk sighed and opened his eyes. The tray and the woman were gone, but two men in suits stood at the foot of the bed, looking at him.

"*Bonjour,*" said one of them.

"Hello," said the other.

Charging Elk recognized both greetings but he said nothing.

The one who had said hello said, "Charging Elk?"

Charging Elk considered a moment. He knew it would be futile but he asked how long he had been in the sickhouse. Both men just exchanged glances. The one who had said hello was dressed in a bulky brown suit. He had a mustache that curled down around the s of his mouth. The other wore a dark neat suit. His tie was knotted between the collar points.

an you speak English? American?" The man in the brown suit leaned closer, and said again, in a loud voice, "American? Do you speak American?"

Charging Elk gestured toward himself with his hand. "American. Lakota." As he thought of something else to say, he remembered how he had gotten there. "Pahuska. Buffalo Bill." Then he remembered the Lakota who had been appointed the chief of the show Indians. He had no power over the Indians—only the white bosses did—but the *wasicuns*, the fat takers, liked him because he was very handsome and his buckskins were heavy with beadwork. Surely these men would know him. "Rocky Bear," he said. "Big medicine. Oglala. Wild West."

"Buffalo Bill, yes. But you are Charging Elk." The man spoke slowly and loudly.

"Charging Elk. Yah." But it was becoming clear that he would not be able to communicate with these men, even though he knew of their languages. He could do nothing but look at their suits, even though his eyes took in their somber faces.

After Crazy Horse's death, the Oglalas were taken from the Red Cloud Agency to their own agency at Pine Ridge. The children were put into the white man's school, and so Charging Elk became a student and learned some of the American words. But less than a year later, when he was thirteen winters, he and Strikes Plenty ran away and went to live with Strikes Plenty's people at the Whirlwind Compound, far from the agency and the school. Later they would move again, when the *wasichus* threatened to come get them, along with the other children. They moved to a place in the badlands called the Stronghold, a long tall grassy butte with sheer cliffs on three sides that could be easily defended. But the white men, soldiers and settlers alike, were afraid of the Stronghold. The

Indians out there were considered bad Indians, even by their own people who had settled at the agency and the surrounding communities. Charging Elk and Strikes Plenty lived off and on at the Stronghold for the next nine years, hunting game, exploring, learning and continuing the old ways with the help of two old medicine people. Sometimes they rode into the Black Hills, Paha Sapa, and stole things from the gold miners. They visited Bear Butte, a lone cone-shaped holy hill where many Oglalas had sought their visions in the past but which was now surrounded by settlers and mining claims. Charging Elk had had his *hanblechia* in the badlands surrounding the Stronghold. He had been prepared well by his *wicasa wakan*, an old man who made many prayers in the sweat lodge, and when he turned sixteen he went out and made many prayers to Wakan Tanka to help him dream his power animal. He never told anyone what the animal was, not even Strikes Plenty, but he later killed a badger and made a small necklace of its claws.

Now Charging Elk tried to ask the two men what happened to the necklace, and he suddenly remembered the holy card the white woman had given him in Paris, which became his *wasichu* medicine, but he knew it was impossible. For the first time in his life, he wished he had stayed in school and learned the brown suit's language. "Buffalo Bill," he said, without hope. "Wild West."

After the two men left, Charging Elk sank down into himself. He was alone, and the enormity of what that meant hit him hard. He had no friends here. He couldn't tell the men in suits where his home was. But they had to know that he was an Indian and he came from across the big water as part of the Wild West show. He was an Indian, an Oglala from Pine Ridge, his home.

Even in his despair, Charging Elk found his mind clearing and he remembered more things. It was like waking up after a night of drinking *mni wakan,* the white man's holy water, but this night seemed to have lasted a long time.

Charging Elk almost felt the impact again as he remembered falling from his horse and landing on the packed earth. That was the last thing he remembered before he was brought to this healing house. He had been chasing the small buffalo herd around the arena with his friends, an act he had performed hundreds of times since coming to this country of the Frenchmen. They liked to see the wild Indians chase the buffalo because it was one of the few acts in the show that was dangerous. And the Indians themselves made it more dangerous by eventually catching up and riding at headlong speed among the thundering animals. Charging Elk remembered a young bull, one that he had become familiar with in the several moons they had performed in the big Paris arena, suddenly swerve and swing its head. Its horn caught the horse on the left shoulder and the horse squealed and almost went down and Charging Elk tumbled past its head. And that was all he remembered until he got to the sickhouse.

But he had been sick before the evening's performance and he became more ill during the course of the several acts. The night chill of December went right into his bones and his back was so tight it felt like someone had strapped a lodgepole to it. But he had performed the several acts before the chase—burning the settler's cabin, chasing the Deadwood stage, fighting with the soldiers in the big show of Custer's Last Fight. But as he waited behind a barrier for the buffalo to be released, he suddenly felt very weak and almost fell from his horse as he leaned over and vomited. He knew then that he had the sickness that had swept through the Indian camp as well as the village of the white performers and workers. Badface had eased his horse next to Charging Elk's and he asked if Charging Elk was all right, but just then the gateman pulled back the barricade and the Indians leaped forward, digging their heels into their horses' flanks, yipping and yelling to the roar of the crowd.

But there was another Oglala in the sickhouse when Charging Elk arrived. As the helpers were lifting him into the bed, he had a sudden moment of intense pain which cleared his head and he saw a friend in the next bed. It was Featherman, an Oglala who had three winters on Charging Elk and who had caught the sickness two sleeps ago and now was quiet and unmoving as his eyes followed the activity of the helpers as they lifted Charging Elk from a rolling bed. The eyes seemed not to know what they saw.

Even as the pain of movement was subsiding into a deep ache, Charging Elk had looked over at Featherman and seen that his friend was going away. "Featherman," he whispered as he looked into the flat eyes. "Stay. Don't leave me." But he could not hear his own words and soon he too was gone.

But Charging Elk did come back, several times, and now he knew he was back to stay. He knew he was back by the heavy throbbing pain in his left side. Now he felt that side, those ribs, through the bandage that had been wrapped around his torso. His breath wasn't so shallow now, even though the bandage was tight against his chest. He had broken some ribs before in another fall from his horse. That time had been in the badlands, a hot summer day, when his running horse had stepped in a badger hole. He and Strikes Plenty were heading for the Stronghold after some trouble with the miners in Paha Sapa. Sometimes the miners shot at them, either to keep them away or just to kill them. Charging Elk had been laid up for a few days with those broken ribs but they healed up, with the aid of the *yuwipi*'s medicine, and he soon was out riding again. Sometimes he and Strikes Plenty sneaked back to Pine Ridge

Agency to visit his parents. They would make the two-day ride and wait for dark before entering the small settlement.

And always it was the same. His parents would try to talk him into staying. They told him there would be no punishment, that the white chief just wanted the young ones to come back and stay, go to school and learn the ways of the white god. They lived in a one-room house with a door and two windows, neither of which contained glass. Squares of canvas were tacked to the top of the windows and rolled up to let in light. They had a table and two chairs and a white man's sleeping bed. And a cross on the wall beside the cooking stove. But no children. Charging Elk's brother and sister had died, a year apart, one of the great cough, the other of consumption.

Charging Elk loved his mother and could understand why she wanted him to come live with them and go to school and to holy ceremonies. He was all she had left. Sometimes he felt guilty and thought how it would be to eat her food and watch her do her quill-work. But he couldn't figure out his father. Scrub had been a shirtwearer, one of the bravest and wisest of the Oglalas. He had fought hard at Little Bighorn and had provided meat when the people were running from the soldiers. But that winter when the people were starving and sick, he had become a peacemaker, just like the reservation Indians who were sent out by their white bosses to try to talk the band into surrendering. Charging Elk had been ashamed of his father that winter. And when he saw his father sitting idly in his little shack, drinking the black medicine and sometimes telling the holy beads, he could not believe his father had gone from shirtwearer to this. It was always this image of his father that drove Charging Elk time and time again back out to the Stronghold.

Charging Elk had to take a leak and he did not want the iron pissholder. It shamed him to have one of the healing helpers roll him onto his side so he could hit the slop pan. And it was hard to piss with the helper standing there, looking away but listening. He didn't like their face coverings. Although he had become adept at looking at their eyes without them seeing, he couldn't tell the hidden expressions and this troubled him. Furthermore, he hadn't taken a crap since coming to the sickhouse but he still didn't need to and this worried him.

He pulled himself higher in his bed until he was sitting up without the aid of the pillow. His ribs ached and the bandage seemed even tighter against his chest, but the pain was bearable and he could breathe a little deeper. He watched another man get out of bed, put his robe on, and walk down the corridor between beds. He too disappeared through the swinging door at the end of the room.

Charging Elk threw back the covers and tried to swing his legs over the side of the bed. It was the first real bed he had slept in in his life. Even in France, the Indians slept in blankets and robes in their lodges. Charging Elk and his friends used to make fun of the soft white men who needed to sleep in feathers on a platform of wood or iron. Now, Charging Elk couldn't make his legs obey him. He pursed his lips into a straight seam, put his arm under one knee, and pulled it sideways. A sharp pain in his side made him inhale sharply, deeply, almost a cry, but he kept his lips tight. He lay back on his elbows and worked his legs one way, his upper body the other, until he could feel the cold floor with one foot. He stopped, panting, and looked around, but nobody seemed to pay attention. He worked his other leg over the side and, with a sharp intake of breath, he slung himself up, until he was sitting on the edge of the bed. The pain in his ribs was intense, his whole side seemed on fire, but he held himself rigid, eyes and lips closed tightly, trying to concentrate on staying conscious. Then he opened his eyes and looked down to the other end of the room, where at night he saw the yellow light. He expected someone, maybe the woman with the white wings and gold cross, to come running. But again, he was undiscovered.

He stood slowly, awkwardly, using his hands to push himself up from the bed. He leaned against the bedframe for a moment, then drew himself up to his full height, aware of the stiffness in his back. His legs were heavy and his head felt light, but he could breathe easier and his ribs didn't hurt so much. He knew he would have to move soon, before one of the healing helpers spotted him.

He took the robe from its hook and wrapped it over his shoulders. He was wearing a thin gown and the heavy robe felt good on him. He glanced down and saw the shoes tucked under the bed. He slid into them and they felt stiff and fuzzy, but warm. He slowly turned and began to make his way down to the foot of the bed, where he grasped the footboard and looked up and down the long room.

He was surprised to see so many beds, maybe a hundred of them, virtually all of them occupied. As he surveyed the room, he suddenly remembered Featherman. The night he had come to the sickhouse, Featherman had been in the next bed. Now there was a *wasichu* with a waxy face and thick sandy hair in the bed. But where was Featherman? Had he really been there? Or had he been a dream? Charging Elk's heart fell down as he remembered the dull, flat eyes. Yes, he had been there. And now he was dead. But perhaps there were other Buffalo Bill Indians in the other beds. His heart lifted again and he thought he might shout "All my relatives!" in Lakota, but he knew the healing helpers would come running if he did. So he began the slow journey down the aisle between beds, moving from one iron footboard to the next. Each time he stopped to rest he would glance at the faces in the beds. Most of them had beards or mustaches, all of them were pale. Some of the faces watched him with great curiosity, perhaps even apprehension. By the time he reached the end of the beds, his heart was as heavy as his legs.

The thin hope that someone from the Wild West show, perhaps the interpreter, Broncho Billy, along with a couple of white chiefs, or even one or two of his Oglala friends, would come and take him away with them was a flickering, surely impossible dream. He knew that the show was only scheduled to be here in this town for eight or nine sleeps before moving on to another land. He felt certain that those sleeps were gone and he had been abandoned. He almost collapsed from the weight of such a thought and he thought how foolish he was to want to travel with Buffalo Bill. He should have stayed at the Stronghold, in the badlands, where he knew his way around. He thought of those sunny hot days with Strikes Plenty, riding to who knows where, but free to go. Not like the reservation Indians. They had laughed and mocked those Indians who had given up and lived in the wooden houses at the agency, collecting their meager commodities, their spoiled meat, learning to worship the white man's god, learning to talk the strange tongue. Now he would have given all his good times, all his freedom, to be one of them, home in the little shack with his mother and father in the village of his people.

Two nights later, Charging Elk sat up in his bed, alert and considerably stronger. He looked down at the yellow light and could just make out the shape of a human being. He had explored that part of the long room that afternoon and knew that there was a smaller room with a cage for a window and a door that they kept closed. Here the healing helpers sat, smoking, talking, making marks on their paper. They were very comfortable in this room, but he noticed that they became quiet and attentive when one of the women with the white wings came among them. These women seemed to be *yuwipis*, but even they became obedient when the man with the steel in his ears was around. He was the real *wicasa wakan*.

But he was never around at night, only one or two helpers. And they never left the caged room unless one of the sick ones cried out in pain or panic, which happened often. Charging Elk had kept awake most of the night before, watching their routine, but there didn't seem to be a routine, just the response to a sudden commotion.

Charging Elk had also scouted the big hall outside the sickroom that afternoon. The toilet room was on the other side. After he took a long painful shit, his first in many days, he wandered down the hall toward a large window at the end. If the helpers caught him, he would pretend that he was lost. But his eyes were as sharp as a horsetaker's in an enemy camp. He noticed the doors that led off the hall, some of them closed, others open. One room in particular interested him. It was a long narrow room, darkly lit by a single yellow wire, and it was filled with hanging clothes.

At the window, the hall turned in opposite directions. One way was long and looked exactly like the hall he had come down. The other way was short and led to a pair of swinging doors that went from the floor to the ceiling. Each door had a small window. Charging Elk walked quickly toward the doors. He stopped and touched one of them. It moved slightly. Then he looked through the window.

It was a large room. Unlike the sickroom, it was as wide as it was long and it was filled with soft chairs and soft longseats. A few people sat on this furniture, some reading, some talking, some just looking off into the distance. To the right, Charging Elk could see a long wooden platform, about waist-high. He could see two heads behind the platform, but they were bent over, looking at something behind the platform. Neither of the women had white wings on her head but they seemed to be of higher station than the helpers.

No one had indicated to Charging Elk that he was a prisoner in the sickhouse, but he knew if the women saw him they would call for the helpers. And if he protested, they would strap him down again. No, he had to be cunning and wait for his opportunity. These people who didn't know him, who gave him the orange juice, the food, and lately the coffee, would become his enemies if they knew he wanted to escape.

Charging Elk looked again across the room and he saw large windows and beyond them trees, a road, and a building across the way. He saw horse-drawn carriages and men pulling high-wheeled carts. He saw women in their strange dresses with the big butts. Then he saw an omnibus go by, with its two levels of passengers, and he remembered that he and some of the other Indians had ridden in such a wagon before, when the interpreters took them on the rare tour, first in Paris, then once in this city. He remembered that they had been afraid to ride on top, out in the open, exposed to danger. But after they became used to these high wagons, they never rode inside. Featherman had liked to ride in front, just behind the driver. He liked the smell of the big horses. He would make jokes about the driver in his high hat and wave at the women with big butts and feathers on their heads. He made the others lighthearted, and sometimes they would all wave, or whoop, at a pretty woman or a cart full of meat. There was never enough meat. But the young Indians enjoyed the spectacle of themselves reflected in the astonished eyes of the French people.

Charging Elk returned his gaze to the room and he saw instantly what he had been looking for. Past the wooden platform, at the far end of the room, were two large glass doors which let out onto the cobblestone walking path. Even as he watched, an old one was being helped inside by two women. He had a white beard and a small black cap on his head. One of the women held a cloth to his mouth.

Late that night, two of the men helpers came into the dark room, pushing one of the wheeled beds. They were very quiet as they passed Charging Elk's bed. They stopped three or four beds away and turned the platform so that it came to rest between two beds. Then they made small whispering noises, a bed squeaked, and something made a heavy thump. Then the platform rolled down the aisle in the opposite direction, toward the yellow-lit room.

Charging Elk could just make out the body beneath the white cloth. One of the helpers, a fat one, was breathing hard and grumbling in the French tongue. The other one was tall and thin and bent over the platform, pushing it slowly and quietly, indifferent to the fat one's complaints.

As Charging Elk watched the strange procession make its way to the yellow-lit room, he felt his whole body shiver, as though he had once again pulled himself out of the icy river in his country. For the past two sleeps, he had again harbored a desperate hope that someone from the show would come and get him; or that the two men, the American and the Frenchman, would take him home across the big water. But now, seeing the dead body spooked him and he thought that he would get sick again, that this healing house was really a deathhouse, and the only way he would leave it would be on a rolling platform covered with a white cloth.

He thought of poor wretched Featherman. To die here alone! What would happen to his *nagi*, his spirit? How would it find its way to the other side, to the real world beyond this one? And what about himself? His own *nagi* would run restless over the land here, far from his people, far from the real world. He could not stay here, waiting to die. He would not wait. With the help of Wakan Tanka, he would find his own way home.

As Charging Elk threw on his robe and slipped his feet into the fuzzy shoes, the thought struck him that the Wild West show was still on this side of the big water. They were going to tour all winter and summer, even until next winter—that's what the white bosses told him when he drew his name on the paper back at Pine Ridge. Maybe they weren't so far away. Maybe they would come back for him. If he left this sickhouse, how would they find him?

He sat down on the edge of the bed. His ribs didn't hurt so much now. He took a deep breath, then sighed, caught somewhere between hope and despair. He thought of his mother and father and their little shack; he thought of his dear friend Strikes Plenty, and their wanderings in Paha Sapa; and he thought of the old *wicasa wakan* at the Stronghold, who had prepared him so well for his *hanblechia*. He trembled to think that he had lost possession of his badger-claw necklace, his war medicine. He had no power. But that wasn't true—he had his death song. If he sang it well at the proper time, there was a chance that his spirit would make it to the other side, even if he didn't.

Charging Elk stood and looked down toward the room with the yellow light. He had made his decision. He wouldn't stay in this deathhouse one more sleep. As he walked silently between the rows of beds in the other direction, he felt alert and expectant.

He crept down the dim hall to the room with the clothes, flattening himself into doorways, looking, listening, but he saw and heard nothing. He began to feel lucky, just as he had that night he and Strikes Plenty had sneaked into the gold miners' tent while they slept and stolen their rifles, a box of bullets, and their work boots. Charging Elk smiled in the dim light, and it was his first smile in many sleeps. He smiled to remember that several miles away they had thrown the boots into a ravine. They had laughed to think of the miners waking up and trying to find those boots. Then discovering that their rifles were also missing.

Charging Elk wished that Strikes Plenty were with him now.

Together, they would know how to get back to their country.
Strikes Plenty was good at finding his way home to the Stronghold.

The door to the clothes room was closed, and Charging Elk's
heart fell down for a moment. He knew that the white people liked
to keep things locked up, that they stole from each other whether
they were enemies or not. He was almost resigned to returning to
his bed but he grasped the knob and turned it and his luck held.
The door swung open with a soft creak. Charging Elk quickly
slipped inside the room and fastened the door behind him. The click
sounded very loud to him.

The room was pitch-black and Charging Elk stood for a moment, not breathing but listening. The shoes these *wasichus* wore
made loud noises and you could hear them from a long way off. But
he heard nothing and as he stared into the darkness, he wondered
how the white men made the yellow wires glow. He felt to one side
of him and grabbed a heavy cloth object. It was hanging from one
of the sloped wires that they used for coats. It was a coat. Charging
Elk shrugged out of his robe and put the coat on. But the shoulders
were too small and his arms stuck out of the sleeves.

Charging Elk was a big man, one or two inches over six feet. He
and the other Oglalas had towered over the small people of this
city. The people here were shorter than the ones in Paris — and
darker. Rocky Bear, who had toured much with Buffalo Bill and
considered himself plenty savvy, said these people came from a jun-
gle in another land. The people in Paris and New York and another
city he had been to, London, were the true *wasicuns*.

Charging Elk finally found a coat that would almost fit him —
roomy enough in the shoulders and the sleeves only a little short. It
was a heavy coat, and he was grateful as he remembered how cold
it had been that night in the arena when he had gotten sick.

He moved deeper into the room but now he couldn't see a thing.
He walked back to the door and, after listening for a moment,

opened it a crack and let the dull glow from the hall in. Then he moved back, brushing his fingers along the coats, until he found a series of shelves. And here he found the other things he was looking for. He tried on four of the white men's trousers until he found a pair that again almost fit him. They were a little loose, so he took the cord from the robe and tied it around his middle. He searched for the other things that the *wasicuns* wore — the shirts and shoes — but all he found was a round brimless hat. He was grateful for it, because he had been thinking that his long hair, which was now loose, would attract attention when he got outside. Now he tucked his hair as best as he could under the soft hat until it bloomed like a black bladder on his head.

He was ready. He had no shirt, but the striped gown, tucked into the pants, looked almost presentable. He would have to make do with the fuzzy slippers on his bare feet.

Charging Elk's escape was surprisingly easy. At that hour, the big room was empty, save for one couple and a woman. The couple were staring out the window at the dark street and the woman had her head down, asleep. A basket lay on the soft seat beside her, and she held two needles. Charging Elk had seen women in Paris making thick cloth with the two needles as they sat in cafés or parks.

There was only one head behind the tall platform and it was bent over. A light came from somewhere behind the platform. Charging Elk crouched and sneaked close beneath the lip of the platform. He could tell that the head was that of a woman by the smell. Once past the platform, he turned a corner, stood tall, and walked quickly out of the deathhouse into the cold night.

As he gulped in the sharp air, he looked up and down the street and, for the first time in a long time, he wanted a smoke.

CHAPTER TWO

Charging Elk spent his first night of freedom in a narrow alley behind a bread bakery that fronted on the street two blocks from the sickhouse. The smell of the baking bread made him hungry, and he remembered those times in Paris when he and some of his friends would go to such a house to buy the puffy things filled with fruit or chocolate. *Boulangerie.* It was one of the words he recognized. And *charcuterie*, where they would buy sticks of greasy meat. *Brasserie* and *café*. The interpreters always named things.

He had found a place near the building where the warm air came out to the alley through a wooden grate. He had to be careful because there was a small door that was open, in spite of the December cold. Once he saw a cigarette arc out of the doorway and land, a small orange glow, on the rough cobblestones. By the time he thought it was safe to retrieve it, the fire was gone. It was still night, but Charging Elk could sense, more than see, a slight lightening in the sky above the alley.

He wasn't as strong as he'd thought he was. Only two blocks from the sickhouse, his ribs hurt so bad he thought he would collapse if he didn't lean against a building. It was while he was recovering his breath, breathing so shallowly he thought he might pass out from lack of air, that he had spied the alley beside the *boulangerie*. As he crossed the street, he could see a man in a white cap carrying a tray of small breads to the glass case and he wondered how he could get one of the breads.

He had no white man coins. Centimes. During the good days in Paris, he almost always had centimes. Although Buffalo Bill sent most of his money to his parents, he got a handful of centimes every other week. Also, some paper money. Frogskins they were called in America. Here the paper money was of many different colors and sizes and was called francs. Charging Elk got five francs when he and some of the others on their days off were taken to look at the sights of Paris. Once they looked at statues or pictures in a long house of wood floors and stone stairs; once they went to a showhouse and listened to a lady with large breasts sing high and big; another time, on a hot day, they went into a house of many prayers and sat in the cool gloom while the interpreter, who spoke French and a funny kind of American, told Broncho Billy, who spoke American and Oglala, what it was they were seeing. Charging Elk and the others listened patiently but he didn't remember much in particular—just that the church belonged to a virgin mother. Sees Twice, a reservation Indian who had become a believer in the white man's god, tried to make them believe that a virgin could become a mother, and in fact was the mother of their savior, whose father was much bigger than Wakan Tanka. Nobody believed him, but when he dipped his fingers in the holy water and crossed his chest in four directions, they did it too. Featherman tasted his fingers to see if the holy water was really *mni wakan*. The others laughed at his joke.

Charging Elk opened his eyes and it was lighter. He didn't know if he had fallen asleep or had just quit thinking. He was sitting on a piece of heavy paper he had found, but now his whole body was stiff with cold. The wall behind his back was cold and the warm air of the bakery didn't seem to be enough. He could smell the bread, the heavy sweet smell, as intense as dewy sagebrush in the morning when the sun first strikes it. Charging Elk liked to go out behind the lodges then and take a piss and listen to the yellowbreasts tune up for the day. He became good at imitating their clear trilling song. On these mornings he would whistle and one of them would answer, then another. The sun burning the dew off the sagebrush made him light-headed with the sharp sweet odor and he thanked Wakan Tanka for giving him another gift.

He had been a child then, nine or ten winters, and his people were on the run but free. Now he was twenty-three and lost in a big white man's town. For a moment or two he pitied himself, but the smell of the bread was making his guts rumble and he knew he would have to do something about it.

Just a few days ago, he had been part of Buffalo Bill's Wild West show and he had had plenty of centimes in his new purse, enough to buy coffee and chocolate bread and ice cream, and on the sly, *mni ʃha*, the forbidden wine. When he and the others walked down a street in their blue wool leggings and fancy shirts and blankets, with their earrings and feathers and brass armbands, the French would stop and stare. Sometimes they would clap their hands and cheer, just like the audiences in the arenas. But the Oglalas would walk by as though they were alone in their own world. Only Featherman would smile and wave. He was never sick for home. More than once he said that if he found the right woman who would take care of him, he would stay. There was nothing left at home. The American bosses were making the *ikce wicasa* plant potatoes and corn. What kind of life was that for the people who ran the buffaloes?

Now Featherman was dead. He had no woman but he got to stay here. And his *nagi* would never go home to be with the long-ago people. Charging Elk felt a sharp shiver go up his back and he knew he would have to stand up. As he contemplated his move, he wondered if he could find Featherman. In Paris, he and the others had toured a big stone field where the white men buried each other in the ground. If he could find Featherman's stone, maybe he could perform a ceremony, just as he had seen the *wicasa wakan* do many times at the Stronghold, to release his friend's spirit. The thought brightened him for an instant, until he remembered how many stones there were in such fields.

Charging Elk steadied himself against the wall, rolling his shoulders and flexing his knees. He was too cold to feel the pain in his ribs. He had thought earlier, after his escape from the sickhouse, that he should undo the tight cloth around his abdomen, but he hadn't, and now he was grateful for the skimpy layer. But the coat was good and heavy and he soon felt a little warmer. He pulled the lapels closer under his chin and looked at the yellow light coming from the open side door. The smell of the bread made him weak and he knew he would have to try for some or he might go hungry all day.

Just as he took a step toward the door, he heard the clop-clop-clop of a horse's hooves against the cobblestones of the street. He flattened himself against the wall and listened to the clop-clop-clop come closer. Then he saw the horse. It was pulling a wagon filled with something under a bulky covering. A man sat bundled up in the seat, holding the reins, a pipe between his teeth. As Charging Elk watched the wagon disappear beyond the alleyway, he smelled something sharp and unpleasant. It was a smell he recognized. The smell of the sea.

But now he knew it was light enough for anyone coming by to see him, so he eased himself toward the door. He held his breath, alert and unafraid. He glanced quickly around the corner and he saw a woman bent over a table. She was rubbing some raw bread into a long shape. As he stood against the wall, he thought of what else he had seen. Two heavy black ovens in the wall, a sink, another table, three or four long baskets. Then he heard a voice, a man's voice. The woman said something and the voice answered, then it was quiet. Charging Elk peeked around the corner again. And he focused on the baskets. There were three of them and they were filled with the longbread. He knew this bread. Sometimes he and his friends would eat at the big grub tent at the Buffalo Bill compound in the Bois de Boulogne and they would have this longbread. It was crackly and soft at the same time and it was good to dunk into their *pejuta sapa* in the morning.

The woman was of middle age and small. Her sleeves were rolled up and her arms were strong and wiry. Her hair was tucked up under a white cap and she wore a white apron. She was standing sideways to the door and Charging Elk knew that she would see him right away if he tried to sneak behind her. He thought of just running in, and if necessary, throwing her aside and grabbing a longbread. But he knew he couldn't run in, much less run away, and they would catch him and take him back to the sickhouse, or worse, the iron house, where they kept the bad ones.

Just as Charging Elk thought of getting away from there, he heard the man's voice calling from another place. He heard the woman answer and she sounded annoyed. He peeked again and he saw the woman wiping her hands on her apron. Then she walked slump-shouldered and grumbling to the front of the store with its glass cases. Charging Elk wasted no time. He stepped up into the room and sneaked as quickly as he could to the baskets. He took two longbreads, tucked them into his coat, and left as quietly as he had come.

The cobblestones of the narrow alley were damp and grimy as he hurried away in the direction opposite that which he had entered.

It was dark in the lee of the tall buildings and he had to watch his step, but the bread felt warm against his chest. Any moment he thought he might hear some shouting and steps running after him. He couldn't run and even now his ribs were aching with a sharpness that caused him to catch his breath in shallow gulps.

Finally he reached the opposite end of the alley and he slipped into an alcove that had been a doorway but was now bricked up. He glanced back. There was no one there. He stood for a moment until he could breathe almost normally, then he slid down until he was squatting on his haunches. He didn't want to sit because it took so long to get up.

He reached into the coat and broke off a piece of longbread and chewed it greedily. It was warm and good and it reminded him of his mother's bread. Doubles Back Woman had learned to bake bread in the iron stove in her little shack. When he and his good *kola*, Strikes Plenty, went to visit his parents, she would bake bread for them. They would eat bread with butter and honey and drink *pejuta sapa*. She always had a pot of black medicine on top of the stove and they would drink it out of tin cups with handles. Then she would fix some boiled meat, if they had meat, and turnips and potatoes. Even as his mouth was full of good bread, he longed for the boiled meat. He and Strikes Plenty could eat as much food as his mother put in front of them.

Charging Elk now chewed less greedily and more thoughtfully as he remembered the day Buffalo Bill's scouts came to Pine Ridge to select the young Oglalas who would go away and tour with the Wild West show. Charging Elk and Strikes Plenty had been visiting his parents when his father, Scrub, casually mentioned that the young men of the village were to gather in three sleeps to show themselves off for the scouts. They were very excited because the show would take them to a land beyond a big water. It was the favored land to the east where the white men came from. They had never seen Indians and they would treat the Indians like important chiefs. A handful of the men had gone to another land across the water two years before and they saw Grandmother England and her man. This Grandmother had many children in many lands. She was called a queen and her man was a prince. The prince had ridden in the show's stagecoach while the Indians chased it around the arena. Then all the white chiefs wanted to be chased by the Indians. They may have been important bosses in their land but they were like children who wanted the Indians to chase them. One of the Indians, Red Shirt, even got to shake hands with these royal chiefs. It was he who told the Oglalas that the queen was Grandmother to all the Indians across the medicine line to the north. He said it was a small world to the white men.

Charging Elk and Strikes Plenty went back into the hills after learning this news, but they did not return to the Stronghold. Instead, they camped along a small creek and talked for two days. The second day it rained, a light cold spring rain, and they built a small shelter of willows, draping their canvas groundcloths over it. They sat before a fire and chewed on drymeat and frybread that Charging Elk's mother had given them. They were young and had never been out of their country. The thought of crossing a big water frightened them. Scrub had told them that, according to Red Shirt, it took several sleeps to cross this water in a big fire boat. Sometimes the water was angry and tossed the boat like a twig on a river during runoff time. That's when everybody got sick and wanted to die. This is what Red Shirt said.

Such a frightening prospect was tempered by many good things: The Indians were treated well, they got enough to eat, they saw curious things, they got to show off before thousands of people, and they made more of the white man's money than they could spend. The bosses sent much of their money home to their parents.

Still, Charging Elk had hesitated. The thought of dying on the big water terrified him. What good would such a journey be if you didn't come back from it?

Strikes Plenty, though, was tired of life at the Stronghold. Sometimes the meat was scarce. The winters were always harsh in the badlands. He was beginning to feel isolated from his family at the Whirlwind Compound. When he went there, he felt more and more like a stranger, as though he were of a different band, the Stronghold band. "What good is this life we now lead?" he had said to Charging Elk. "What good will come of it? One day we will be old men and we will have nothing but memories of bad winters and no meat and no woman. I do not want this."

Charging Elk had been surprised to hear his *kola* talk like this. They had never spoken of leaving the Stronghold. It was true that Charging Elk himself had had these very thoughts, but when he visited his parents and saw the way the people lived on the reservation, he quickly put them away. "And if we go, and if we come back, how will we live? What will be here for us?"

Strikes Plenty had looked down at his moccasins that were drying beside the small fire. In the silence, Charging Elk thought himself wise to bring up such a far-seeing concern. He pitied his friend for dashing his excitement. But then, Strikes Plenty had looked up and said, "What if we don't come back?" He had a grin on his face.

It was a great shock when the Buffalo Bill bosses did not choose Strikes Plenty to accompany the show to the land across the water. Charging Elk and Strikes Plenty had looked at each other in disbelief when Strikes Plenty's name wasn't called. They had participated in the horsemanship contests and they were both good, the best. They had been riding hard for ten years, while the reservation Indians only rode for work and pleasure. They had the fastest horses, they rode bareback while the others used saddles made of sheepskin and leather. They were both lean and hard from the years of living on meat and turnips and sometimes with nothing.

The people who had come to watch the contests at the powwow grounds cheered them, the women trilling, the men shouting. There was a recklessness about the way the two friends rode, as though they had not been tamed by the white bosses. Even their soiled, ragged deerskin leggings and shirts seemed to suggest a life lived the old way. The other riders wore their best clothes, beaded and fringed buckskins, blue felt leggings, calico blouses, some even full headdresses. They painted their faces and their horses and they rode their woolly saddles with a practiced recklessness. Charging Elk and Strikes Plenty grinned at each other.

But when the twenty-five names were called, Strikes Plenty's wasn't among them, and so Charging Elk decided not to go. He would persuade his friend to return with him to the Stronghold. Whatever that life lacked, it was better than living among these reservation people.

The two friends rode out of Pine Ridge and rode for another couple of hours in silence. Strikes Plenty had fallen several paces behind and Charging Elk glanced back once in a while to make sure he was still there. It saddened him to see his *kola* slumped on his horse, with his head down, thinking how miserable he was. But after a time, Charging Elk heard Strikes Plenty's horse break into a trot, and soon his friend rode up even.

"I've been thinking, brother," said Strikes Plenty, with his familiar grin. "You must go back and say goodbye to your mother and father. They won't be seeing you for a long time and they need to remember you clearly."

Charging Elk looked at his friend's grin and he felt his own jaw drop in disbelief.

"When you go across the big water to the land where the sun comes from, they will miss you."

"I'm not going. Right now I'm going to the Stronghold."

Strikes Plenty looked at his friend for a moment, his grin gone now, replaced by a look of resigned determination. "No. You must go with Buffalo Bill. You have been chosen and if you do not go, you will become doubtful and melancholy. In one sleep's time, or seven sleeps, or two moons, you will wish with all your heart that you had gone. You will be at the Stronghold but your thoughts will be in the faraway land. I will not like to be around you."

"My thoughts will be here," Charging Elk said. He was angry that his friend presumed to know so much about him. His red horse gasped and lunged forward with the force of the kick in its ribs. Then it began to trot with an easy gait that it could maintain for hours at a time. Many times High Runner had carried Charging Elk through the badlands to the Stronghold at just such a pace.

But Strikes Plenty rode up and grabbed the twisted rawhide rein just behind the horse's neck, turning its head. Both riders stopped then and looked at each other. For the first time ever, something crackled in the air between them. Charging Elk started to say something he would regret, but Strikes Plenty held up his hand to stop him.

The two friends were alone on the plain. There was nothing around them but the rolling hills and swales. There were no trees, no shacks, no animals. Only a lone hawk, circling to the north of them, a speck of a bird that caught Charging Elk's eye for an instant, then was gone into the space of blue sky.

"I am not going back to the Stronghold," said Strikes Plenty, looking away, his voice soft but determined. "I have been thinking this for a long time. It is no use for me out there anymore. At first, it was fun, for a long time it was good to be free, to have good times, but last winter, during the Moon of Snowblind, I went out hunting and I saw one of the older ones—he was hunting beneath another ridge far off—and he was dressed in coyote skins with a wolf cap on his head and his *ʃunka wakan* was gaunt beneath him, and I thought, That will be me. My brother, Charging Elk, will be married, he will have a warm lodge and children, and I will be out here alone with others like me, starving and cold in the winter, wandering in the summer." Strikes Plenty was now looking off toward the long-setting sun. His eyes were narrowed against the yellow glare and his lips were tight, as though he had said what he wanted to say and was waiting for a response.

But Charging Elk didn't know how to respond. He suddenly felt unsure of himself. Strikes Plenty was right—not about Charging Elk being married and his friend wasting his life at the Stronghold, but about the past couple of years not being fun. The two *kolas* had become increasingly concerned with filling their bellies with meat and surviving the winters. If they went back out now, they would lose touch with their relatives for another winter. Charging Elk didn't want that either.

"If I go with Buffalo Bill, what will you do?"

Strikes Plenty brightened, his grin returning. "Find a woman, settle down. There are plenty of women out at Whirlwind."

"But what will you do? After you find your woman? Plant potatoes?"

Strikes Plenty laughed. "Maybe. Maybe I'll have my woman plant potatoes. They say the *wasichu* makes his woman do the planting. He plants something else when he goes to town."

Charging Elk's horse grew restless beneath him, alternately trying to graze and hopping around, making great shuddering snorts. High Runner wanted to return to the Stronghold. There were mares out there.

"It is for the best," said Strikes Plenty. "You will see the land where these white men come from. You will see many great things, make money, enjoy yourself. Me, I will become fat with potatoes, and maybe I will have a *winyan* and many children when you return."

"I will miss you too much. I will miss our good times, brother-friend."

"Those times are gone, Charging Elk. We must follow our eyes and see what lies ahead. Today we go our separate paths and we are not happy about this. When you come back, things will be changed. But we will not be changed. We have been brothers together for many years, we have raised ourselves from children, and we are still young. Much lies ahead for us, but we will be strong brothers always." Strikes Plenty rode closer and leaned over and hugged his friend. "When we are old *tunkashilas* together, we will laugh at this moment."

Charging Elk stood in the alcove and remembered how he had felt when he watched his dear friend ride away that early spring day in the direction of the Whirlwind Compound. It was the end of nine winters of brotherness and he felt a great emptiness, as though Strikes Plenty had taken away half of him.

Two days later, he had ridden High Runner in the procession of riders and wagons down to the iron road in the town of Gordon, Nebraska. His parents had ridden in a wagon, and while the young men were unloading their bundles of clothing and equipment, Charging Elk had handed the reins to his father. "He is yours."

In return Scrub lifted a bundle out of the wagon. He unrolled the blanket and lifted up the hairpipe breastplate. Charging Elk recognized it. His father wore it when the Oglalas were free on the plains. He wore it when he took the horses of the Snakes and Crows. He wore it during ceremonies. He wore it when he fought the soldiers at the Greasy Grass. And he wore it when the Oglalas surrendered at Fort Robinson.

Charging Elk ate a last bite of bread as he remembered holding the bundle on his lap during his first train trip in America. He had had his badger medicine and his father's protection and he had felt ready for what lay ahead. But he had been a little unnerved by the look in his mother's eyes as she watched the iron horse and the big wooden wagons pull away from the station. He had seen that look when he was a child, twelve winters earlier, when the Oglalas came in to Fort Robinson. But the music of the peace song had made Doubles Back Woman strong then, and even as the train made the lonesome sound and picked up speed, she had been singing a strongheart song with the other mothers and fathers, brothers and sisters and old ones on the platform. Still, he could not get her frightened eyes out of his mind. He was her only remaining child. He prayed to Wakan Tanka to bring him home safely, so he could honor his mother for all the days of her life.

Later, on the train ride from Omaha to the big New York, Rocky Bear, the Indian leader who had crossed the big water once before, had come to where Charging Elk was sitting, looking out the window at the new country. He still held his father's breastplate in his lap.

"Your *kola*—Strikes Plenty," said Rocky Bear. "He should be with us, Charging Elk. He was tough—and he could ride. You and he made these reservation boys look puny. You raised yourselves in the old ways out at the Stronghold." The leader glanced around the wagon at the young Oglalas sitting on the wooden benches. "These boys will do. But we are not taking our best."

"Why did the white bosses leave Strikes Plenty behind?" Charging Elk leaned forward in his seat. "He was the one who wanted to go see the other side of the big water."

Rocky Bear leaned down. "He was not Indian enough for these bosses."

Charging Elk looked up with rounded eyes.

"These bosses think they know what an Indian should look like. He should be tall and lean. He should have nice clothes. He should look only into the distance and act as though his head is in the clouds. Your friend did not fit these white men's vision."

Charging Elk looked out the window and saw a big white house surrounded by trees. A herd of black-and-white cows grazed in a field beside it. He had not seen this kind of cow before.

Strikes Plenty was not tall and lean; he was short and broad and his face was as round as *hanhepi wi* when she is full in the night sky. Charging Elk liked his brotherfriend because he didn't act as though his head was in the clouds. He always had a grin on his face, even if they were caught out in a blizzard or had to ride two sleeps with nothing to eat. He wanted to tell Rocky Bear to tell his white bosses that Strikes Plenty was more Indian than all of them together on this iron road, that he had lived the old Lakota way until two sleeps ago, when he rode off to the Whirlwind Compound. But he didn't. At that moment he almost envied Strikes Plenty and the new life he had envisioned. Out at the Stronghold, the idea of having a wife and a life of peace and comfort had seemed far out of reach. Charging Elk felt the bundle in his lap and looked out at the black-and-white cows. One of them was trying to mount another, even though both had bags full of milk.

Now it was full light and Charging Elk was beginning to feel vulnerable. The bread had filled him up and his thoughts of home had comforted him to some degree. He had not thought much about his plan, except to get as far away from the sickhouse as possible. Still, he was hesitant to leave the alcove. He did not know this town, this country. He was now sure there was no one who could speak Lakota here. But if he could find the right people, the brown suit and the black suit, they would send him to Buffalo Bill. Except for his ribs he was well. They would see that.

Charging Elk broke the remaining longbread into four pieces and tucked them into his coat pockets. Then he stepped out into the street.

Marseille was a large city and it smelled of the sea, of salt and winter, of smoke and food, from the chestnuts roasting on braziers on street corners to the golden *pommes frites* in the brasseries to the thick honey sweets in the tea shops. The big street Charging Elk walked along was noisy with carts and wagons and carriages and omnibuses, all pulled by horses or oxen, or in the case of the carts, pushed or pulled by men in blue coats and pants. Men and women walked on the sides of the street, the men carrying big baskets on their shoulders, the women smaller baskets on their heads. The broad walkways on either side of the street were filled with people who seemed to come from everywhere there was an opening. They appeared, moved, and disappeared. Others appeared. Some walked purposefully, others idled along, while still others stopped to look into the windows of the stores. Some of them were well-off, the men with their dark suits and topcoats and top hats, the women wearing the big-butt black dresses, mantles, and hats with feathers and black spiderwebs that partially hid their faces. They carried umbrellas to shield themselves from rain and sun. Others of the pedestrians were poor, dressed in rough coats and flat caps, in long simple dresses with shawls and plain bonnets. Children were dragged along by mothers or rode in their fathers' arms.

Charging Elk saw a group of people standing before a big window. They were talking and gesturing and pointing at various groups of small figures. Some of them were animals—cattle, sheep, and pigs. Charging Elk remembered the family that raised pigs along the road to Wounded Knee. He remembered it because he had never smelled such a sharp, sour odor. It seemed to ride with him for many miles afterward.

Other figures in the window were of men and women and children, dressed in costumes Charging Elk had never seen before.

Some of the figures were light-skinned, others dark-skinned. One of the dark ones had a cloth tied around his head, a blackness over one eye and a knife between his teeth. He had a fierce scowl. The others were either sad or happy or without passion.

In the middle of the window, he saw a group of figures that seemed to be apart from the others and quite a bit larger. Three bearded men in different dress stood or kneeled. One had a tall cloth wrapped around his head. Charging Elk recognized this figure. At the show in Paris, at the foot of the naked iron tree they called the Eiffel Tower, he had seen real men wear these big hats. They came from even farther to the east where they rode the long-necked, big-humped beasts that he had first seen in a pen at the exhibition. They had looked hot and ugly, but when he touched the chewing muzzle of one, he was surprised how soft and pleasant it felt.

Sees Twice had told him that the Eiffel Tower had been built so the French could honor their five generations of freedom from cruel kings. All the surrounding buildings and fountains and gardens were part of this honoring ceremony. He said the white men of America had a similar honoring. They had defeated a cruel king many years before. Featherman had wondered aloud if all kings were cruel, but Sees Twice couldn't answer that. He only knew that the Grandmother England was kind. Maybe only woman kings were good to their people.

Charging Elk almost smiled at this recollection—he had begun to enjoy his memories more than his life. He looked into the window again and he recognized black men with naked chests and big red lips. He had seen black men in Paris and New York but he didn't think they had red lips. And the sheep. And the small horse with big ears. He had seen these big ears first in the gold camps of Paha Sapa, and later in the Wild West show. They were part of an act that made people laugh.

But his eyes were again drawn to the big figures in the middle of the window. All of the animals and men were looking at a man and woman and baby. The man wore a brown cape and was sitting on a rock. He held his hands out, as though he wanted something from the others. The woman was dressed in a long blue dress and a white cloth that covered her head. She was looking down at the baby with just a hint of a smile. The baby lay on some straw that filled a wooden box. Its hair was yellow like the straw and its naked body was bright pink. Its arms and legs were sticking up and it had no expression on its face.

Charging Elk ate one of the four pieces of bread as he walked along the street. His stomach was constantly growling now as he smelled food everywhere he turned. The longbread filled his stomach but he wanted more than bread. He wanted one of the sticks of meat from the *charcuterie*. He wanted *pejuta sapa* and a flaky chocolate bread.

He passed through a narrow street that was lined with outdoor tables. Many people crowded the alley and he found he could move only by slipping through a narrow passage in the center. He was almost glad for the crush of healthy humans after the many days in the sickhouse. He noticed that all the tables were filled with the little figures of animals and various people. He was surprised at how lifelike some of them looked. He was especially struck by a figure of a policeman with its blue high-collared tunic and round flat cap. He stopped to look it over, although he had been avoiding real ones all day. A child next to him was holding one of the yellow-haired, pink babies. This one too had its legs in the air as though it were kicking. The girl, of perhaps four winters, was looking up at her mother with a hopeful smile, but the mother shook her finger and said some words, and the girl put the figure back on the table. Then she looked at Charging Elk, and he saw her mouth go wide open. She looked up into his face, then turned and buried her own face into her mother's coat.

Charging Elk suddenly remembered how different he was from

any of these people and he grew tense. He had earlier let his hair fall free from under the cap, although he kept the cap on his head. He was at least four hands taller than the tallest of them and his wrists stuck out beyond the coat sleeves. He looked down and he saw that his ankles were exposed, his bare feet covered only by the woolly slippers. He noticed how much darker his skin was than the little girl's. She had black hair and dark eyes but her face was the color of snowberries. But Charging Elk was dark even for an Oglala. Many of his friends had teased him about his color when he was a child. He was embarrassed and even ashamed of his darkness, until his mother, Doubles Back Woman, told him it meant that he was the purest of the *ikce wicasa*, that Wakan Tanka favored him by making him so dark.

He now began to notice the people glancing at him as he squeezed through the crowd. They looked him up and down, starting with his hair, then following his length down to his feet. One old woman, her bent body leaning on a cane, looked up at him with a sideways glare and said something that made the others around her turn from the tables to look at him. He thought how different it was when he and his friends walked the streets of Paris in their fancy clothes and the people looked at them with awe. Although he wanted to get away from these suspicious, even hostile stares as quickly as possible, he walked deliberately with his head high, his eyes level above the heads of the small humans.

Charging Elk finally made it to the street at the end of the alley. It was a small street but not as narrow as the alley. He leaned against a building and breathed sharply. He had been jostled in the ribs and now they ached. His stomach had tightened into a hard knot from lack of real meat. He felt as miserable as he ever had in his life and he saw no end to his misery. He wished with all his being that he could step out of his body, leave the useless husk behind, and fly to the country of his people. He would become his *nagi* and join the other Oglalas in the real world beyond this one. At that moment, leaning against the building with his eyes closed to shut out the world around him, he would have gladly died, no matter what happened to his spirit.

But when he opened his eyes he was still there. And he was looking at a pine tree in a large shop window across the street. There were things on the tree, ribbons of red that wound around the branches, white sticks that stood straight up from the needles, and little figures and shiny round balls that hung from the prickly twigs.

Charging Elk almost grunted in his sudden recognition that it was still the Moon of the Popping Trees, the same *hanhepi wi*, nightsun, that had shone on them the night the Buffalo Bill show had come to this town from Paris on the iron road. He remembered that this town was called Marseille and it was on the same big water that they had crossed from America. The fire boat had landed somewhere in a town north of Paris. Marseille was south of Paris, a different piece of country but on the same water. Rocky Bear had told them so. They could take a fire boat from here to America if they chose. Charging Elk's spirit rose a little as he thought this. He wondered if Wakan Tanka had been testing him with such adversity. Sometimes the Great Mystery worked that way. The medicine people at the Stronghold had told him that while they prepared him for his four-day fast. Bird Tail, the oldest and most powerful, had told him, when they were purifying themselves in the steamy *inipi*, that he would see many things in his suffering, many frightening things, but to keep his eyes open for the real vision. He would know it. And Charging Elk did. When the badger came to him one night, he held out his hand and the badger placed its power there. They talked all that night, the badger sang to him and smoked with him, and when he woke up, the badger was gone. But Charging Elk had the badger power in his hand.

Charging Elk suddenly felt both apprehensive and hopeful. If this was all part of Wakan Tanka's plan, he would have to see it through. He would have to listen carefully and make good decisions. Above all, he would have to pray for guidance. He no longer had his badger-claw necklace but he still had his death song. If he sang it well at the right time, his *nagi* would find its way home. But would he still have the power on this side of the big water? One way or another, time would tell.

He stepped away from the building and crossed the street. He felt warmth on his head and shoulders and he looked up to see the sun shining down on the street. He took that as a sign that the Great Mystery was watching him and he looked up and stared at *wi* for a moment. He felt its warmth bathe his face and he felt both powerful and small. And for the first time in many days, fully alive. He would not wish to die again, lest Wankan Tanka take him at his word.

On the other side of the street, in the shadows again, he studied the dressed-up tree. He knew about this tree. He had seen it in the gathering house in Pine Ridge on a visit to his parents' shack, and another time in a miners' town in Paha Sapa. He and Strikes Plenty had sneaked up to a big eating house there and had seen it through the window. In Pine Ridge, it had stood in a corner of the gathering house, and the Oglala children sang soft songs to it.

It was the season of the white man's holiest of days and they worshiped this tree as though it were the sun. The white sticks were lit at night and the tree came alive and sparkled. Charging Elk decided that the little figures in the alley had something to do with the holy days. He had a vague recollection of seeing the woman in the blue cloth and the yellow-haired kicking baby, the men with the big hats; he knew they possessed much power but he didn't know quite what they had to do with this season of the holy pine trees. He didn't know what the policeman and the dark man with the eye patch had to do with it.

Charging Elk remained free for five more sleeps. Although he had
no centimes, he managed to fill his belly a little with things he stole
or picked out of trashbins behind restaurants. A couple of times he
came upon a neighborhood open-air market and he walked among
the stalls, smelling good things—rough dark bread, red glistening
meat, stacks of oranges and nuts, trays of olives, and cheeses of
every color and size and shape. He had seen such markets in Paris
and he and the others often bought cones of the hard white nuts
with the green meats. Charging Elk didn't like the cheeses—some
were dry, others smelly or sticky on his teeth, all gave him diarrhea.
But the reservation Indians, who were used to the white man's
commodities, ate the cheeses whole and farted all night, much to
their enjoyment.

That first day, in spite of attracting so much attention, Charging
Elk did steal a small bag containing four apples from beside one of
the stalls. And that night he found some bird bones behind an eating house that still had some of the pale meat on them. But after
that the pickings were slim—orange peelings, cabbage leaves,
pieces of hard bread, a few soggy *pommes frites* in a paper wrapper
that had small white man's words written on it. He decided not to
try to steal anymore at the outdoor markets, because he was afraid
of the many stares. He stayed off the large boulevards for the same
reason.

He was growing weak again—he had to stop more frequently to
rest. The days had been sunny and warm, but the nights were cold.
Even the heavy coat was not enough to keep him from shivering
when he stopped walking and tried to sleep. So he slept very little,
but when he did he dreamed of the feasts when he was a boy on the
plains. The Oglalas ate real meat then. There were still buffaloes
around the Tongue and Powder rivers, along the Missouri and the

Milk rivers, and the men would come back to camp with their pack-horses covered with meat and hides. Charging Elk dreamed of buffalo hump, of belly fat and boss ribs, of brains and marrow bones. But just as he was about to dig in, just as his mother passed him a bowl of sarvisberry soup, he would awaken to find himself on a stoop in an alley, or under some bushes in a park full of stark trees. Then he would walk again and look up at the darkness and recognize many star people, but they would be in the wrong place in the sky.

On the fourth day, he came upon a boulevard that he recognized and his heart jumped up. He couldn't believe his good fortune. He forgot his weakness and homesickness for a moment. He and some of the others had ridden in an omnibus on this very boulevard in their only sightseeing ride. And he knew that the show arena was a couple of miles up the boulevard.

He looked the other way, and he knew that the omnibus turned onto another boulevard that he could even see in the distance. He recognized the spires of a holy building on the corner. That boulevard would take him down to the big water, where the fire boats rested.

But he began to walk out toward the arena. His ribs felt good now, and although he was aware of the tight knot in his belly, he seemed to have plenty of strength. And he dared to hope—foolishly, he knew—that there would be someone left at the arena site. Perhaps that was where the American in the brown suit lived. Perhaps some of the workers were still there, taking down the tents and the corrals. Charging Elk walked with purpose but he was light-headed from the hunger and weakness. He began to imagine that the show would be there, that he would soon hear the loud voice and the cheers of the audience. He imagined himself breaking free of the barrier and riding hard after the buffaloes. The audience was always thrilled at the excitement and danger of the event. But it wasn't really very dangerous—the herd was small and young, most of them yearlings or two-year-olds. It would have been dangerous if all the animals were full-grown—given their bulk and speed, they could have made short work of a weaponless rider and his horse in such a confined space. It would have been just as dangerous to be in the audience. In Paris, one of the young bulls had climbed the barricade and hooked two people before it was shot by one of the handlers.

By now it was midafternoon and Charging Elk, while bemoaning his misfortune that night in the arena, began to notice something curious: There were hardly any people on the boulevard, and the stores, even the cafés and brasseries and tobacco shops, were closed. There were very few carriages on the street. Just the day before, Charging Elk had to stay on the small streets to avoid the crush of people. Just that morning, the shops had been open and people had sat outside in the cafés, soaking up the warm sun. He thought he must be on a dead street, that the people for some reason had decided this street was bad medicine, but when he came to a big cross street, it too was empty.

Charging Elk walked on, part of him happy that there were no people to stare at him, another part becoming fearful that he was alone. Maybe it was against the law for humans to be out just now. Maybe something had happened to the big town. But he did see the occasional humans—a shopkeeper locking up, a woman pushing a pram, a couple of young men turning a corner to disappear.

After a couple of rest stops, Charging Elk found himself at the big round square where the wagons and carriages went around and around to go to many streets—Rond Point du Prado. He knew the name because the interpreter had made him and the others say it before they left on their sight-seeing trip. If they got lost, they were to say it to a gendarme or an omnibus driver.

Now Rond Point du Prado was quiet, only one taxi entering a

street angling off to his right. Charging Elk listened carefully for a loud voice, a cheering crowd, but all he heard was the clopping hooves of the horse pulling the taxi through the narrow, echoing street.

Charging Elk crossed the roundabout, circling around the big stone statue that spit water. On the other side, he hurried up a wide street on the edge of a large park until he reached the field across from the greensward where the show had set up.

There was nothing there. Not one tent, not one hawker's stand, not even a fire pit where the Indian village had stood. He walked over to the large trampled circle of earth where the portable arena had been set up. The ground had been raked smooth. There was not a hoofprint on it, not one sign that the Indians, the cowboys, the soldiers, the vaqueros, the Deadwood stage, the buffaloes and horses had acted out their various dramas on this circle of earth.

Charging Elk stood on the edge of the circle, not wishing to disturb its raked perfection, and looked across the wide street into the vast park. There was not a soul among the trees and rolling grass hillocks. The walkways and green meadows were empty.

He looked back across Rond Point du Prado and he saw yellow lights coming from some of the windows in the buildings above the storefronts. The light was failing now and he dreaded another night in the big town. Especially this night when the people had disappeared. Just as he felt a wave of despair grip his heart, as it had so often in the past several sleeps, he remembered the train station. It was a foolish hope, but the foolish hopes seemed to come as often as the despair, and he realized that he had become weary with the suddenness and frequency of both emotions. Up and down, up and down went his heart until he walked numbly through the streets without a thought or feeling.

But he felt obliged to follow up on this slim chance. As he

crossed the field to the street that led to the station, he noticed that his fuzzy slippers had become wet with dew. He almost chuckled at this latest problem. Wakan Tanka was not content with just the hunger and weakness of his pitiful child—now he was giving him cold feet. Charging Elk looked up at the sky to beseech the Great Mystery and he saw rain clouds where once had been sun. Nevertheless, he stood at the edge of the field and sang a song of pity and prayed with all his heart that Wakan Tanka would guide him home to his people, to his own land. He asked for a little food too. Then he began to walk again.

And he could not believe what had become of him in such a few short sleeps. Just a little while ago, he had been on this very street, dressed in his finest clothes—dark wool pants with painted white stripes, black sateen shirt with his father's hairpipe breastplate over it, brass earring and armbands, and two eagle feathers hanging from a beaded medallion in his hair. His badger-claw necklace hung around his neck, he had the holy card the French woman had given him in his breast pocket, and he had painted his face with his own medicine signs and had tied three feathers in his horse's mane, just behind the ears. He knew he was quite a sight.

He was one of over seventy Indians in the parade from the iron road to the field at Rond Point, most of them Lakotas, principally Oglalas. And they were just part of the larger procession of cowboys, soldiers, vaqueros, and wagons filled with elk, deer, and buffaloes. There was even a brass band on horseback, the Cowboy Band, filling the street with such noise that Charging Elk had to keep his horse's head high and back to keep him from skittering all over the cobblestones. Still he couldn't help feeling a great pride that he was part of such a spectacle. People were lined up in throngs on the broad walkways on either side of the street.

Of course, Buffalo Bill rode at the head of the procession on his great white horse, waving his big hat and bowing to one side of the street, then the other. Annie Oakley, the one Sitting Bull had named Little Sureshot, and her husband and the big bosses rode behind him. Then came the cowboys, some with the woolly chaps, and the soldiers with their neat blue uniforms and the vaqueros with their big upturned hats. And finally, the Indians, led by Rocky Bear, who had been designated chief by the bosses. From the Paris shows, Charging Elk knew that next to Buffalo Bill, the audiences wanted to see the Indians most. They called the Indians Peaux-Rouges—redskins. When the Indians rode by, the people whooped and pointed at the dark painted faces. Some of the women threw flowers, but the Indians rode by without recognition of such enthusiasm.

Charging Elk remembered that day as one of the longest of his life. They had ridden the iron road all night after a performance in a big town somewhere south of Paris. It was late night when the workers finally struck the tents and grandstands and awnings, packed up the food and furniture from the large eating tent, shut off the generators, and took down the lighting and the immense rolls of canvas backdrop painted with endless scenes of mountains and plains and rivers and villages and forts. They disassembled the booths and seemingly hundreds of other small structures and took it all by wagons to the train station. There they loaded up the thirty-eight big wagons of the special train with equipment and animals and human beings for the all-night trip.

Some of the Indians complained because they had been to this side of the big water before and they knew that, unlike the white performers and crew, they were riding in third class, where the benches were harder and the wagons noisier and rougher. Charging Elk noticed that Rocky Bear was not among them. On this side of the water, the big bosses treated the chief well because the French people liked him better than the Americans had and considered him a noble leader. But the bosses didn't hesitate to lodge the other Indians in the last wagon before the animals and equipment. Even Featherman, the *iktome* who joked, grumbled as he tried to stretch out on a bench.

The show had reached Marseille an hour before first light and all the wagons were unloaded and the equipment was taken to the field to be set up. Charging Elk had been surprised to see the crowd of people watching the predawn activities.

By then Charging Elk was a seasoned performer. The show had not only played in the American town of New York, but had played for close to seven moons in Paris. He was used to the curiosity of the big town people—in both New York and Paris, they had wandered among the lodges of the Indian village, watching the women cook or sew or repair beadwork. They stood over the squatting performers and watched them play dominoes or card games. Some even entered family lodges, as though the mother fixing dinner or the sleeping child in its cradleboard were part of the entertainment. Rocky Bear said that Buffalo Bill and the other bosses approved of this rudeness because it made the people hungry to see the Indians in the arena.

At midmorning, the performers lined up to begin the parade. It was a cold, gray day, and Charging Elk, like the other Indians, wore his blanket over his shoulders. He was tired and sleepy and he wasn't looking forward to performing that day.

But when the Cowboy Band on their matching white horses broke into the song they called "The Girl I Left Behind Me," a song he had heard hundreds of times, and the procession began to move slowly forward, Charging Elk folded his blanket and draped it over his horse's shoulders. And by the time the Indians entered the street, and the crowd gasped and applauded, he felt a familiar shiver of excitement that made it difficult to sit his horse as calmly as he wanted. Nevertheless, he managed because he knew the French people wanted the Indians to be dignified. And too, the young Indians wished to be thought of as *wichasa yatapika*, men whom all praise, men who quietly demonstrate courage, wisdom, and generosity—like the old-time leaders.

As Charging Elk rode his painted horse in the procession, he couldn't help but think how fortunate he was. Instead of passing another cold, lonely winter at the Stronghold, or becoming a passive reservation Indian who planted potatoes and held out his hand for the government commodities, he was dressed in his finest clothes, riding a strong horse, preparing himself to thrill the crowds with a display of the old ways. Of course, he knew that it was all fake and that some of the elders back home disapproved of the young men going off to participate in the white man's sham, but he no longer felt guilty about singing scalping songs or participating in scalp dances or sneak-up dances. He was proud to display some of the old ways to these French because they appreciated the Indians and seemed genuinely sympathetic. Rocky Bear had once told him, while they were sitting around a fire after the evening show, that these people on this side of the big water called the Indians "the Americans who would vanish," that they thought the defeated Indians would soon disappear and they were very sad about it and wanted to see the Indians before they went up in thin air—unlike the real Americans, who would be only too happy to help the Indians disappear.

So Charging Elk had entered this city in triumph and the people had welcomed him. Now they looked at him with suspicion, even with hostility, just as the Americans did.

But Charging Elk had quit these thoughts, and now, as he hurried through the dark street toward the Gare du Prado, he entertained no other thoughts and very little hope.

And as he crossed the empty staging field, where the parade had formed itself, he felt the flicker of hope go out entirely. The station was dark, except for a small yellow light in a window.

The Gare du Prado was a freight station, with a series of long brick buildings, each with a wide loading platform. There were many switching tracks, and even now, several lines of freight wagons sat idly in the darkness.

Charging Elk stepped up on a loading platform and walked without sound to the lighted window. He saw a man dressed in a dark uniform sitting at a table. The room was small and lit by a single yellow wire which hung from the ceiling. The man was breaking off a piece of longbread. Then he sliced a piece of cheese from a wedge. Two small dark apples sat on one corner of the table next to a tiny pine tree. The tree had some glittery red rope wound around it. The tips of its branches were white, as though it had just snowed in the small room.

Charging Elk watched the man eat the bread and cheese and he thought about knocking on the window. But what could be said or done? Besides, judging by his uniform, the man was some kind of soldier. He might think Charging Elk was a thief, or an enemy, and try to kill him. On the other hand, he might know what had happened to Buffalo Bill's train.

Charging Elk almost raised his hand to the window but the uselessness of the action and the potential danger stopped him. Instead, he walked quietly to the end of the platform and looked off to where the iron road disappeared into darkness. He felt more resigned than disappointed because he didn't really believe that the Buffalo Bill train would be there. He almost felt better for having not believed it.

He was about to jump off the platform when he heard a noise behind him. He glanced back and saw the large yellow light of an open door. The man in the uniform was standing just outside the door, lantern in hand, looking up at the sky. Charging Elk dropped to his hands and knees and slithered down off the platform. The hard cinder earth was four feet lower than the dock. He hunkered down and after a few seconds peeked up at the yellow light. But the door was closed again and all he could see was the small window. Then he saw a circle of light bobbing along the platform away from him. In the dark, he could just make out the man's legs.

Charging Elk waited until the light disappeared off the other end of the dock; then he wasted no time, shinnying up onto the platform, walking quickly toward the room. He tried the doorknob and it turned. He slipped inside, closing the door behind him. The first thing he spotted was the food—half the longbread, the cheese wrapped in heavy paper, and one of the apples. He stuffed these things into his coat pockets, then opened the drawer beneath the table. He looked over the small things, things he didn't recognize except for a writing pen and a ticket punch, just like the ticket sellers at the Wild West show used. He was about to close the drawer when he noticed a small metal box near the back. He pried the lid off and his heart leaped up. Three silver coins and a handful of centimes gleamed in the light of the yellow wire. Charging Elk quickly dumped them into his pocket, then closed the box, then the drawer. As he turned to leave he spotted an umbrella and a wool scarf hanging from a hook. He wound the scarf around his neck and gripped the umbrella like a weapon. But when he opened the door and looked up and down the platform, there was no sign of the bobbing lantern.

As Charging Elk hurried away from the railroad yard, he too looked up at the sky and made a silent prayer thanking Wakan Tanka for guiding him to such good things. Then he ate the apple and thought of the chocolate bread and tobacco he would buy the next morning.

CHAPTER THREE

Charging Elk sat on a fruit box in a small funnel-shaped arcade that led to two shop doors and ate the bread and cheese. He was too hungry to remember that he didn't like cheese, and in fact, the creamy cheese tasted strong and smoothed the tight ball in his guts. The windows on either side of him were shuttered, but he could see through the iron mesh and he looked into the one that seemed to have nothing but hats in it. There were the tall hats and the round hats that rich men wore, and some others that looked like cowboy hats with the brims turned down or level as a tabletop. Most of the men at Pine Ridge Agency wore hats like this now. The older men wore black hats with beaded or horsehair hatbands. They wore old *wasichu* clothes given to them by white holy men and their helpers, and black shiny scarves bought from the trader. Charging Elk had been surprised, when the Oglalas came in to Fort Robinson, to see some of the very men who had fought at Little Bighorn only a year before dressed this way. They seemed to have

58

picked up the style from the reservation Indians, most of whom had quit fighting eight years before.

It almost shocked Charging Elk to remember that he had gone to the school at the agency for nearly a year. He had sat in one of the rows of long tables watching the freckle-faced white woman write her words in white chalk on the black board: Boy. Girl. Cat. Dog. Fish. She showed them colored pictures of these creatures. The humans were pink, the cat yellow, and the dog black-and-white. The fish were orange and fat, unlike any he had ever seen. But he was most interested in the cat. He had seen the long-cat and the tufted-ear-cat, but they were wild and only once in a while seen. The cat in the picture was small and had a happy look. He had just seen his first small-cat right there at the agency, but it had been rangy with frostbitten ears and it ran away from people and dogs. Still, it lived among humans.

He remembered the word "Indian." She had pointed directly at him, then at the board, and said "Indian." She made all the children say "Indian." Then she showed them a picture of a man they could not recognize. He had sharp toes, big thighs, and narrow shoulders; he wore a crown of blue and green and yellow feathers and an animal skin with dark spots. His eyes were large and round; his lips tiny and pursed. The white woman said "Indian."

Charging Elk and Strikes Plenty were three years older than the other students, a fact that made them ashamed. All the things they had learned out in the buffalo country were of no use here, and their smaller classmates had to help them spell, and add and subtract the red apples. About the only thing the two older boys—they were thirteen winters then—were good at was art. The woman gave them colored sticks and they drew pictures of the life they had just left—villages of lodges, men on horseback, buffaloes, mountains, and trees. Charging Elk once drew a picture of himself, Strikes Plenty, and Liver cutting off the finger of the dead soldier at Little Bighorn to get his agate ring. The woman had scolded him and torn the picture into little pieces, which she made him pick up and put in the wood stove. He didn't bother to explain, even if she could understand, that the soldier's knuckle was too big to slip the ring off. Instead, he remained silent, and when the Moon of the Red Grass Appearing came, he and Strikes Plenty took off for the Stronghold. And that was the end of his white man's learning.

Charging Elk looked out and watched the rain bounce and puddle on the rough cobblestones of the street. The arcade was dry and the night was warmer than it had been the last four sleeps. He looked up at the shuttered windows in the buildings above the shops. Most of them leaked slivers of yellow light, and he imagined the rooms filled with people, eating roasted meat, talking their strange tongue, laughing, smoking tobacco, playing dominoes. Charging Elk liked the game of dominoes. He liked the feel and design of the tiles and he liked to put them together in the proper way. But the poker games were more exciting. He and some of the other performers played poker and dominoes every night in Paris after the evening performance. They weren't supposed to play for money, so they played for matchsticks. Ten matchsticks equaled one centime. Late at night when they cashed out, some of the Indians went to bed with no centimes in their purses. When this happened to Charging Elk, he was grateful that the white bosses were sending most of his money home to his mother and father.

One night, not long after they arrived in Paris, Charging Elk and Featherman and three others were outside their lodge playing poker by lantern light when they heard a loud commotion across the compound where the wide trail from the arena entered the village. Several people were shouting and rushing toward the path. Charging Elk saw Rocky Bear and his wife come out of their lodge and turn to the sound of the excitement. Then Rocky Bear let out a great yell.

The young men scooped up their matchsticks and stood, watch-

ing a group of people coming toward them. Buffalo Bill was in the
center of the crowd. He was wearing the fancy black clothes that
the rich men of Paris wore in the evening, with a stiff white shirt
and a little white tie with wings. His goatee looked yellowish
against the shirt.

Rocky Bear and his wife were on one side of him, with big grins
on their faces. On the other side, an Indian man, dressed in a rough
suit, smiled sheepishly.

"Black Elk," whispered Featherman. "It is Black Elk."

Charging Elk couldn't believe it. Even out at the Stronghold, the
word had gotten around that Black Elk and three other Oglalas
had been lost in Mother England's home a couple of years earlier.
They hadn't come back to Pine Ridge with the other performers
when the show season ended. Most thought they must be dead, that
they had met a treacherous end across the big water. There were
even ceremonies to release their spirits and people mourned them
in the old way. And in a new way—in the white man's holy house
at Pine Ridge, where the white *pejuta wicasa*, wearing his golden-
and-white robes, said many solemn words about their lost brothers
and sons. When Doubles Back Woman told Charging Elk about
this ceremony, and praised it, he had become angry that she and his
father had even entered this holy house, much less believed what
the blackrobe said. He had ridden back out to the Stronghold and
vowed never to enter such a flimsy house.

And now here was Black Elk, two years later, looking surprisingly thin and pitiful under Buffalo Bill's arm. Charging Elk hadn't
really known Black Elk, who was three years older, because they
had grown up in different places. But he had known of him when
they were out in the buffalo country many winters ago. Both were
boys then, but the three-year difference in their ages meant they
played with their own peers. At the big fight on the Greasy Grass,
Charging Elk had seen him and his friends wandering among the

dead soldiers, looking for things to take. But after the surrender at Fort Robinson, he didn't see much of the older boy.

The big fire in the center of the camp was built up and two women came with a large pot of coffee, which they put on a stone on the edge of the flames. Somebody brought Buffalo Bill a stool and the others sat on their blankets. It was a warm spring night and the fire felt good and so did the cool air on their backs. Charging Elk and the other young performers sat on the opposite side of the fire and studied both Buffalo Bill and Black Elk. The women passed cups of hot coffee to the leaders.

Buffalo Bill talked to Rocky Bear, glancing from time to time at Black Elk. He had a big voice that seemed to include all the Indians around the fire.

Rocky Bear turned to Black Elk and said, "Our leader, Pahuska, welcomes you back to his family. He has been sad these past two years that his brother has been lost. But he never gave up hope that one day he would find you. He was a great scout in his younger days and he had no doubt that he would track you down. But now it seems that you have found us. Welcome to our camp, Black Elk."

Black Elk seemed almost dazed that he was sitting at the fire with Buffalo Bill and his people once again. He looked at all the faces as he thanked Buffalo Bill and Wakan Tanka for bringing him here. Then he said, "Pahuska knows that Black Elk is an honorable man who would aspire to become a *wichasa yatapika*, perhaps even a *wicasa wakan*. I have lived in the *wasichu* world for two years and I do not like what I see. Men do not listen to each other, they fight, their greed prevents them from being generous to the less fortunate, they do not seem to me to be wise enough to embrace each other as brothers. I have learned much from this experience, much that will help me teach our people the right road when I get back to my country. I am glad to see Pahuska and my brothers and sisters, but now I am tired of this land and my heart is sick for home."

Rocky Bear translated for Buffalo Bill, but the showman seemed to have heard the gist of it in the Lakota tongue. He nodded at Black Elk and said, "Yes, yes," as he listened. Even after Rocky Bear had stopped, Buffalo Bill continued nodding. Then he spoke more words in his own tongue, occasionally signing to Black Elk. He was a decent sign-talker and all the Indians watched for the signs. He made the sign for friend, for travel; later, he signed for big water and iron road.

Then Rocky Bear said to Black Elk, "Pahuska understands you. He too gets sick for home. This night he was with the big royals and the big bosses of this great nation. He drank their wine and ate their food, but all the time he thought of his home and his relatives at North Platte. But Pahuska is a big man too and he knows he must teach these French what the *ikce wicasa* are like. They have become too modern with all their powerful engines and big buildings, their fire boats and iron roads. Even tonight they boasted of their progress in the hundred winters since they killed their king and took over. They build their big iron tree so they can look over all that they own. They forget where their people came from; that they too were *ikce wicasa* in the long ago. Pahuska thinks Black Elk could help him teach them the wisdom of the simple life."

Black Elk had stayed with the company for two sleeps. During that time he told the story of himself and his companions missing the boat home; then wandering around the big English town of Birmingham, until they took the iron road to London. One of the Lakotas could speak English and he found a Wild West show called Mexican Joe. It was a small show, but the Indians were paid in cash and got enough to eat. Eventually they came to Paris, then traveled to other cities in another country, then back to Paris. After a time, Black Elk fell ill and couldn't perform any longer. A French family took care of him, but not before he almost lost his *nagi*. His body did die and he dreamed of many things that only the dead are allowed to see. He didn't say what—only that he had journeyed home and had seen his mother and father and the pitiful *ikce wicasa* and now he knew how to help them to regain their dignity and honor. He didn't say how he would do this, but the young men did not question the power of Black Elk's death vision.

After a big feast on the second night, Buffalo Bill gave him some American frogskins and a policeman took him to the iron road to reach a place where a fire boat would carry him across the big water. He was subdued as the people embraced him but he looked happy. After having died, he was happy to go home.

Charging Elk stood and stretched. The rain had diminished to a fine mist and he felt that he should go down and scout around the harbor where the fire boats rested. Of course he didn't have enough francs to cross the big water, but he wanted to see if any of them flew the flag of America. Now that his belly was almost filled up, his mind was clearer and he had begun to think of other possibilities. The boat they came to this land on was big, with many little rooms and the big ones that held the animals and equipment. There were many little nooks that might hold a man if he didn't require much room. He would have to have food and water to last him many sleeps. But at night, perhaps he could stretch his limbs and relieve himself.

Charging Elk gulped back a sudden rising in his throat as he remembered the first three sleeps out of New York. The fire boat had crashed up and down and rolled from side to side and he had become sick almost instantly after losing sight of the big town. The farther away from land they went, the rougher the ride. The Indians shared rooms down in the bottom of the boat and they could hear the creaking and groaning and crashing as they lay in their swaying rope beds. There were many Indians in each room and they swung and wept and vomited and sang their death songs. Charging Elk, when he thought back on it, had never seen and heard such fear in his life—not at the fight on the Greasy Grass, not at the surrender at Fort Robinson.

But then the big water calmed down, and the people, exhausted and weak, had come out in the open air and they saw nothing but water and sky forever. At that point they thought they would never see their mother earth again and were frightened all over—but they were alive. And in five more sleeps, the ship was moving slowly along the coast of France to the big port in the north. And the people gave a thanks-giving song to Wakan Tanka and once again were excited by the adventure that lay ahead. They had performed in New York and had liked it and were excited to perform for these new people. But when they set foot on the stone quai, their legs felt strange and they became dizzy and had to stand or sit for some time before *maka ina* forgave them for leaving her bosom.

Charging Elk now thought that he could take a few sleeps of near-death if it meant that he would be on the home side of the big water. If he didn't cross over, he would never get home, and that was the truth of it. It would be a hard thing, but if he found an iron boat that flew the flag of America and if he could find some more of the francs for meatsticks and bread, he could do it.

The rain was no longer ticking on the umbrella that Charging Elk held over his head, so he closed it and hung it on his arm. His feet were wet inside the fuzzy slippers and his toes were numb with the cold. But he had made it to the harbor and there were more lights here, tall lights on big poles, and a few humans. Most of them were men and they walked in groups, talking loudly and laughing and striking each other on the back and head. They were drunk and happy, but Charging Elk stayed away from them, sometimes crossing the street to stand in a dark arcade as they passed.

At first, he had been dismayed to see hundreds of boats in the small harbor. Most of them were sailing boats, some small, some large. Their tall sail poles looked like a thick forest of slender skinned trees. Not even in Paha Sapa had he seen such a strange forest. The boats were tied to each other, so that some of the men that Charging Elk watched had to climb over two or three boats before they could disappear below the deck of their own.

As he looked at the harbor full of so many boats, he began to feel confused and he felt the old familiar hopelessness begin to set in. He didn't see a single iron boat among them, much less one that flew the right flag. The only encouraging thing he noticed was the ease with which one could get on one of these boats.

He started to walk farther along the stone quai, out toward a large tower on a promontory. To his left were a series of restaurants, some with tables and chairs stacked outside under canvas awnings. Of the several that he passed only two were lit up. One of them was empty and the chairs rested upside down on the tables while a solitary *wasichu* swept the floor. But the other held a large round table just inside the window. Many people, men and women, even a few children, were crowded around the table. Charging Elk saw a big chunk of cooked beef being carved by a waiter in a white shirt and black vest. Bowls of potatoes and other things were being passed around, and Charging Elk felt his mouth water. He watched them all raise their glasses toward the center of the table, then gently strike their glasses with their neighbors. It was for a good wish. Sometimes in Paris, the Indians had gone to big houses with their bosses and had learned that it was necessary to make wishes with the glasses. Now Charging Elk became thirsty for the *mni sha*. The Indians weren't supposed to drink it—just as they weren't supposed to make friends with the French women—but they sometimes managed to sneak a few bottles back to camp. At first,

Broncho Billy, their interpreter, would buy it for them for a few centimes that he would put in his pocket, but after a while Charging Elk and his friends realized that they could walk into a wineshop and pick out some bottles by themselves. The shopowners didn't know that Buffalo Bill frowned on the Indians who drank. He had even sent two of the Oglalas and one Brulé back to America for drinking too much.

Charging Elk smiled as he remembered the first time he had tried to pull the cork out of a bottle with the piece of curly iron. Somehow only the top half of the cork came out, and when he tried to capture the rest with the iron screw, he pushed it down into the bottle. And when he tipped it up, the half cork plugged up the neck. It caused great laughter among his friends, as each time he tipped the bottle nothing came out. Featherman solved the problem by pushing the cork into the bottle with the stiletto knife he had bought in Paris and pouring the wine into a tin cup.

Charging Elk stood in the shadows outside the window and watched the platter of meat being passed around. He imagined that he could smell it and that he could taste it. He had gorged on meat the size of the roast by himself, when he and Strikes Plenty killed an elk in Paha Sapa. But mostly they lived on rabbits and porcupines and sage hens; sometimes deer. The big animals had become increasingly scarce in the years he lived at the Stronghold. Many times in winter he had been as hungry as he was just before he stole the iron road policeman's bread and cheese. Strikes Plenty was right. Their friendship probably couldn't have survived another winter of near starvation at the Stronghold.

Although the rain had stopped, a wind had come up from the northwest and now Charging Elk could hear the harsh snapping of pieces of cloth tied to the tall poles of the big boats. Strings of white lights slung from the tops of the poles to the ends of many of the boats swayed and cast moving shadows on the water. The wind was fresh, but because of the clouds, Charging Elk wasn't as cold as he had been during the earlier starlit nights when he would awake with white frost on the papers he would drape over himself.

Charging Elk had torn himself away from the family of eaters and was now walking farther along the quai, away from the big street he had followed from Rond Point du Prado. He would keep that street in mind as a landmark, but now he wanted to make sure there were no fire boats tied to the wooden ones. He prayed to Wakan Tanka to give him a sign, to show him the flag of America. Or the name of the fire boat that had brought him to this land. The *Persian Monarch*. Before they left New York, before they boarded the giant boat, Broncho Billy had pointed out the name on the front. He had said Persia was way to the east even of the land they were going to. People there wore shiny clothes and the monarch—some kind of king that the people didn't hate—kept large flocks of comely women for his pleasure. They just lay about and waited until he called on one or two of them. The Indians were used to Broncho Billy's lies and they didn't believe this idea; still, some of the Indians, like the Blackfeet, were said to have as many as four or five wives if they could afford them. The Lakota men could rarely afford two wives. Maybe a king, who commanded many people, could have as many of the women as he wanted. Featherman joked that he would stay on the boat when it got to their destination and see if it would take him to these women. That was before the near death of seasickness.

As Charging Elk walked along the quai, he idly looked up a street that led away from the port. He stopped and looked again. In the distance of two street corners, he could see soft but bright yellow light. And he saw small figures, many of them, all walking one way. The yellow light seemed warm at this distance, warmer than the white lights of the port. By now, the wind had begun to bite through Charging Elk's coat, and his feet tingled in the now-soaked fuzzy slippers. He had become increasingly preoccupied with his health the past few sleeps. He knew if he had to go back to the house of sickness he would lose this opportunity to find his way home. And he had the gnawing feeling that he would just become sicker there. Death visited that house too often, and he felt certain it would take him away next time.

Charging Elk passed a large building made of iron and glass. It looked different from the stone buildings, light and open like the cages for birds he had seen in some markets. It stood apart from the others on the quai, almost at the water's edge, and it smelled of sea creatures. It too was dark but he could just make out long rows of tables which seemed to be covered with shiny metal, and he wondered if this was where the women washed their clothes. Everything smells of the fish, he thought, and he felt queasy as he walked on the edge of a basin filled with small wooden boats. Each one had a single skinned tree and was open to the weather. Some were filled with small wooden cages; others had piles of knotted string beneath a piece of canvas that hung like a tent from a wooden pole attached sideways to the skinned tree. Charging Elk knew that these were devices to catch the fish and the hard-crusted creatures he had seen in markets. The Lakotas were surprised and disgusted with the things these people ate. Especially the slimy many-legged thing that seemed to melt into itself. Featherman had said something obscene about it and everybody laughed. Still, they were horrified.

By now Charging Elk found himself standing on the edge of a cobblestone square surrounded by three- and four-story buildings. At one end was a large holy house with two towers. A bell was ringing in one of the towers, and he realized that he had been hearing it for some time. But it was the din of hundreds of people in the square that muted the bell and caused him to shrink into a doorway. Some of them carried torches which gave off warm golden flames. In the center, several men carried a woman dressed in blue and white silken cloth. A golden circle hovered above her head and she was seated on a golden chair, and at first, Charging Elk thought it was a real woman, but she didn't move. Her hands were clasped, palms and fingers pressed together, and he knew she was one of the holy statues that he had seen in the small street those few sleeps ago. These French worshiped her and were taking her up the steps to the holy house. He looked around for the man in brown robes, the kicking baby, and the men with shiny cloth wound around their heads. Perhaps they came from Persia; perhaps Broncho Billy was right; perhaps this town was where the *Persian Monarch* came from. For just an instant, he thought he might be in Persia. But this town was only a train ride from Paris and these people were dressed like all the other French. No shiny clothes, no big cloths on their heads. And no monarch with his many women.

Charging Elk watched the procession make its way slowly up the wide steps of the holy house, and he realized that the voices of the people were not loud, just constant. They seemed to chant the same things at the same time, all the while crowding around the statue and a man in a red gown carrying a gold cross with red fire glistening at its center. As the procession ascended the stairs, Charging Elk could see that the leaders were holy, with their golden robes and tall stiff hats. One of them held a long coupstick which swayed slowly above the crowd. Two of them were swinging iron boxes that made smoke and caused the watching people to bob up and down and move their right hands over their bodies, just as they did that day in the dark cave of the holy house in Paris.

The people followed the golden men into the big house and then the doors closed. The bell had quit ringing and suddenly it was as quiet as it had been that afternoon and evening. The golden torches were gone too; only the lights on posts cast their cold white circles on the wet cobblestones.

Charging Elk wondered what kind of ceremony this was that the white people held during this Moon of the Popping Trees. He knew it was holy; perhaps as holy as the *wiwanyag wachipi*. But the Dance Looking at the Sun was held during the Moon of Red Cherries, when it was warm and Sun looked down on his people for the longest time of his yearly journey.

Now the people were forbidden to hold the Sun Dance, just as they were forbidden to speak Lakota. But many of the people from Pine Ridge came out to the Stronghold to participate in the Sun Dance. The whites never bothered with the Indians out there and so they were free to perform their holiest ceremony in the old way.

Charging Elk had sacrificed his flesh before the *wagachun* when he was seventeen winters, one winter after his visit from badger, who gave him much medicine. The pain of the thongs in his breast as he danced before the sacred tree was unbearable and he was certain he would disgrace himself, but just as he was about to cry out, the pain ended and he was in another world. It was as though he could see himself dancing and blowing the eagle-bone whistle and, at the same time, entering the Great Mystery, where he saw the ancestors and the great herds of buffaloes under the wind and sun and moon. He saw many sacred beings in this world and he knew it was the real world. He heard the beat of the drum and he knew it was the heartbeat of the *can gleska*, where all becomes one. As he danced, he heard the pounding rhythm in his feet, the shrill arrow of his whistle, and he felt the darkness take him. Later, in the *pejuta wicasa*'s sweat lodge, he had vowed to always live in the old way, to participate only in Lakota ceremonies, to avoid and ignore the holy ceremonies of the *wasichus*. And he had fulfilled that vow as best he could.

But now he had witnessed one of the white men's ceremonies and he found himself wishing he could go into their sacred house and see some more. He wanted to be with these people, inside where it was warm and holy. But he knew that as soon as he entered, the people would stare at him, or maybe they would throw him out because he wasn't one of them. Or worse, they might think he was an enemy.

Charging Elk was sunk inside of himself, thinking of his loneliness in the cold dark while the *wasichus* were in the sacred room with their holy woman and the golden leaders, and he didn't notice the slow, measured steps which clumped dully on the wet cobblestones. If he had heard the steps, he could have just stepped farther into the shadows or walked deliberately around the corner and toward the harbor. He had observed that people who walked deliberately in these big towns were seldom seen.

But he was caught unawares and he jumped when he heard the voice behind him. *"Pardon, monsieur."* The voice was calling for his attention, and so he turned.

The man wore a shiny dark cape that fell down past his knees and a small flat cap with a visor and a curtain that covered his neck and ears. He said something else, something that seemed to be a question. Charging Elk looked down at the man's silver buttons, which were attached to a tunic beneath the cape. He shrugged uselessly and he saw that the man carried a long stick. He knew that the man was an *akecita,* for he had seen many of them patrolling the streets of Paris, and even Marseille. He had avoided them these past sleeps and now he was disappointed that he had been surprised by one. Again he shrugged, and again he avoided looking into the policeman's face. But he had sized him up and saw that the policeman was taller than the people of this town, but still half a head shorter than Charging Elk. He was also slighter and the knuckles that gripped the baton were sharp and white. Charging Elk thought he could take him with a quick move that would allow him to spin the man and get a grip that would break his neck or his windpipe. One of the older men at the Stronghold, one who had fought many times with enemies, had shown him and Strikes Plenty how he had used this move when an enemy thought he had him cornered.

But Charging Elk stood, still looking at the buttons, while the *akecita* continued talking. The voice was becoming louder and faster, slightly more threatening, and Charging Elk felt his body go tense with anticipation of the policeman's first move.

He had been in three or four fights in his life, only one with a white man, a miner who had caught him stealing food from his shack. He had knocked the miner down and hit him on the head with a half-full coffeepot. Then he had run away. He and Strikes Plenty had laughed about the incident, but afterward Charging Elk had wished he had lifted the miner's hair. But the thought had not occurred to him then as he sought only to escape. Anyway, there was no glory in scalping enemies anymore. There were no real enemies anymore. The old days when one rode into camp with an enemy's scalp and the people sang an honoring song were gone. Now the reservation people would be angry and frightened of reprisal.

Charging Elk felt the rush of anticipation leave his body. He knew he was just as powerless in this country beyond the big water as the people were on their own land. He knew that his badger medicine would not help him here. All he had left was his death song and now was not the time to sing it.

The policeman grabbed him by the biceps and pushed him toward a street that led away from the square.

Charging Elk sat for a long time under a single yellow wire in a small room in a place of many rooms. He sat on a hard chair with his coat buttoned to his neck and his beret pushed back so that it perched on the crown of his head. His long hair fell over the coat collar to his shoulders and his eyes were slitted and without expression.

Many policemen came to look at him, in twos and threes, chatting among themselves, gesturing toward him, then going away. None of

them addressed him, but one was bold enough to offer him his tobacco and papers, which Charging Elk took. He rolled a cigarette,
accepted a light, then nodded at the man, and the man shrugged and
almost smiled as he left. A moment later, Charging Elk could hear
much shouting and laughter in the passageway outside the room.

As he smoked, Charging Elk looked at the table before him, with
its neat stacks of papers and a jar filled with writing instruments.
On the wall behind the table, he saw a photograph of a white-
bearded man in a dark suit with a sash draped over one shoulder
and thought he must be the boss of these police. He studied the
three-colored flag which hung from a pole in the corner. He knew
it was the flag of France. During the grand entry to begin the daily
Buffalo Bill shows, soldiers carried it along with the American flag.
Then after the troupe circled the arena a few times on their horses,
the Cowboy Band would play the power songs of the two countries
and the audiences would rise and put their hands over their hearts.
Charging Elk had grown to like these songs because afterward the
crowds would cheer and clap their hands. Then they would be
ready for the Wild West show. And the Indians would be ready to
accommodate them. Wearing only breechcloths and moccasins and
headdresses, they chased the buffalo, then the Deadwood stage, attempted to burn down a settler's cabin, performed a scalp dance,
and charged the 7th Cavalry at the Greasy Grass. Buffalo Bill always rescued the *wasichus*—the settlers, the women and children,
the people who rode in the stagecoach—from the Indians, but he
couldn't rescue the longknives. They died every time before Buffalo
Bill got there. And when he came on the scene of the dead bodies,
he took off his hat and hung his head and his horse bowed. By then,
the warriors were behind the long canvas backdrop, which was
painted with rolling yellow hills and the many lodges beside the
wooded river. They were hidden from the audience and so they
smoked and drank water and told jokes.

It had been good in Paris. The days had been too hot sometimes, but the women were handsome, and there was much excitement all the time. Except for a few bouts of longing for the peaceful seclusion of the Stronghold, Charging Elk had enjoyed the whole experience. He had even come to know and make friends with some of the reservation Indians, who didn't seem so weak after all. And after all the daily riding, they could sit a galloping horse almost as well as Charging Elk. But he still took the most chances, counting coup on the buffaloes, taking a fall from his horse after being "shot" with more vigor, fighting hand to hand with the soldiers with more spirit. He took pride in his performances, sometimes too much pride, and the others, led by Featherman, would tease him without mercy, calling him a black Indian because of his dark color, or a scabby *tatanka* because he lived in the badlands like an old bull. They played jokes on him, putting scratchy grass in his sleeping robe or the strong sand that goes on meat in his *pejuta sapa*.

Charging Elk smiled for a moment as he recalled the jokes, but the reality of where he was abruptly jarred his consciousness. Except for the table and the chair Charging Elk sat upon, there was one other chair and a tall box with many drawers in a corner. The single yellow wire in its glass globe and a window which looked out into the corridor provided a harsh light but the corners of the room were shadowed. He had been sitting in the chair, almost without moving, for two hours and now he had to piss. He had not seen the *akecita* who had brought him here since their arrival.

The tobacco he had smoked had made him dizzy and his guts were rumbling because he had not eaten for many hours. He closed his eyes and made himself think again of Paris and he saw the young woman who had come to look at the Indians in the village. That first time she was dressed in a long metal-gray dress which did not have the big butt and which was tight around the middle, almost like shiny skin. She was slender and her small breasts only slightly interrupted the smooth line of the tight material. She had come with an older man and another man about her age. At first, Charging Elk didn't pay much attention to her. Many people, many handsome young women, came to the village to look at the Indians. If there was anything interesting about this one, it was her hat; or rather, the shiny green and blue and yellow feathers that surrounded the crown of it. It looked as though a strangely beautiful duck was sleeping on her head, its own head tucked under a wing. Charging Elk stared at the hat, then looked at her face and was a little surprised to see such a clean simple face framed by vermilion upswept hair. Her lips were pale and her eyes were the green of ice in the wind caves of Paha Sapa. He looked at her for some time and decided that she was nice to look at. Then he went back to playing dominoes.

She returned the next day, just before the afternoon performance. Charging Elk was on the verge of entering the lodge he shared with five other young men to change into his buckskins and the long headdress he was given by the man in charge of costumes, which he wore during the grand entry and during the dance scenes. She was standing on the worn earth path between his lodge and Rocky Bear's, looking at him. Although, like most of the other Indians, he didn't like to look at the eyes of these *wasichus*, he did look directly at her, at her clean face, then into her icy-green eyes. She smiled at him and his heart jumped up and he ducked into the lodge. When he came out, adjusting the feathers of the headdress, she was gone.

She came one more time after that—four sleeps later. Charging Elk had been counting because he had come to realize that he liked the attention that seemed beyond the bare curiosity of the other French women. He liked the way she had looked at him and he liked the smile that he saw many times after that, if only in his mind. For three sleeps he had worn his black sateen blouse with the brass arm and wrist bands, his father's breastplate, a beaded vest, and the silver earrings he had taken from Cuts No Rope in a poker game. He carefully braided his hair with otter skin and red yarn. Then he waited in a variety of poses designed to show he didn't care if he saw her again.

The fourth sleep he decided she would not return, so he wore his worn calico shirt, a pair of baggy-kneed white man's pants, and a black vest. His braided hair was tied off with bits of rawhide. The day had been hot in that close damp way that made Charging Elk wish for the open air of the plains. He was tired and his young bones ached from all the riding and fake fighting he had done over the three moons since their arrival in Paris.

He was playing dominoes with Featherman. It was just after the daytime performance and there would be no evening performance because this was the day the *wasichus* went to their holy houses and rested and ate long meals at home. Several of the performers were going to town to see the sights with Broncho Billy that evening. As tired as he was, he looked forward to eating a big meal in a brasserie that Broncho Billy had been told had plenty of American beef.

As he studied his next move, he felt more than saw a shadow that covered his face and hand. He thought it might be one of the other show Indians come to watch the game, but when he looked up with mild annoyance at the closeness of the shadow caster, he saw the clean face of the young woman looking down at him from beneath a simple white bonnet.

He stood quickly, all thoughts of his aching bones a thing of the past, and she involuntarily took a step back and made a noise that he knew was not a word. He was a head taller than she was and she seemed almost frightened at his size. But she recovered in the time it took for him to realize this and she stepped forward and offered her hand. It was a small hand in a white lace glove without finger pockets. Her nails were small and shiny, the skin unlined, even around the knuckles. Charging Elk didn't know what to do with the pale hand. He had seen men kiss their women's hands, or take the hand and bow. Both gestures seemed too demonstrative, and he didn't want to shake her hand as men did, so he brushed her fingertips with his own dark hand while looking at her white bonnet.

She drew her hand back and touched her dress just above her breasts and said, *"Je m'appelle Sandrine. C'est mon nom."* Charging Elk looked at her lips and they were the color of wild rose. *"Sandrine,"* she said. *"Moi."*

Then Charging Elk heard Featherman's voice behind him. "That is her name, I believe. Sandrine. Now you must tell her yours. In American."

He looked at the young woman called Sandrine and touched his own chest and said, "Charging Elk."

She said, "Charging Elk." When she said it again, the first part of his name was soft and flowing, but the Elk was firm and emphatic. He had not heard it that way before. "Sandrine," he said, pointing to her. Then he laid his fist against his chest. "Charging Elk." And he heard Featherman's high laughter ring out in the closeness of the afternoon heat.

Charging Elk opened his eyes and he was still in the small room with the glaring light from above. He was thirsty and hungry and he had to piss. He hadn't had a drink since he had stopped at a fountain sometime before dark. It seemed a long time ago that he had sat in the arcade and eaten the bread and cheese. He unfastened the bottom two buttons of the coat, crossed his legs, then closed his eyes again to block out the cold light.

Sandrine had led him out in back of the camp into an airy forest of tall trees with heavy leaves and hard, green trunks. Bushes grew among the trees but there were cinder paths that wound around and among the bushes. They came to a lake with an island in the middle. On the island, he could see a cave carved out of a large boulder. He had been to this lake several times before—the show

Indians often took walks out here to sit and smoke, to eat bread and meat sticks, away from the curious white people, although they were often followed by children. It was out here, while smelling the grass and looking at the cool surface of the lake, that the young men talked openly of home. The relative peace of the forest reminded them of all the quiet land of home, the open plains, the river bottoms, the pines of Paha Sapa. Quite often they would talk and smoke for an hour, then fall silent, each remembering home in his own way, all sick for home. But when they returned to camp to dress for the next performance, they would make self-conscious jokes, tease each other, perhaps wrestle, all the time putting on their bravado, along with their paint, for that evening's show. And when they entered the arena for the grand entry, they were dignified young warriors, ready for anything.

Sandrine and Charging Elk sat in the grass on the edge of the lake, looking at the island but stealing glances at each other. Sandrine picked up a small stone and looked at Charging Elk and said, "*Caillou.*" She held it between two fingers and repeated the word. Then she gave him the stone, dropping it into his palm. "*Inyan,*" he said. She said, "*Inyan,*" and they both smiled. It was the first time he could remember feeling warmth for a *wasichu*. She looked up at the hazy blue sky and said, "*Ciel.*" And he said, "*Mahpiya.*"

They had spent a pleasant hour naming things for each other— horse, dog, earth, water—but rarely looking into each other's eyes. If she looked at him, he was looking at the cave. If he stole a glance at her, she would be looking down at a blade of grass between her fingers.

Finally she stood and brushed the back of her flower-print dress. Charging Elk watched this and he thought, She is a different woman from the one I first saw—the formidable one with the tight metal-gray dress and the hat that looked like a many-colored duck.

He liked this one better. He wished they could have stayed there into the evening and then the night. Even when they were quiet, he had felt at ease, as though they were two people with one *cante*, with one being. He had never felt like that with a woman. He had never really been with a woman, except the crazy woman out at the Stronghold who lived alone and opened her thighs for a bottle of holy water. Only twice was he able to bring her the *mni wakan* and those were the only two times he had entered a woman.

He stood reluctantly and watched Sandrine sort through the contents of her bag. He heard the click and clatter and jingle of things and he told himself he didn't want this woman as he had wanted the crazy woman. It was enough to be with her on a warm afternoon in this gentle forest. He watched a small boy duck behind a bush and he thought of a conversation with Strikes Plenty, the time they were trying to decide whether to try out for the Buffalo Bill show. When he had asked his *kola* what they would do when they returned home from the tour, Strikes Plenty had said, with his challenging smile, "What if we don't come back?"

Charging Elk had thought the idea of not returning was foolish talk, but now, as he looked at the sorrel hair of the busy Sandrine, he thought the unthinkable and it frightened and thrilled him at the same time. Would it be possible? Would she take care of him, here in her own land? Foolish, he thought, this is foolish to think. . . .

Sandrine had been muttering to herself as she clattered around in the bag. Suddenly she cried out with pleasure and held up a small, square piece of paper. She looked at it for a moment, then kissed it and handed it to Charging Elk. It was shiny and hard. He looked at it and saw that it was a picture of a bearded man in a red robe. He wore a white gown beneath it and on the white gown was a heart. The heart had a cross growing from its top and there was a woven chain of thorns around it. Blood dripped from the heart.

He looked at Sandrine, his eyes blank with ignorance. Her own eyes were green and moist with some sort of pleasure. *"Jésus,"* she said. Then she took the card from him and turned it over. It was full of the white man's neat looping writing. She said something long, something he didn't understand, but he knew her words came up from her heart and he felt slightly embarrassed. She put the card into his hand and closed his fingers over it with her own small hands. They stood there for a moment, looking at their hands, then she said, *"Adieu, Charging Elk—mon ami,"* and walked away, up the path toward the arena and Paris. That was the last time he saw her.

But he kept the picture of the man with the bloody heart. He carried it with him, in the pocket of his vest or in a small leather sleeve he made to attach to his belt when he was performing in his breechcloth. He didn't understand the picture, but it had been given to him by Sandrine, the woman who had warmed his spirit, and so it had become part of her *nagi* that he must carry always, just as he always wore his badger-claw necklace.

Charging Elk's thoughts were interrupted by the sound of heavy footsteps, and he looked up to see three men entering the room. Two of them were dressed in the *akecita* uniforms, but it was the other one who made his eyes go round. It was Brown Suit! The American. But now he was wearing a black suit with the winged white tie that *wasichus* wore for dress-up. A round black hat with a short upturned brim rested on his head. Only his mustache that curled around the corners of his mouth was as it was that day at the sickhouse.

"Charging Elk. Hello, my friend." Brown Suit stuck out his hand, and Charging Elk lifted his. The man pumped the Indian's limp hand up and down and he smiled, but he was startled to see how thin and drawn Charging Elk was. The hollows under his cheeks were almost black beneath the harsh light. He turned to the younger policeman with the sergeant's stripes on the collar of his tunic. "Have you given this poor man anything to eat?" Franklin Bell's French was quite passable, despite his having been the American vice-consul in Marseille for only two years. He was annoyed. It was Christmas Eve—or had been—and his last guests had been walking out the door when the gendarme arrived with news that an American, a Peau-Rouge, had been arrested.

The other, older man wore several ribbons and three medals on his tunic. He was a small, neat man with sparse graying hair parted in the middle and combed straight down on either side. His mustache was a startling chestnut-colored bush beneath his sharp nose. He was Chef de Police Guy Vaugirard, who was equally annoyed at having been awakened in the middle of the night after a pleasant Christmas Eve with his grandchildren for such a trivial case. He spoke quickly and firmly to the sergeant, who snapped his heels together and hurried away. The men listened to his hurried steps in the hall. Then they heard him speaking with great authority to someone at the front desk.

"Why is this man being detained?" Bell's voice was still truculent but careful. He knew that Vaugirard was the chief of police, a much-needed hero of the disastrous Prussian war and a favorite of the conservatives of the Third Republic. But Bell was outraged that an American had been arrested; he also felt a certain amount of guilt that he had not done more to contact the Buffalo Bill show before Charging Elk left the hospital. He had waited three days before he wired Barcelona—he had more pressing problems involving a disagreement between a Marseille soap manufacturer and an American distributor—but by then, the company was on its way by ship to Rome. And Charging Elk had left the hospital and was nowhere to be seen. It had surprised Bell that Charging Elk, sick with influenza, and with two broken ribs on top of that, could disappear so completely during the four days he had been on the loose.

It didn't surprise him that the police would pick him up at the first opportunity. But now it seemed that Charging Elk was being charged with some sort of crime.

Chief Vaugirard opened a small leather case and offered Bell one of his slender black cigars. Bell said, *"Non, merci,"* and he watched the chief light one with a silver lighter. He looked at Charging Elk and saw that the Indian was looking at the cigar. On an impulse he said, "You might offer one to your guest."

But Vaugirard returned the leather case and lighter to his tunic pocket. At that moment the sergeant returned to the room. "My man is bringing food," he said.

"Why is this American being held?"

"Vagabondage, Monsieur Vice-Consul," the sergeant said. "My man found him wandering in Place St-Victor outside the Basilique. He behaved suspiciously, he could produce no papers. My man acted according to his authority."

Bell had become accustomed to this authority during his tenure in Marseille. One of the unpleasant parts of his job as vice-consul was acting on behalf of Americans, usually sailors, who ran afoul of this authority. They were guilty unless they could prove their innocence. Napoleonic Code. Unfortunately, the French system was just as rigid as the American. "And did your man ask him for his papers?"

"Of course, Monsieur Vice-Consul. He did his duty in a very correct and professional manner."

"And did this man understand what was being asked of him?"

"I don't follow, monsieur . . ."

"Do you understand this man?"

"But he has said nothing—not one word—"

"This man, Charging Elk, is a member of the Wild West show of America. Perhaps you took your family to a performance? Or read about it in the newspaper?"

"Ah, yes, Monsieur Vice-Consul. I did not have the honor to attend a performance, but my brother-in-law—"

"Monsieur Charging Elk is a very important American. He took ill during a performance and was hospitalized. He was still in the hospital when the show left for Spain. I was in the process of reconnecting him to the show when I learned of his detention." Bell felt uncomfortable in the small, sterile room. He had been here before, trying to get a sailor released so he could sail with his ship the next day. He hadn't been successful—the sailor had gone to trial for public drunkenness and destruction of property and had served six months in jail. It had cost the consulate sixty dollars to send the sailor home on a steamship. And their budget didn't provide for such random expenditures.

Bell looked at Vaugirard, who had not said a word and seemed quite content to let his sergeant take care of the matter. Bell would not let him get away with it. "As you may have deduced, Chief Vaugirard, Monsieur Charging Elk is not a vagrant. He is an important member of the Wild West show who had the misfortune to fall ill in your city, a victim of the influenza epidemic. Now he wishes nothing more than to repatriate with his American comrades, who are performing in Rome. If you would be good enough to release him to my custody, the consulate will guarantee his immediate passage to Italy."

The sergeant set an ashtray he had retrieved from the top of the filing cabinet on the table before the chief of police. Vaugirard looked up at him and said, "What do you think, Borely?"

Sergeant Borely's eyebrows lifted in surprise as he watched the chief tap the ashes from the little cigar into the ashtray. But he was quick-witted and recovered his composure. "Monsieur Charging Elk is charged with *vagabondage*. And it has been reported to us that he left the Hôpital de la Conception without permission. These are serious offenses, I think, *chef*. Especially with the influenza epidemic in full bloom. Perhaps he is contagious, yes? To leave the hospital before he is pronounced well and to wander our streets— it is very dangerous to our citizens, I think."

Vaugirard continued to tap the little cigar on the lip of the ashtray as he digested this information. He was a deliberate man and now he had to make a decision. On the one hand, it would be easy to hand over the Peau-Rouge to the vice-consul. It would be a quick resolution and within his power, with a little fudging on the official report. And it would be good for relations with the Americans, who were great consumers of the products of France. On the other hand, the law was the law, and by rights, the man should stand before the legal system. And too, Vaugirard was known for his faith in the professionalism of his officers. He very seldom interceded in their actions or countermanded their decisions. The morale of the Marseille Police Department was very high as a result. He saw no reason to throw his weight around now.

"As you can see, Monsieur Vice-Consul, my sergeant has given a great deal of thought to this matter and I have to agree with him. If it was just the *vagabondage*, I think we could look the other way. But to leave the hospital without being properly discharged is a very serious matter." Vaugirard stubbed out the cigar and looked at Charging Elk for the first time since a cursory glance when they had entered the room. "We have no choice but to hold your citizen in detention until he can appear in court. You see, it is the only way."

"May we at least take him back to the hospital where he can receive proper care? It would be a courtesy to an American citizen and his government." It occurred to Bell that Charging Elk wasn't a citizen of the United States. Because of the treaties, the Indian tribes were their own nations within the United States. But the individuals were wards of the government and as such were entitled to diplomatic representation in foreign countries. He had read the directive only some months ago in conjunction with the Wild West show's appearances in France. "I'm sure my superior, the consul general, would be most amenable to placing Monsieur Charging Elk under a doctor's care. Then, when he is pronounced fit, we will send him at once to Italy." Bell tried to act hearty, as though his suggestion put the matter to rest, the end of it, they could all go home well satisfied with such a just resolution to this surprisingly sticky problem.

But Vaugirard was up to the bluff. "No, no, that is not possible, Monsieur Vice-Consul. He has already left the hospital once. No, I think it would be best if Monsieur Charging Elk remained with us."

"But it is Christmas. . . ."

"I am aware of that, monsieur," Vaugirard said with more force than he meant to. He pulled out his watch. Three-thirty in the morning. His grandchildren would be up in a few hours to open the presents that they hadn't torn open last night. His only son was a poor surgeon in Orléans and he very seldom had time or money to bring the family to visit. Vaugirard was damned if he was going to waste any more time with the problems of the Americans. "Sergeant Borely will make sure your citizen is cared for. I'm sure a tribunal will hear the case next week, probably a slap on the wrist, nothing more. *Bonne nuit*, Monsieur Vice-Consul."

"Thank you for your kind attention to this matter, Chief Vaugirard. I'm sure Monsieur Charging Elk would thank you too, if he could. *Joyeux Noël*, Chief Vaugirard!" Bell had meant to sound sarcastic but his French wasn't good enough.

Borely turned to follow his chief out the door; then he stopped and said, "I will inquire about the food, monsieur."

"Thank you, sergeant." Bell turned to look at Charging Elk, but the Indian had his eyes closed and he was rocking almost imperceptibly on the wooden chair. Bell couldn't tell if he was asleep or simply trying to block out the world.

The American Consulate was on Boulevard Peytral in the Sixth District, only a few blocks from the Préfecture. It was four-thirty in the morning and Bell was walking in that direction. His spacious apartment on the second floor of a grand residence was right next door to his workplace. The apartment had been furnished with antiques from the Empire period. Bell didn't know how the consulate had acquired such grand furnishings, but after his time in the shabby tenement in Panama, his last posting, he wasn't about to look a gift horse in the mouth. His dinner that evening had gone quite well—he had even toasted Napoleon for providing such magnificent craftsmen that could build such magnificent furniture: "To the emperor of good taste and bad judgment." Margaret Whiston had laughed, to his delight. She was the cultural affairs attaché and a very ample piece. One of the few unmarried Americans (like himself) in Marseille. She did have a fiancé in the embassy in Constantinople, but the distance, and the unwillingness of both to give up their jobs, had created a crisis in their relationship that Bell was only too happy to exploit. So far it had been just talk, but she was considering his offer to spend next weekend in Avignon. She was a very bold young woman.

In spite of the lateness of the hour, Franklin Bell was in relatively high spirits. He had promised Charging Elk that he would return the next day with cigarettes and food. He thought Charging Elk had somehow understood that, but he couldn't be sure. The Indian had simply nodded without really looking at him. In fact, Bell couldn't remember the Indian ever looking at him. They were a strange race of people, he thought, still attempting to live in the past with their feathers and beads. But perhaps that was understandable, seeing that they had no future to speak of. He had read an article in *La Gazette du Midi* just the other day about "the vanishing savages," and that just about summed it up. They were a pitiful people in their present state and the sooner they vanished or joined America the better off they would be.

Still, he now wished he had gone to a performance while the Wild West show was in Marseille. He had read *Buffalo Bill, King of the Border Men* when he was a kid, twenty years ago. He had grown up in Philadelphia, and like all kids then, he had wanted to go west to the frontier to fight Indians. And in 1869, there were plenty of Indians to meet in battle.

Bell crossed into Boulevard Peytral and saw his apartment, with the soft glow of light in the French door behind the wrought-iron balcony. He still hadn't gotten used to closing the shutters every night the way the French did; he hated to wake up in the morning in a still-dark apartment.

As he fished his keys out of his pocket, he thought again of Charging Elk, but only in the abstract. He had finally met an Indian, but not in the heat of battle; rather, he had met a poor wretch in a shabby coat that didn't fit him and hospital slippers that were soaked through; he was alone in a country where he could not speak the local language, and worse, he couldn't speak the language of his own country. He would sit in a French jail for at least four days until the Christmas weekend was over, and maybe longer, given the crowded nature of the French courts. So much for the romanticism of youth. This Indian was thoroughly defeated.

Bell suddenly thought of the other Indian — Featherman. He had been brought to Hôpital de la Conception as an influenza case even before Charging Elk, but it turned out he had consumption, which had turned virulent. So he was moved to the tuberculosis ward. It hardly mattered. He would be dead soon enough. And it would be up to Bell to notify his relatives. How does one notify the relatives of a savage? He would have to catch up with the Wild West show somehow. It was all too much.

Bell turned the key and the door swung inward. If only Margaret were there, waiting for him in bed. But—maybe next weekend, in Avignon. He made a silent prayer as he climbed the stairs to his spacious apartment filled with Empire furniture and the pervasive odor of a delicious bouillabaisse that his landlady had created. He would sleep as long as he wanted and perhaps he would dream of Margaret and her abundant offerings. It was Christmas, after all.

CHAPTER FOUR

Martin St-Cyr *hated Marseille in the winter and he wondered at* the turn of events that had landed him here. He wondered quite often, at least once a week, but he never came up with a satisfactory explanation. The simple explanation was that he had followed a girl here. After their graduation from university in Grenoble in 1886, she had taken a teaching job in a lycée here. Because she was a brave Christian girl with a missionary spirit, she had chosen a school in Le Panier, an old working-class section of Marseille that now attracted immigrants from the Barbary States and the Levant, who worked the worst jobs in the soap and hemp factories, the abattoirs and tanneries.

St-Cyr had graduated with a degree in economics and had been accepted into law school at the Sorbonne for the next semester. But he hadn't counted on falling in love with Odile despite the fact that his best instincts told him that they were not at all compatible. She was deeply religious and felt compelled to spend at least this part of her life helping the less fortunate. He was not religious at all, in spite of being raised in a Catholic household. His third year in college, he fell in with a group of socialists, many of whom (like him) were more in love with the idea of the working classes than with the actual people who constituted the oppressed. St-Cyr attended the meetings and rallies, passed out leaflets, and played a small part in attempting to organize the meat workers and the draymen in Grenoble. But when the police entered the Place St-André, where the workers and students had gathered to protest the arrest of three leading organizers, two students, and a meatcutter, St-Cyr had ducked into the Palais de Justice, just off the square. From there, he watched the trunchion-swinging gendarmes charge the overpowered, if not undermanned, protest. Much blood was spilled that hot autumn afternoon, and after that, St-Cyr had eased himself to the fringes, then out, of the movement.

But St-Cyr had never been a socialist, activities aside. He told his friends he was going to law school to further the goals of democratic socialism—the movement could always use good, committed lawyers—but he still believed in many of the bourgeois values—his own father was a capitalist, a silk merchant in Lyon, and had provided his family a very good life.

So what was St-Cyr doing, sitting in a small drab café on a Wednesday morning in Marseille, sipping café au lait and eating a brioche? He couldn't really answer that. Odile had, in fact, become a missionary and was now in Algiers, emptying bedpans in a charity hospital. At the end of one year, she would decide whether to continue her work or come back and marry St-Cyr. But lately he had wondered at the idea of marriage, of committing oneself to another for an eternity on earth. And there was the subject of sex. Although they had their romantic moments—picnics along the Promenade de la Corniche, day trips to the Camargue to see the flamingoes and the agile black bulls that were the stars of Provençal bullfights, overnight to Avignon to tour the Palais des Papes, evenings at the opera or the theater—sex had refused to rear its head, at least for Odile. No matter how much or how fast St-Cyr talked about the joys of the subject, she had remained inviolate. Saving it for their wedding day. Forcing him to frequent the prostitutes on Rue Sainte. In fact, he had visited his favorite whore just the night before, a heavy dark girl named Fortune, who invariably smelled of cigarettes and cassis.

Odile the good versus Fortune the bad—what a contrast, thought St-Cyr, the one tall and fair and clean-edged, slim as a boy, except for the swell of hip and breast, a virgin; the other dark, built low to the ground, musky in her ample nakedness, a whore.

St-Cyr sighed and drank off the last of the café au lait. He had become concerned lately that perhaps he preferred the prostitutes. One didn't have to spend eternity with them, and they were always waiting in the Rue Sainte for the next visit. St-Cyr pulled out his gold watch, a graduation gift from his father, and popped it open: eight-thirty. Time to make his rounds. He lit another cigarette, stood up, and dropped a few sous on the metal table. He stood for a moment outside, looking out from under the awning at the putty-gray clouds above the buildings. At least the mistral had blown itself out overnight, after three days of whining. St-Cyr did hate Marseille in the winter, maybe in any season. He flipped his cigarette into the gutter, then he walked across the rain-slick street to the Préfecture.

"Bonjour, Sergeant Borely. Lovely to see you, as usual. Lovely day, is it not? And what have you got for me this exquisite day?"

Borely looked down at the young reporter. He was seated on a platform behind a tall counter, and even as short as he was, he was a head taller than his guests. The arrangement was meant to be intimidating, and it worked, except with this scamp.

"Ah, *bonjour*, St-Cyr. It is a cold, wet morning, as usual. And I have nothing of interest." Borely looked down at the log book. "Two wife-beatings, a stabbing, the usual vagabonds, and a cutpurse a citizen brought in after beating him up. His face looks like an *aubergine*, but he will live to atone for his sins."

St-Cyr took down the superficial particulars of each case as the sergeant recited them: both wife-beatings were fueled by alcohol, as was the stabbing. A Levantine tannery worker, drunk on absinthe, had slashed an Algerian sailor in the face, nearly severing the tip of the nose—the only angle there was that the Algerian was also drunk, a rarity among the North Africans, most of whom were Muslims. The cutpurse entry would be good—the citizens of Marseille were always pleased with vigilante justice. St-Cyr was just about to close his little bound notebook. Not a very good haul, but Tuesdays, even Tuesday nights around the seaport, were pretty quiet. "Anything else, sergeant—anything at all? *S'il vous plaît?*"

Borely looked down at the young police reporter. There was something about him he didn't like. St-Cyr had been on the beat for almost two years now, and in that time he had done nothing to offend Borely. He was unfailingly polite, filled with the *joie de vivre*, and quite bright, and he always got his facts right—something that had never concerned St-Cyr's predecessor. Yet there was an air of privilege about the reporter that annoyed Borely—even the way he dressed. Today, in the middle of winter, he was wearing a yellow tattersall waistcoat and a scarlet poet's tie, and a ridiculous wide-brimmed hat that would have embarrassed an Italian. True, he was a handsome devil, with his sparse but trim goatee and small white teeth, and his slim, foppish frame. But it was more at the manners, the politeness, that Borely took offense. They bespoke of good breeding, of—what else?—a life of privilege with that faint tinge of contempt for authority.

Borely himself barely had two sous to rub together, what with a wife and six children, and his consumptive mother who lived with them in a too-small flat behind Cours St-Louis. The plumbing was always broken and the small street was full of garbage from the open-air market. And now the neighbor was threatening to call the police because her cat was missing and she was sure Borely's oldest boy had thrown it out the hallway window. Imagine that. Calling the *gardiens* on their own sergeant. Borely shook his head at the thought.

"Well, thanks for the information, sergeant." St-Cyr seemed to interpret this gesture as a negative. He had put his notepad in his pocket and was screwing the cap on his fountain pen.

Borely watched him with a sigh that was almost affectionate. He did like the young man, in spite of, or perhaps because of, those attributes that annoyed him. And as a police reporter he made far less than even Borely. But perhaps he needed something to do more than he needed money. "We still have the Peau-Rouge," he said.

St-Cyr had started to leave, but now he turned back, his face blank with confusion.

"The Peau-Rouge. We arrested him Christmas Eve, or rather, early Christmas morning." Borely smiled. "Of course! You were off for a few days, weren't you?" While I have been pulling double shifts throughout this season of the nativity, he thought.

"Yes, I went to spend Christmas with my family. In Lyon." The words were almost abstract, uttered without inflection, as St-Cyr uncapped his pen. "What about this Peau-Rouge? What is he in for?"

"Nothing to get your hopes up about, St-Cyr. *Vagabondage*. And he left hospital without permission."

Now St-Cyr was thoroughly confused. "But how does a Peau-

Rouge . . ." He stopped himself. The Wild West show. Of course. But how . . . ?

"He was with Buffalo Bill. According to the American vice-consul, and to the records of *Hôpital de la Conception*, he contracted the influenza, and he suffered broken ribs in a fall from his horse. He was hospitalized with these afflictions." Borely stopped himself to watch a young secretary cross the room to the captain's office. She wore a long-sleeved white blouse with ruffled shoulders and a long, slim black skirt that just brushed the tops of her narrow-toed shoes. Her black hair was done up in a bun with Chinese sticks shot through it. But it was the front of the blouse that caught Borely's eye.

"The Peau-Rouge is here, now? In the jail?"

"He has a court appearance next week, or possibly the week after that. With all these holiday revelers, the courts are much backed up, I think." Borely pursed his lips in a gesture of disdain. "This is not the holy season anymore, Monsieur St-Cyr. It is a season to get drunk and beat your wife or stab a North African, do you not agree?"

"Yes, of course." But St-Cyr had been writing with careless haste: Peau-Rouge. *Vagabondage*. Leaving hospital—Conception—without permission. Christmas Eve. Crossed out. Christmas morning. "And does this American Indian have a name?"

Borely pretended to study the logbook, but he was looking right at the name. He was enjoying the suspense of the moment, but he was also a little intimidated by the American language. He didn't want to butcher the word in front of this young man of privilege, so he ended up spelling it out.

"Charging Elk," said St-Cyr, who had studied the English language in Grenoble. His father had said English was becoming more and more the *lingua franca* of commerce, especially the American tongue. St-Cyr had no intention of becoming a capitalist like his father, but he did learn the language to please him. "Does he speak English?"

"According to the vice-consul, he does not. He does not speak English or French. In fact, he has not spoken a word since his arrival. Perhaps the man is a mute."

St-Cyr tapped his pen against his teeth. This was a story! An American Indian all by himself in Marseille without the ability to communicate with anyone. It didn't seem possible that it could just fall into the lap of Martin St-Cyr. "You mean, Sergeant Borely, that the Wild West show just left town without him? He's stranded here?"

"Absolutely. The vice-consul says the show is in Rome, even as we speak. He wanted to send this, this Charging Elk to Rome by ship, but of course that is impossible until the legal matters are settled. You understand, monsieur, that we can't just turn him loose at the whim of the vice-consul."

But St-Cyr was writing again and didn't respond. Finally, he looked up at Borely with a thoughtful smile that showed his small, even teeth. "Would it be possible to have a look at this *indien*, Sergeant Borely? I would like to write a small story about him, nothing much. I think my editor would find it of some small interest." He laughed what he hoped was a charming laugh. "I will make sure I spell your name right—in the first paragraph." St-Cyr didn't really have much hope that the sergeant would allow such an unusual request from a lowly police reporter. Or that his editor, whom he only knew by sight, would allow much more than a few factual words. More likely he would send a feature reporter to write the story.

But Borely actually seemed to be considering. St-Cyr didn't think Borely was a vain man, but the thought of seeing one's name in print can be enticing. The desk sergeant was in control of his own little world here in the Préfecture, but when he went home in the evening to his flat, to his civilian clothes and squabbling brats, he was as anonymous as the dock worker who lived above him.

Borely called out to two policemen who were standing in the hallway that led to offices and interrogation rooms. They had been chatting quietly, but at the sound of Borely's voice, they both came at a fast clip, their shoes clicking smartly against the marble floor.

"You, Dugommier, take Monsieur St-Cyr down to the cells. Tell the jailer that the monsieur wishes to see the Peau-Rouge." He turned to the reporter. "This is very irregular, St-Cyr—but you are a police reporter and it is incumbent upon me to offer the cooperation of the department. I could do nothing less."

"*Merci beaucoup, sergent.* My newspaper always appreciates the cooperation of the Marseille Police Department." St-Cyr fought back an impulse to laugh at Borely's puffed-up language. "And may I have your Christian name, sergeant—for the story?"

St-Cyr thought that Ambrose was not a name he would have associated with Borely, as he followed the policeman down the narrow, winding stairs to the depths of the Préfecture. Francis or Jerome, perhaps even Michel. Not Ambrose. Patron saint of—what? Desk sergeants?

The basement smelled of cooking, of rancid oil, onions, and cabbage, with a strong hint of disinfectant. The combination was not agreeable to St-Cyr's nose, and he felt the brioche and the sweet café au lait move in his stomach. He began to wonder, as he looked at the dark, sweating walls of the low, narrow corridor, if this was such a good idea after all. The place was medieval, right out of the Spanish Inquisition. He imagined torture devices in special rooms inhabited by men in brown hooded robes. Again, he felt a surge in his stomach as a wave of claustrophobia hit him.

But the corridor opened out into a larger hallway, and a man sat behind a desk beneath a tall skylight. He was wearing a collarless shirt with the sleeves rolled up. His tunic was draped over the chair.

"Monsieur is here to see the Peau-Rouge. It is cleared with Sergeant Borely."

The man behind the desk was obese, a condition not at all usual with the Marseillais. He had a periodical spread open before him. St-Cyr could see an illustration of a young woman in a corset and black stockings that came to just above her knees. A fringed mantle was draped across her lap.

"And what is monsieur's capacity?" The man carefully folded the periodical and pushed it to the side of the desk. It was clear that he was in charge here and took his orders from a higher authority than Borely.

"I am a reporter with *Le Petit Marseillais*. I cover the activities of the police department. Today I have been sent to interview the Peau-Rouge—with the kind consent of Sergeant Borely and, of course, yourself." St-Cyr didn't find it necessary to tell the truth, to explain that he had heard of Charging Elk just moments before.

But the fat man had quit listening to St-Cyr. He lumbered to his feet, pulling his suspender straps over his shoulders with a satisfying snap for each, all the time grumbling to the other policeman about the lack of communication between those lilywhites upstairs and the poor bastards who had to work in such a shithole as this.

He shrugged into his tunic, which he did not bother to button, then opened a small cabinet on the wall behind the desk. He continued his diatribe against those upstairs as he lifted a heavy ring of keys from a metal hook. "Insufferable bastards," he grumbled as he walked across the hall to an iron door. He fitted one of the keys into the lock, then pushed the door inward. The groan of the iron hinges made the hair stand up on the back of St-Cyr's neck.

The jailer told the other policeman to wait outside, then slammed the door shut behind himself and St-Cyr. The corridor before them was even dimmer than the one that had brought St-Cyr to the jailer's desk. There were no windows, no outside light, just the occasional lightbulb in a wire cage hanging from the high ceiling. St-Cyr was almost surprised to see that the jail had electricity. He had half expected to see gaslights, perhaps even torches flickering on the walls.

One side of the corridor was a stone wall; the other side, another stone wall interrupted by metal doors with no windows. St-Cyr had not been down here before and now he wished he hadn't been so eager to come. He pulled his coat tighter to afford some protection from the damp chill. He thought, This *is* right out of the Inquisition. He had always had a touch of claustrophobia—since that day as a child when he and his class at the lycée had toured an ancient dungeon and had to walk single-file through the narrow passageways and the small winding marble stairs that were lit only by small slits in the stone walls. Now he felt the familiar panic and he made himself look at the jailer's broad back.

"These are the doors to the cells, then, monsieur?"

"*Oui, oui,*" said the jailer.

"And is there a prisoner behind every one?"

"*Oui, oui.* Some. Not all."

St-Cyr was annoyed by the man's abruptness but he knew that the jailer was equally annoyed by his presence. He obviously didn't approve of civilians in his fiefdom. The man was practically sub-human, a grouser and a bully, just the type that St-Cyr might have imagined working in such misery. Still, he couldn't help but be somewhat comforted by the broad back before him.

St-Cyr was trying to imagine what this American Indian would look like—would he be dressed in feathers and fur, in war paint? Would he have a fierce scowl? More important, would he be dangerous, a wild savage from the American frontier? St-Cyr had not gone to the Wild West show of Buffalo Bill. He really had no interest in the wild west or the cowboys and Indians—at least up to a half hour ago. When he was a boy, his playmates would often play Indians and soldiers, enacting the violent scenes they had culled from the pages of illustrated adventure books. St-Cyr was more inclined to collect insects. He had had a large butterfly collection from his family's August vacations to their chateau in Périgord.

The jailer grunted something and stopped and rattled his keys. St-Cyr had been so deep in thought he almost ran into the broad back, but now he pulled back in fear of this damp, cold, dimly lit place and its Gothic keeper. What in the name of God was he doing here? He was only a police reporter who went around the city to the various precincts to gather small facts about mostly small crimes. As he watched the jailer insert a key in one of the iron doors, he had the irrational fear that this whole business was a trap, that he was going to be locked up, that he would never see the light of day again.

The jailer swung the door open, then stepped inside. St-Cyr was surprised to see a shaft of light from the open doorway; still, he held back, just ducking his head around the corner to look inside.

The light came from a small window in the opposite wall up near the ceiling. The window was covered with woven iron, but it was high enough that a man could not reach it, even standing on a chair. St-Cyr edged forward until he was standing in the doorway, ready to bolt back the way they came at the slightest movement.

But the scene was almost tranquil—the shaft of light, the jailer standing quietly on one side of the room, his tunic now buttoned against the chill, and a figure on a bed that was suspended from the wall. It was a close room, perhaps two meters by three meters, but its height gave the claustrophobic St-Cyr great relief after the perilous journey down the low, narrow corridor. Out of nervous habit, he slid his notebook out of his coat pocket.

"Here is your Peau-Rouge, monsieur," the jailer said, his voice rough-edged but almost hushed.

The first thing St-Cyr noticed was the long, dark hair. It was parted in the middle and fell past the man's shoulders, almost to the small of his back. Even St-Cyr's whore, Fortune, did not have hair so long.

"Charging Elk?" said St-Cyr.

The Indian turned to the sound of his name, but he did not look directly at St-Cyr. He seemed to be looking at the door behind the reporter. His eyes were dark and there were shadows beneath his cheekbones. His mouth was closed tightly, like a seam in a burnished leather glove.

At first, St-Cyr was glad that the Indian did not look threatening—in fact, he did not look capable of violence at all. In his black coat, buttoned to the neck, and short pants and slippers, he looked almost pitifully thin. His bare ankles seemed especially vulnerable. The more St-Cyr studied him, the more concerned he became.

"Does he eat?" he said.

"Like a bird," the jailer said. "He eats his soup and drinks his tea—that's about it. He leaves all the vegetables in his soup bowl. He has no taste for bread. I think the Peau-Rouge does not eat like real men."

"I think he's starving, monsieur. Look at him. Perhaps you are not feeding him the right food."

The jailer, who had been almost civil since entering the cell, now rattled his keys against his leg and blew an abrupt puff of air, obviously angry. "We do not operate a restaurant here, monsieur. We are poor jailers. We do not sit behind fancy desks upstairs and decide whether we will have bouillabaisse or couscous for lunch. Perhaps *gigue de chevreuil* for dinner. No, we do not operate like that. This one will eat what the others eat—or he will go hungry."

St-Cyr now looked at Charging Elk. "Do you understand English?" he said in English.

Charging Elk almost responded to the word "English." But he remembered Brown Suit, the American, and his inability to communicate with him, and he remained silent.

"How can I help you, Charging Elk? Would you like something different to eat? Eat?" St-Cyr tried to will the Indian to understand with loud, correct pronunciation, but the Indian just stared at the door behind the reporter.

St-Cyr could feel the jailer's impatience, and he knew that his time was just about up. But he didn't want to leave. He wanted to make the Indian understand that somehow he would help him. And this was surprising to St-Cyr. He was not a cold man—he helped beggars with a sou every now and then; he gave his landlady a tin of very expensive foie gras for Christmas; he brought the old man who lived across the hall from him and was dying of consumption packets of pastilles and reports of new remedies that he read about in his newspaper. Still, he let little in the way of universal human suffering affect him.

But Martin St-Cyr was almost desperate to help Charging Elk. It was plain that the man was dying. He could be dead in hours or days and nothing would be known of him. The brutish jailer and his comrades would dump the body in a cart and wheel it out to Cimetière St-Pierre, where it would be buried in the indigents' section without a cross or a name.

St-Cyr tried to identify what it was about the Indian that affected him so. Surely some of the other cells were filled with men in equally desperate circumstances. His own countrymen who were being held in such squalid conditions, possibly starving too. Even now, he could smell a damp, ashy odor that spoke of illness, even death.

Perhaps it was that the Indian could not speak any language but his own, and his countrymen were thousands of miles away on the other side of the earth, that made St-Cyr desperate to do something that would help the Indian survive, until at least his court date. But, as Borely had said, the courts were backed up, and the Indian didn't look like he would last another day.

"Perhaps, monsieur, if I left a little money, you could see that the Peau-Rouge gets something substantial to eat? Perhaps some sausage and cheese and peasant bread?" St-Cyr dug in his pocket and found several francs.

"We do not dispense special privileges here, monsieur. He eats what everyone else eats."

But St-Cyr was prepared for this response. He opened his wallet and pulled out a twenty-franc bill. "A little something for your time, monsieur," he said, offering the bill.

The jailer glanced quickly, instinctively, toward the door; then he stuffed the bill and the coins into his tunic pocket. "I'll see what I can do."

"Soon?"

"*Oui, oui, monsieur.* Soon."

St-Cyr didn't trust him, but there was nothing he could do about that. But there was something he could try to do about the Indian. About Charging Elk. He made himself think the man's name. He made himself look into Charging Elk's face. He was a man, a human being, and he would likely die if St-Cyr didn't do something.

But for the moment, he could only drop his packet of Gauloises and a box of matches on the bed beside Charging Elk's brown hand. "For you," he said in English. "Don't worry. I will help you out of this wretched place. Don't worry, Monsieur Charging Elk."

Charging Elk listened to the key turn in the lock and heard the bolt thrust home with a thin echo. Then it was quiet. He drew his feet up onto the bed and watched the newly disturbed dust motes circle and float in the shaft of light.

He had no idea how long he had been in the stone room of the iron house. In spite of the cold he had slept much of the time, and he had dreamed of home. In his dreams he saw the golden eagles soaring over the Stronghold; he heard the bark and howl of coyotes in the night; he smelled the sage in the spring wind, and the crisp chunks of venison cooked over an autumn fire; he cupped his hands in the clear stream of Paha Sapa and felt the cold water take his breath away as he splashed his sweaty face. He dreamed of home, and so he slept much. He saw his mother picking berries in the Bighorns and his father cleaning his many-shots gun in the lodge on the Greasy Grass. His brother and sister played games with rag balls and slim bones in the evening quiet of the big camp. And he and Strikes Plenty caught the winged hoppers they threw into the water for the slippery swimmers.

Sometimes the dreams ended in the blackness of night; sometimes in the light of the high window. Sometimes they ended happily; other times with images of soldiers attacking the big camp on the Greasy Grass, or with the people descending into the valley of the Fort Robinson, with its many soldiers and the big flag of America.

Once he dreamed of Crazy Horse, and the great warrior chief told him that one day he would go to that land where the sun rises, across a big water, where the favored *wasichus* came from. Crazy Horse had told him that he could not accompany Charging Elk because he would be killed soon by his own people. Charging Elk had reached out for the *wichasa yatapika*'s arm, but it was not there. Crazy Horse had become a cloud in the sky above the badlands.

Some of the dreams disturbed Charging Elk; others comforted him. But all were welcome, for Charging Elk knew he was very close to joining his ancestors. And that is why he sang his death song all day and dreamed of home all night. And each night he prayed to Wakan Tanka that this would be the night that he would finally make the journey across the big water. He even prayed to badger to give him strength for the journey, but he was sure that his power was gone, that his animal helper would not hear him in a far-away iron house.

His hand brushed the packet of cigarettes as he smoothed his coat tighter against his knees. He picked it up and looked at it. The pale blue of the packet reminded him of clear skies over Paha Sapa and he thought of the sacred beings that roamed there and he remembered the ceremonies of the old *pejuta wicasa* out at the Stronghold, which always began with a smoke.

Charging Elk held one of the smoke-sticks and pointed it to the sky and to the earth and to the four directions, offering prayers for each. He prayed to the sacred beings and the ancestors, just as the holy man had done. He offered prayers to the four-leggeds and the wings of the air; then he prayed long and fervently to Wakan Tanka, vowing to serve him always in the real world behind this one. He lit the cigarette and smoked it halfway down, then smudged it out in his palm. He rolled the cigarette between his thumb and forefinger until the remaining tobacco shreds fell into his hand. Then he put them in the pocket of his coat so that he would have something to offer badger when he returned home.

Charging Elk lay down on the iron bed. He wasn't cold anymore and he felt at peace with all his being and with the world around him. He stared up at the high ceiling and he heard himself singing. It was a powerful song, and he thanked badger for giving it to him. He closed his eyes, singing.

CHAPTER FIVE

⟡

wo days after Martin St-Cyr's account of the "lost soul" in the "entrails" of the Préfecture appeared in *Le Petit Marseillais*, not much had happened, which was disappointing to the young reporter. In his wilder daydreams, he had imagined a monstrous public outcry—rallies on the steps of the Préfecture and in the *place* of the Palais de Justice; marches by trade unionists and socialists; candlelight vigils by religious and social justice groups; perhaps even a visit from Paris by the Minister of Justice. In his more sober moments, he thought there would be a small but vigorous protest by ordinary citizens, who often gathered to demonstrate against one thing or another. Usually these citizens chose small issues, such as the price of baguettes going up another centime. Or a new ordinance that restricted the amount of garbage that could be left at the curb.

While St-Cyr's article didn't create the massive reaction that he would have liked, it did bring several people down to the

Préfecture. An old priest led them, and he did talk of the outrageous and inhuman treatment of the Peau-Rouge, one of God's simplest creatures. He spoke of compassion and mercy, of prayer and forgiveness. Soon he was rambling, preaching a sermon that had less to do with the plight of this particular Peau-Rouge than with the fate of uncivilized savages the world over, all of whom were God's simplest creatures.

St-Cyr stood at the back of the small group, counting the disappointingly obedient, well-behaved heads. There were no more than twenty-five of them, also disappointing, so he decided to double it in his follow-up story. There were five *gardiens* stationed like pickets before the great doors. Perhaps he could mention something about suppression, the potential for violence, but even as he took notes he began to have doubts about his career as a writer.

His editor had at first seemed unmoved by his account of Charging Elk's imprisonment. But one might chalk that up to a deficiency in the man's personality. He didn't seem to have one. And when St-Cyr had asked to be allowed to write the story himself, even though he was merely a police reporter, he had expected a terse rejection, perhaps a sharp bark of mirthless laughter. But the editor sat for a long moment, perhaps two, with his fingers steepled before his grim face. In his black suit and with his bald head gleaming under the overhead light, he looked like an undertaker lost in thought while the mourners wept.

Just as St-Cyr was thinking of trying to walk out the door of the small office backward, retracing his footsteps as if to erase this awful moment, the editor stood and slapped his palm on the desk. St-Cyr almost jumped straight up at the gesture.

"Can you do it?" the editor said in his even undertaker's voice.

"Yes, of course, Monsieur Grignan. I will do my best."

"Very well." The editor looked at the small crystal clock on his desk. "You have two hours. Take it to Fauconnier when you are finished. Tell him to make the necessary adjustments."

St-Cyr had been pleased that Fauconnier, the veteran journalist, had not found it necessary to make too many changes. He crossed out "brutish" in St-Cyr's description of the jailer ("He might eat you next time") and "cold-blooded" in reference to the whole police department ("We have to work with them even if they are cold-blooded bastards").

In the end, Fauconnier had clapped St-Cyr on the shoulder and said, "I think you are in love with this *indien*," a comment that the young journalist took as a compliment.

That night he celebrated with champagne and *fruits de mer*, followed by a visit to Fortune, who swore she had seen the Peau-Rouge the other day, poking in the refuse piles near the Quai de Rive Neuve. As she slipped into her kimono, she said, "He was a small wiry sort with stiff hair, like a Levantine—except he wore a suit of feathers."

The next morning, St-Cyr read his story and was quite impressed with his first effort at real journalism. It appeared as he and Fauconnier had left it, except that the typesetters had left out a letter in Borely's Christian name—Ambose. Ah well, Ambrose would see the humor in this; he was a decent cop. But when St-Cyr went on his rounds of the police stations, he was met with a kind of stiff hostility. Borely was not on duty at the Préfecture, a fact which disappointed the reporter. But as the day wore on, he became increasingly glad that he did not have to face the desk sergeant. After all, it was Borely who had let him venture down to the cells to see the Indian.

St-Cyr had miscalculated the police reaction to his article. What he thought was merely a plea to save the Indian from the inhuman conditions of the jail was taken as a slap in the face by the police department. St-Cyr got his police reports that day but with little enthusiasm.

Now, as he folded up his notebook, he became unsure of himself and wondered if he could write a follow-up article on such a pitiful reaction to his first one. Even if he doubled the crowd size and made it more enthusiastic, he had little to write about. And too, he had not been able to find out anything about Charging Elk. The desk sergeant at the Préfecture had said he knew nothing about the Peau-Rouge; inmates in the jail were none of his concern.

What if he was dead? St-Cyr felt a sudden rush of panic that made his upper lip tingle with sweat, in spite of the chill of the building's shadows. Perhaps the sergeant was covering up the fact that Charging Elk was already dead—that already a hole had been dug in the indigents' cemetery! Of course, that was it. That was why he had not been given any information about Charging Elk. The jailer, brute that he was, had not used the money to buy food— he had pocketed it to buy wine and salacious magazines. But what did St-Cyr expect? That the police cared about the savage?

But even in his panic, which was now becoming a churning in the pit of his stomach, St-Cyr was formulating the follow-up story in his head: "Where is the Peau-Rouge? Why have the police denied a humble reporter access to the savage called Charging Elk? Do they have something to hide? Could it be that the *indien* has died of starvation, or perhaps even more likely, a broken heart, in the gloomy dungeon of the Préfecture? The citizens of Marseille demand to know the answers to these and other questions. The church is up in arms, as witnessed by the large demonstration on the steps of the Préfecture, led by the holy fathers of the city and its outlying reaches. Unionists and socialists were seen in the audience—an unholy alliance that has united the distressed citizenry in its demand that the Peau-Rouge be freed, or, at the very least, released to the care of a more humanitarian institution. It is clear, even to a disinterested observer, that the hearts of the Marseillais have gone out to this pitiful savage, who apparently remains in his cold, damp cell in the bowels of the Préfecture. However, it is the duty of your humble servant to report that several of the protesters were advocating violence, if violence be the only means to attain justice. Let the police consider themselves fore-warned."

St-Cyr stood in the shadows of the buildings across from the Préfecture, scribbling as fast as he could, as the story came to him. It was as if the first story were merely a warm-up for this one. In his haste to get it all down, he had forgotten entirely the small gathering listening to the rambling priest, who was now telling the story of Christ and the money changers in Jerusalem.

If St-Cyr had really thought about it, he would have realized that there was a small war going on inside of him. He had suffered for three years a rather humble, boring life in a town he didn't like, waiting to marry a girl he now didn't think of more than once or twice a week, doing the most beggarly kind of reporting, and now he had a chance to write the story of his life. It was all there—he couldn't write fast enough to keep up with all that he had to say, and he had plenty to say. This was not merely the bare bones story of a wife-beating, or a drunken Levantine cutting off the nose of a Muslim. This was the story that would make St-Cyr a legitimate journalist—perhaps even a notorious one.

On the other hand, he had been genuinely moved by the sight of Charging Elk in his cell. He could not forget the dark, sunken eyes behind the cheekbones, the flatness of them and the way they avoided looking directly at St-Cyr. They were the eyes of a dying animal, of an animal that had resigned itself to death. St-Cyr had always thought that eyes, when they were alive, reflected hope, no matter how mean the circumstances.

St-Cyr, in his fevered state, did not realize that he had come to think of the creature in the cell as an animal that had been cornered. And in a way, he cared more for the animal than the man. If the man had been French, he would have thought of him as an unfortunate creature who had suffered an injustice at the hands of the law. But Charging Elk, like an animal, had no inkling of what had happened to him, why he was there, and he couldn't voice a protest, could not explain his circumstances or mount a defense.

St-Cyr was not aware, at the moment, of this war going on inside him between the cynical young reporter and the human being who feared for the welfare of a fellow creature. That he had come to think of Charging Elk as a somewhat lesser animal did not enter his consciousness. He was inventing a story—based on the small demonstration—that would eventually release the Peau-Rouge from his hellish isolation. And wasn't that a noble thing?

Once in a while Charging Elk could see trousered legs walk by the high window of his small stone room. At first, they appeared as thin shadows on the opposite wall, an almost imperceptible blurring of the light. But when he gradually realized that the brief shadows belonged to something outside the cell, he began to stare up at the window. For long periods of time, he stared at the window, and his heart jumped each time he saw the legs. He looked forward to seeing legs. They gave some definition to the world outside his stone room—a world of light and fresh air, of trees and sky, of people. He could imagine the legs walking up a flight of stairs to a warm room full of padded chairs and good things to eat, or down to the port to climb aboard one of the fire boats that would steam off to America, to take their owners to the wide-open country of the Lakotas.

It had been three sleeps since the man with the cigarettes had entered his room to look at him. The man had called him by his name and had worn a yellow vest that reminded Charging Elk of the yellowbreasts that called so sweetly on summer mornings at the Stronghold. Those mornings when he and Strikes Plenty had lounged about their cooking fire, drinking coffee and talking of women and game and good times seemed so long ago, although less than a winter had passed. Charging Elk continued staring at the window and thought that it was good that Strikes Plenty—and his parents—could not see him now.

For two days, Charging Elk had lain on the sleeping platform and sung his death song. It was a powerful song and it took him away to his own country. He did not feel the cold or see the close stone walls. He did not notice when one of the *wasichus* brought him soup or emptied his slop bucket. Once, one of the helpers, the fat one, grabbed him by his coat and pulled him to his feet and screamed and made threatening signs with his fists. Charging Elk had sung on, scarcely noticing the hatred in the small pale eyes. But this day, the third sleep, his song was weak and he was afraid it was losing its power. He no longer felt his *nagi* lifting inside of him, hovering, waiting to be freed for the long journey home.

Then, around midday, something happened that caused him to quit his death song entirely. One of the helpers entered his room, carrying a small platform and a tray. He smiled and talked soothingly, pointing to the window, then to the shaft of light on the opposite wall. He pointed to the tray and rubbed his belly, and Charging Elk followed the man's finger and he saw real food. A cooked bird and several small potatoes, accompanied by a large chunk of bread and a piece of chocolate. He saw the usual mug of pale tea, but he also saw a small bottle of what looked to be *mni wakan*. It had no paper with the French writing stuck on it, but he could see the dark juice through the deep green of the bottle. A clean squat glass stood beside the bottle. The helper noticed that he was looking at the wine. He pointed to the bottle and put his thumb against his lower lip, tilting his head backward. Then he left, laughing.

Charging Elk had not eaten anything solid for several days. He had drunk the liquid from the soup and swallowed the tea because he was always thirsty, but he was anxious to be dead and away from this stone room, this foreign land. It had been easy to quit eating the things that floated in the soup and the sour bread, but the sight and smell of real food made him almost grateful that he had not gone away. As hungry as he was, he didn't know if he could eat anymore. His stomach felt small and dry inside him, like a leather pouch that was drawn tight.

Charging Elk looked at the bird for a long time before he found the strength to swing his legs over the edge of the platform and stand up. His sudden dizziness, almost a blackness before his eyes, made him think briefly of the sickhouse and the first time he had tried to get up from the white man's bed. His ribs no longer hurt, but he felt just as weak. He stood for a moment, waiting for his sight to come back; then he reached down and touched the bird gingerly, almost a caress. It had been roasted and its smell filled the small room. He pulled a piece of skin from the carcass and tasted it. He thought it might be a *wasichu* trick, that it might be poisoned or diseased. But the skin tasted good. It was greasy and he realized that he had not had any real grease for a long time.

He picked up the plate and sat down on his sleeping platform. He had had chicken meat several times when the show was in Paris and he didn't particularly like it. It did not have the strength of the red meat of buffalo or elk. But now he ate all the skin off the chicken, licking the grease from his fingers. Then he pulled a leg off and ate the tough meat from it.

After he finished the chicken, he popped the small potatoes, one by one, into his mouth, mashing them with one or two bites, then swallowing them. He chewed the dark bread, which had become dry in the cold of the stone room. The mug of tea was barely warm and he drank it down in two gulps, all the time eyeing the bottle of wine.

He reached into his coat pocket and pulled out the blue packet of cigarettes and the matches Yellow Breast had given him. There was one cigarette left. He studied its almost perfect shape—the roundness, the cut-off ends. He and the other Indian performers rolled their own tobacco and they never attained such perfection as this one. He put it to his lips and struck a match. The thought of making prayers, of performing the *yuwipi*'s ceremony with the tobacco, did not occur to him. And for the first time in several sleeps he felt warm and satisfied with this life and did not wish to end it. He did not know what would become of him, but for the moment he was at peace and didn't care about tomorrow.

Charging Elk leaned back against the stone wall and watched the smoke curl up into the shaft of light toward the window. He saw Yellow Breast's eyes in the smoke and he saw that the eyes were troubled, almost frightened, with what he saw in Charging Elk's face. He had given Charging Elk this tobacco to make prayers with; and now he had given him a meal of real food and a bottle of *mni wakan*. Charging Elk would drink it after he finished his smoke because he knew that Wakan Tanka had sent Yellow Breast to help him. Charging Elk smiled. The Great Mystery had almost taken him away after testing him most severely. He had made him sing his death song in an effort to be rid of this life. But now, He wanted Charging Elk to live, to continue to breathe the air of this strange country among these strange people. Just a short time ago, this thought would have caused Charging Elk great heartsickness; now he was content to smoke the cigarette and think of his life as here and now—no matter what, he would survive. And when the time came, he would go home to his people. Wakan Tanka would see to that.

Madame Soulas sat beside her husband in Captain Drossard's large office in the Préfecture. The captain was speaking of the poor fishing this winter—nothing but *rouget* and *hareng* for sale and those at outlandish prices. The *coquillages* were poor and tasteless, and what few *crevettes* there were cost an arm and a leg. The captain was sure that the fishmongers were taking much too big a cut—they seemed to think that they had not only caught the fish themselves but had created them out of clear blue water. Next, it would be loaves of bread from the sky.

Madame Soulas listened to her husband, René, protest. He was not only a fishmonger, he was an official in the Association. He had been hearing complaints all winter long, both from the fishermen and from the customers, for it had been a poor season and the prices reflected that. Only this morning, a group of men who fished out of Vallon des Auffes had threatened to sell their catch elsewhere if the Association wouldn't give them a fair price. They would spend the rest of the winter in Toulon or Nice. They heard the fishermen there got what they deserved.

Madame Soulas listened to her husband try to explain that if they set the prices too low, the fishmongers would be out of fish in an hour and out of business in two. But the captain would have none of it. He was sure the Association needed a thorough investigation, it was the scandal of Marseille.

Madame Soulas let her mind wander, until the argument became so much buzzing in her thoughts. She was still opposed to the matter at hand, but René had insisted it was their duty as Christians: "Dear Madeleine, did not Christ die on the cross for us? Are we to leave him there, weeping in despair, crying out for his Father? Did he die for nothing?" And when she protested that they already had two young mouths to feed and scarcely enough room to turn around in, he dismissed her with one of his usual pieties: "If we are true Christians, we will not mind a little sacrifice. Did not Christ call on us to help our less fortunate brothers? Is it not God's will? Besides, it is only for a day or two."

It was difficult to argue with René, not just because of his pieties, but also because of his genuinely pious nature. It was this quality that had attracted Madeleine in the first place. They had met at a retreat for young people in the Ardèche, sponsored by the parish of St-Laurent. Madeleine had been fifteen and René sixteen. Madeleine went to a convent school in another part of the city and so she had only seen René at church and in his father's fish stall. As the fates would have it, she fell out of a tree at the rustic retreat, injuring her shoulder and tearing her skirt on a broken-off branch. The sight of her white underthings caused much giggling, among boys and girls alike. But as she lay on the ground, trying to gather her senses, she heard a loud, scolding voice and thought it might be the young priest who supervised their recreation. But when she looked up, a short, square boy with thick hair and a stubby nose was squatting down beside her. There was something quite serious in the boy's appearance, a lack of expression, and she recognized him as the fishmonger's son.

That had been twenty-one years ago. It had been five years from that moment until they were married. In fact, they never spoke another word to each other for two years after the incident. Madeleine learned, after they were married, that René had sought out the older priest for advice on entering seminary that very week. Father Daudet was encouraging and gave René special religious instructions for the next two years while he finished lycée. But the week before René was to enter the seminary, his father was killed by an insane sailor while he was at the quai, bidding on fish.

Madeleine had accompanied her parents to the funeral, and they sat only two rows behind the bereaved family. She was surprised that while the others gave in to their grief, René had sat quite erect, clear-eyed, seemingly emotionless.

And the next day, she saw him again, at the fish stall this time, working alongside some of the other fishmongers, who had volunteered to man the stall while the family recovered. He never missed a day after that.

Madeleine had been puzzled then, and slightly angered, by the boy's lack of feelings for his own father. Could this be the same boy who had been so solicitous of her injury and her dignity? It was only after they were married that he revealed his one overriding principle in life—everything that happened was God's will, good or bad. But even in the bad, there was good, for it was God's will, and was not God good? Did He not do things for the betterment of mankind even though they seemed bad, often tragic? Madeleine tried to understand this mishmash of simple reasoning, but in the end she could not. She considered herself a devout Catholic—she and René took the children to mass every Sunday and every holy day—but she could not bring herself to feel that all the tragic things that went on around her were good simply because they were God's will. She often thought that René had the temperament of a priest—grave but not undone by bad things. Perhaps even uplifted by tragedy.

So she sat in the captain's office, waiting, rueing the day that she and René had followed Father Daudet and the other parishioners down to the Préfecture to protest the imprisonment of the Peau-Rouge. She had felt quite virtuous in offering up her prayers for the well-being of the savage. As Father Daudet had said, he was one of God's humblest creatures. And René was right, of course—it was their Christian duty to offer shelter to a fellow human being. She didn't object to that. They had, after all, housed an engineering student from Montpellier for nine months, and while he had paid a small amount for rent and a little for food, they hadn't gotten rich — nor had they expected to. And there was the little nurse from Apt before that.

But this was a savage! Surely God didn't intend for Christians and savages to live together! Madame Soulas shook her head and looked at her husband, who was patiently explaining how the mistral and the tramontane were keeping the fishermen from going out as often as they normally did. The captain was snorting in disgust. One would think that René had committed a crime against the state, instead of being guilty merely of foolishness in this foolish endeavor.

And yet, here it was — the moment at hand. They had already been to the Palais de Justice and signed the temporary custody papers. The tribunal had questioned them — or rather, René extensively. Could they provide the savage with creature comforts? Were they prepared for such a person in their house-hold? How would the children adjust to such an exotic creature? How did they think a savage would respond to living in a civi-lized neighborhood? Finally, the *président du tribunal* had turned to Madame Soulas and said, "And you, madame, are you prepar-ed for — how shall I say it — for whatever unusual needs this savage might require?" She remembered the look on René's face —the smile that was somewhere between Christian joy and pure apprehension — but he needn't have worried. She was his wife. Now she wondered what would have happened if she had said no. She was quite sure the tribunal, given the severity of the questions, would have turned them down. But René — what would it have done to him, and to them? She couldn't understand why he would want to bring this *indien* into their home. But he was almost uncharacteristically insistent, as though his own family were not enough for him. Sometimes his piety was a burden.

For the fiftieth time in the past three days, Madame Soulas asked herself, Why us? She understood that there were other families, not to mention relief agencies and church organizations, that would have been only too happy to take in the savage. Just the day before, two nuns from the Vieille Charité had appeared at their doorstep. The older one was severe and erect in her habit and the younger one wore thick wire-rimmed glasses that made her eyes too big for her face. Both were quite reasonable in their request that the Soulases give up their claim to the Peau-Rouge. They were equipped to deal with vagabonds and orphans, it was their calling to care for indigents. When René scoffed at the notion, the nuns became more insistent and threatened to talk with Father Daudet about the moral fitness of the Soulases. And that enraged Madeleine as much as it did René, and it was she who escorted the nuns out the door. In spite of Captain Drossard's questioning the honesty of the Association des Poissonniers, René was the most moral man she knew. He never put his thumb on the scale or failed to put his tithe in the collection plate. And besides, it was Father Daudet who had recommended to the tribunal that the *indien* be placed in their care! Those were the final words hurled by Madeleine at the retreating nuns.

Later, when she had calmed down, Madeleine found herself wishing that things had turned out a bit differently. Perhaps if René had seen the nuns' point that they were in a better position to help the savage, it all would have worked out for the best. Their life would be normal, the children wouldn't be threatened, and the savage would have the best of care. And besides, he had been arrested for loitering. Didn't that make him a vagabond and therefore eligible for care at the Vieille Charité?

Madame Soulas sighed. The solution to this problem had been at hand just yesterday, but René had offended the nuns. He was a good man, but sometimes she wished he had a little more sense.

What a mess we are in, she thought.

All of this because they had gone to the Wild West show of Buffalo Bill one Sunday afternoon. René had sat on the edge of his seat during the whole of the performance. He had clapped and cheered at the big carriage and the pursuing Indians. He had let out a howl of delight when the Indians rode among the running bison. And he had actually made savage whoops when the Peaux-Rouges had killed the brave soldiers. Madame Soulas had been horrified at his behavior until she noticed many of the other spectators doing the same thing!

But Madame Soulas was more concerned about the children. Many of the acts had frightened them. Chloé had wept when the bison pounded by, shaking the long portable bleachers, followed by the half-naked, flinty-eyed savages. She had hid her face in Madeleine's skirt at the sound of the guns and the cries of the soldiers as they fell. Mathias had tried to act brave, as thirteen-year-olds will, but she had noticed how he flinched back when the action got too close or too noisy. The Americans seemed to think that violence was just a way of life. The announcer had said as much. But it was not the French way.

Madame Soulas was astounded all over again as she thought that one of the Peaux-Rouges who had chased the bison and killed the soldiers was actually coming to live with them. What could René have been thinking? What about our poor children? Poor Chloé was only nine! And Mathias was impressionable to a fault. To have a savage sit down at their table, to sleep in their home, it was too much. And what of the neighbors? Did they deserve to have a savage frightening their children half to death? And Mademoiselle Laboussier—would she ever come again to give Chloé her piano lessons?

Madame Soulas found herself caught between the states of high anxiety and sullen misery when she heard the sounds of several footsteps outside the captain's office. She suddenly felt her heart pound and flutter and skip all at once as she prepared for her first sight of the Peau-Rouge.

But only one person entered the room, a tall man in a brown suit with long bushy sideburns and a neatly trimmed mustache which curved down around the corners of his mouth. His thick sandy hair was rumpled, but he had the air of someone important. He strode to the captain's desk, took the official's hand, and pumped it a little too vigorously. Madame Soulas noticed that his ears were small and close to his head. Beneath the hair, his face was quite delicate with hardly a line on it. He seemed very young to carry such authority. As she listened to the two men exchange greetings, she noticed that the man's French was quite simple and quite bad. There was something of the north in his accent, a smooth clipped accent, but the words were not smooth. It was clear that French was not his natural tongue.

The captain introduced him as the American vice-consul Franklin Bell to Monsieur and Madame Soulas, and the vice-consul insisted on shaking hands with both of them. He was the first American she had seen outside of a few sailors carousing around the Old Port, and of course Buffalo Bill and his cowboys. Americans never came to her neighborhood and she seldom left it. *"Enchanté, madame,"* he said, as she looked into his blue eyes and thought they were the color of the ceiling of Notre Dame de la Garde, a pale but lovely blue that seemed impossible. Madame Soulas felt a tingle in her cheeks as he bowed over her hand.

"And so, madame," he said to her, "would you like to meet your new ward? He is quite a gentleman — although they tell me he eats like a horse. Finished off a whole chicken by himself."

Madame Soulas was taken aback by his familiarity and a little embarrassed that he was addressing her so directly. She looked toward her husband, her eyes wide with confusion. She was not really a shy woman, and certainly not helpless—she sold fish right alongside René, although she didn't engage in the banter and insults of the market like many of the other wives. But this man—this American—was far too familiar for a complete stranger.

"Yes, of course we would like to meet Charging Elk, Monsieur Bell. But could you tell us about him first?" René glanced nervously at Madeleine, but kept his attention on the American. "It is my understanding that he speaks neither French nor American."

"Only too true, monsieur. He does know a few English words— Buffalo Bill, Wild West, and, of course, his own name—Charging Elk. He speaks the Siouan tongue, but unfortunately I have been unable to locate an interpreter. Nor am I likely to." Bell shook his head regretfully. "I'm afraid all the Sioux and their interpreters left with the Wild West show."

"But why don't you just send him to wherever they are?" The words were abrupt and desperate—and out before Madame Soulas could catch herself. She felt her face tingle again.

Bell looked at her for a moment, his unguarded expression caught somewhere between annoyance and amusement. "A very good question, madame. Very good. One that I have asked myself. But, you see, madame . . ." He paused, glancing at the captain. "I'm afraid your government will not let Monsieur Charging Elk leave the country. At first, it was because he had to appear before a tribunal to settle some petty charges. He did that. But now they say he entered the country illegally—he is not a citizen of the United States, he does not hold a valid passport—and so he must remain in your country until the justice system decides otherwise."

"It is the way the law works, Madame Soulas," said the captain. "The French Republic would be overrun with undesirable types if we didn't secure our borders."

"But will he ever be allowed to go home?" René seemed almost stunned at this kind of law that would keep a human being who apparently had done nothing wrong from returning to his country.

The captain raised his shoulders in an elaborate shrug. "I am only a guardian of the peace, monsieur. It is up to a higher authority. Who knows what they will decide?"

"But the law is misguided in this case, *capitaine*. The Peau-Rouge is clearly a citizen of America. He is the original citizen. Buffalo Bill said so."

The captain had attended a performance of the Wild West show too, and he had heard the speech about the original Americans, these *indiens*. At the time, he thought it must be true. But now the government said that the *indiens* were not real citizens of their own country, so this must be true too. It was all very confusing, but he was duty-bound to uphold his country's laws. He was about to shrug again, but the American stepped between him and the fishmonger and his wife.

"This will all be sorted out, monsieur, madame. Please rest assured that Monsieur Charging Elk will be with you only for a short time. Then he will be allowed to return to his own people and we can all get on with our lives. In the meantime, let me extend the heartfelt appreciation of my government for your kind generosity." He turned to the captain. "May I bring in our citizen now?"

Madeleine Soulas felt a little foolish riding in the fancy carriage up La Canebière and she hoped that none of her friends were on the boulevard that late morning. But somebody was bound to see them — and of course when they got to their neighborhood, they would be the talk of the market. Still, she felt very comfortable in the cool black leather seat. The slender white horse was a beautiful animal with its jingly black tack and the red pompom on its head. Its clipped gait rang out on the cobblestones, unlike the ponderous clop-clop-clop of the drayhorses that pulled the wagons and omnibuses.

Franklin Bell sat opposite her and René, facing backward, and beside him sat the savage, looking at nothing, seeing nothing. At first, Madame Soulas could not bring herself to look at him directly. When he had entered the room, she had glanced out of the corner of her eye and seen shiny black leather shoes, a gray suit with matching vest, a white shirt with cellophane collar, and a black tie. The clothes fit well, although the large hands seemed to hang helplessly from the cuffs.

When Madame Soulas allowed herself a quick glance at the face, she was quite surprised to see how calm and benign it looked. The savage's hair had been cut and parted in the middle. The eyes were more impassive than threatening. The thin lips were neither curved up or down, just set in an unreadable straight line. He didn't seem to respond to anything that went on in the room, and Madame Soulas wondered if perhaps he wasn't a little dumb. It wouldn't surprise her—after seeing the way the savages comported themselves in the arena, all that yipping and yowling, the fierce way they rode their horses. They did seem to be part beast.

But René had seemed to brighten at the sight of the Peau-Rouge. Perhaps because he was dressed as a normal man, even a little finer than normal, almost like a merchant or an official. It was only when one looked at the dark, almost black face with its high cheekbones and squinty, unseeing eyes that one realized he was far from being a normal man.

And now here he was, dressed in fine clothes, riding in a fine carriage, looking over the top of Madame Soulas's head toward the Old Port. What was he thinking?

Madame Soulas found herself getting more fidgety as they neared the neighborhood, and when they turned off La Canebière into the narrow Rue d'Aubagne, she was glancing nervously at the many pedestrians, hoping that she wouldn't see a face she recognized—and of course, she looked right into the eyes of Mademoiselle Laboussier, Chloé's piano teacher. Mademoiselle was a large young woman who wore too much makeup and gaudy clothes and spoke with a rapid ferocity. Many times Madeleine was tempted to terminate her daughter's lessons when she heard the staccato voice raised in protest — *"Non, non, non, ma chèrie!"* — but both she and René wanted their daughter to be accomplished enough to attract a smart young man when the time came — a lawyer, perhaps, or a merchant, someone bourgeois. They were quite content to be fishmongers but they wanted more for their son and daughter.

And now, Mademoiselle Laboussier was staring at the occupants of the carriage with an exaggerated look of astonishment. Strangely, that look not only did not disconcert Madeleine, it amused her almost to the point of laughter — the big red mouth pursed into an O, the large blue-rimmed eyes and the overly rouged cheeks. In the bright daylight of the street the large young woman looked like an escapee from the circus sideshow — the fat lady, perhaps.

Madeleine Soulas was tempted to wave, perhaps even to call out to Mademoiselle Laboussier, but she resisted, riding the rest of the way with her eyes to the front, studying the back of the driver's black beaver top hat. For the moment, at least, she didn't care what the neighborhood thought. In fact, she used the time to imagine herself as the kind of lady who would be driven in such a fine carriage. She stiffened her back and smiled kindly at the top hat.

Franklin Bell was surprised at the spaciousness of the fishmonger's flat. He had no idea of the kind of money a fishmonger might make, but the large flat was clean and gracious, with its soft velvet furnishings and trimmed and tasseled drapes, its polished wood tables and cabinets, the doilies and antimacassars draped in strategic spots. There were even a couple of electric lamps. This was a home.

While Madame Soulas occupied herself in the kitchen with the teakettle, Monsieur Soulas took Bell and Charging Elk up the stairs to the next floor. Charging Elk carried a half-filled seaman's duffle, while Bell carried a small cloth valise. They walked down a wide hall, lighted by a bright window at the end. At the last door on the left, Monsieur Soulas stood aside. *"Voilà,"* he said, indicating with his outstretched arm that they should step inside.

Bell entered first. "This is very nice, monsieur. Quite adequate."

The room wasn't large, but it was almost excessively clean and contained a single iron bed covered with a bright duvet, a small hemp rug beside it, a bureau, a washstand, and a small closet hidden behind muslin curtains.

Charging Elk entered more cautiously, glancing around at the furnishings, then walked over to the window. It looked down onto a small walled courtyard. He was surprised to see other, similar courtyards behind other buildings. The buildings seemed so solidly stone from the narrow street, and yet here was an open space, with trees and bushes, tables and chairs and umbrellas. There were even carriage sheds at the far end attached to a stable area. Charging Elk's heart lifted as he counted seven horses. The window contained a view quite unlike that of the high window in the stone room.

Bell had come over to join him at the window. "Lovely, isn't it?" he said in English. "I know you will be happy here, Charging Elk. These are good people—they'll take care of you for now. And soon you will be on a steamer for America. I promise you."

Charging Elk looked into Bell's eyes for the first time. His face seemed to register some kind of emotion, but Bell couldn't tell if it was desperation or gratitude or just plain confusion. Bell patted him on the shoulder. He didn't know what else to do.

After a tour of the rest of the flat, they had tea in the parlor. Madame Soulas served honey-soaked cakes on small china plates. She was not quite sure what the *indien* would do with his, but he ate it with a fork. She didn't know that Broncho Billy and the reservation Indians had taught him how to eat his food from a plate with a knife and fork. They had laughed at him when he speared his piece of roasted meat with his own knife and bit a large hunk from it. Finally, it was Sees Twice who told him to put the meat back on the plate, then showed him how to cut it with the many-pronged fork and the dull knife which lay beside the plate. That was in the train station in Omaha, and it was the first of many times that Charging Elk had wished that he had never left the Stronghold.

Franklin Bell watched Charging Elk eat the sweetcake and he was surprised at how deliberately, how delicately, the Indian ate. He made the sweetcake last a long time. And he didn't touch his tea until the cake was gone. Then he sipped it down, carefully replacing the cup and saucer on the table.

Bell wondered if all the Indians in the Wild West show had such good table manners. They had performed in Paris for seven months. They must have picked up the niceties of civilization. But what did they think of the white man's civilization? Did they consider it an improvement over their own primitive ways? They must have liked the money and the food—and of course, the attention—but what about the rest of it?

Bell suddenly remembered the money issue. He would have to wire the officials of the Wild West show to see if Charging Elk had any pay coming. The consul general's secretary had insisted that they needed that money to defray the cost of clothing the Indian. Thank God the Soulas did not want any money from the consulate—Monsieur Soulas would put him to work at his stall in the open-air market. But had Charging Elk ever done any real work? Hauling fish at five in the morning and cleaning up after market was a little different from riding horses every day pretending to do harm to civilized people.

Bell pulled out his pocket watch and made a show of looking at the time. He had told his driver to return in one hour and now he had ten minutes.

"So, I must be off presently. I believe we've covered everything." He looked at Madame Soulas. "Is there something else, something I've not told you? It has been quite a few days—you must be weary of bureaucrats. Madame?"

Madeleine glanced at Charging Elk, as though she were just now realizing the fact that they would soon be alone with him. Strangely, his impassive face and calm demeanor almost tricked her into believing that he would be no trouble.

"I think everything is covered, monsieur," said René. "I believe Monsieur Charging Elk will be of no trouble to us. *N'est-ce pas*, Madeleine?"

Madeleine shrugged as she acknowledged René. His beaming face at first surprised her—it was so genuine—then it annoyed her. All she could think of was the trouble, the disruption in their daily lives, the strangeness with which they would be viewed by their neighbors, and he was absolutely radiant with anticipation. She had learned to be wary of that look. She was annoyed, but at the same time determined to put the best face on the situation. She didn't want to begin this strange relationship as the sour fishwife. Still, there were so many questions that couldn't be answered just now. Time would tell if they could ever be answered. But the savage— she made herself think of his name, Charging Elk—would be with them for only a short time. Then they could resume a normal life.

Madeleine realized that both men were looking at her, and she suddenly wondered if the *indien*—Charging Elk—could tell time. Would he know when to wake up in the morning? Did he know who they were, what they did, what was expected of him? But she said, "We will do all we can to ensure that Monsieur Charging Elk is comfortable, Monsieur Bell. We are Christians." Then she added: "That is all we can do."

"*Superbe!*" Bell slapped his knee and stood up. He pulled a small card from his vest pocket. "Here is my calling card, Monsieur Soulas. You can see the address of the consulate. If anything should come up, please call on me." He tugged down the front of his vest and adjusted his tie. "And I will call back in a couple of days to see how things are working out. It's a fine thing you are doing, Soulases. *À bientôt, mes amis*."

In his haste to leave, Bell forgot to say goodbye to Charging Elk. It was only when he was stepping into the carriage that he realized this omission. But it was too late—he did have to get back to the office for a meeting with a trade group from the Vaucluse. They wanted to expand the American market for their special essence of lavender. There was no real problem—lavender was very popular with the ladies—but the perfume makers in America needed to be assured that the consulate was looking out for them.

Bell had learned more about the art of diplomacy and facilitation in his two years in France than he had in the previous ten in such hellholes as Panama City and Lima and Marrakech, haggling over coffee, bananas, and spices. He felt that he was ready to become consul general somewhere, but he feared he would be sent to one of the second-rate countries he had just fled. Marseille wasn't the finest place in the world—there was very little in the way of art, or ancient, or even old, architecture—but it was one of the great seaports. He was getting a real education in the area of trade agreements.

As the carriage turned onto La Canebière, Bell tugged on his mustache and watched a couple of boulevardiers entertain a small gaggle of young ladies in uniform long dresses and coats and hats. Probably shopgirls or office workers. One was particularly attractive, small but shapely, standing aloof from her giggling friends. Aplomb, he thought, such aplomb—and dignity. Why couldn't he meet a young woman like her?

Bell knew he was still fairly attractive. He had always been ath-
letic—he had played squash and boxed at Yale. He had even been
a member of the first-ever lacrosse club. Now he smiled and sat
back in his seat. He almost laughed as he remembered the lacrosse
coach, a Seneca Indian who worked as a groundskeeper at his college and whose main instructions were "Run, boys, run" and "This
is war, young men!"

Funny, Bell thought, how the Seneca was completely integrated
into America—he spoke the language, dressed properly, and attended chapel every morning—but this Sioux, Charging Elk, was a
babe in the woods. Bell had even had to show him how to knot his
shoelaces this morning! My God, what about tomorrow morning?
How long would it take for this Indian to learn how to tie his own
shoes? Would Monsieur Soulas assume that responsibility? And
what about brushing his teeth? You'd think after all those days of
being in the hospital, of wandering the streets of Marseille, of being
in the jail, he would have been only too happy to brush his teeth.
But he hadn't seemed very interested in this simple act of hygiene.

Bell was suddenly filled with misgivings. The Soulases were nice
people, but Charging Elk was his responsibility. What if the Indian
decided to run away? What if he ended up in jail again? Or met
with some unfortunate accident? Or—the unthinkable—decided to
visit violence on a French citizen, on one of the Soulases? It would
all end up back in his lap. And of course, it would go on his record,
which was, up to now, spotless, if undistinguished. Bell knew how
easily he could be buried in some small Latin or South American
country—or worse yet, North Africa, which was always dangerous.

Bell was leaning forward on the seat, his back stiff and his
hands clenched over his knees. All it takes is a small series of mis-
takes or one big fiasco and you're exiled, he thought. Or drummed
out of the corps. Now Bell realized that his big mistake was not
involving the consul general more. If he had just kept Atkinson ap-

prised of the situation, perhaps any repercussions of the Indian's behavior, if it was unacceptable, could be deflected. It would be the old man's fault as much as his.

Bell sat back, glumly watching the pedestrians along La Canebière. He saw a young couple step into a shop that had a big eye painted on the glass. Several candles burned in the window, and behind them, tired red velvet drapes hid the rest of the shop. The man wore jodhpurs and tall brown boots and a turban, the young woman such a large, gaudy bustle she could scarcely fit through the door. Bell was used to such odd sights in the strange seaport, but now he wondered what these extravagant creatures were seeking from the fortune-teller. He had never been to a fortune-teller but he made a note of the location of the shop. He could use some help with his love life.

As the carriage turned onto Boulevard Peytral and slowed to a stop before the consulate, Bell made a mental note to look in on the Soulases the next day and every day after that, schedule permitting. Bell knew that the red tape would be maddening, but he was optimistic that the Charging Elk matter would be resolved in a week or two. Meanwhile, he would baby-sit the Indian at every opportunity.

"*Voilà*, Monsieur Bell."

Bell looked up. He had been studying his brown hightop shoes. They needed polishing.

"*Le consulat, monsieur.*"

Bell smiled. After two years he didn't need to be told where he was. But he must have been sitting there awhile. "*Merci*, Robert." He stepped down and the carriage moved away, the white horse with the red pompom seeming to move faster as it thought of the stable. Or perhaps Robert was in a hurry to end his day.

But it was a fine winter day, and Franklin Bell took one last look at the sharp blue sky and smelled the heady brine of the Old Port before he hurried in to his meeting with the lavender processors from the Vaucluse. As he pulled open the heavy wooden door, he thought once again of the small, shapely French girl and decided that she wasn't very pretty after all. Something of a pleasant illusion, not unlike the powderpuff boulevardiers of Marseille. Goddamn, he envied them.

CHAPTER SIX

Charging Elk stood at the window of his small room and looked down at the stable and the horses. It was night and the horses looked dark and indistinct beneath a single gas lamp. All of the other flats around the inner square were shuttered and dark. One of the horses walked around the pen, circling it again and again, while the others stood sleeping in the middle. Charging Elk thought the horse must be new to the pen, still spooked by the unfamiliar surroundings. Perhaps it was from the country. There was plenty of country between here and Paris. All of the Indian performers were fascinated by the country they passed through, even at night when they might see a gentle hill marked by rows of grapevines rolling away from the iron road, or a big stone building surrounded by smaller buildings, all the slate roofs glinting like ice in the moonlight, all the windows dark. And when they passed through a town, they watched for people and horses with quiet curiosity.

The train stopped often to take on water. Broncho Billy said it was the water that made the smoke, and the smoke made the train go. During these stops the Indians and the other performers were allowed to get off the train and walk the stiffness from their legs. Charging Elk never walked very far from the train, and when the whistle sounded, he was among the first to get back on.

Sometimes Charging Elk would see Buffalo Bill standing at the far end of the stone platform, usually accompanied by three or four other men in fine clothes, all of them smoking cigars. Once in a while, if the stop was long, he would come to stand with the Indians. Rocky Bear would also come from his carriage to interpret, even though Broncho Billy, who was married to a Lakota woman and spoke the language quite well, was always with the Indians. Once Buffalo Bill had talked with Charging Elk.

"How'd you learn to ride like that, young man?"

When Rocky Bear had interpreted the question, Featherman said, "He is a wild Indian from the badlands. He never surrendered."

"But how is this? This young man came in with Crazy Horse, hell's bells, twelve years ago. All the Oglalas came in."

"There were some who could not accept the ways of the *waᶴichuᶴ*," said Sees Twice. "This young man had never seen the inside of a church until we went to Notre Dame in Paris." Sees Twice had said this in English, so Rocky Bear interpreted for Charging Elk.

"Well, you saw yourself one hell of a church, Charging Elk. That's the greatest church on the face of the earth, next to the Pope's house. You'll see what I mean when we get to the land of the Eye-talians."

Just then, the whistle sounded and Buffalo Bill clapped Charging Elk on the shoulder. "You're going to see a lot of things on this trip, son, things that will make your head spin round and round. Enjoy it all—but just remember, when you're in that arena you're a wild Indian from hell's fire."

Charging Elk had watched him stroll back to his carriage. He was dressed in a heavy wool suit and he wore a gray hat with a narrower brim than the one he used in the show. Except for his mustache and the little puff of hair on his chin, one wouldn't have recognized him as the great warrior who thrilled the audiences with his buckskin suit, beaded gauntlets, and shiny black boots that came halfway up his thighs.

It had always puzzled Charging Elk that, in the daily reenactment, Buffalo Bill was the first *wasichu* to find the dead longknives on the Greasy Grass; yet none of the Indian performers, even those who had fought there, could remember any of the Lakotas talking about him then. Surely, such a big man would have been talked about. But Broncho Billy swore up and down that Pahuska had been a buffalo hunter and a scout for the longknives. Even now he was a big chief with the army of Nebraska.

Charging Elk watched the restless horse continue its path around the pen. There was something about the horse, as indistinct as it was, that reminded him of High Runner. It was taller than the other horses and it held its head up, as though it smelled open country and longed to be there.

It seemed like only a couple of moons ago that Charging Elk had handed the reins to his father and said, "High Runner is yours now. He will make you look like the shirtwearer you are." Scrub's own two horses were poor in color, with broad bowed backs and hooves as big as buffalo chips. They were meant to pull a wagon, not to ride with dignity. Charging Elk now regretted that he had not seen his father on High Runner, but when the iron horse shuddered and slowly began to grind away from the station, the reins were tied to a wagon wheel and Scrub stood on the platform, singing a braveheart song with the others.

Charging Elk looked above the rooftops with their many dark chimneys silhouetted against the dark sky. They reminded him of the stumps in Paha Sapa that the *wasichus* left when they took the trees to make their houses and hold up their mineholes. Once he and Strikes Plenty had ventured a long way into a dark hole in search of the precious gold, but all they found was wet rocks, a broken pickax, and the squared-off wooden braces. Later, when they rode back to the Stronghold, they became afraid because they had entered one of the *wasichu*'s wounds in *maka ina*'s breast. They went directly to Bird Tail, the old *pejuta wicasa*, and told him what they had done. The holy man had simply looked off toward the strange shapes and colors of the badlands—although his eyes were frosted over and he had to be led around by his wife—and told the boys to fast, to think about what they had done, and to return the next day. Neither Charging Elk nor Strikes Plenty got much sleep that night. But the next morning, Bird Tail told them that he had had a dream in which a buffalo wandered through the forests of Paha Sapa and came upon a cave carved into a scarred rockface. The buffalo turned around four times, as a dog does before it lies down, each time looking back at the world. It seemed to be looking at everything, as though it wanted to remember all that was there. It looked for a long time, through the many winters of its ancestors, over the plains and rivers and mountains that they had crossed; it looked at times of good grass and times of hunger; it looked at times of trouble and times of peace. Finally, it looked up into the sky at the sun and its eyes turned as white and hard as polished stone. Then it whirled and entered the cave.

Bird Tail had picked up his pipe then and lit it with a match he struck across a piece of rough stone. After a couple of thoughtful puffs, he said, "I want to thank you two boys for going into the *wasichu*'s wound in grandmother's breast. You didn't know it at the time, but you were sent there for a reason. Wakan Tanka knew that you would tell me and that I would dream about the buffalo with the stone eyes. The Great Mystery works that way. All things have a reason, but he chooses to let his children figure them out.

"You see, the dream I had was of the future. All this time, we have mourned the passing of the buffalo. We have thought the sacred hoop was broken when the *wasicuns* came into our country and our people lost their way. But now I have seen that the buffalo are not gone forever; they have only returned to their home deep in the heart of Paha Sapa. There they will remain until the hoop is *wakan* again."

"And how will they know when that time comes?" Strikes Plenty spoke in a voice that was at once excited and skeptical.

The old man smiled as he knocked the tobacco ashes from his pipe into the smoldering fire. "They will know, young man. They will tell us." He put the pipe into its beaded pouch, then opened an ancient parfleche that was painted with faded vermilion-and-green designs. He helped himself to a braid of sweetgrass, a twist of tobacco, and a buffalo-tail flyswatter. "Now you boys help me up. We'll go have a sweat and ask *maka ina* to forgive you for entering the *wasichu*'s wound in her flesh."

That night Charging Elk dreamed of returning to the Stronghold. He rode High Runner and the tall bay danced through the badlands, in a hurry, as always, to return to the good grasses and the cunning mares. As they ascended the high butte, Charging Elk could see many people, on horses, in wagons, some walking, all going toward the Stronghold. And when he got on top, he saw many lodges and he saw many people dancing in a circle. He didn't recognize the dance. It was not rhythmic and graceful like the old-time dances; rather, the people hopped and twirled in place, men shouting and wailing, women ululating and crying out. The drum group pushed the people even faster, until some of the dancers fell to the ground, where some lay motionless while others twitched and rolled around as though they were struggling to leave their bodies.

It was still night when Charging Elk heard a light rapping sound. He had quit dreaming and had been lying on the sleeping platform, covered with a heavy quilt. After much thought, he had decided that the crazy dancers were not Oglalas, not even Lakotas. They came from somewhere else. But who were they and what were they doing in the land of the Lakotas? The White Buffalo Cow Woman, who brought them the sacred pipe and the sun dance, had promised that the Lakotas would prosper and thrive as long as they sacrificed and performed her ceremonies correctly. But had she foreseen the coming of the *wasichus*? Why didn't she warn the people so that they could prepare? If the people had done something bad, something that would anger Wakan Tanka and cause him to turn away from the people, why didn't she intercede on their behalf? Charging Elk tried to understand but he knew that the Great Mystery was beyond understanding. He could only play out his role and hope and pray that the circle would become *wakan* again and he would live to be an old man among his people. He thought again of Bird Tail's dream of the last buffalo and he thought that it must be roaming deep in the bowels of Paha Sapa, perhaps reproducing itself, perhaps learning new ceremonies from the White Buffalo Cow Woman. Perhaps one day they would emerge, leading a river of the great animals out into Lakota country. The thought made his heart jump up, just as it had that morning when Bird Tail told his dream. Through the window at the other end of the room he could just make out the white sliver of the new moon and he knew it was the Moon of Frost in the Tipi. It was the coldest of all moons—at the Stronghold only the hunters and those who had run out of wood or buffalo chips would get up early to go out. If Charging Elk and Strikes Plenty had meat, they would huddle around the fire and drink coffee, draping their sleeping robes over their backsides. Those were the long, lonely days that were so hard to endure. Sometimes when the wind blew and the snow piled up, they would be stuck inside the lodge for five or six sleeps at a time. Five winters ago, when Charging Elk was eighteen, they were stuck for nearly all of the Moon of Frost in the Tipi. They ran out of meat and coffee and tobacco and had to boil the rawhide they used to patch their moccasins.

There were seventeen lodges out at the Stronghold that winter, around seventy people all together. Some were families, others were young men a little older than Charging Elk and Strikes Plenty. They were "bad" Indians and so they had to be careful. If they ever came in to Pine Ridge they would be arrested. The men would be sent away to Fort Randall, the women put under guard, and the children taken by the agent to a home of many children. But that winter, as they ran out of food and firewood, there were many who would have liked to come in, no matter what the punishment. But there was no way they could move. The usual two-day journey would have taken five sleeps, if they made it at all. As it was, eight of them died of starvation that winter—four children, three old ones, and a wandering Sans Arc who had been gutshot by a miner. Bird Tail had kept him alive for two moons with his medicine, but the cold and starvation had been too much for him.

Charging Elk closed his eyes against the dark. He would have gone through ten such winters just to be back home. But this time he would be with his mother and father. And then he would find a wife. By now Strikes Plenty would have found his *winyan* out at the Whirlwind Compound. He had family there. And there were many young women looking for a husband.

Charging Elk didn't feel much like a "wild" Indian anymore. He remembered the pride he had felt when Featherman told Buffalo Bill that he was a wild Indian. He had thought then that Pahuska had appreciated the fact that he was not a reservation Indian like his compatriots. Perhaps he had. But where had it gotten Charging Elk? Most of the reservation Indians could speak the American tongue; all of them adapted to this new life of strangers better than he did; and all of them were still with the Wild West show, wherever it was—perhaps at the Pope's house.

No, Charging Elk's wildness counted for nothing now. He felt like the fire boat out on the big water, no land in sight, no end in sight. Just the vast, swelling water that played games with the suddenly small boat.

But where was Yellow Breast? Wakan Tanka had sent him with tobacco. Surely that was an offering, a sign to let Charging Elk know that the Great Mystery had not forgotten him. He had tried to smoke the cigarette in the right way, but he was no *pejuta wicasa*—he had no real power in the spirit world. And it was clear that his animal helper did not have the power anymore to talk with Wakan Tanka on his behalf. So where did that leave him? Had Yellow Breast abandoned him too?

He heard the light rapping again and he became alert. He looked toward the door and saw it open a little to let in light from the long-room.

"*Bonjour, Charging Elk. Est-ce que vous avez bien dormi?*"

The door opened a little wider, and Charging Elk swung his legs over the side of the bed and sat up. He was still wearing the suit and shirt he had had on yesterday, minus the collar and tie and shoes.

A head peeked around the door and he saw it was the Frenchman who lived here.

"*Ah, très bien. Ça va?*"

Suddenly an electric wire came on above them, making the room look hollow and cold. Charging Elk stood and narrowed his eyes against the glare.

The short, stocky man was dressed in blue pants and a black sweater. He was carrying a heavy pitcher. He smiled at Charging Elk, but he was also looking at the rumpled suit. Then he made a gesture that seemed to excite him. All the time he was speaking the tongue of the French. He pointed to the duffel and the small valise, which had remained unopened at the foot of the bed. He asked a question, but Charging Elk could only look at him.

Charging Elk watched the man and he guessed that he had lived about thirty-five winters. His slick hair was thin and combed back over a patch of skin at the back of his dome. Charging Elk had noticed the day before that the man's hands were surprisingly big for his size. They looked red and nicked in the pale light. But Charging Elk was most interested in the man's face. It had no mustache or beard. Even the sideburns were cut short, barely reaching the lobes of the ears. For some reason Charging Elk didn't mind looking into this *wasichu*'s face. Although the nose was flat and two of the man's lower front teeth were missing, there was something in the eyes that the Oglala recognized—the kind of sad wisdom that some of the older people possessed. Their eyes expressed a kindness, a forgiveness of mankind's trangressions, that comes from a hard life, from understanding what human beings go through to become better— or sometimes, even worse. The eyes of these old people did not condemn. And now Charging Elk was seeing it in the eyes of this small man, who was talking and gesturing almost nonstop.

Charging Elk stood aside as the man carried the pitcher over to a little stand that had a large bowl on top and a cloth hanging from a peg on the side. The man looked around, exclaimed, then pulled the duffel over to a box of drawers. He opened up the drawers, each time gesturing and saying *"Et voilà!"* Then he dumped the contents of the duffel into the drawers and muttered to himself as he pawed over the clothes. Finally he held up a long gray shirt without a collar or buttons and handed it to Charging Elk. He found a pair of new blue pants much like his own. Then a white-and-blue-striped sweater. As if by magic, he produced a pair of big, rough shoes from the duffel. And a rolled-up wool jacket. He opened the top drawer and found a pair of gray stockings tucked together. He looked at Charging Elk with a satisfied grin. He pointed to the clothes, then to the tall Indian. He poured some of the warm water into the bowl and made signs of washing his face. "I will wait just outside," he said. Then he spied the valise. "Let us see."

The valise held a comb and brush, a razor and strop, and a toothbrush, among other things. *"Très bien, très bien, très bien,"* said the small man, as he held each item up to the light before placing it on the box of drawers. Then he drew out a hand mirror. He held it up to Charging Elk's face and laughed. *"C'est un bel homme, n'est-ce pas?* I will wait just outside."

Charging Elk was glad to get out of the suit. It was warm but it made his legs itch. He put on the new clothes, and although the pants were stiff, they didn't make him itch. He put on the stockings and the rough shoes, tying the knot just as Brown Suit had instructed him. He was relieved that these new shoes were bigger than the ones he had worn the day before. The toes were wider and he wriggled his foot gratefully.

He washed his face with soap and water; then he dipped the toothbrush into the soapy water and brushed his teeth. It felt good to clean his teeth, even with the bitter water. Then, looking down into the hand mirror on the box of drawers, he lifted the brush to his hair, then stopped, shocked to see that his hair had been cut off to just around his ears. Of course, he had touched the short hair in disbelief many times since yesterday morning, but to see it now filled him with fear. How would Wakan Tanka know him? Charging Elk suddenly felt ashamed of himself. He had gone from being a wild Indian to this creature in the mirror. He glanced down at his new clothes, his new rough shoes. What had happened to him? Just a few sleeps ago, he had possessed his father's hairpipe breastplate, his own badger-claw necklace, his skin clothing—above all, the long hair that had never been cut. Even when he put on the *wasichu's* blouses and pants, he wore brass armbands, earrings, and the two eagle feathers in his hair. He wore moccasins and wrapped his braids in ermine and red yarn. Now, this creature that looked back at him in the mirror didn't look like the Oglala from the Stronghold. The face had grown thin, the eyes seemed unsure, and the mouth looked weak. How would Wakan Tanka know that it was Charging Elk? How would Charging Elk again become the man he once was? Would he always look like this—like a weak, frightened coward?

Charging Elk turned the mirror over on the box. He walked to the window. It was still pitch-black and the horse that had circled the pen earlier had stopped. All the horses stood under the arc of the gaslight, heads down, indistinct, indistinguishable one from the other, sleeping. Above them, the beginning sliver of the Moon of Frost in the Tipi hung over the big town like the curved awl his mother used to sew moccasins. Charging Elk made a morning prayer even as he wondered if she was looking at the same moon. He had lost track of time but he sensed that this moon was still to come in his homeland far to the west. Perhaps his mother and father would know that he had seen this moon and they would make prayers for him. Perhaps they would ask Wakan Tanka to send a dream that would show him the way home.

René Soulas watched Charging Elk stir five lumps of sugar into his café au lait and thought, He is a beautiful human being. Even in the clothes of the workingman, he is above the humble station of the *prolétaire*. The way he moved, the way he held his head, the long fin-gers—he was like a prince, a very dark prince. René had noticed Charging Elk in the Wild West show because he was so much darker than the other Peaux-Rouges. He was almost as dark as a *nègre*. And he was the one who took the most chances—who rode among the stampeding bison as though they were his pets.

Réne had been stunned when Charging Elk had walked into the captain's office at the Préfecture. Here was the one *indien* that he recognized out of the whole lot—except for the great chief, Rocky Bear—and he was coming to live with them! But then, he thought sadly, it is only for a short time. Monsieur Bell, the American, could come at any time—today, tomorrow, next week—to take this mag-nificent creature from us. It is sad that in such a short time, we will not learn to communicate. He could tell Mathias and Chloé so much about the wild west. According to Buffalo Bill, the wild west was not even in Les États-Unis, but in some vast land beyond. Perhaps someday Mathias would go there to see Charging Elk in his *habitation* and learn the skills of survival. It was not out of the question. Mathias had a nose for adventure.

René watched the *indien* eat his baguette with apricot jam heaped upon it and he wished the children could be here now. But Madeleine had insisted that Mathias and Chloé spend this first night with her parents. She was convinced they would have night-mares or that they wouldn't be able to sleep for fear of being scalped. René had scoffed at her fears, but now he acknowledged that the scalping scenes in the show were very gruesome. And he had seen Chloé hide her face in her mother's skirts when the *indiens* danced around with the scalps on their spears. But it was all a trick. The "dead" soldiers still had their hair. Anybody could see that.

He glanced toward his wife, who was making a fish stock on the stove. René had insisted that they have a traditional bouillabaisse for dinner that night in honor of their guest. After all, he might be with them just a short time. René had already traded a good-sized hogfish to Monsieur David, the spice trader, for a few strands of saffron and some pink pepper. Madeleine had insisted that the saffron was too dear, but how can one make a decent bouillabaisse without it?

Poor Madeleine. How she suffered—and so needlessly. "Think simply, dear one, and put your trust in God." René didn't know how many times he had told her that over the course of their marriage. And didn't it always work out? Even when Chloé came down with the influenza and it was necessary to call the priest for extreme unction, René had simply prayed hard and long into the night—and the next morning she sat up and took some broth and a bit of biscuit. René didn't like to talk about it, but he sometimes had visitations from the Virgin Mary. This time she told him to tithe a little more, to sell more fish and put more francs into the collection plate, and Chloé would live a long life of blessedness, perhaps even become a nun. Of course, Madeleine was furious when he dropped the extra francs into the basket, but that was all right. She got over it and even seemed a little proud when he put the extra in the basket. Out of the corner of his eye, he noticed her looking around at the other parishioners with a somewhat superior smile. Even René enjoyed the look on Monsieur Gaspard's face, a look of surprised disapproval. Gaspard was a very high official in the Mairie, very bourgeois.

René loved Madeleine now more than he ever had. She had given him two beautiful children and she was still beautiful herself. It always saddened him that his father could not be alive to see his family. If God had not found it necessary to take him, he would have approved of Madeleine. She could still fit into her wedding dress, and her dear face was as unlined and plump as it had been the day he picked her up off the ground when she fell from the cherry tree.

René Soulas was a lucky man. True, this winter the fishing was off and they would all have to tighten their belts a notch, but his family had always been agreeable to whichever way the wind shifted. And soon it would shift again—the mistral did not blow forever—and there would be lamb and pork on the table. So what if they had to live on fish? Did not the fish provide them with a livelihood? What's wrong with eating a little of the profits? René sighed. Perhaps a hogfish for saffron was not a very good deal, but this was a very special occasion. And bouillabaisse without saffron was just fish stew.

René pulled his watch from his vest pocket: ten minutes after five. They had twenty minutes until the first boats came in with their catch. "Come, Charging Elk, we must be off. I will show you how I earn my living. Perhaps you can be of some help, my friend." René still hadn't decided if Charging Elk was strictly a guest or a contributing member of the family. Would he want to work?

"He doesn't understand a word you're saying." Madeleine still had her back to the table. "He doesn't understand anything. Don't you realize that? The American says he is ignorant of any common language. Besides, you speak French to him, then *langue d'oc* to me. How do you expect him to learn?"

"French, Provençal, perhaps not the words—but I believe he is a very intuitive fellow. They say the Peaux-Rouges have a sixth sense." René stood, and Charging Elk followed suit. "See? He knows it is time to go."

"You are a foolish man to believe that. But you were foolish to want him in our home. I just hope poor Chloé won't be scared out of her wits."

René walked around the table and put his hands on her shoulders. He kissed her on the ear. "You are foolish to be worried, my dear wife. Our children will have an excitement to last them all their lives. They will tell their grandchildren that they slept under the same roof as a wild *indien*."

"If they live that long."

René laughed. Then he stopped, as abruptly as he began, and said, "Buffalo Bill says they are disappearing—like the bison. He says their culture is dying and soon they will be gone too. It is a tragedy that such things happen."

Madeleine continued to chop an onion for the stock. For a moment it was the only sound in the kitchen. Then it too stopped and she turned away from the cutting board. She was only a few centimeters shorter than her husband, but she looked up to his hair and ran her damp fingers through it. "You mustn't think about such things, René. You are a simple fishseller. You have a loving family. That is enough for you to think about." The words were calm and instructive, but there was a years-deep affection in the voice. They often argued, as Provençal people will, but it meant nothing to how they felt about each other. Madeleine smoothed his hair, then turned toward Charging Elk. "We will treat him well—for the short time he is with us. Now go. I will see you at eight-thirty. Perhaps we will bring home a hogfish for your bouillabaisse."

René laughed for a second time, this time in real mirth. He knew she was chiding him for trading off a choice hogfish for the saffron. Now she was suggesting that they would lose two hogfish for this latest of his foolish enterprises. He smiled up at Charging Elk and took him by the elbow, steering him toward the door. "See you at the market, my dear one. And don't forget the cashbox."

"Have I ever? Do you really think me irresponsible, or do you make yourself important in the eyes of a savage who can't even understand you? Now go. Leave me in peace to prepare your precious bouillabaisse. *Á bientôt*, foolish one."

It was still dark when the two men turned the corner from Rue d'Aubagne onto La Canebière on their way to the Old Port. They passed the wide Cours Belsunce and Cours St-Louis, where the cafés would be bustling in a couple of hours. It was the time of day, or night, this dusky hour, that René enjoyed more than any other. He had been walking this route now for twenty-five years, since he was a child accompanying his father. Even when he was a student at lycée, he had helped his father and his helper cart the fish to the stall before he went off to school. They did it by hand, his father pulling the big-wheeled cart, René and the helper pushing. Some people never realized how steep the grade was up La Canebière, but René did. When the catch was good and the citizens had plenty of francs, the cart would be loaded to the top with fish. It took all three of them to deliver the slippery, wet cargo to their stall in the open-air market.

Now, René had a horse-drawn cart that his own helper, François, kept in his field on the northern edge of Marseille, not far behind the Gare St-Charles. The big dun mare wasn't much to look at, just an old dray animal, but she was strong enough to carry Mathias, when he was a small child, and pull a full cart at the same time.

François had been with René now for some ten years and had eased the fishmonger's life considerably. He knew what to do, he was prompt, and he took orders easily. Even now, he would be waiting with the cart. The baskets would be clean, the block of ice would be waiting for them back at the stall, and the selling boxes would be set up at a slight angle, so the customers could see the bounty of the sea easily. René was assiduous in arranging his fish and crustaceans in the most attractive way. He even arranged lemon halves artfully in the beds of chipped ice, although this time of year they came from Africa and the southern portion of the Levant and were too expensive. Madeleine scolded him for buying the lemons, which were only thrown away at the end of market, but René knew it was these little touches—like laying the hogfish on its ice bed with its mouth propped open to show its cavernous maw, or arranging the shrimps so that they seemed to be spilling from a wicker cornucopia—that attracted customers to his stall. René did not stand in the dust when it came to new methods to tempt the browsers. The women, who were the lifeblood of his trade, especially appreciated his artistry.

By the time René and Charging Elk reached the sloping stone ramp of the Quai des Belges, a dozen boats had slid up to the edge and the fishermen were unloading their catches. The men were bundled up in wool jackets and caps, oilskin pants, and long boots. For the most part, they were silent as they carried the deep wooden boxes up the ramp. René sighed and pursed his lips. In the twenty-five years he had been coming down to the quai, he had learned to immediately read the mood of the fishermen. Sometimes they were loud and bantering. That meant that the boats were loaded with fish. Other times, they were thoughtful and the conversation was subdued. And that meant the catch was so-so, disappointing but not cause for grave concern. Now, the almost complete silence of the fishermen meant that the catch was not good at all and they were worried about their families, their boats, their livelihood.

René, with Charging Elk in tow, spent the next few minutes examining each catch. He looked out into the black open water between the rows of moored skiffs and yachts and saw three more fishing boats drifting toward the quai, their sails already down, powered only by their momentum. He was looking for one in particular, a larger boat named *La Martine,* which went out farther and caught the bigger fish, as well as the most *hareng.* But it was nowhere to be seen. Not surprising. Sometimes it stayed out for two or three days at a time.

"It is nothing," said a slender younger man. He had his coat collar buttoned to the neck and his arms wrapped around his torso. His wire-rimmed glasses glinted beneath the light of an electric lamp. "It is worse than nothing. Can it get any worse?"

René recognized him. He bought fish for half a dozen of the best restaurants around the port, including his own. None of the fishermen or the other fishmongers liked him because of his disdain for the quantity or quality of the fish. If there were plenty, he would remark on the poor quality; if the catch was meager, he would imply that the quality of the fishermen was poor. Nonetheless, the fishermen saved their best fish for him. To have their fish chosen for the finest restaurants in Marseille was truly a mark of honor, not to mention good advertising. On the other hand, the fishmongers resented the fact that he didn't buy from them, as did the other restaurateurs.

"It will get better, Monsieur Breteuil," René said, wondering if he really meant it. "January is always the poorest month, especially for the shellfish. You'll see. Things will pick up when the mistral dies and the water warms."

But Breteuil was looking beyond René. "What's this?" he said, his voice suddenly soft and wary.

René looked behind him, past Charging Elk. He saw only other fishmongers and the marketmaster. Several carts stood in the street behind them, the horses' muzzles buried in their feed bags. François was coming toward them with the baskets balanced on his shoulder. René saw nothing out of the ordinary, but when he turned back to Breteuil he saw the chef staring at Charging Elk.

"Only my new helper," he said with a taut grin that seemed to start at the lower edge of his mouth, revealing the dark space where the two bottom teeth were missing. He glanced around and saw a group of three fishmongers staring at his helper, and his smile widened. "Monsieur Charging Elk, messieurs, late of Buffalo Bill's Wild West show."

"But how is he here?" said Breteuil.

The three fishmongers had moved closer and were staring up at the big-boned stranger with the dark face. Although Charging Elk had lost a great deal of weight, he was still an imposing figure, with his wide shoulders and long arms and legs.

"Introduce us, René," said one.

"Does he speak French?" said another.

The third one simply stared.

René introduced them, and each stepped forward to shake hands.

"Doesn't have much of a grip," said the first one, a stout man who sold fish at the base of Le Panier. "He could use some honest work."

"But the Peaux-Rouges are not used to shaking hands, Jean-Claude. I believe they clap each other on the back. I have seen them do this at the Wild West show." To demonstrate, René reached up and recklessly slapped Charging Elk on the back. "See?" he said, the smile broadening even more, so that he looked like a happy gargoyle under the pale light.

But he hadn't seen the *indien* cast a sharp glance at this sudden gesture.

Breteuil had noticed, but he had noticed more the large but slender hand that had slipped so neatly into his. Despite its limpness, it was not a soft hand. He could almost feel the potential power of that hand, and it excited him and frightened him at the same time. He had known the same kind of thrill with some of the *nègres* that sailed up on the ships from West Africa. Many of them were as tall and powerful as this *indien*, but they were little more than slaves. Some of Breteuil's friends had been with the *nègres* and had encouraged him to do likewise, but to see the large *nègres* being ordered about by Arabs had left Breteuil with a feeling of frustration and contempt. It disgusted him to see them accept such humiliation; yet, he found many of them quite beautiful. He looked at Charging Elk and saw that the *indien* was looking right at him. The narrow eyes glistened in the electric lamplight and Breteuil almost stepped

back in fright; still, he felt a warmth surge through his body, in spite
of the chill of the dusky hour.

By six-thirty, all the boats, including *La Martine*, were in, and their
catches were lined up neatly in large wooden boxes at the top of the
Quai des Belges. The marketmaster rang the brass bell and the bidding began.

Most of the fishmongers gathered around the boxes from *La
Martine*, hoping for hogfish and tuna, as well as herring. The boat
was fitted for trolling as well as for seining. When the fishing was
slow, the captain put out the net. When the herring ran out, the
lines were put down. When the tuna were feeding on schools of sardines, the crew cast the shiny hooks into the turbulence they created. Seeing what *La Martine* would come in with was almost
always a happy adventure for the fishmongers.

But René didn't harbor much hope in the big ship's catch this
morning. Instead, he started at the other end, where he was pleasantly surprised to see several boxes at least half full of herring and
rouget, as well as a decent supply of anchovies. The shrimpers had
had a little luck, but the langoustine and shrimp were in short supply. And there were only a couple of dozen octopi in the whole
catch.

By now, two other fishmongers were bidding with him, and so
René got down to work. He enjoyed this part of it—to pay as little
as possible, occasionally bidding the price up, then leaving another
fishmonger to pay a little extra for his booty. Next time he might be
a little shy and bid too low. In the end, René purchased twenty-
eight kilos of herring, seventeen kilos of *rouget*, a basketful of anchovies, and one octopus—mostly for display. He paid too much
for it, but it would go by the end of the market, even if René had to
take a beating on it. He bought what few squids and sea urchins he

could find. Breteuil had been partially right—it was not exactly
nothing but not a lot either. René estimated that he had enough fish
to last about half of the four-hour market, just enough to keep the
people in his neighborhood—at least the early birds—from grous-
ing too much. Ordinarily, he could sell well over a hundred kilos,
but he would make do with what God provided him. At the last
minute, he walked down to *La Martine* and bid successfully on a
twelve-kilo tuna, which he would cut into steaks. As he was leafing
through his roll of francs, satisfied that he at least had a decent variety of fish, he glanced around, looking for Charging Elk. In the
excitement of the bidding, he had forgotten his ward. He saw
François walking toward the cart with two heavy baskets. François
had been bidding for scallops and mussels at the other end of the
quai. By the look of the baskets and the awkward gait, he had been
somewhat successful.

Then René spotted Charging Elk. He was helping Breteuil load
his fish on a cart. Damn that Breteuil! He was an abomination in
the eyes of God, with his effeminate ways and haughty manner.
René knew by hearsay the kind of crowd the chef ran with. They
were all *polissons*, all bound for perdition in the next life—but in this
life they were more than a simple thorn in the side. They were evil
beyond compare.

René finished paying the fisherman, then hurried over to his baskets, dropping the tuna in with the anchovies. He was almost running by the time he reached Breteuil's cart. "Monsieur Breteuil!
What are you doing with my new helper?" René felt his heart beating in his chest and he knew that he was more worked up than he
probably had a right to be. And he realized that he was more scared
than angry. Charging Elk was like a puppy. He could be led by anyone with nothing more than the promise of a treat. Even now, he
had a long, thin cigar clamped between his lips.

"He offered to help me, Monsieur Soulas. It is nothing, just a helping hand." Breteuil wiped his glasses on his coat. It had begun to mist, and both he and René instinctively looked up at the graying sky. Both seemed mildly surprised, after yesterday's brilliant winter sun.

"But it is not done, monsieur. You have a helper. You must not take mine too." René laughed and immediately felt ashamed of himself for being deferential to an insolent pervert. He tried to recover. "You must never do it again, monsieur. It is not done on the Quai des Belges. Look around." He waved his arm toward the men loading the carts.

Breteuil hooked his spectacles behind his ears. "It is nothing, Soulas. He was just standing here, so I invited him to help me lift my baskets. My helper was bringing the langoustines from way over there." Breteuil pointed off into the vague darkness. "I thought your Peau-Rouge could use some exercise."

But René was already leading Charging Elk away toward his own baskets. "You must stay away from that creature. He is an evil one. He and his fellows prey on the uninitiated. They are the devil's own spawn, a pox sent by Satan to tempt young men of limited intelligence and morals. . . ."

Charging Elk stopped, freeing his sleeve from the tugging hand, and looked back at Breteuil. He suddenly knew who the man reminded him of—the pale skin, the slender body, the spectacles. Yellow Breast. And this man had given him a smoke too. Perhaps they knew each other, or were sent by Wakan Tanka to help him. Perhaps they were *heyokas*, sacred clowns, come to show him the way. The little man tugged more forcefully, all the time chattering at him, and Charging Elk allowed himself to be separated from the pale *heyoka*. But he knew he would see him again. He would watch for him, for surely, somehow, he or Yellow Breast would give him a sign.

René was almost beside himself with excitement. He had been

surprised when the *indien* had looked back at the evil Breteuil. He seemed to have known what René was saying and looked back to confirm his judgment. Charging Elk could understand! Madeleine had been wrong to doubt the man's intelligence. *"Oui, oui, mon ami,* you are a bright one. You see what I say is true. A severe lesson. But come, René Soulas will show you how to sell fish."

By midmorning the drizzle had stopped and the dark clouds were giving way to the high gauzy puffs that would soon blow off to the south. The tall gloomy buildings across the way were lit with streaks of sunlight. To the left of the market, where the street narrowed, a woman began hanging her wash on a line between buildings. She leaned out of her third-floor window, pegging clothes to the line, then moving it on little wheels at either end.

Charging Elk watched her with a neutral interest, much as he had taken in the activities of the market. He had been standing on the duckboards behind the tables full of sea creatures, watching the little man and his wife scoop up quantities of the slippery fish, then put them into a metal tray that hung from a hook beneath the canopy. They would slide a piece of heavy metal along a rod until the metal and the tray would hang in balance; then they would yell at the customer until she gave them money in exchange for the fish. At first Charging Elk had been confused by all the yelling back and forth; one man in particular, who was dressed in white beneath his blue coat, yelled back at the little Frenchman. He made faces and threw his hands about, at one point walking away with a disgusted wave. But soon he came back and yelled some more. Finally he bought several kinds of creatures and he and the little man shook hands. When the man in white turned to leave with his baskets full, the little fish man glanced back at Charging Elk and smiled.

Charging Elk knew that the fish man was Ren-ay. And that the taller dark man was called France-waa. The little man had pointed to Charging Elk and said, "Charging Elk," in a way that Charging Elk barely understood. Then he had pointed to himself and said, "Ren-ay." When the dark man came to the cart, the little man had pointed to him and said, "France-waa." Then he repeated the process twice more, the last time seeming to want Charging Elk to repeat the words. When Charging Elk mumbled the odd sounds, he was more surprised at his voice than the act. He had not heard his own voice since he had sung his death song in the iron house. How many sleeps ago was that? Then he thought of the girl in Paris and how she made him repeat her name—Sandrine. She had given him much power with the picture of the man whose heart bled. Later Broncho Billy had told him the picture was *wakan*. The man was *wakan* to the white people, but many Indians now worshiped him too, just as they did Wakan Tanka. Charging Elk should have been angry—the girl had tricked him into worshiping this strange, bearded *wasichu*—but he wasn't; in fact, he thought of the girl as a spirit-giver who had presented him with his own *wotawe*, a good luck charm which he should keep with him always. He didn't have to worship the man, only the power of the charm.

But now both the girl and the *wotawe* were gone, and he was in another place—a place where people walked among the stalls with straw baskets and bags, many already filled with cabbages and olives and dates and rough bread. Right next door to the Soulases' stall was a stand that sold every type and shape of cheese. Some of the pieces were small and round, covered with a moldy white rind. Others were cut into wedges or large squares. The flesh was creamy or hard, white or yellow or orange. A young woman stood behind the raised counter, smoking a cigarette in a rare lull, several bills woven between her fingers.

From his vantage point behind the fish boxes, Charging Elk could see that one of her legs was shorter than the other. A shoe had been built higher to compensate for the deformity. He was surprised to see that her foot seemed much like the other one. In Paris he had seen people, mostly men, with one leg gone. Once he and Featherman had almost been run over by a man with both legs cut off at the thigh. He was seated on a low wood platform with small wheels and he moved by swiping his knuckles along the sidewalk. The strips of cloth wound around his hands were dirty and ragged, but his beard was neatly trimmed and his coat and shirt were fairly clean. He didn't even seem to notice the two Indians looking down at him as he sped along.

Now Charging Elk looked up and saw that the young woman was staring at him, a crooked smile creased around the cigarette. He looked away, unnerved by the frank stare. At the same time, he knew how odd he must look, a hulk of a man among these people, much darker than any of them. The stature that had once made him so proud in Paris now made him feel as freakish as the man with no legs. He glanced down at his new clothes—the wool jacket, the blue pants, the sweater, the rough shoes. He had stumbled several times on the rough cobblestones with his new shoes. They were stiff and hard and he couldn't feel the cobblestones. Ren-ay had laughed each time and held him by the arm, chattering up to him with that wide smile that showed the gap in his lower teeth.

Charging Elk didn't like the feel of the stiff new clothes, but he was relieved to see that the other men were dressed similarly. If the coat and pants were a little longer, he would feel almost like one of them. At the very least, if he stood perfectly still he would feel almost invisible.

Charging Elk suddenly looked around the market with a clarity that made his heart jump. He almost exclaimed in Lakota as he remembered that this was the same town that he had come to with the Wild West show. That was so long ago that he had come to think of it as another town. He suddenly saw the parade from the train station to the arena. He had been proud then, proud of being a Lakota, proud of being in the show, proud of his appearance. He had been eager to put on a show for these new *wasichus* that they would talk about long after he was gone.

Charging Elk watched the little man—Ren-ay—argue with an old woman in a black scarf over a pile of small silver fish. She pointed a crooked finger at the fish man and said something in a quavery voice. Ren-ay threw up his hands and laughed, then scooped a mess of anchovies into the measuring bowl. The old woman regarded the scale with a suspicious eye but she seemed to be getting what she wanted.

Charging Elk watched the exchange, but he seemed to see nothing. The enormity of his changed situation had hit him in the chest as hard as a horse's kick. He had put on a show, all right, a shameful display. He had taken many falls from horses in his young lifetime but never in the arena, unless he was "shot" and had to tumble off the horse. And he had never been so helplessly sick that he almost crossed into the real world. Now, instead of being with his Lakota mates, wherever they were, he was standing in a market with the smell of fish in his nostrils.

Charging Elk had thought of running away during the night before. It would have been easy to sneak out of the dark flat—the man and his wife were in their own room on the other side of the stairs—but where would he go? He had had his taste of freedom after escaping from the sickhouse and he hadn't liked it. He had been cold and weak and hungry and still sick. If the *akecita* hadn't taken him to the iron house, he probably would have died. But then, death would have been a good thing, something he had wished for; on the other hand, how would his *nagi* have found its way home? That was always the question that prevented him from accepting death or seeking it.

Charging Elk glanced up at the now blue sky, then at the little fish man's back, and he didn't feel like a prisoner, not as he did in the iron house. As far as he knew there was no lock on the door to his room. He had listened carefully the night before when the little man had escorted him up to his room after the night meal, but he heard only a soft click as the door closed—no key turning, no final clank of a bolt. But why was he with these people? He seemed to be with them the way he was with Strikes Plenty out at the Stronghold, or with his parents before they surrendered at Fort Robinson. He seemed to be free, yet he was with them, as though he and they had become relatives.

Even as he thought this, he knew the woman did not like him. He could see it in her eyes—the way she watched him—and he could hear it in her voice. He had sensed it immediately upon stepping into the *akecita* chief's big room with Brown Suit, the way she had turned her eyes away when he glanced in her direction, the rigidness of her mouth. And why should she like him or not like him? What was he to her? What did surprise him was the way the little man held on to him, the way he chattered in his tongue, even though he must have known that Charging Elk did not understand anything. Ren-ay seemed to like him very much. But why? He was no longer an important man, a man who made the audiences stare with their mouths open, their eyes wide.

"Monsieur?"

Charging Elk had had his eyes fixed on a golden horse's head above a shop across the street. Below it, a man with hair only around the sides of his head and wearing a white bloody apron was cutting chunks of dark red meat for his customers. The meat had made Charging Elk's stomach rumble. He couldn't remember the last time he had had real meat.

"Monsieur?"

He turned and saw the young woman with the short leg. She was standing on the other side of a stack of wooden boxes that separated the two stalls. She had her hand extended toward him. He saw a cloth tobacco pouch and a small pack of cigarette papers in her palm. She raised her palm slightly and nodded. He moved toward her and realized that he had been standing in one position so long his legs had grown stiff from the cold. But now a streak of sunlight had reached the woman's stall and her face was bathed in the sharp glow. He took the pouch and papers from her, tapped out some tobacco on one of the papers, and handed the makings back to her.

"Merci, madame," he said, without thinking. Broncho Billy had taught the Indians that *merci* meant gratitude, just as "thank you" did in the American tongue. Charging Elk was surprised at how easily the words had come to him. *"Tabac,"* he said. *"Merci beaucoup, madame."*

The young woman struck a wooden match and held it to his cigarette. Then she said something that he didn't understand. *"Merci, madame,"* he said, and he surprised himself again by allowing his eyes to take in the woman's face. She smiled at him and he smiled back. Her face bore the marks of the affliction that Indians called the white scabs or white man's disease. Many of the people of Charging Elk's parents' generation bore similar marks. Many others had died of the white scabs, including most of his relatives. He had not known any of his grandparents and only an uncle and two cousins on his mother's side. His uncle had married a Hunkpapa woman after the fight on the Greasy Grass and lived with her people at Standing Rock. He had not seen his uncle and cousins since he was eleven winters. Now twelve more winters had passed and he thought of them only briefly, as though his past were too far away to think of.

"Il n'y a pas de quoi," said the young woman. In spite of the pockmarks on her face, when she smiled, she was quite attractive to Charging Elk. "Marie-Claire," she said, but he didn't know that the

words made up her name. She did not point to herself, as the others had. She said it again and he smiled slightly. He liked her long hair, which flowed over a checked mantle that covered her thin shoulders. It was shiny and made him think of obsidian from Paha Sapa. He thought of his own black hair and he almost reached to touch it, but it barely showed below the soft round cap. He felt his face flush with shame and he looked away from her. He smoked and wondered if he would be allowed to have his long hair again. Perhaps he *was* a prisoner of the gabby little Frenchman. He stole a glance at the young woman—suddenly he was grateful to her for not being afraid of him—but she was engaged with the old woman with the crooked finger.

Madeleine Soulas had left the market early that day. She was only needed when there were lots of fish and lots of customers. François was a good helper but he didn't have the personality to sell the fish. He was quiet and withdrawn, more at ease setting up the stall, filling the display trays, stacking boxes, chipping ice, and keeping the work area clean and uncluttered. Nevertheless, she liked François and when she baked, which was infrequently, she always brought him a large portion of sweetcake. He had never set foot in the Soulas flat, although René had invited him more than once. Perhaps he didn't feel comfortable around families, since he seemed to have none of his own.

Now Madeleine was making a raisin-and-honey cake. She had come to realize that she only baked when she was upset. The act of putting a sweet together, all the small steps, the measuring, the folding, the beating, the decorating, allowed her to think things through without really thinking. But now she had much to think over. Although Charging Elk wouldn't be with them for very long—and the shorter time the better—she was worried about how the children would react when they saw this savage. Furthermore, she was angry with René for subjecting them to such a shocking discovery when they returned home from school. Thank God she had had the presence of mind to send the children to their grandmother's last night. They would have had nightmares all night long. Madeleine could almost see the future nightmares in the back of her mind—painted, screaming savages chasing the monstrous bison, or worse, the brave pioneers, through their troubled sleep. As she beat the batter a little more ferociously than usual, she thought, Well, Chloé can sleep with me tonight. She didn't care where René slept. Just so long as her children were safe.

Madeleine Soulas wiped a loose hank of hair away from her eyes with the back of her hand. Please, blessed Mary, please. And she was surprised and angry to see a tear fall into the batter.

CHAPTER SEVEN

Franklin Bell *sat in the uncomfortably small Empire chair and watched* the consul general's secretary, Agnes Devoe, pour tea at a sideboard. He had a feeling that something unusual was in the air, but he had no reason in the world to feel that way. Perhaps it was the hour—four-thirty on a dark, wet late-January afternoon— that seemed unusual. Archibald Atkinson was normally out of the office by midafternoon, off to tea with visiting American dignitaries or attending a function with representatives of this or that French organization—or to his penthouse flat on Rue de la République. He was an avuncular man of limited energy because of his girth and age, and he often went home early to be with his wife, who suffered from allergies to just about everything. He once had confided in Bell that her doctor had told him that she would do better in a dry climate. The doctor had said Marseille was probably the worst place in the world for her allergies—dry but weedy in the summer, wet and windy in the winter. Of course, Bell had happily interpreted the statement to mean that the old man was ready to move on, perhaps to retire back to the States. But a year and a half later he was still here and Bell was still vice-consul.

Now he possessed something of the same feeling as he had had then, a feeling of almost breathless excitement. So little really happened to him at the consulate, other than the business of bureaucracy, that Bell had taken to manufacturing his own excitement, the occasional burst of hopefulness that was invariably dashed by the reality of business as usual. With a little sniff of disgust, he thought of his futile effort to woo the lovely but now stone-cold Margaret Whiston, as he watched Agnes set a cup of tea on the desk before Atkinson.

At least Agnes was reliable, steady as an old horse. She was only three or four years older than Bell, but he thought of her as something of a spinster aunt, probably because she had been at the consulate through three consuls general and showed no sign of ever having been attached to any of them—or anyone else, for that matter. She was tall, erect, and unfashionably thin, but her dark blond hair was luxuriously done up in a bun.

"Well, Frank, how are things going with that hemp business?" The consul was still breathing hard from a trip to the bathroom. Bell estimated that he weighed at least 250 pounds, most of it straining the buttons on his waistcoat. With his small, shaved head, pug nose, and pudgy fingers, he looked like a fat, healthy baby with muttonchops. In spite of his ridiculous appearance, he commanded the respect of all those who talked with him for more than ten minutes. At sixty-six, his mind was strong and incisive.

"Same as always. Monsieur Latrielle wants to ship the finished product, but the cordage outfit in Boston wants the raw material. It's a real stalemate, but we're working on it." Bell watched Agnes set the cup of tea on the desk before him. The backs of her hands were ridged with thin blue veins and were a bit more waxy

—almost translucent—than he had noticed before. "Thank you, Agnes."

"That's good, Frank. We have to resolve this thing as soon as possible. You know those Irishmen back there—they're almost as stubborn as these Marseillais."

"I have a meeting with Latrielle tomorrow at noon. I think he's softening a little—although he still says it's to his disadvantage to ship the raw stuff. I think this might be his last shot." But Bell had noticed an air of distractedness about Atkinson, not at all usual. He wondered if the consul's wife had taken a turn for the worse. Again, that feeling of excitement, this time accompanied by a modest guilt, wormed its way into his bones. He took a sip of tea to occupy the momentary space that had developed between him and the old man. He half expected Atkinson to say something like "I've been here too long, Frank, it's time to go home, you can take over here." Had the moment arrived, at last? He sneaked a glance over the rim of his cup toward Agnes, who sat at a little desk where she took notes of meetings. Her face betrayed nothing, as always.

But Atkinson pushed a piece of paper across the polished mahogany desk toward Bell. "We've got a problem," he said in a weary voice.

Bell picked up the paper. The first thing he noticed was the name in the upper left-hand corner, handwritten in a neat script: *Charging Elk*. Beneath it was a round stamp: Ville de Marseille—Archives. To the right of the name and stamp, he saw a standard form, but the words that caught his eye, written in bold letters, were "ACTE DE DÉCÈS," followed by *"de Charging Elk."* He glanced at Atkinson, barely seeing him but noticing that the consul's eyes were fixed firmly on him. He quickly returned to the death certificate. *"6 Janvier, 1890 . . . décédé à Marseille, ce matin, à quatre heures à l'Hôpital de la Conception, âgé de trente-neuf ans. Indien de la troupe de Buffalo Bill. Célibataire; né dans le Dakota (États Unis d'Amérique); de passage à*

Marseille; Fils de . . ." This last space was left unanswered. Who knew who his parents were? Even if it was Charging Elk.

Bell looked up at Atkinson with a smile. "Somebody made a mistake. This is Featherman. He died on the 6th. And he was thirty-nine. I saw the information the representatives of the Wild West show provided the hospital."

Atkinson had made a steeple of his fingers, his elbows resting on the arms of his leather chair. His eyes weren't quite closed but they seemed heavy. Bell wasn't used to seeing Atkinson like this and he suddenly felt a wave of alarm come over him. Why was the consul so grave over a simple case of mistaken identity? "I'll go to the hospital first thing in the morning and straighten out this mess. Obviously, they've made a mistake. It's a simple matter, really."

Atkinson broke the steeple by curling one hand into a fist. He covered it with the other hand and cracked the knuckles. He picked up his teacup and swiveled toward the long windows that looked out over a courtyard. Bell looked beyond him toward the closely pruned limbs of a wintering plane tree. If nothing else, the French were immaculate gardeners. The public gardens were always put away nicely for winter.

"I've been here for nine years now, Frank." Atkinson seemed to be talking to the plane tree. "And I've come to realize—often to my amusement—that nothing here is simple. That's why we, the American Consulate, exist—to make things simple, if we can. We try to facilitate these trade agreements, we try to grease the wheels, to make sure Americans are treated right, without offending the government bureaucrats or the manufacturers or the growers. Sometimes we even resort to bribery—not the flashy money under the back table stuff, but you'd be surprised what I have to promise these people, Frank." Bell heard a little sound, almost like a chuckle, come from the shiny head just visible over the tall back of the chair. "Things get done eventually, but sometimes I wonder at what cost, Frank."

Now Bell was more puzzled than alarmed. What had brought all this on? Surely the matter of the death certificate was not a problem. Perhaps the old man was just plain tired of the constant battles, the pressure to promote, i.e., sell, relations between the French and the Americans. It was true that Marseille was unlike any of Bell's previous postings. Panama had been and still was virtually a colony, ripe for the taking—the Americans took out all the coffee and sugar and bananas for a pittance. Similarly, in Peru, the Americans had almost a monopoly on the guano and nitrate deposits. And Morocco didn't have any resources worth getting into the perpetual conflict with the Spaniards and French and Brits; consequently, it had been the easiest of Bell's previous postings. But it was in Marrakech that Bell realized how easily he could become one of the complacent foreign service zombies he had seen throughout his career. There are some countries, some climates, that seem to encourage a kind of peaceful slothfulness, a desire to end one's career, no matter what age, on the veranda of a tucked-away paradise where employees become servants and drinks are served promptly at five of a hot afternoon.

Bell allowed himself a little smile, in spite of the gravity of the situation—he hadn't moved up the ladder the way he had thought he would when he applied for the foreign service, diplomatic corps, right out of Yale, but getting posted to Marseille was a big step in the right direction. The energy here was extraordinary—ships bringing in products from everywhere, taking away things to other major ports, including those of America. Since the Suez Canal opened, some twenty years ago, Marseille had become the busiest port in Europe. Sometimes Bell just walked around the crowded port, watching the barrels of olive oil, the crates of wine, the tanned hides, the boxes of Marseille soap being lifted onto the ships, and he always thrilled at the commotion of commerce. It was really the place Bell wanted to be for a few more years. He could stand the wheeling and dealing that now seemed to have drained the enthusiasm of the old man. He still had the brio—and now the knowledge if not the experience—to take over running the consulate. He just needed a chance, damn it all.

In the quiet gloom of the tall dark-paneled room, lit only by an electric chandelier, Bell felt quite alone in his revery, though he was aware of the scratching pen of the secretary, but even that seemed less an act of the present duty and more a transcription of his thoughts. The notion that he was so transparent made him uncomfortable, so he quit thinking and confined himself to staring at a plaster bust of Benjamin Franklin, America's first ambassador to France just a little over a hundred years ago. Oddly enough, the familiar bald dome and the fringe of long hair over the upturned frock collar reminded him of the fortune-teller's lair on La Canebière. There had been a bust set on a pedestal between the window and the red velvet curtains—but surely not Benjamin Franklin.

Just as Bell was beginning to think that he had somehow missed being dismissed, he was startled by the energy with which Atkinson whirled about in his chair and clanked his cup down in its saucer.

"But we do have a problem, Frank, and this is what it is. I've already sent a man—Horgan, in domestic affairs—over to La Conception, and he was informed, quite emphatically, by the doctor who signed this piece of paper"—he stabbed a freckled forefinger at the death certificate—"that the man who died on the sixth of January was your Indian, this Charging Elk."

Bell noticed that the consul general had said "your" Indian, and the familiar sense of dread—that he was responsible for Charging Elk, for good or ill—returned and sent little pricks of fear up his spine. But he determined not to accept responsibility for something he had no control over: "It's clear that the doctor's wrong. I'll go over and talk to him myself. We know it was Featherman who died on the sixth. Its indisputable." Bell had used "we" purposely to defray responsibility. But he still didn't know what the problem was. My God, what *was* the problem?

"You don't understand, Frank. The doctor is covering his hind end—excuse me, Agnes—and will not accept that he made a mistake in identifying the Indian. Horgan said he made quite a scene, accusing us of questioning his integrity, his professionalism, and so on. He practically threw poor Horgan out into the street." Atkinson again sounded that strange chuckle that seemed to require no change of expression, certainly no mirth. Bell was surprised that he hadn't noticed this mannerism before.

"So, as far as the good doctor, and the city of Marseille, and, of course, the Republic of France, are concerned, Charging Elk is dead, plain and simple." Atkinson again made a steeple of his fingers and stared over them directly at Franklin Bell. "What are you going to do about it, Frank?"

Bell didn't know what to say. The consul was apparently blaming him for the doctor's intransigence. Bell tried to figure out what he had done wrong. The only problem he could see was that Charging Elk had escaped from the hospital. I suppose the old man might think that was my fault too, he thought. Of course, I had visited the Indian in the hospital, along with our French liaison officer, but how were we to know he couldn't speak English or French? Bell turned his attention to the bust of Franklin and pursed his lips. Damn, he thought, if I could only have communicated with Charging Elk. If I could just have assured him that he would be joining the Wild West show again, he would have relaxed and stayed in the hospital. But how could I? Anyway, how would that have prevented the doctor from reaching the same conclusion, that it was not Featherman but Charging Elk who died at the Hôpital de la Conception?

A strange combination of fear and anger crept into Bell's mind. He had really not been put in this position before. But he remembered that some of the older hands in the consulate, at some festivity or another, had said straight out that Atkinson was frustrated because he had not been offered an ambasssadorship to any country worth a hill of beans. He had a spotless record and had got things done wherever he had been. At one time, he had been a bright light and moved rapidly through the ranks. But now he was stuck in Marseille and would likely end his career here. Of course, these old hands had sneered at the notion that Atkinson thought he could beat the politics of such appointments. Hardly any career diplomats became ambassadors, especially those in the Consular Service. That was a pure fact. But now Bell felt a little abused that he should become the object of Atkinson's frustrations. It just wasn't fair.

What really hurt Bell was that he considered himself Atkinson's protégé. He had learned more in his first three months on the job here than he had in his previous nine years in the foreign service. It was true that he and Atkinson hadn't become bosom friends, but one doesn't expect that kind of relationship with one's superior, especially given the age difference. Still, Bell thought they had a relationship of mutual respect and understanding, perhaps even a kind of amiable—dare he say it?—father-and-son, or at least mentor-and-student, relationship. And now this.

"Sir, am I to understand that I'm being accused of—what?—lack of judgment, failure to follow procedures? What? As far as I know, Charging Elk is alive, living temporarily with the French family, awaiting the opportunity to rejoin the Wild West show. I assume that the French authorities are still moving ahead with the documentation and will allow him to leave as soon as possible. It all seems very cut-and-dried."

In the momentary silence, Bell could hear Agnes Devoe's pen scratching dryly on her pad. In that curious way the mind works in tense situations, he suddenly thought she must be French. Devoe was a French name, wasn't it? But her English was perfect. And a French national would not be allowed this close to the consul general.

"First of all, I'm not accusing you of anything, Frank. Certainly not." Atkinson sat back with a smile and threaded his fingers behind his shiny head. The waistcoat gapped between the buttons, showing ellipses of starched white shirt. Atkinson suddenly seemed at ease, almost puzzlingly so, and Bell dared to hope that the worst had passed. But the old man went on: "The problem we have before us is quite simple—according to the French authorities, Charging Elk is dead. You and I know, of course, that this is utter nonsense, but I'm afraid we are going to have to convince them that this is the case. And I'm afraid that is going to be quite a chore, one requiring a bit of tact—we don't want to offend the doctor further, but we need him, or perhaps the local medical board, if necessary, to change his verdict. Otherwise"—and here Atkinson actually lowered his voice, as though the room might be unsecured—"there is no way that we can get Charging Elk documented and out of the country."

"But what about Featherman?" An idea was beginning to form in Bell's mind. "Two Indians stayed in Marseille, one died, the other lived. Could we have documented Featherman if he had lived?"

"Good point, Frank. Yes, I suppose so. According to the doctor—whose name, for your information, is Durietz—Featherman is the Indian we have on our hands."

"Then who's to know our Indian isn't the one named Featherman?"

"I see where you're going with this. I don't know. I don't know if I like it." Atkinson had swiveled to face the window again. By now the stubby limbs of the pruned plane tree were barely visible in the darkness. The limbs reminded Bell of the menorahs in the windows of the Jewish neighborhood next to his in Philadelphia. Forbidden territory.

"I don't think the French care which Indian lived and which died. I hate to say this, but one Indian is as good as another to them—no insult intended."

"And what about us, Frank?" Atkinson's voice had become reedy with fatigue. "Do we care?"

Bell realized that his remarks must have sounded a little too cold-blooded. He hastened to correct that impression. "Of course, sir—I was just thinking of how to expedite Charging Elk's return to his show. If he has to assume Featherman's identity to do it, wouldn't that be more expeditious than trying to fight through this red tape? Really, I have Charging Elk's interest in mind. I'm sure he would want us to hasten his repatriation, no matter how." Bell thought of something else, perhaps not true, but possibly so. "I sense the Soulas family is a bit impatient with the progress of things. I believe we suggested that his stay with them would be brief—a matter of days—and already it's stretched into nearly three weeks. Madame Soulas especially seems a little anxious."

For the first time, Bell's argument seemed to arouse a positive reaction in the consul. He swiveled slowly toward his desk, picked up the death certificate, then slowly raised his eyes to stare at Bell. But this time, there was just a hint of amusement, maybe even a little admiration. At least, Bell interpreted it that way.

"Maybe you've got something here, Frank. Tell you what—talk it over with James, then get back to me. We'll clear this up, one way or another."

Bell almost moaned in despair. Winton James was the legal affairs attaché. He was just about Bell's age, a Quaker and an unwavering bureaucrat. He would never fall for this scheme. Atkinson could override James's objection, but he wouldn't. The only hope Bell could see was that James might think the whole idea was the consul general's—with a little help from Bell.

Atkinson was already shrugging on his coat, an expensive black wool coat with a brown seal-hair collar. He looked at himself in the hall-tree mirror beside the door, setting his bowler hat at just the right angle on his slick head. He picked an umbrella out of the rack and leaned against it, glancing at Frank in the angled mirror. "Good night, Frank. See what James thinks about this idea of yours. Could be interesting, to say the least." The consul opened the door and stepped into the hall. "*À bientôt*, Agnes. Put that death certificate in the safe, will you? And don't forget your umbrella. *Bonsoir*, all."

Bell watched the consul amble down the quiet hallway. The steel-gray stucco of the walls looked especially cold under the dim glow of a high chandelier. He turned to say good night to Agnes. She was straightening out the old man's desk, her thin face with the almost hawkish nose handsome but impassive. In her long skirt and high-collared blouse, she looked almost schoolmarmish. Bell could imagine her washing the blackboard and dusting the erasers after the last student had left.

"Have a nice evening, Agnes."

"Good night, Mr. Bell." She didn't look up from her task.

Bell stood there for a few seconds more, wondering what he wanted. He looked beyond the desk and saw the long streaks of rain on the tall windows. He wondered what Agnes thought about when she took the notes for meetings like this. Did she admire the way the men conducted consular business? Did she think it was all silly and the men were fools? More important, what did she think of him? Had he really been so conspicuously devious? Suddenly, her opinion of him seemed important.

She picked up the death certificate and began to walk toward the large safe set in an alcove behind the open door, then noticed him. "You're still here," she said, without surprise.

"Yes, I was just thinking . . ." Bell racked his mind. "Yes . . . it's raining. Might I have Robert call you a cab?" The plane tree had vanished in the darkness outside the blurred windows, but Bell could almost smell its damp wood, the wet earth at its base. He felt humiliated and he didn't know exactly why. It was just business, this whole thing. So why did he feel this way? He stood for a moment waiting for Agnes's answer. Then he left, almost running.

freedom of the Stronghold. Of course, they had been children themselves, just fourteen winters, but they had no choice—or at least, they thought so at the time—but to live like grown-ups. They didn't want to turn into *wasicuns* like the other children and even their own parents. So they grew up quickly out at the Stronghold, with the help of some of the older people, who provided them with a lodge and who fed them until Strikes Plenty was able to "borrow" a gun from a relative at the Whirlwind Compound. Later, they stole amunition and another gun from miners, but they prided themselves on their ability with bows, shooting birds and rabbits with the steel-tipped arrows. Most of the others, even those at the Stronghold, had long since given up this traditional weapon. And when they ran out of bullets, they had to tighten their belts.

Charging Elk still could not believe how self-sufficient he and Strikes Plenty became at such an early age. But they had lived a strange life together for eleven winters—no family, no other friends. Occasionally they were invited into another lodge for a feast or a council, but for the most part, they had lived away from others; consequently, Charging Elk had felt uncomfortable around families, especially children. Now, this boy, Mathias, was not tough the way they were—in fact, he was a thin, pale boy with eyes like a deer and a shock of thick brown hair that stood high on his small head—but he was smart and helped Charging Elk learn new things. Just two sleeps before, he had taken Charging Elk to a shop that sold reading books and had shown Charging Elk a round ball with many strange shapes and writings. He had pointed to the town they were in, Marseille, to the big town, Paris, and across the big water—*"Atlantique, Atlantique, Atlantique"*—the town of New York, where Charging Elk had boarded the fire boat some time ago. Then he pointed to a long buckskin shape flanked by blue on two sides—*"Amérique"*—then pointed to Charging Elk. He repeated the gestures, until Charging Elk understood. Then he tapped his finger on the ball, in the middle of *"Amérique." "Dakota,"* the boy said. "Dakota," Charging Elk said eagerly. The Dakotas were relatives of the Lakotas. In his excitement, Charging Elk had asked the boy how he could go home—in Lakota—but the boy simply smiled in shy amazement at the unfamiliar words.

Charging Elk lit his cigarette with a stick match and crossed La Canebière to Cours Belsunce. He liked this wide street with the rows of knobby trees on the street-side edge of the broad walkway. There were many places where he could look in windows at clothes and sweets and knives and everything a man might want. There were cafés, but he hadn't the courage yet to enter one for a small cup of the bitter *pejuta sapa*. But he always stopped at a particular kiosk with a bright green-and-white-striped awning that sold the flimsy papers with *wasichu* writing on them. Often they had pictures on them, drawings, mostly of men he thought all looked alike, with their beards and stiff collars. But once in a while there would be a drawing that would catch his eye—a horse and carriage, a ship plunging across the water with its sails up. He hadn't drawn anything since the time he went to the *wasichus'* school in Pine Ridge, but one night he had sat at the big table with the tall chairs and watched the girl, Chloé, trying to draw a horse. The head was too big and the legs weren't shapely. He watched her puff air and mutter to herself, running her fingers roughly through her short dark hair, finally throwing the colored stick down. Charging Elk had picked up the stick and drawn a horse that looked more like a horse than hers had. It wasn't very good—he was embarrassed that he wasn't a better maker of horses—but he was surprised at her attention. And when he handed the stick back to her, she smiled and said something. Then she took another colored stick and wrote a word below the horse: CHEVAL. *"Cheval,"* she said, pointing her delicate finger first at the drawing, then at the word. Charging Elk had watched the small, pale finger, but something else entered his mind.

A young woman in a simple dress and a white bonnet, sitting on the grass beside a calm lake, naming things for him: Sandrine. His heart rose in his chest, just as it had then, and he looked at the girl, pointed to the horse and said, *"Sunka wakan."* Then, in English, he said, "Horse." Then he smiled and said, *"Cheval."*

Since he had started working for the fishmonger, he was paid a few francs every Saturday afternoon, which he spent on tobacco, and nougat and licorice for himself and the children of René and Madeleine. Although she hadn't tried to address Charging Elk directly, Madeleine seemed to have become more at ease in his presence. Now, instead of ignoring him except to place food on his plate or to collect his washing, she actually looked at him from time to time, usually when she was discussing something with René. Charging Elk didn't know what they talked about but he took her casual glances to mean that she thought of him as a human being— someone to be considered—not as some strange object or wild animal to be stared at, perhaps to be feared. He knew that some of the Americans and French people thought this way. He had seen it in the wide eyes of the audiences when he deliberately rode at a full gallop directly up to the barricades, only to swerve at the last second, kicking up dust and sometimes mud.

The children were another matter. Since that first time he had seen them—that disastrous meal of fish soup when he had had to go up to his room to throw up in the slop bucket and was sick all the next day—they had grown more and more close to him with each passing day. Mathias, especially, sat with him for an hour or two at a time, pronouncing words, teaching phrases. Sometimes the whole family would sit silently after dinner, listening to Chloé play some simple tunes on the piano. Madeleine frowned as she kept time with her long sticks that made woven clothes.

At nine o'clock the whole family would go to bed. Charging Elk had learned to tell *wasichu* time from the reservation Indians in

Paris, and so when the clock over the fireplace struck nine, he knew that the evening was over and he felt vaguely disappointed that he wouldn't see the children until the next late afternoon. And so he would awaken early—remembering some gesture that Chloé had made or a new word that Mathias had taught him—and wait for René's knock on his door before dawn had broken over the town. Every day was like that except for Sunday. Although they worked on Saturday, that evening was longer and the family seemed gayer. Mathias would play his stringed box with the long stem and he would sing. Sometimes René and Chloé sang with him and René would even dance. Once he pulled Charging Elk to his feet and held his hands and twirled the tall man around and around, all the time singing. And often he wanted Charging Elk to sing, but Charging Elk was too shy. The songs they sang were not his songs. He and Strikes Plenty often sang in their lodge, even on the trail, and they drummed and sang with others at the Stronghold. He understood those songs, he understood the talking drum. But to his surprise, seeing the happy family, he felt almost happy too, although his happiness came, in part, from remembering how his people celebrated that last summer before and after the fight at the Greasy Grass, forgetting for a time their precarious future. He remembered how the traveling camp got bigger by the day that summer as more and more reservation Indians joined them out in the buffalo country. He remembered the singing and dancing every night as the people celebrated their coming together. And he remembered thinking that this happy life would last forever, that the chiefs, Crazy Horse and the great Hunkpapa Sitting Bull, would lead them to a place where there were no *wasichus*, where they could live in peace in the old way. Then he remembered the hunger and sickness, the fights and flights, as winter and the soldiers came. When he thought about it, the only time Charging Elk had been at ease among the *wasichus* was when he was performing with Buffalo

Bill's show. For the only time in his whole life he had been safe from the *wasichus*. Until now.

Charging Elk stopped before a small store that sold many interesting things, even small likenesses of the big iron tree in Paris, not far from where the Buffalo Bill show had performed. Charging Elk and some of the other Indians, along with Broncho Billy, had taken a small cage up to a steel lookout with bars to keep people from falling off. Charging Elk had never been so high, not even in Paha Sapa, and he was not even halfway to the top of the iron tree. He remembered how quiet he and his companions had become—later, all of them confessed that they had been frightened that a big wind would come up and blow the tree down with them in it. Even Broncho Billy, who knew everything, seemed whiter than usual.

But Charging Elk knew what he was looking for in the little store with the many things. Just beside the door, there was a wire rack, and it held the picturecards that one could send across the big water. Several sleeps ago, he had passed this wire rack and the first thing he had seen was a picturecard of Buffalo Bill with Rocky Bear and another Lakota named He-knows-his-gun. Rocky Bear was wearing his blue blanket pants and a blanket tied around his waist, and a calico shirt that Charging Elk had seen him wear many times. They were posing in the picture-taker's house, Buffalo Bill with his hand over his heart and the two Indians carrying pipes in their folded arms. Behind them was a screen painted with palm trees and a big moon. Charging Elk himself had been to the same picture-taker's house in Paris.

Now he walked into the store and found a young man with garters on the sleeves of his collarless shirt. *"Pardon, monsieur."* He pointed back to the rack. *"Combien?"* Mathias had taught him how to ask for the price of things, but he still didn't know many numbers, so most of the time it was useless to ask. To his surprise, he heard the young man say, *"Trente centimes,"* a figure he knew. The clerk put the postcard in a thin glassine envelope and Charging Elk walked out of the store, feeling good about his purchase. He would give the picturecard to René and Madeleine.

Charging Elk continued up Cours Belsunce, stopping to watch a man who hid cards and took money from a large knot of watchers. He had seen this kind of gambling in Paris, and Broncho Billy had told him and the others that the man who hid the cards was a cheat and they must never play the game. But some of the Indians did play and lost their money. They thought because they were good at hiding the bones during stick games, they could figure out the cheater's way.

Charging Elk became aware of the furtive glances in his direction and so he moved on. Even in his work clothes, he attracted as much attention as he had when he was on the run from the sickhouse. But he was becoming used to it; in fact, he had almost recovered the pride he felt when he and the other show Indians walked down the streets in Paris. He had put on weight, so he felt powerful again. And his hair had grown long, although not as long as before the terrifying cutting. That would take some time, but he felt almost comfortable being himself among these people.

He had been in Marseille for the better part of three moons. It was now the Moon of Snowblind, when the sun shone on the wind-slick snowfields just before thaw in his own country, but here there was nothing but streets and buildings and people—and rain. He knew that soon the first thunderstorm would rumble over the Stronghold and Bird Tail would perform his ceremony to welcome the new growing things. It was an old ceremony and it used to be performed to thank Wakan Tanka for bringing the buffalo back once again. Now, it was only to thank Wakan Tanka for allowing them to live through another winter. Charging Elk suddenly stopped. Would this be the spring that the White Buffalo Cow Woman and the buffalo with the stone eyes led the herds out of the bowels of Paha Sapa? But what about the *wasichus?* What about their holes in *maka ina?* Perhaps they would find all the buffalo before they were ready to return. Perhaps they would kill them or make them run deeper into her heart.

Charging Elk felt weak as he made his way to the stone wall of a building. The wall was warm against his back but not warm enough to stop the chill that ran through his own heart. Bird Tail's vision had seemed so true that every time Charging Elk thought of that day he and Strikes Plenty heard the old *pejuta wicasa* tell of it, he felt certain that the Great Spirit would make sure that he got home in time to see it. Now he was not so certain, either about the buffalo or about himself. The thought of his *nagi* hovering aimlessly over this place once again filled him with dread. He closed his eyes and waited for the familiar weakness to pass, which it did more easily these days. Many sleeps he did not think or dream of his home at all, and it surprised him. In the sickhouse and later, on the run, he could think of nothing else. At night he had dreamed of his mother and father, of his life at the Stronghold with Strikes Plenty, of the country that he knew so well and moved so easily in, as though he would be there forever. He had lived then with the terrible constant dread he had just experienced—the dread of not going home, of staying here among these people, of dying here.

But now Charging Elk felt the sun warm his face and he thanked Wakan Tanka for planting the seeds of the plan that had been growing in him every day for the past several sleeps and now seemed so simple: He would work hard for the fishmonger and earn enough money to pay for his trip home. He would wait until he had many francs; then he would find Brown Suit or Yellow Breast or the pale man with the spectacles who bought fish down at the water's edge. One of them would help him find a fire boat that would take him across to America. They were *heyokas*, but Wakan Tanka had sent them to help him.

Charging Elk had closed his eyes to think these comforting thoughts, but now he opened them in a kind of contented excitement. Three small girls stared up at him.

"Bonjour, Charging Elk. Ça va?"

It was Chloé and two of her friends. He was surprised to see them out of their neighborhood, even though it was only five or six streets away. Charging Elk himself had come this far only three or four times, on Saturday or Sunday afternoons.

"Bonjour—Chloé. Très bien. Et vous?" He wanted to ask her how she had found him but he didn't have the words.

Chloé introduced him to her friends, making him say each name. The girls giggled at his pronunciation, but Chloé spoke sharply and the girls stopped and stared shyly at the sidewalk.

Not knowing what else to do, Charging Elk pulled the picture-card from the little sack. He held it before the girls: "Buffalo Bill," he said. He pointed to Rocky Bear. "Rocky Bear."

Chloé leaned closer for a better look. "Rocky Bear," she said. Then she said something to her companions. They looked up at Charging Elk and saw that he was smiling. One of them, a tall girl with long black hair who seemed to be fascinated by his long brown finger, said, "Rocky Bear."

Charging Elk laughed, then held the picturecard before the third girl. She was shyer than the other two, and he noticed that her upper lip had a red welt that ran up to her nostrils. Finally when she said the name in American, the words came out in a breathy slur. Charging Elk knew from the sound of her voice that she had some sort of affliction. One of his childhood friends, Liver, had no ears and his attempts at words were poor. This girl was not much better.

"Très bien," he said, and he touched the small girl on the head. He thought it odd that he could tell that she could not speak the French words very well even though he hardly knew them at all.

He took the girls into a sweets shop and bought them a bag of nougat to share. He felt a certain amount of pride in making his third transaction of the day. He now knew the price of tobacco and picturecards and two hundred grams of nougat. He turned the girls toward Rue d'Aubagne and their own neighborhood and said, *"À bientôt, mes amies."*

The girls giggled at his strange, throaty speech, then thanked him and walked off, their cheeks full of the soft candies.

René Soulas stood outside his doorway and watched the cab come up the narrow street. He had been to the *épicerie* on the corner to pick up a tin of olive oil and a small jar of capers for Madeleine. He often ran errands for her, because he was always restless and curious to see what was going on in the street. Now, several boys who had been playing soccer stopped their game to let the cab pass. Not many cabs came up their working-class street and so they looked inside with great curiosity, but the horse clip-clopped on past them with scarcely a notice.

It was a warm, breezy day in early May and the daffodils were about done in René's garden behind his flat. He was thinking about the tiny green clusters of buds on his geraniums when the cab slowed, then stopped at the curb directly in front of him. The door opened and Monsieur Bell descended with a hearty greeting. *"Bonjour, Monsieur Soulas! Ça va?"*

"Très bien, Monsieur Bell. And you? But what brings you to my house? You have news, I think."

The two men shook hands, and René watched as the American handed a franc note up to the driver. The driver touched his hat, his narrow face impassive, then drove off.

"Please—come in. I'm afraid Charging Elk isn't here. He is off walking, as he does every afternoon." René stood aside and let Bell pass through the doorway into an anteroom filled with coats and hats on wooden pegs. "Please continue." But René was filled with apprehension at the vice-consul's visit. It could only mean that he had come to take Charging Elk away.

Bell walked into the living room. Although he had visited the Soulases' home four or five times since the day he had delivered Charging Elk, he was always impressed by the room and its furnishings. Bell had been on his own so long that he always felt a little uneasy in a French family home. The smells—of cooking, of tobacco, of the horsehair in the chairs and sofas—always reminded him of the home he had left in Philadelphia and had returned to on only a few occasions. Of course, he did have holidays, but they weren't nearly long enough to justify the long steamship crossing, and the thought of the journey home exhausted him. But every time he received a letter from his mother, he felt that old guilt that had been visiting him for over twelve years. He hadn't actually left Marseille since he got here, except for a couple of tours of Provence, principally Avignon and Orange, and a journey to the Costa del Sol in Spain, where he thought he might find romance, and one hurried but long train and boat trip to London for a special training session in international law.

"Perhaps you would rather sit in the garden. It is very nice this time of year. It will be too hot soon, but now it is nice. Perhaps you would like some tea—or coffee?"

René led the way to a tall iron-framed glass door off the dining room. Bell followed, trying to fix the smell that emanated from the kitchen. It was citrus, he decided, as he stepped down into the garden. A clean smell, a spring smell so welcome after a winter of closed-up, unpleasantly stuffy buildings.

"Here we are," said René with a sweep of his arm.

The garden was small, perhaps eight by six meters, surrounded by a knee-high stucco wall with an extended brick cap. The ground was packed earth with a tall plane tree near the far wall, just beginning to leaf out. A row of lavender plants with their narrow sage-colored leaves softened the rough stucco wall. But it was the several geraniums in pots atop the wall that defined the garden and provided the color—green now, but soon to be the bright reds and pinks that Bell associated with the Mediterranean. He wondered idly, as he took in the neat garden, what the people of the Midi would do without their geraniums.

"*C'est parfait, monsieur!* A place to spend your evenings after a hard day of selling fish." Bell hadn't come for small talk, but there were certain niceties to be observed. He had seen how Atkinson could actually make tough Marseillais businessmen blush at his solicitude. Beyond the geraniums he could see the inner courtyards of the surrounding buildings that fronted on the busy streets. All had pots of geraniums waiting to burst into color. "I take it you are the gardener."

René waved his hand in dismissal. "It is nothing. A few flowers for the wife, a place for the children to read." But he was intensely proud of his handiwork.

Bell pulled out one of the chairs from a plain wooden table—"May I?"—and sat down.

"Of course, monsieur. Perhaps you would like a glass of wine?"

"Please don't go to any trouble."

"It is no trouble at all. It will be an honor." René excused himself and hurried back inside. He walked quickly to the stairs and called up, "Madeleine, come, it is Monsieur Bell, the American." But he heard nothing, no sound of a chair scraping, no footsteps. He called again, and again nothing.

That woman, he thought. How can she be gone at a time like this? He needed her support to perhaps convince the American that Charging Elk was very happy with them. And it was true. Madeleine had made her peace with the *indien* when she saw that the children had taken to him immediately. It had taken her a month or two, she was a judgmental woman, but now she wanted him to stay. They hadn't talked specifically about the long term, but he was almost certain about that.

René hurried into the kitchen and found a bottle of Armagnac that he had been saving for a rare occasion. He had had it for two years, as such occasions rarely visited his house. He laughed at himself as he found two brandy glasses. Charging Elk was certainly a rare occasion—the rarest. But René hadn't thought to give him a drink of the liquor, partly because Monsieur Bell had told him not to, but also because Charging Elk was a simple soul—tobacco, sweets, a glass of wine with his meals, that was all he needed. And when he didn't have those, he went without. One could almost forget that he had been a celebrity with Buffalo Bill.

As he carried the bottle and glasses and a small bowl of almonds out to the garden, René looked around his flat; at the dining-room table where Charging Elk watched the children do their schoolwork and drawings; at the parlor where they all listened to Chloé play the piano; at the kitchen itself, where just last night Madeleine had prepared a lamb shoulder and a lovely dessert to celebrate Chloé's twelfth birthday. Charging Elk had given her a small ceramic figurine of a *chinois* with a bright red robe and a cone-shaped hat. René didn't know how he knew to give her a gift, but it was the hit of the evening.

He will be missed, thought René. The house will have an empty place in its heart. But as he set the tray on the table, he said, *"Voilà! I hope you like Armagnac, Monsieur Bell. It is all I could find."*

"It will do very nicely, Monsieur Soulas." Bell watched the small man pour a generous amount of the brandy into two snifters. He noticed that the bottle had no label. "And how is the fish-selling business? Okay? Not so good? I seem to see more fish in the markets these days."

"Still not perfect, but getting better by the day. I have been in this business since I was a child helping my father, and I have not seen such a bad winter. Wind, wind, wind. Rough seas, lots of storms. It's a wonder more fishermen were not killed." René handed a glass to Bell. "I know of seven boats that were lost between here and Toulon this winter, three in one storm—all hands lost, no trace. There will be more ex-votos in Notre Dame de la Garde than one would like."

"It is a tragedy, certainly. You can be sure my government mourns the loss of these brave souls. *À votre santé.*"

René lifted his glass, but the words of the vice-consul struck him as odd—and a little annoying. What did it matter to the widows and children, the mothers and fathers of the fishermen that the Americans mourned their loss? The Americans would go about their business while the widows would grieve for the rest of their lives. René himself made it a point not to get too close to the fishermen, although he would see the same lot of them every morning or every other morning. Theirs was a dangerous occupation. Over the years, he had come to the Quai des Belges too many times to discover that one of the regular boats was missing—usually one of the small skiffs that fished the reefs for bass and hogfish. René shivered slightly as he imagined the water filling boots and lungs, the slow sinking to the bottom of the quiet sea, the white blind eyes, the raging winds and tumultuous waves above. The rare nightmares he had usually centered on such images.

"Well, monsieur, I'm afraid I don't bring good news for you."

René blinked rapidly to rid himself of the images. Then it is bad news, he thought. He was almost glad he had expected it. Even though Madeleine and the children weren't around, he felt fortified by his fatalistic expectations. "And so you have come to take away our guest."

"Yes, exactly so. We will not burden you any longer. You can't imagine the gratitude of the consul general for your kindness these past few months. He asks me to offer you a modest compensation for your and madame's unconditional generosity in taking care of Charging Elk. We understand he was quite happy here."

"Then he is to go back to America, to be with his own people." René tried to imagine how it would be for Charging Elk to be re-united with his tribe, with his parents. Did he have brothers or sisters? Grandparents? René was saddened to think he knew so little of Charging Elk's past life. But he was so close to learning of it. Mathias had been teaching the young *indien* many words of French, and it seemed only a matter of time before Charging Elk would be able to open up his world to them. What a great deal he could say to them!

"It's still a bit sticky," the vice-consul was saying. "There has been a preposterous amount of bureaucratic folderol—insanity, I should say, if you promise not to repeat it—regarding the repatriation of Charging Elk. I won't bore you with all the ins and outs, but it seems your government considers him as dead as yesterday's news. It's beyond belief, Monsieur Soulas."

René was still stuck on the word "folderol," a word he had not heard before, and so it took a few seconds for the latter part of the vice-consul's sentence to reach his consciousness. Now he looked up at the American and said slowly, "Dead?"

"Yes, I'm afraid so. Something of a foul-up, I would say. There was another Peau-Rouge in hospital at the time Charging Elk was admitted. This other *indien*, a man named Featherman, died of consumation just about the time Charging Elk came to live with you." Bell shook his head, his lips stretched beneath the mustache into more of a grimace than a smile. "It's a pity, really. This Featherman could speak my language. It would have been so much easier if he had lived."

"But I don't understand this—what has the death of this

Featherman got to do with Charging Elk? He is alive—he goes to work each day, he plays with my children, he eats at my table . . ."

"Well, you see, this is the foul-up—excuse me, complication—I lapse into *anglais*—the doctor who signed the death certificate used the wrong name. Since both *indiens* were in the hospital together and Charging Elk escaped, I suppose he had no record of Charging Elk's being discharged. So when an *indien* died, he must have assumed it was Charging Elk, who as far as he was concerned had remained in the hospital until he died."

René sat in stunned silence, watching his hand twirl the snifter on the tabletop. He understood only about half of what the vice-consul had said, but he knew that somehow someone or everyone thought that Charging Elk was dead. He looked up at Bell. "But don't they read the newspapers? Was it not Charging Elk who was being held at the Préfecture? I saw his name in *Le Petit Marseillais* myself." Or did I? René thought. It seemed so long ago that he and Madeleine had joined Father Daudet and the other parishioners on the steps of the Préfecture. What was it—January? And now it is May. Four months.

René felt a small flash of guilt run through him as he thought of the happiness he had felt in those four months. And further—of the hope he had felt in the past couple of months that somehow Charging Elk would be forgotten by the Americans, that he would remain with the family, perhaps forever. But the guilt René really felt was that he didn't want Charging Elk to go home, even though he knew that the *indien*'s family must be heartsick over their lost son or brother.

René forced himself out of these thoughts, but not before he resolved to confess his selfishness to the priest this very Sunday.

"Yes, of course I presented those newspaper articles to the officials at the Mairie and the Hôpital de la Conception. But you see, I'm the one who identified Charging Elk when he was being held in the Préfecture—and before that, in the hospital—and now these bureaucrats say I must have been mistaken." Bell let out a puff of exasperation, followed by a quick swallow of the brandy. "Here's the—what, kicker, joker—I don't know what you say in French— now they say there was no *indien* at the Préfecture on Christmas Eve. Can you imagine that? Chief Vaugirard—your chief of police—has no recollection of Charging Elk's ever being there! As far as your government is concerned, there is no Charging Elk."

René thought for a moment. He looked at his geraniums and imagined that he saw little slits of red in the green buds. He glanced up at the clear blue sky above the rooftops across the inner courtyard of the buildings. The clusters of orange chimney pots were lovely against the bright blue. He imagined them filled with geraniums, all of the chimney pots filled with geraniums—all over Marseille. He looked at Bell, a thought growing in his mind. "Then who is living in my house?"

Bell laughed, and it was his genuinely hearty laugh. "No one, Monsieur Soulas, absolutely no one. Forget the big fellow who plays with your children, who eats at your table—he is nonexistent, a ghost you might say."

René waited politely for the American to finish his bout of perverse humor. Then he said, "And what about this Featherman? Is he nonexistent too? Is he too a ghost?"

Again Bell laughed. "Most certainly, monsieur! He is a real ghost—buried in Cimetière St-Pierre on the seventh of January, the day after Charging Elk came to live with you."

"I must plead my ignorance, Monsieur Bell. If this Featherman died in January, wouldn't the officials know it was him and not Charging Elk? I don't understand how such a catastrophe could take place. It seems quite simple even to me, poor fishmonger that I am."

Bell looked at the little Frenchman for a moment, a measuring gaze as he tried to decide how much he should tell him. He probably should tell him nothing, since he would have Charging Elk out of the Soulases' lives forever in a day or two. But the fishmonger had been so good about everything, so patient, he deserved an explanation.

"I won't mince words with you, my friend. My government suspects that the authorities here are covering up a monumental mistake, that they mistook Charging Elk for Featherman. The *acte de décès* that was filed in the archives in the name of Charging Elk should have been that of Featherman. The doctor who signed the certificate made a mistake. Simple as that."

"But now they could correct it, yes?"

"In a way they have—just a little over a month after Featherman died, his death certificate quietly showed up in the records. So he is on record now. Trouble is, so is Charging Elk. According to your government, both are now dead. And as far as they are concerned, that is the end of the matter. I suppose you could say they corrected it in a way that would allow them to save face. We know that they engaged in this deception but we are powerless to prove it." Bell leaned forward, his eyes firmly on René. "Unfortunately, we still have a very real *indien* on our hands."

"Again, monsieur, forgive my ignorance, but couldn't you just take Charging Elk to the proper bureaucrats and show him to them? Surely they would know that he is a Peau-Rouge and that he was a member of the Buffalo Bill show. How many *indiens* could there be in Marseille and how else could they have gotten here?"

Bell sighed. He was beginning to like the fishmonger more and more. For the first time since he had come to Marseille, he felt he was making a real human contact with a Frenchman, that they had something in common besides selfish interests. He reached for the bottle of brandy. "Do you mind?"

"No, no, please, Monsieur Bell. Forgive me."

Bell poured them both a healthy splash of the amber liquid. Then he sat back and again measured the Frenchman with a long gaze. Something was happening here. Bell was getting a feeling that things might work out—if he judged this man right. "Two things about that worry me." Bell had unconsciously thrown off the mantle of the company man, the pretext that anyone in the consulate cared about the Indian but himself. "One, I'm quite sure they would refuse to acknowledge that the man standing before them was Charging Elk, or even an *indien*. And two, I'm afraid that if by chance they did acknowledge him, they might just throw him back in jail. So, you see, damned if you do, damned if you don't." Bell wondered if he had phrased the last part right, or if it even made any sense in French.

But René had been doing some thinking even as he listened to the American. "So what will become of Charging Elk?"

"Well, at this point I am trying to make arrangements with our embassy in Paris. I would like to see them make an international fuss about this. As you see, we seem to get nowhere on the local level." Bell finished his brandy in one swallow. "But the important thing right now is to resituate Charging Elk. We have imposed on you and your family far too long already, for which we will remain in your debt long after this is over."

"But where would you put him?"

"We have made arrangements for a small room not too far from us. Now that the weather has warmed up, he can do odd jobs on the consulate grounds. I'm confident we can clear up this matter in a few weeks. Then we can send the poor devil home—or at least to rejoin the Wild West show, which is now in Germany or Austria." Bell stood up and took a last look at the geraniums on the stucco wall. The Armagnac had given him a slight headache. Without looking at René, he said, "God, what a mess we bureaucrats can create."

René had heard the distance in his voice and he felt a little sorry for the man, who clearly had a good heart. "If you please, Monsieur Bell, my family would be only too happy if you let him remain with us until it is time for him to leave Marseille."

Bell turned, his eyes suddenly bright in the casting shadows of late afternoon. "Are you certain you want him?"

"Of course! It is no problem. My children are quite fond of him, and even now, my wife is knitting him a sweater for next winter. He works with me and my helper at the stall. He walks in the afternoon. He is used to this life we lead, that he leads. To put him in a room by himself—he might as well be in the jail." René's voice had begun to rise in alarm at the thought of Charging Elk living alone. How would he eat? What would he do alone at night? The man needed a family. "We take good care of him," he said, and he was surprised at the tone of defiance in his own voice.

Bell continued to look at the small man without speaking. He seemed to be weighing the Frenchman's sincerity, but gradually his lips broadened into a smile. "I was hoping you would say that," he said. "Yes, he is clearly better off here with you." But the smile tightened a little too much and the brow furrowed over the clear blue eyes. "But I feel I must warn you, I really don't know how long this business will take—a couple of weeks, maybe more. There is the matter of proving he exists, getting him papers—he has no birth certificate, no passport. I just don't know."

This time René smiled. "Time is of no importance, monsieur. I know how these bureaucrats are. You must take your time and do it correctly. He will be at home with my family." He thought he heard movement in the kitchen and wondered if Madeleine had been home all the while, listening. She had come to accept Charging Elk, but he didn't know how much longer her goodwill would last. He had lied about the sweater. "We are the only family he has at the moment," he said, hoping he didn't sound too presumptuous. "Relieve your mind, Monsieur Bell." René poured another splash of Armagnac into their glasses. "Rest assured."

But Bell was looking off toward the neat row of potted geraniums on the low garden wall. He had a sinking feeling that they would be in bloom before Charging Elk went home. If he ever did.

CHAPTER NINE

─────

It was late August in Marseille and the heat pressing down on the port city seemed to force the air out of its citizens. The morning markets stayed busy but by eleven o'clock the streets were empty, save for the stray delivery wagon or plodding omnibus. Even the horses seemed lost and unseeing in the dazzling heat waves of the high Mediterranean sun. The workers putting up the new apartment building on Rue de la République slowed to a crawl by three in the afternoon. The men hauling dusty sacks of cement on their backs, the hodcarriers pushing their heavy wheelbarrows, the masons wrestling the blocks of stone into place—all seemed to be moving in slow motion, as though they were wading neck-deep through the murky waters of the Old Port. With rags tied around their heads, with their skimpy undershirts, chalky blue shorts, and dusty sandals, they looked like dark, weary children.

Charging Elk watched them from the top of the omnibus and noticed how they all worked with their backs bowed beneath the glaring sun, scarcely acknowledging each other, except to give or take an instruction, or share a cigarette in a slim cast of shadow. Work was the way of this town. Everybody worked, most hidden in their shops or the factories and plants, others—the shipbuilders and dockworkers, the street sweepers and deliverymen—out in the open, even when it was so hot that a man could feel the heat of the cobblestones through his shoes, as though a constant fire burned beneath the city. That August of 1893, one of the hottest months anyone could remember, the days were filled with an almost desperate desire to stay alive—and in fact many old people did not survive. The fine black funerary carriages were supplemented by plain carts and wagons, carrying more and more caskets out to Cimetière St-Pierre. At night the people took what small relief the darkness and breeze could offer. They strolled slowly, almost hesitantly, along the Canebière or sat, exhausted from the day's heat, in their own courtyards with citron candles burning to repel the small mean mosquitoes, or in the outdoor cafés around town. Many of them came to the cafés and restaurants around the Old Port to sit and drink *citron pressé* or anisette and watch the strollers and the quiet, looming ships. This had become Charging Elk's routine for the past four months.

Now the sun on the top of his head made him dull, almost sleepy. He had been watching the workers for some time now, ever since he had moved from the Soulas home into his own flat in Le Panier, near the Old Port. He had been working at a soap factory on the northern outskirts of the town for eight months. When he went to work at five in the morning the apartment building would be deserted. When he came back at three in the afternoon the workers would be crawling over the rubble of stones on the sidewalk, hauling the sacks of cement from wagons on heavy cloths draped over their bent backs. From day to day it was hard to tell that they were building anything, but in the four months Charging Elk had lived alone, he had seen two floors go up, and now they were making the stone stand up for the third.

Just the week before, Charging Elk had calculated that he had been in France for four years—more than three and a half of those years in Marseille. Of course, it wasn't the first time he had made such a calculation. Mathias had taught him how to read the numbers on the heavy round watch the family gave him one Christmas. Then he had learned to read the calendar, to learn the days, the weeks, the months—and the years. He was surprised at the speed with which the seasons passed—first it was hot, just like now, then cool, then cold, and cool again, and finally hot. He still watched the moons carefully and he kept a crude winter count on a small pad of paper that he had bought on Cours Belsunce, each page representing one moon—the Moon of the Black Fish, the month he had discovered that fish had spirits; the Moon of the Long Walk, when he had walked clear to the Plage Prado and back one Sunday, the Moon of the Home Look, when he had climbed the dry hill to Notre Dame de la Garde, the high church, and looked out over the longest view he had seen in this country. Even though the landscape included blue sea and many buildings, it made him as homesick as he had ever been. The scabby limestone hills to the north reminded him of the badlands and the Stronghold. He drew a picture of himself on High Runner, standing on a square butte. With Mathias's help, he backdated his winter count, starting with the moon he had left his parents standing on the train platform in Gordon, Nebraska.

Charging Elk stood and clumped wearily down the small circular stairs at the rear of the omnibus. Place de la République was just ahead and the horses were slowing. As he swung down off the platform, he tried to understand what these last years meant to him, but he was too tired and hot to think of anything more than the many steps he would have to climb to reach the high Panier neighborhood. A woman looked up at him for an instant before she clutched the handrail to step up into the bus. Charging Elk barely noticed anymore the startled looks as people took in his size and appearance.

He crossed the almost deserted *place* to the steps at the base of Le Panier. He smelled of lye, and of fat and coconut oil, acrid and sweet at the same time, and his face and neck were oily with coal dust mixed with his sweat. He was anxious to get out of his work clothes and wash himself, then nap until it was time to think of his dinner. His small flat—only one room but with two windows and an alcove containing a too-short, too-narrow bed—was adequate, even comfortable, for the most part. He had an oil lamp and an oil burner to cook on. But when it came time to eat, he often wished he were still living with the Soulas family. Now the only meal he took with them was the Sunday midday meal. There was always plenty to eat, plenty of fish, sometimes meat, with potatoes and tomatoes and olive oil, washed down with the *mni ʃha* and gassy water. He enjoyed the meals, even the fish now, but mostly he enjoyed the company. Although he could speak a little French, there was nobody other than the Soulas family who really understood him. Mathias and Chloé especially understood him because they had taught him the tongue. But he had no friend like Strikes Plenty and he had no woman who might learn to listen for the words beneath his thick accent. So he occasionally spoke sparingly and haltingly to the *charcutier* and the *boulanger* in his neighborhood, to the old waiter at a small café called Le Royal down at the Old Port. He worked alongside a young Frenchman, maintaining the fires under the great vats of oil and fat, and they talked a little, as much as Charging Elk could understand and make himself understood. They ate their lunches together in the shade of the loading dock, in the open air. Even the stagnant air of summer seemed like a blessed relief from the fires. The man's name was Louis Granat and he came from a village in the great mountains known as the Hautes-Alpes, somewhere to the north and east. He had come to Marseille to become a sailor and journey off to see the world, but he had fallen in love with a laundress and taken a job at the factory to be close to her. Louis Granat drew a figure of soft curves in the close air of the loading dock, said *"Mal d'amour,"* then kissed his fingers. Two weeks later, Charging Elk learned the laundress had left his friend—Granat had put his hand over his heart and bent his head in sorrow. Just as Charging Elk was beginning to feel sorry for the pitiful young man, Granat had raised his head and grinned. He put his lips together and made a farting sound. *"Fini,"* he said, grinning. *"C'est dommage."*

Charging Elk was glad his young friend had recovered so quickly from the heartbreak, but he began to be troubled about his own life. He had never fallen in love with a woman; had never felt all of the emotions pantomimed by his friend. He and Strikes Plenty had talked about having women of their own many times, but neither had had one. Now, he wondered if something was wrong with him, if he would ever have a woman to love, to have children with. And he began to see the impossibility of his life here in this city in France. How could he meet a woman who would be happy with him? Even Marie-Claire from the market seemed unattainable, although he knew that she was not considered attractive by the Frenchmen. None of them flirted with her, as Charging Elk had seen them do with other young women. Yet, Charging Elk used to watch longingly as she and an elderly couple who would appear almost silently at the end of the market packed up the cheeses to go home. Then he thought of something else that further depressed him—in spite of the show Indians' crude jokes about attractive women, in spite of the admiring glances they got from women, in spite of their proud vanity, none of them had come close to touching one of the Frenchwomen, not even

Featherman, who had hoped to settle down with one and become a Frenchman.

So Charging Elk became almost resigned to a life without the love of a woman. He fell into a routine of working six days a week and of eating his Sunday meal with the Soulas family. Most evenings he would walk down the long, steep stone steps and from Le Panier to the Old Port to sit at one of the small metal tables outside Le Royal and drink anisette while he watched the young women stroll by, arm in arm with each other or with a lucky young man. Once in a while, a gesture or a giggle, a toss of the hair or the wiggle of hips, would fill him with a sudden surge of desire, but when he climbed the steps back up to Le Panier he felt only a quiet, echoing aloneness.

Charging Elk and Louis Granat remained working friends until one day, just before quitting time, one of the bosses called the young Frenchman aside. Charging Elk watched the exchange out of the corner of his eye, afraid that his friend would be scolded or fired, but he saw the sudden happy grin of a child and he sensed that Louis Granat would not be tending the fires the next morning. A week later, Charging Elk learned that he had been transferred to another part of the factory where the sheets of soap were cut and pressed into bars — one of the better jobs in the factory. And although they saw each other once in a while after that, they were very formal, almost shy, in each other's presence. The new man was a Turk, who did not talk at all.

Charging Elk had been on the job for eight months. It had been difficult to leave the fishmonger's world, but he had realized that he was becoming almost a child to the Soulases when he had lived his own youth as a man, independent and free of any authority. René had not said anything for some time after Charging Elk made clear to him that he wanted his own place to live and his own job. In truth, Charging Elk wanted the freedom to look for a woman. Marie-Claire had been a good companion to him in the market. It hadn't taken him long to get over the facts that her face was pocked with the aftermath of the white scabs and one leg was shorter than the other. He enjoyed watching her banter with the customers, sometimes scolding them, sometimes sharing a big laugh, sometimes doing both at the same time. They gave each other cigarettes and she taught him the names of her cheeses and gave him samples of the big round ones. René had joked that she had her eye on him, but when the market ended, the old couple showed up to help her cart the leftover cheeses away. And Charging Elk was left to wonder where she lived, what her home was like.

But René, even though he thought the young *indien* was ungraciously deserting him after all he had done, one Sunday introduced Charging Elk to a large man who was dressed in a black cutaway and striped pants. His tie was full around his neck and held down with a gold pin. His silver hair was greased and combed back so that it ended in a mass of oily curls at the back of his neck just above his collar and below the brim of the top hat. His mustache curled up away from the corners of his mouth and was pointed on the ends. Charging Elk had not seen such a fine-looking man before in Marseille. The man reminded him of Buffalo Bill when he got all dressed up to meet the big bosses of France.

Charging Elk had been waiting on the church steps for the Soulas family to finish with their ceremony. He often met them there so that they could walk a little before returning to the flat for Sunday dinner. René had quit encouraging Charging Elk to join them in the holy house, and that was good, although he was often tempted to go in and see what their ceremony was like. But he could not go in, for he feared that Wakan Tanka would abandon him for good. He still believed that the Great Spirit had plans to bring him home when the time came. But time was getting long and he still hadn't managed to save much money. The little Frenchman paid him just enough to buy tobacco and sweets, with a little left over for an occasional anisette or café. Charging Elk had only twenty-four francs tucked away. He knew it would cost many francs, perhaps a thousand, to board a ship for America. Mathias had told him so.

So when René had introduced him to the big man who reminded him of Buffalo Bill, Charging Elk had instinctively brightened up. For some reason he knew that the man was strong medicine and that he might help him. He was more important than Brown Suit or Yellow Breast; perhaps even more important than Buffalo Bill.

Charging Elk started work at the soap factory three sleeps later. René had ridden out to the factory with Charging Elk on an omnibus that morning. He left the fish stall with Madeleine and François, the first morning he hadn't shown up for work since he was sixteen years old, the day after his father had died. He didn't like the way things were turning out, but he had had a visitation from the Virgin Mary one evening while he was pruning his geraniums and she had told him, not through words but through her sad smile, that he must free the dark one to cross the waters to his people. She didn't exactly accuse him of selfishness but he knew what she meant.

Unfortunately, René could not pay Charging Elk enough to save up for a ticket on the ship, then the train he would have to take across America, and he could not afford to pay for these things himself. But he did sit on the diocese board with Monsieur Deferre, the wealthy soapmaker, who paid decent wages and who took an immediate interest when René suggested that Charging Elk not only was a strong worker but was a Peau-Rouge who had been a member of the Wild West show. And when he met Charging Elk on the steps of Ste-Trinité, he was impressed by the man's size and color, the dark chestnut face with the cheekbones that almost hid his slanted eyes, the flowing black hair tied with a length of red yarn. He was truly a savage, but one dressed in a rumpled wool suit and a clean white shirt with a poet's tie around his neck. Monsieur

Deferre, who had started his soap factory from scratch and now employed two hundred men, shook the *indien*'s hand and told him to report for work in three days.

As Charging Elk began the long climb up the stone stairs from Place de la République, he remembered that meeting with Monsieur Deferre. He had been full of high hopes then—the thought of earning enough money to go home, coupled with the thoughts of living alone and finding a woman, had been almost too much. That night he had fasted and prayed long to Wakan Tanka, thanking him for showing his troubled child the way out of his misfortunes.

But Charging Elk was disappointed when he walked up to the pay window at the factory after his first full week to learn that he had earned only twenty-four francs. René had said Monsieur Deferre was very big with money and Charging Elk thought he would pay him as much as Buffalo Bill had. Charging Elk was still confused about the value of money, but he knew that the American frogskins were worth more than the francs. The thirty frogskins he earned with the show each moon were worth far more than four weeks' worth of francs.

One night Mathias had calculated how long Charging Elk would have to work in order to buy a ticket on a fire boat. He made many money signs on a piece of paper and finally said, "Three years, all told. If you save all your money, which you can't now."

Charging Elk had reached his apartment building in Le Panier. It was on Rue des Cordelles, a narrow street which buzzed with many tongues, mostly North African and Levantine. Children played in the street until late at night, sometimes keeping him awake. But more often than not, he found the laughter, the squeals, the cries, the barking dogs somehow comforting, as though the constant flurry of noise proved that he was not really alone. Now he watched a small group of girls in long dresses and scarves (in spite of the heat) playing a game with a small rubber ball and a pile of pebbles. Le Panier was always more lively than the rest of Marseille. René said the Africans enjoyed life more than most because they were not sensible. Charging Elk noticed that the men argued a lot, throwing their hands about, and the women cried out to their children in scolding voices, but nobody seemed to take offense. He couldn't tell if that was enjoyment of life or sensible, but they all got along. In some ways, this neighborhood reminded him of the village out at the Stronghold. Even the cooking smells seemed much alike, although the food was different. He had eaten a couple of times in a small dark restaurant around the corner which had a beaded curtain for a front door. He had eaten a dish they called couscous, but he didn't use his fingers like the others. But as he watched the other diners, he was again reminded of feasts in the village, the intense eating, the laughter, the teasing, even the dogs that lay patiently at their owners' feet, waiting for the scrap of flatbread or chicken skin. Despite René's protests, he was glad he had chosen to live in Le Panier. These people were closer to his own than any of the others he had come across since he left Pine Ridge.

Charging Elk awoke and it was already dusk. He lay there for a moment, his naked body wet with sweat. Although his two windows were thrown open, there was not yet the familiar, faint breeze that began a couple of hours after the sun went down. As usual his first thought was of food. He didn't have an icebox, so each evening he had to decide whether to go out to the *charcuterie* or the *épicerie* to buy a meat stick, or sometimes a rotisseried chicken, or pâté and rough bread. If he didn't, he would eat stale hardtack and sweating cheese, a pomegranate or an orange. Since he never seemed to have enough food around, he usually ended up going out to the shops.

As he weighed his options, he suddenly remembered that it was Saturday. He had been so dazed from the week's work and the heat that he had forgotten that he had drawn his money from the man in the little window and tomorrow he didn't have to work. He stood and walked over to the small bench beneath one of the windows where he had thrown his work pants. He pulled a handful of bills and coins from a pocket. He smoothed and counted the bills, then counted the coins, arranging them in neat stacks: twenty-eight francs and thirty centimes. He counted again, not believing his arithmetic, but he came up with the same sum. Had the payman made a mistake or had he received a raise in his wages? Over four extra francs. That was half of his room rent for the week.

As surprised as he was, Charging Elk suddenly knew that this was all part of Wakan Tanka's plan for him. He wanted his child to come home to him even sooner than the original plan.

Charging Elk felt a surge of energy and excitement that caused him to shiver in spite of the heat. Although he hadn't seen Brown Suit in well over a winter, perhaps two, and had never seen Yellow Breast again after he had first visited Charging Elk in his stone room, Wakan Tanka had taken it upon himself to see that his child would return to his people. Charging Elk made a prayer of thanks as he tucked the money into a purse he kept at the foot of the duffel bag. Then he opened the purse again and took out five francs. He would go out tonight. He would celebrate his newfound good fortune.

Le Petit Zinc was a small restaurant on the Quai de Rive Neuve, not far from the Quai des Belges, where Charging Elk had helped René load his fish only eight months before. The man who owned the restaurant, Monsieur Valentin, was a close relative of Madeleine's, perhaps even her brother, although Charging Elk didn't know for sure. But sometimes the family and he ate at Le

Petit Zinc, the only restaurant they went to—the only restaurant Charging Elk had been to in Marseille before the few meals at the North African hole-in-the-wall in Le Panier.

Now he sat at a small outdoor table, near a low iron fence garnished with pots of geraniums, the only barrier between the customers and the passersby. Across the street was the broader promenade that led to the ships and boats moored in the brackish water of the Old Port. During the day, nets were spread out as men, and sometimes women, sat on the stones, mending them. But tonight it was a promenade for families, for friends, for lovers.

Charging Elk smoked a cigarette and waited for his dessert. He felt good and not a bit lonesome. He even allowed himself to think of what his homecoming might be like. It was still a long way off— he had only eighty-five francs saved in the purse. It would take him some time to get up to a thousand. But with his new wages, he was that much closer; hence his feeling of well-being, his lack of self-consciousness as he watched a fancy open carriage with gold trim and brass oil lanterns rattle rapidly over the cobblestones. And perhaps Mathias was wrong—perhaps his passage would cost less than the boy thought. Charging Elk put a reminder in his *cante iste* to have Mathias help him find a fire boat bound for America. Together they would find out exactly how much it would cost.

Charging Elk was now of twenty-seven winters. He was not the same young man who had crossed the big water with Buffalo Bill and Featherman and the others. Lately, he had been thinking of Black Elk and that night he had come to the camp in the Bois de Boulogne. All of the Oglalas had welcomed him heartily, yet he seemed almost haunted, even fearful of all he had seen. His eyes had seemed young with apprehension but his body looked stooped and weak. Charging Elk had now been gone two years longer than Black Elk. What would Charging Elk be like when he arrived in Pine Ridge? Would his parents be happy to see him? Surely, they would believe that he had returned from the dead. But what if they themselves were dead? No, not in four years. They would be themselves, just a little older. His mother would hug him and cry and hold him close, then make him a big meal of roasted beef and the potatoes they were now undoubtedly planting. His father would also hug him, then tell him all about High Runner as they sat and drank *pejuta sapa*. And the people—they would feast him with honoring songs, perhaps even give him a new name, but would they know him? Perhaps he had changed more than he knew from living among these strangers.

Charging Elk watched the waiter set the dish with a slice of apricot torte before him. His thoughts were so far away he didn't see the waiter staring rudely at his dark face and his long hair, but if he had, his only reaction would have been a small amusement. The waiter scraped the breadcrumbs from the tablecloth with a knife, then took the empty half-liter and glass away, along with the cheese plate, all the time looking at the lean dark face.

After his *prix-fixe* meal, which came to two francs twenty, Charging Elk walked farther along the Quai de Rive Neuve, again lost in thought, and because it was dark now, he began to have a memory that at first puzzled him. Although he had been this way a couple of times before, it had been crowded and noisy, just as it was this night. But the farther out he went, as the numbers of people diminished he began to have a memory of a cold, dark night in winter. It had been raining and the cobblestones were shiny under the gaslights. His feet were wet and cold. He was weak and his ribs were tender and ached with the constant throbbing of his heart.

He suddenly stopped and looked up a side street that led away from the Old Port. He saw a basin full of small ships with folded masts just a short distance from the side street. And he saw a yellow glow in the longer distance and he knew where he was.

A wave of fear swept through his body, threatening to reverse the bouillabaisse and the torte, as he remembered that night, his last night of freedom before the stone room in the iron house. He remembered the procession with the holy men and the statue of the woman in blue. He remembered the torches bobbing as the people climbed the steps up to the high church. And he remembered the voice in the darkness behind him: *"Pardon, monsieur."*

The warm summer night came clear and vivid with memories of the sickhouse, his escape, his search for the Buffalo Bill show, which ended with him staring at the empty train tracks at the Gare du Prado. The small room with the single bright light, the *akecita* and Brown Suit, and finally his cold stone room. And then he heard himself singing, not singing really, just a low rumbling as he mouthed the words to his death song.

He had wanted to die then. He had sung his death song for two, three, four sleeps, and he had fully expected Wakan Tanka to call him home. But he had also been fearful, afraid that his *nagi* would not know the way home, that it would wander here in this country of strangers. Now he felt a wave of shame creep over his face like crawling ants as he remembered his pathetic attempt at a ceremony, using one of the cigarettes that Yellow Breast had given him. He was no *wicasa wakan* and he had no right, other than to sing his death song and make his prayers, to pretend to be a holy one of such power.

Charging Elk was overwhelmed by his memories of those early times in Marseille. For the most part, especially after he came to live with the Soulas family, he had learned not to think of those days. When he did, he became fearful and ashamed and was haunted by nightmares that left him exhausted in the morning. So it was out of self-preservation—because he had to get up early each morning to accompany René down to the Quai des Belges—that he had put such thoughts out of his mind.

Now he swallowed against the threat of the meal coming up and

turned back, toward the people and the lights. But he didn't stop at
Le Royal, as he usually did when he came down to the Old Port.
He walked by and climbed the several stone steps up to Le Panier
and kept walking until he reached his building. Once inside his
room, he tore off his sweat-drenched clothes and sat on the bench
before the window. He sat there for a long time in a shaft of moonlight until his mind finally became a blank, erased of the kaleido-
scopic images of loneliness and despair. Only then did he creep
over to his narrow bed in the alcove. His legs were heavy and his
back had stiffened up, as it always did at night from the hours of
shoveling coal into the fires beneath the vats, and he vaguely remembered wondering if he would be able to sleep, or if the images
would come back in his sleep, but when he laid his head tentatively
on the bolster and closed his eyes against the moonlight, he was
gone into a dark world of blessed nothingness.

The next Saturday, after another insufferably hot week of work
and eat and sleep, Charging Elk put his pay, which again totaled
twenty-eight francs, thirty centimes, into the purse and tucked it
into the bottom of the duffel bag.

He walked down to the end of the hall and filled his pitcher from
the faucet, scarcely noticing the foul stench from the squatter
across the way. He had become used to the smells of sewage, of rot-
ting meat and fruit, of garbage piled at the curb. The Old Port had
a particularly bad smell from all the sewage pipes that emptied into
it. At first, such smells had offended his nose—he was used to the
clean air of the plains—but now he was almost used to it. He was
used to the garbage scows, gathered on one side of the Old Port,
that would be filled with offal and dead rats and dogs and other rot-
ting things to be towed out to sea and dumped. It took an unusual
smell to make him take notice—like the dead baby his nose had

scouted out in the alley earlier in the summer. The smell attracted his notice because it was an overpoweringly sweet, yet sour smell. And when he investigated, he almost cried out in horror. But as he made a prayer for the small bloated infant, he noticed a curious thing: The pale baby lay with its arms and legs in the air, and he recognized it. It was the same baby as the one in the windows and in the markets at Noël. It was the baby Jesus. René and his family had such a baby, along with its parents, who weren't really its parents, and some shepherds and animals and men in turbans. Every Noël they set up the small immovable figures beside the fireplace. The season was an honoring time for the infant.

Back in his room, Charging Elk put the image of the dead baby out of his mind as he washed his body with a cloth he dipped in the soapy water. There was a bathhouse on the street around the corner, but the only time he had gone there, all the other men had stared at him as though he were a giant, so he cleaned himself in his flat. It took three or four basins of water to get all of the coal dust out of his pores and his hair, but he had become adept at making a little water go a long way.

He was already sweating by the time he got his clean white shirt buttoned. In spite of his fearful episode the week before, he was going down to the Old Port, but this time he would eat in the cheap brasserie on the Quai du Port beside the Café Royal. It was a big place and most of the customers were sailors and the kind of people who hung around a port, who wore rumpled suits and tatty dresses but had enough money to eat out. He had studied the posted menu one night after his anisette at Le Royal and he recognized pork and lamb.

Charging Elk often wished he could read. Sometimes he bought illustrated magazines to look at the pictures, but when he tried to figure out what was being said of them, he just saw neat black marks, in spite of Mathias and Chloé's patient teaching. Once he saw a picture of *tatanka* and he did recognize the word "bison" in the writing beneath it. He took the magazine to Mathias, who told him that the magazine said that all the bison were gone, all that was left of them was bones and memories. Mathias was alarmed at this thought, because he had been thinking of going to America with Charging Elk, although he was only fifteen at the time. He had wanted to see the Indians in their homeland and perhaps become one. Charging Elk had assured him that one day he could go to the land of the Oglalas and become a brother by ceremony; furthermore, he assured Mathias that the words beneath the picture were wrong, that he knew where the buffalo had gone. At first he wouldn't tell Mathias how he knew this because it was not good to tell of another's dream, but when the boy grew more and more despondent, he finally told the story of Bird Tail's dream of the buffalo entering the cave in Paha Sapa. He drew a picture of the mountains, the cave, and the buffalo entering. Then he swore the boy to secrecy.

The Brasserie Cherbourg was large and full of noise. Charging Elk sat at a rickety table near the open windows that looked out over the Old Port and watched the waiters dart by with trays of food or liters of wine over their heads. He marveled at their agility as they squeezed between tables and swerved to avoid a carelessly flung arm or another waiter or a drunken sailor. Most of the tables were occupied by men, mostly sailors, some with young women, who seemed to enjoy the chaos. But it was the noise that made Charging Elk happy—the constant hum of voices, the barely heard accordion of a roaming musician, the occasional clatter of dishes or the shouted toast. Although he was dining alone, he felt that he was part of the festive crowd.

He ordered the *rôti de porc* because he recognized "roast" and "pork." Most of the other items he didn't recognize, although he was sure Madeleine had cooked some of them at one time or another—especially those dishes listed under *poisson*. Now he only ate fish on Sunday with the Soulas family. He had grown to like some of Madeleine's fish dishes, especially those with crisp skin and firm white meat, but he never ate fish on his own. He had a small oil burner but the only time he used it was when he could afford a piece of beef.

When the waiter brought his half-liter of red wine and poured a glassful, Charging Elk looked up and said, *"Très bien, monsieur, merci,"* but the waiter had already turned his back and was threading his way back to the kitchen. The visit had been so brief, Charging Elk couldn't remember what the waiter looked like, beyond the hairy arm and square fingers below the rolled-up sleeve.

As Charging Elk drank his wine and waited for his meal, he studied the people around him. He had come to recognize sailors around the port. Usually there would be three or four of them and they would be dressed in a way that suggested a life on the sea— canvas pants and shoes, striped shirts with no collars, or if they were Arab, long dresses of white. But the more he studied his fellow diners, the more he was aware that they were all *wasichus*. They had turned the color of walnuts from the days in the sun, but they were white men, like the ones in New York and Paris and the miners he had seen in Paha Sapa. Not one of them was dark like him or the Arabs or the *nègres*.

Charging Elk began to feel uneasy. He had become so used to the people of this town and his own uniqueness that he had not thought of himself in terms of color. He had no one to identify with, no group that he belonged to, and so he thought of himself as one who had no color, was in fact almost a ghost even though his large dark presence always attracted attention from both light and dark people. But now he felt that he was in a place where he did not belong. He took a sip of the *mni sha* and stared out the window at a juggler in face paint who was entertaining a crowd down by the ships. He was tempted to just slip out of the eating house—he was only a couple of tables from the door—but he knew if he was caught, they would send him back to the iron house. No, he would stay and eat his roast pork, pay up, and leave quickly.

But halfway through his meal, a young man approached his table and stood, feet planted and arms crossed. Charging Elk had seen him coming—he was aware of everything now—but chose to ignore whatever trouble this young man might bring. He speared a chunk of pork with his fork and sprinkled some salt on it, seemingly engrossed in the act, but his eyes were seeing more than the meat. The man stood so close to the table Charging Elk could see the curve of his penis under the canvas pants. Above a large silver belt buckle, the man wore a blue shirt, which was open halfway down his chest. His forearms were heavy and naked and one of them had a raised welt from a knife wound. A blurred likeness of an eagle decorated the other.

Charging Elk chewed the piece of pork deliberately, and when the sailor said something, he swallowed and took a sip of wine. The man said something else and it seemed to be a question. Then he repeated the words and Charging Elk looked up at him. His face was surprisingly youthful, round and red from the sun, with a wispy blond mustache above his thin red lips. Charging Elk knew that the man was somehow challenging him, but at first he didn't recognize the language. It was not French but there was something familiar about it.

Charging Elk lifted his shoulders and made his face blank and said, *"Je ne comprends pas votre langue."*

"I said are you a goddamn bloody Indian."

This time Charging Elk recognized the word "Indian." The

young man said it the way Brown Suit and other Americans said it.

In spite of the sailor's aggressive stance, Charging Elk was for an instant overcome with a desperate hope. "Indian, yes, him," he said, pointing to himself with his thumb. "Oglala. American. Buffalo Bill." He searched his mind for more American words but all he could think of was "Broncho Billy," which he didn't say.

The sailor turned to his companions, who were seated at a table just behind Charging Elk and toward the interior of the noisy room. "He is a goddamn ignorant blanket-ass. He admits it. Was I right?"

"Ask him to give us a war whoop, Teddy," shouted one of them.

"Go ahead. Give him a punch. If you've got the balls for it," said another.

Charging Elk had turned around in his chair and smiled at the men. The idea had come to him that if they were American sailors they would know how to get to America. Perhaps they were on a fire boat that was leaving for America. Perhaps they would help him. It was a desperate hope, he knew, but perhaps they would at least tell him how much it cost to go back to America. *"Bonsoir,"* he said. "America."

But as he looked at their faces and felt the presence of the one standing over him, he began to realize that they were not friendly. Charging Elk was used to a certain amount of hostility—sometimes he noticed it in the eyes of other workers in the soap factory, or in the way he was ignored by some shopkeepers or the way some women gave him a wide berth on Cours Belsunce or La Canebière—but now he looked up and he saw hatred in the round young face of the sailor. The set of the thin lips and the narrow eyes reminded him of the miners he had encountered in Paha Sapa, those who wanted to kill him and Strikes Plenty. Back then, Charging Elk would have taunted them and laughed at them, while riding for safety. They were rough men with no wives and no families and no home, except for a straight-sided tent with a stovepipe or a shack made of flat wood. They hated the Oglalas and would gladly have killed him if they could have gotten to their rifles in time.

Charging Elk sat for a moment, looking down at his half-eaten meal, confused. He understood why the *wasicun* miners in Paha Sapa hated him, but why would these sailors hate him in Marseille? There were many people of many colors here. Why would they choose him? He had spent the past three winters making himself invisible, yet they knew him right away. He looked up and glanced around for the waiter. The noise in the brasserie was suddenly a crashing hum in his ears and he became tense. Many of the other sailors were now looking at him and the young man standing over him. Some were shouting in his direction. Suddenly, he saw the crowds in the stands at the Wild West show with their big eyes and shouting voices as he rode hard after the buffaloes.

But this was not a show and these people were not cheering him on. Now the young man was standing sideways, addressing the room. Charging Elk heard the words "goddamn" and "Indian." He knew "goddamn." The *wasichus* said it when they were angry, although it made the show Indians laugh. Featherman would say "goddamn" and everybody would laugh. He would say "shit" and "horse's ass" and all the Indians would laugh. But the sailors weren't laughing.

Charging Elk tried to stand and the young man whirled around and pushed him back down. He felt a sudden flash of anger and he gripped the table to stand, but the anger had taken him by surprise and he was confused. It was the first real anger he had felt since coming to France almost four winters ago. In a way it felt good— he had lived a passive, even submissive life since he left the Stronghold—but it was also confusing. What could he do with his anger here in this room full of *wasichus?* He had only a knife and he was only one. The anger he had felt subsided as suddenly as it had come, replaced by the beginnings of fear. As he glanced around the room at the white faces, he began to fear for his life. And his *nagi*. What if they killed him? What would happen to his *nagi*? It would never find its way home. But he could see no way out. He began to hum, first under his breath, then a faint, thin falsetto, then he began to sing as though he were alone, as though he had staked his sash to the ground and meant to make his final stand; as though he were alone on the plains, surrounded by enemies, suddenly calm and determined, as though he meant to take as many as he could before he was killed. Then he stood.

The young sailor with the round face and thick forearms had taken a step back and now looked up into Charging Elk's face. The sailors at the surrounding tables now stopped their jibes and laughter and listened in disbelief. The accordion player squeezed his box in a hushed, toneless accompaniment, as though he had forgotten the lively tunes he played every night without end.

The waiter and another man, dressed in a lumpy white suit, approached Charging Elk cautiously. They each took one of his arms, gently urging him toward the door. They were alert to whatever violence might erupt inside the large man, but they needn't have worried. Charging Elk was in another country, a quiet country, and he was strong with meat and song. He had remembered that he was a man, and a man who sings his death song in a proper way is a man to be reckoned with.

Once outside, the man in the lumpy suit spoke to him in a rapid French, at times apologetically, nervously, at other times admonishingly. Charging Elk knew he was telling him not to come back to the brasserie, but he didn't care. His body felt light, even in the evening heat that had been stored up in the cobblestones during the day, and he felt good, somehow different. He looked toward the juggler with the white-painted face, who was now throwing flaming sticks in

CHAPTER TEN

C harging Elk became a little reckless after that night at the Brasserie Cherbourg. He began to go out more during the work week, staying out later at night, drinking a little more wine at cafés other than Le Royal. In fact, he purposely stayed away from the Royal, not because it was next door to the Brasserie Cherbourg, where the sailors would take over on the weekends, but because he didn't want the old waiter to see him drinking several glasses of wine rather than his usual one anisette. Although they didn't talk much, Charging Elk had come to regard the old waiter, with his iron-gray mustache and cratered face, as something of a guardian—like René. He was always polite, he always asked after Charging Elk's well-being ("How are you this evening?") and remarked on the heat ("Hot again, I'm afraid" or "We will sleep well tonight"), and that was that. Unlike René, he left Charging Elk alone to enjoy his anisette and his thoughts. But he was never far away, serving near-by customers or standing solemnly at his post beside the inside door.

The incident at the brasserie was one of the things that Charging Elk thought about. Although he knew he had been lucky, that his death song had thrown the whole crowd off-balance and he had managed to escape before they regained their equilibrium, he also thought that the song had had a magical effect. He hadn't become invisible as he would have wished, but somehow the song had frozen the sailors, rendering them powerless in their effort to harm him. Charging Elk began to think of the song as a magical weapon, rather than a means to make him strong and brave in the face of certain death. He knew that the purpose of the song had become distorted into a kind of defense mechanism, but he didn't know why—only that it worked this time. And it hadn't worked in the iron house. Perhaps he *was* meant to live, and to live here, at the edge of the great water that stood between him and his home. Perhaps this had become home.

Consequently he carried himself with a little more assurance; he began to look people in the eye; he took to going to the bathhouse around the corner from his flat; and he ate out almost every night. He felt stronger at work and he worked harder at making himself understood. After the incident, he lost his reluctance to be noticed and began to walk proudly, the way he had when he and the other show Indians went around the big towns to promote the performances. He even replaced his good beret with a felt hat with a floppy brim that he purchased in the very hat shop that he had cringed in front of that rainy night four years ago before the *akecita* had arrested him. He had enjoyed walking into the shop, then trying on hats while the clerk and the other customers looked on nervously. He had hoped to find a reservation hat with the stiff brim, but now he decided that the floppy brim made him look as dashing as a boulevardier. That same day he bought a black walking stick with a silver duck's head in a flea market on Rue St-Ferréol—not far from the Préfecture where he had been a prisoner. Thus decked out, he strolled the streets of Marseille in the evening and sat in the cafés at night, doing his best to imitate the slender young men who attracted admiring glances from the young women. And in truth, he did cut an admirable figure, just not the type nice young women would feel comfortable with. They looked at him as a large, possibly dangerous North African or Turk, the kind of brute their mothers—just before they crossed themselves and said a fervent prayer to the Virgin—told them to avoid.

One night in the middle of October, the Moon When the Wind Shakes Off the Leaves, Charging Elk found himself in a part of town that he was not familiar with. It was not far from the Old Port, only three or four blocks, but it was in a direction that he had not taken before. He recognized the monumental Opera House, but as he ventured into the blocks behind it, he noticed that the gas lamps were farther apart and the streets narrower and darker. He was a little surprised that the streets were still lit by gas lamps, because most of the streets in the Old Port vicinity were now illuminated by the electric lights that glowed white and cold.

In the dim flicker of a gas lamp he could just make out the street sign at the corner two blocks behind the Opera House—Rue Sainte. He knew these words "Rue" and "Sainte" but had never seen them together before. He stood for a moment, already having decided to turn back to a large outdoor café he liked at the juncture of the Quai des Belges and the Quai de Rive Neuve. It was always exciting to sit outside La Cigale and watch the other patrons and the strollers, and even though the evenings had turned a little chilly, there were plenty of braziers burning among the tables. After the deadly heat of summer, the Marseillais did not mind a little chill with their wine.

It was a Sunday night and except for the Old Port, most of the big town was quiet. Rue Sainte was no exception. The street was empty, the doors were dark, and the windows on the upper floors were shuttered. Just as Charging Elk was deciding there was nothing of interest in this neighborhood, he looked up the street toward the east and he saw, in the next block, three or four squares of light that flooded out onto the cobblestones. The warmth of the light intrigued him, so he began to walk in that direction. The breeze that came every night now had suddenly turned into a brisk wind off the sea. Charging Elk held his long coat with the black fur collar closed with one hand while the other held his floppy-brimmed hat tight on his head. He did not like the winters in the port town—the constant winds, the rain that often turned into sleet, the dampness that turned the cobblestones shiny by night and lurked in corners even on sunny days. It was on those sunny winter days that he missed the Stronghold the most. He had not forgotten the grim blizzards, the deep snow that kept the people in their lodges for days on end, but he thought more about the sunny warm days when people would sit outside the lodges and the children would play their winter games. He and Strikes Plenty would often sit with a group of men on canvas tipi liners and smoke and talk about everything under the sun. Or they would ride into the draws and canyons of the badlands in order to give their horses some exercise, with the vague hope of scaring up a couple of rabbits or even a deer. Those days with the sun warm on their backs were always with Charging Elk as he endured the cold and damp of Marseille. He would give everything he had here for just one of those days.

But now he put the sweet thoughts of home out of his mind as he stopped before the first doorway. It led into a narrow room with a long bar on one side and a few tables and chairs on the other. It was what René called an American bar because people, mostly the rough crowd, came here to drink alcohol. Even now, a couple of men were standing at the bar, drinking beer and smoking. A woman in a tight striped shirt was behind the bar wiping glasses with a towel. Her hair was piled on top of her head but several strands had escaped and hung limply over the nape of her neck and around her ears. Charging Elk studied the woman for a moment, marveling at the striped sailor's shirt—he had never seen a woman wear anything so bold—then he walked down to the next doorway.

This place was a replica of the first one, except that there were no customers and the man behind the bar, a short, stout man with small wire glasses, was bent over a newspaper. A cat was perched on the bar beside him. Charging Elk was tempted to go in and have a glass of wine but he didn't like cats. Le Panier was overrun with cats and they howled and fought almost every night. In the morning when he went to work, they would be crouched in doorways and on window ledges, watching him. He didn't like the way they watched him.

He hurried down to a third doorway, which was closed and curtained with an opaque material. A large window beside the door glowed with a gauzy warmth. He had to stand close to see into the interior and he saw a large, cheerful room filled with couches and chairs. Two chandeliers with electric lights lit the orange walls and the red furniture. A small, shiny wooden bar backed up against one wall. Behind the bar, a large mirror reflected the lights of the chandeliers. Shiny glass decanters filled with amber and golden liquors stood in a row before the mirror.

At first Charging Elk thought he was looking into the main room of a small hotel, but there was no writing on the window, no sign over the doorway. Could it be a home, like the Soulas home? Perhaps a rich man lived here, but why was it open to the street? And why were there no people in the room? He decided that it was a furniture house for rich people, even if it did seem to be in a peculiar location. And he decided that the owner must have forgotten to snuff out the lights and lower the grates when he left.

Charging Elk started to walk back toward the Old Port, but he stopped and looked back. There was a fourth light back on the corner just beyond the furniture house. It was probably another shabby bar, but his curiosity was piqued, so he walked back and peered into a leaded-glass window that flanked the doorway. It was a bar, dimly lit and smoky, but he was surprised to see that it was not shabby. The bar was of polished dark wood and the chandeliers were made of many-colored glass. The men standing at the bar were dressed in long dark coats and top hats or derbies. Charging Elk watched the men for a moment, then he saw a row of small tables and chairs and more men sitting, leaning close toward each other, talking, laughing, smoking.

One of the men glanced in his direction, but Charging Elk knew the man could not see him. When the man turned back to his companion, Charging Elk caught the glint of spectacles, and he sucked in his breath. He leaned in closer to the window, his nose almost touching the cold glass and his breath leaving a small frosted circle, and the man lit a thin cigar with a flint lighter. It *was* him! The pale man who bought fish at the Quai des Belges. The *heyoka,* the holy clown, who Charging Elk had thought might help him at one time. Charging Elk stepped back from the window. It was him. But why? Had Wakan Tanka sent Charging Elk on this journey to the dark street to finally meet the *heyoka* again? Charging Elk had long ago given up the notion that this spectacled one or, for that matter, Yellow Breast was really a *heyoka.* He had come to believe that they were just men who had come into his life briefly, then vanished. They were no more or less *wakan* than the dead baby Jesus he had found in the alley.

But now he began to believe that he had been mistaken, that perhaps they were *heyokas* after all. There seemed to be nothing holy about them, but that is the way of *heyokas*. They act crazy, but deep within them they possess much power. They are to be respected but feared.

Charging Elk was now thoroughly confused. A gust of wind blew the floppy brim down against his cheek. Should he enter the bar and present himself to this *heyoka?* Would the spectacled one remember him? After that morning when Charging Elk helped the pale one load his fish into his cart and accepted a cigar in return, René had made him wait with François while René bid for the fish. Furthermore, René had called the *heyoka* many bad words and made a bad face while doing so.

While Charging Elk was trying to decide what to do, he heard footsteps, and he turned and saw two men coming up the street. He walked the few steps to the corner and stepped behind the building. He waited for a moment, glancing up and down the cross street. In one direction he could see the scabby hill with its dwarf pines where Notre Dame de la Garde stood as a lighted beacon above the city; in the other he saw the dark, skeletal masts of ships in the Old Port. The sight comforted him. Then he looked into the side window of the bar. He was less than two meters from the pale *heyoka*. He saw the glint of the spectacles above the laughing mouth, the thin cigar—just like the one he had given Charging Elk that morning—between two slender fingers.

Charging Elk slipped away quickly, rounding the corner again, intent on walking as fast as he could back to the safety of the Old Port. He didn't know why but he knew that this street was *sica,* a bad place, and the one he thought was a *heyoka* was really a *siyoko,* an evil spirit. He could feel the evil grip his heart, as surely as if it had come to him in a bad dream, and, in fact, he felt as though he were in the clutches of the pale *siyoko* now.

He ducked into another gust of wind and felt the floppy brim flutter and snap against his face. He lifted his eyes just in time to avoid running into the two men he had seen earlier, who were now standing before the door of the furniture house. Just as he stepped wide of them, the door opened and he saw a small fat man in a dark suit and an immaculate white shirt and tie. He saw the smile and heard the words of welcome—*"Bonsoir, messieurs. Bienvenu, mes amis"*—and then he was beyond the door.

Near the entrance to the first bar he had encountered on the street, he slowed, then stopped to look back. The street was empty. He looked into the bar and saw the same two drinkers and the woman with the loose hair. She was eating something with her fingers.

Charging Elk stood for a moment. He wanted a drink of the *mni sha*, but he was undecided whether to stop here or continue on to the Old Port. The more he attempted to decide, the more he knew that he should go back to his flat in Le Panier. The evening had become strange, as though the treacherous *siyoko* had called him to this street and now would wish to do him great harm, perhaps to steal his *nagi*. What loss could be greater?

But even as Charging Elk thought these thoughts, he was walking slowly, carefully, back to the furniture house, only now he knew that it was not a furniture house, but something that was open to the street. Perhaps the *siyoko* lived there and made it attractive to entice men like himself to enter.

Now he was at the window with the gauzy curtain. He glanced up and down the street, but all he saw was the yellow lights of the doorways. Inside, he saw the two men. They were sitting on a divan, drinking amber drinks in round glasses. One of them was smoking a cigarette and talking to the round man, who stood before them with his hands clasped before his belly. He seemed to be the owner of this house. He turned to the back of the room and clapped his hands two or three times. Charging Elk could hear the faint, hollow claps above the wind and he ducked back away from the glow. When he looked again, he saw a curtain part and five women emerged and walked single-file into the room. They were dressed in long, shimmery robes and they walked slowly, cheerlessly, as though they were on their way to the iron house. Then they stopped and the round man, twirling his hand, had them turn around, and around again. One of the young men on the divan stood and walked around the women. The other sat back among the plush red cushions with his legs crossed, blowing smoke into the air. He seemed uninterested in the young women.

But Charging Elk was very interested in the women. He knew what he was seeing now. In Paris, some of the *wasichus* who worked with the Wild West show went to places like this. Broncho Billy had told the Indians to stay away from the loose women of Paris. But most of these women stood out on the street or in doorways and called to the Indians when they walked by. Some of the Indians went with these women to their rooms, in spite of Broncho Billy's warnings about disease, even robbery by the rough "hombres" these women consorted with. Buffalo Bill himself had made a speech when they got to Paris about the evils of life in the city. He told the story of one Indian, a Shyela, who had gone with one of these "whores" in the Grandmother's big town of London and when he came back, he was all skin and bones with sores all over him. They buried him a few days later in the Grandmother's country. By then his arms and legs had melted from his body.

Now Charging Elk was seeing the very whores that infected men with such horrible diseases. But they looked nice in their robes. They looked like the young women that he longed for day after day and dreamed about at night. Even as he thought this, one of the women opened her robe and twirled around. She was wearing only a white shift and black stockings and lace-up shoes. As she twirled in his direction, he could see the bulge of her breasts above the lace top of the shift and the flesh of her thighs above the rolled stockings. His mouth went dry and his cock stiffened almost in the same instant. She was not much more than a girl, but her figure was stout and her face pretty beneath a shock of dark curls that cascaded down over the collar of the light blue robe. She wore a velvet band around her head and her lips were painted a deep red. Charging Elk thought he had never seen such a wondrous sight as this nearly naked girl with the big thighs. He had seen pictures of completely naked white women in Paris—you could buy them in kiosks. Featherman had quite a collection of them and would let you look at them at night for a few centimes. The young Indians marveled at the pale amplitude of these women as they passed the pictures around.

Charging Elk was embarrassed by his stiff cock and again looked up and down the street but it was still deserted. When he looked back, two of the girls had sat down beside the men while the other three, including the desirable one, were filing back to a curtained doorway. They walked with that same slow, almost defeated gait they had displayed earlier. He watched until the light blue gown disappeared behind the curtain.

Charging Elk was saddened that the girl had gone away. He had desired her so fiercely he could almost taste her creamy flesh as one tastes a *glace à la vanille* on a hot August day. He had an overwhelming need to taste her and fuck her. Without thinking, he looked down at his crotch, but his erection was hidden by the thick wool coat. Fuck. In spite of his almost keening need, he stifled a breath of laughter. "Fuck" was one of the words he had learned in Paris. Many of the young Indians, whether they were playing cards or waiting on their ponies to enter the arena for the show, talked about fucking. It was all bravado, of course. When they were around the white women, they were reserved and even a little fearful.

Charging Elk thought of the young white woman in Paris, the

one named Sandrine. He knew now that she was a holy person and the card she had given him was a picture of Jesus, the savior of the *wasichus*. He had saved them by telling them to worship his father, who was named God Almighty and who Sees Twice had said was even stronger than Wakan Tanka. Although he hadn't believed Sees Twice then, now he wasn't so sure. After all, the *wasicuns* ruled the world.

Sandrine. He tried to picture her in his *cante ista* that day on the edge of the little lake in her simple dress and white bonnet, but all he saw was the stern gray dress and the hat with the sleeping duck. For a long time he thought he would never forget her, but he now realized with some shame that he hadn't thought about her for more moons than he could count. Now he closed his eyes and he saw the stout young woman in the blue gown, her swelling breasts and white, chunky thighs, the velvet band around her hair, and his desire became fierce again.

During the next several weeks, Charging Elk made a point of staying away from Rue Sainte. In fact, he seldom left his room after work, except to buy food and bathe at the bathhouse around the corner. He still took his Sunday meals with the Soulas family and he enjoyed his conversations with Mathias and Chloé, but they were growing up and had many interests that did not include him. He knew he was being foolish, but it hurt him to listen to Chloé go on about her friends in the church group or Mathias talking about a train trip with his classmates to see the wild bulls of the Camargue. He listened politely and understood most of their talk but he could see the shine in their eyes as they told of their new adventures and he knew that they no longer considered him a big part of their lives.

After dinner, he and René would walk on Cours Belsunce, stopping for an anisette along the way in René's favorite café. Here the little fishmonger would exchange insults and laugh with his friends while Charging Elk sat and smoked, waiting for an opportunity to escape.

Ironically, it was Madeleine who made him feel most at home during his Sunday visits, as she set food before him or darned his socks or prepared a packet of sweets for him. Charging Elk realized that the two of them had become friends at long last. Once he brought her an embroidered shawl in a box tied with a satin ribbon. When she opened it and held up the shawl to admire the embroidery, he saw that her eyes glistened with pleasure. And when she stood and kissed him on both cheeks, he thought happily that although it had taken a long time to reach this point, he did not know of a better woman in Marseille. He was surprised to think this.

But all in all, this was not a happy period in Charging Elk's life. He was not happy with his job—shoveling coal all day, day after day, had become a dreaded chore. He hated to come home covered with coal dust and smelling of oil and lye. He had not made another friend at the soap factory since Louis Granat of the Hautes-Alpes had been sent away to cut soap bars. In spite of René's constant reminder that he was fortunate to work for such a man as Monsieur Deferre, he wished desperately for another job. But how would he find one?

And Charging Elk was discouraged with the amount of money he was managing to save. He had only 140 francs tucked away in the bottom of his duffel bag and he had figured out, with Mathias's help, that it would take him at least another two years, more likely three, to save the money necessary for the trip home. He had begun to have serious misgivings about ever seeing his country and his people again.

More than anything, though, he was tired of living alone in the one room, of eating the tough chickens from the rotisserie or the rough country pâté and the goat cheese on baguette. Once a week he ate at the North African restaurant around the corner, always the couscous and flatbread. He was even tired of that. But most of all, he hated the early, cold nights when he would sit and smoke and wait until it was time to turn off the oil lamp and crawl into bed. The only satisfaction he got during this period was when his mind began to drift into sleep. Often, he would see the clean morning sun as it cleared the distant craggy hills of the badlands, or he would see a golden eagle circling above the plain, its cries so sharp and haunting he would sit up and listen—only to hear a cat fight or footsteps echoing on the cobblestones. He enjoyed these memories, the immediacy of them, but they only led to a more desperate loneliness.

One chilly Saturday evening in early December, the Moon of the Popping Trees, Charging Elk decided that he had had enough of his stark life in the little room and thought a walk down to the Old Port would cheer him. He had already washed himself at the bathhouse, but now he clicked open his push-button pocket knife and cleaned his fingernails, which were always black from the coal grime. He put on a clean shirt and tied his poet's tie loosely around his neck. Then he slapped some scent he had bought during his dandy days on his face and took five, then ten francs from the purse at the bottom of the duffel bag. He put on his good shoes, his long coat, and his hat. He glanced at himself in the mirror above the washstand and almost liked the dark, chiseled face, which was no longer the face of youth, and the hair, which hung shiny and black down past his shoulders.

Night came early now and the wide stone steps that led down from Le Panier were already glistening beneath the gas lamps. They felt greasy beneath the slick soles of his shoes as he took them two at a time. But he was becoming more and more excited as he thought of a Saturday night away from his room, out among people again, the smells of roasting chestnuts and brazier fires filling his nostrils, the sounds of people laughing and chattering. It was near the time of Noël and the Old Port would be lit up, strings of electric lights draped from mast to mast of some of the larger ships, garlands of evergreens and fruit decorating the shopfronts. The cold would keep down the stench that usually came from the sewage of the port.

Charging Elk stopped suddenly at the base of the steps, a short block from the Quai du Port. A dark thought had intruded on his growing excitement, one that filled him with a familiar dread. This was almost exactly the time of year he had gone to the sickhouse four winters ago, the time he had almost gone away from this life, the time the show and his companions did go away and left him here to die. He remembered the moaning men in their beds, the cold night streets when he was on the run, the emptiness of the Gare du Prado, the touch of the gendarme — *"Pardon, monsieur."* And he remembered lying in the stone room singing his death song.

Charging Elk, since moving out of the Soulas home, had lived mostly with the isolation of his own thoughts, his memories, good and bad. He did not have the luxury of intrusions into his life, of children like Mathias and Chloé making demands on him, of a woman like Madeleine making jokes of his ambitions as she did with René, of René himself constantly talking even when he'd like to be quiet. He did not haggle with the fishmonger or the greengrocer; nor did he exchange jokes and jibes with the other men at work. He listened but he didn't talk, couldn't talk like ordinary men. He had no real language to share with these *wasichus*. So he carried the freight of his thoughts and memories around with him and sometimes welcomed them and sometimes hated their insistence.

Now he tried to tell this latest thought to go away, to leave him to enjoy this evening, but as he tried to roll a cigarette he found that his fingers were trembling. In disgust, he threw down the paper and tobacco. It was no use to go out this night. No matter where he went his thoughts would go with him. But just as he gathered himself to climb the stairs, he heard a whining sound behind him, like one of the cats of Le Panier. He grew even more disgusted, but when he turned to shoo it away, he saw a thin figure dressed in dirty heaps of cloth. Even the feet were wrapped in damp cloth. The figure was bent to the side, as though it were deformed, but when Charging Elk looked, he saw that a smaller figure was riding almost upright on its hip. The figure yowled again and stuck out its small, clawlike hand.

As though a great wave of cold air rose up from the cobblestones of the narrow street, Charging Elk felt his back twitch uncontrollably, almost violently. He had not felt such cold since he had escaped from the sickhouse. But now he saw that the figure was a young woman, her dark face shiny with grime. Her upturned palm was pale and delicate and the baby on her hip was no larger than the dead baby Jesus he had found in the alley.

His first inclination was to run, to bound up the stairs as quickly as he had descended. He felt vaguely ashamed of his fear of this woman and her child, but he couldn't help but feel that her sudden appearance was a bad sign, that she possessed some of the *siyoko's* power, had perhaps even been sent by the bespectacled one to harm him. He knew about gypsies. He had seen the women begging around the Old Port—some were old and bent over on their canes and moved as though their legs were made of stone; others were young, like this one, usually with a child. The men could take one's purse and disappear before the victim knew it was gone. Once Charging Elk had heard a man shout and saw a gendarme chase a gypsy through a crowd on the Canebière. The gypsy dodged and wove his way through the people as dexterously as a big cat. Then he suddenly vanished, as though he became the very air that the people breathed.

Charging Elk had been astonished at such an act, but he shouldn't have been. René had told him that the gypsies contained *l'esprit malfaisant*. They could see deep into a man's spirit, they could tell his future and put a curse on him. Charging Elk and René had passed a fortune-teller's room every dark morning on their way to bid for fish and René always crossed himself in the way that made these Frenchmen *wakan*.

Now Charging Elk dared to look into the wraith's eyes, and they were dark and large, like the musky pools the beavers made in Paha Sapa. The small claw was raised before her, almost touching his coat. He glanced at the child but its eyes were closed, as though they were sealed shut with a line of white paste. The face was nothing more than a skull with dark skin, an old man's face.

Again Charging Elk felt ashamed of himself, but this time for fearing the frail woman and child. He dug into his pocket and then pressed the first coin he found into the woman's hand. In the same gesture, he gently curled her small birdfingers over the coin, a one-franc piece. It was too much to give to a beggar, but he was now almost grateful for the simple human contact on that dark street. *"Vous voilà, madame, pour votre bébé Jésus."*

The woman hung her head and backed away, wailing as though her heart would break, and Charging Elk recognized the sound. He had heard the Oglala women wail that way when they lost a husband or child. His own mother had wailed when his brother and then his sister died of the coughing sickness. But he was surprised that the woman had reacted that way to his generosity. Perhaps he shouldn't have touched her.

Nevertheless, Charging Elk felt his spirits rise as he watched the young woman hobble away into the darkness. In some way, he felt that he had passed a test, that he was once again free to become the man of the streets again—perhaps even become a whole man finally—for the first time in a long, long while.

But when Charging Elk entered Rue Sainte he began to have second thoughts. The street was crowded with men, mostly sailors enjoying their Saturday night on the town. The two shabby bars were full of laughing, shouting men in short wool coats, some with caps with the little pompom on top. Glasses of beer in various stages of fullness rested on the bar or swung in slow movements between bar and mouth. There were other men too in their long coats and derbies or top hats, drinking wine and watching the sailors.

Charging Elk had been so sure of himself as he walked alongside the Opera House only two short blocks from this scene. But now he thought of the incident in the Brasserie Cherbourg, the hostile sailors, the jeering women, and he became a little afraid. René had told him several times to stay away from the American bars. It was not unusual for men to fall in with the wrong crowd or the wrong woman or even to be killed in these places. Marseille was full of bad men from all the lands of the world, men who were not civilized like the French and who would slit your throat if you looked at them in the wrong way. René had slid his finger across his own throat when he said this, and Charging Elk had recognized the gesture immediately. And so he had stayed away from the places where these bad men congregated. Until now.

But the men were so involved with their drunken behavior, even those on the street who brushed by him, that the young Indian was beginning to feel invisible again. And his confidence began to grow. Still, he wished he had brought his walking stick with the heavy silver duck's head.

He walked deliberately down the middle of Rue Sainte, away from the two rowdy bars, until he came to the fancy whorehouse. He wove his way through a crowd of men, stepped up on the narrow stone walkway and looked into the window.

The room looked just as he had memorized it the past several weeks in his own shabby little flat—the warm painted walls, the bright chandeliers, the mirror over the elegant wooden bar, the plush red divans. And just as he had envisioned over and over in the same length of time, he saw the girl with the blue robe. She was sitting on one of the couches, looking down into a tall glass of amber water that she held on her lap. She was wearing the same black velvet headband, and dark curls partially hid her face. Her legs were crossed, the robe falling away from one white thigh just visible above her stocking.

She was not alone. This night, the room was filled with men in long coats and ties, some of them in the black evening clothes that rich men wore. Charging Elk had seen men like these escorting their ladies into the Opera House or sitting with others in some of the fancier restaurants in the Carré Thiars just off the Old Port. Nowhere could he see any sailors or any of the rough men that seemed to patronize the other establishments on Rue Sainte.

Several young women sat with the men, in groups or singly, much livelier now than that night a few weeks ago. One of the women had short straw-colored hair and wore a gown the color of a summer peach. She was surrounded by five or six of the men, all leaning forward, all bathed in the glow of her light laughter. She held a cigarette in a holder before her face and sipped from a small flat glass. Charging Elk thought she had some kind of power to make these fancy men pay so much attention to her. Perhaps it was her hair. He had not seen such yellow hair in Marseille.

The girl in the blue gown was sitting with a young man who seemed to be talking into her ear. He was facing her on the divan but she was looking into her drink. Once he put his hand on her crossed leg, running his finger from her knee to the top of the stocking. But she pushed his hand away and turned away toward the front of the room. She seemed to be looking right at Charging Elk, but he knew she couldn't see him through the curtain. He didn't move as he might have that other evening. Perhaps it was the noise and movement on the street that made him bold, invisible to the girl and to the crush of men behind him.

Charging Elk walked two steps to the door, opened it, and stepped up onto the threshold. The warmth of the room came over him instantly and he realized that he had been holding his body stiff since entering this street, and not just because of the cold. But he had put all thoughts of evilness out of his mind. He wanted to be close to the girl with the blue gown.

"May I help you, monsieur?"

He was not the short fat man of the other night. This one was not much taller but his chest was broad beneath the white shirt and wing tie. The dark suitcoat was tight over his upper arms and his flat face had a scar that ran from his ear to the corner of his mouth. The lips were set in a faint smile that did not look real.

Charging Elk was not prepared to answer the man's question. Instead, he looked into the room, trying to find the girl, but she was not there anymore; nor was the man she had been with.

"Perhaps monsieur is lost?"

Charging Elk continued to search the room. Then his eyes caught sight of the heavy wooden bar. "I would like a drink of the red wine, if you please."

"But that is not possible, monsieur. This is a private salon. I'm afraid we don't let just anybody walk in off the street."

Just then the small fat man whom Charging Elk had seen the time before from the window hurried over from his perch at the end of the bar. His bald head gleamed beneath the chandelier. "What is the problem, Gérard? For heaven's sake shut the door. My girls are getting goose bumps."

"I was telling monsieur that this is a private salon. He insists that he wishes a drink, but I was just about to escort him outside."

The fat man looked up at Charging Elk's face, then his eyes swept down the Indian's body, even to his shoes. Charging Elk took off his hat and held it before him, close to his chest. Like most people of his class, Charging Elk had a healthy contempt for those in authority; at the same time, like the others, he knew that he must be respectful. Nevertheless, he looked the owner in the eyes.

But the fat man seemed to like what he saw. He enjoyed men and prided himself on his ability to size them up correctly. In spite of the shabby attempt at finery, the ill-fitting coat, the cheap shoes, the ridiculous hat and fraying shirt cuffs, there was something almost *distingué* about the set of the gentleman's dark face, something oddly attractive about him. Certainly, he was a foreigner, and the fat man rarely allowed foreigners into his establishment, but this one had an air about him. He might be interesting, a welcome relief from the vain *haute bourgeoisie* that came to preen their feathers and fuck his girls.

"You are welcome to Le Salon, monsieur. Gérard, take his coat and hat. You mustn't be rude to such a gentleman. Only two years ago, you were fighting for your meals. Now you think you eat better than our clientele."

Charging Elk understood that the small fat man was scolding his worker, and it made him uncomfortable. In fact, now that he was inside the smoky, cheerful room, he wanted nothing more than to leave as quickly as possible. It was clear that these men were gentlemen. Surely they would be able to look right through him and see that he was a coal-shoveler in the soap factory.

But the little fat man had taken him by the elbow and was steering him toward the end of the bar. "Permit me," he said. Then he called to the man behind the bar. While they waited, the owner introduced himself. "I am called Olivier. And you are . . . ?"

Charging Elk was about to say his name, but then he thought better of it. Whenever he said his name, people reacted with a puzzled look and a vain attempt at saying it. "I am . . ." He searched his memory and the first name that came to mind was that of René's helper in the fish stall. "I am François."

Charging Elk shook the moist little hand that appeared from a curtain of ruffles below the shiny coat sleeve. His fingers felt a large ring, and when he looked down, he saw a deep red stone in a gold setting. "*Enchanté,* François. I am honored to make your acquaintance."

The man behind the bar set two glasses with flat bowls and delicate stems before them, then poured them full with a liquid that bubbled and hissed. The one who called himself Olivier picked up his glass and waited for Charging Elk to do the same. Then he said, "Welcome to my salon. Cheers."

The bubbly liquid seemed to dance in Charging Elk's mouth. It was difficult to swallow and he coughed and felt the bubbles shoot up into his nose. His eyes watered as he tried to snort the liquid out of his nose. Then he coughed again. He coughed and snorted, then snorted and coughed.

Three men less than two meters away had been throwing dice but now stopped to watch this display, at first attracted by the odd appearance of the newcomer, but now amused by the even odder behavior.

"Olivier, you must teach your friend to drink with his mouth like a gentleman," said one.

"Is he all yours, Olivier?" said another.

"He's a big one—just your type, eh?" said the third.

Olivier chided them gently. "You mustn't make fun, gentlemen. This man is not of our culture." He suddenly smiled brightly. "The gentleman is a prince of the Orient."

The three men looked at Charging Elk, their mocking smiles suddenly frozen on their faces.

Charging Elk raised his glass, a little embarrassed but now in control of himself. "*Bonsoir, messieurs. Enchanté.*"

The three, in spite of themselves, raised their glasses, but they didn't drink. "If he's a prince, I'll eat my hat," said the first one, picking up the dice. The others turned away to their game.

"If he is a prince, I'll eat your hat—but I wouldn't touch those clothes of his."

"It would be an act of public safety if Olivier burned them while he is fucking one of the sluts."

"See which one he goes with. Perhaps we will have to burn her."

Their comments were meant to be heard, but Charging Elk only understood that they were talking about clothes and fire. He wasn't paying much attention. He was looking for the girl.

"They are pigs, but their money is as good as any. I am forced to take their money but I do not like their kind in here." Olivier laughed as he offered Charging Elk a cigar from a box he retrieved from behind the bar. "Unfortunately, they are the only kind who come here. They come from excellent families. Without them, I would be out of business."

"They are pigs," said Charging Elk, as he leaned over the match Olivier held before him. He puffed in the smoke and said again, "They are pigs. From the country."

Olivier glanced up at him. He suddenly realized that he had no idea of the man's nationality, much less race. He had not seen such a human being in Marseille. He had not been to the Wild West show that winter of 1889—such things were uncouth to a man of his sensibility—and the only *indiens* he had seen had been in illustrated tabloids and they had worn feathers and war paint. A most disagreeable race of savages.

Olivier also wondered about the man's language. His French was very rudimentary and his accent almost swallowed the simple words. Now he wondered how much the man had understood of the three boors' comments. Perhaps he *was* from the Orient—or the South Seas—or even America.

Just then, Olivier felt a slight chill and glanced behind him at the door. Although he had been watching the door all evening—just as he had every evening for the past twelve years—to see who came and went, this time his heart suddenly lifted in his chest until it made his head pulse with its rapid throb. It was Breteuil. My Lord, he thought, he is still so beautiful, even after eight years. When they first met, Breteuil had been a young sous-chef in a mediocre restaurant down at the Old Port. Since then he had become the most famous chef in all of Marseille, perhaps all of Provence, his small exclusive restaurant on Rue des Catalans catering to the corrupt politicians, the phony aristocracy, and the *haute bourgeoisie*. Olivier hated them all, for he had once been a politician, a representative for the port district—the most important district in all of Marseille—in the Assemblée Nationale, until he had been caught with an Arab boy, *en flagrant délit*, in a small shelter on the Quai de Rive Neuve. Although he himself was a member of the bourgeoisie, albeit a somewhat shady member because of his sexual proclivities, he had been thrown out of office and shunned—but his salon was still patronized by the hypocrites, many of whom were themselves entertained by Olivier's boys in the back parlor. Including Breteuil. And to think he was once mine, thought Olivier. It always filled him with a mixture of bitterness and sadness to escort Breteuil to the back parlor. But to be close to him for just a minute or two again was worth the humiliation.

"Excuse me, François. Enjoy your champagne, my friend." Olivier almost ran to greet the tall, beautiful chef with the glittering spectacles.

Charging Elk did not see Olivier and the pale *siyoko*, arm in arm, wind their way through the crowd to the curtained back rooms. He was waiting for the girl with the blue wrapper to appear again. And after a half hour she did appear, looking a little weary, and when she sat down on a divan, she did so with a heavy sigh and a plonk.

The room had been emptying in the half hour that he had waited. Now only a dozen men and half that many women were still there. Charging Elk had been listening to a man in gartered shirt-sleeves play songs on the piano. In the earlier crush, he hadn't noticed the music. He also had been watching the yellow-haired woman, who was still there and still surrounded by men. As far as he could tell, she didn't go through the curtains with any of them. They seemed content to light her cigarettes and listen to her laugh.

Charging Elk waited for a few more minutes, watching the girl in the blue wrapper out of the corner of his eye, and when he was satisfied that no other man seemed to want her, he moved away from the bar and approached her. He had no real plan—he didn't know how to deal with her—but he still had eight francs in his purse. Did he just give her the money, and if so, how would she react? Perhaps she just went through the curtains with certain men. Perhaps he would scare her.

Charging Elk was acutely aware of his shabby clothes now, his dark skin, his long, loose hair. He might have felt a dandy on the dark street, but here under the bright chandeliers, he could see his scuffed shoes, his frayed cuffs. He wondered what he must look like, in the middle of the room, away from the safety of the bar. But he was determined to be near the girl now, for he knew that he would probably never be allowed in here again. He had sensed that the little fat man thought of him as an evening's curiosity.

He sat down only a meter away from the girl, but he might as well have been in another room. The divan was circular and so he was facing in another direction, toward the front door and the muscular Gérard, who was watching him with the bland alertness that seemed to be his natural state.

Charging Elk rolled a cigarette, lit it, and dropped the extinguished match into a standing ashtray. Although several people had been sitting here over the course of the evening, the ashtray was perfectly clean and the tile floor gleamed like marble. As he smoked the cigarette, Charging Elk tried to think of something to say, something that would be polite yet hint at what he wanted. Finally he slid a little closer to the girl so that he could at least see her profile. His mouth went dry as he breathed in a heavy scent of lavender. Strangely, he thought of Strikes Plenty. He saw the round face of his friend and he heard the teasing laughter—"Go on, are you afraid of a woman now?"

"Bonsoir, mademoiselle," he said, not daring to look at her yet. "Are you tired from your labors?"

She remained silent, staring toward the bar. The three men who had been playing dice were gone. The piano player had quit playing and was now drinking a glass of wine at the end of the bar, his satchel full of music resting at his feet. He stood alone, an employee in a frock coat that was too shiny at the elbows, in trousers too baggy in the knees, ignored in a house that catered to the rich and the indolent.

Marie had often watched the piano player, at home in his little corner of the large room, playing one song after another, basically forgotten in the loud drinking and the constant journeys to the back rooms. Once in a while, one of the patrons would request a particular song, or a group of tipplers would gather around and sing a popular song or two, and at least once a night someone would stand and lead a lugubrious version of "La Marseillaise." The piano player would dutifully provide the music, the heavy chords vibrating the glasses on the bar. Afterward the drunken men wept or clapped each other on the back in brave camaraderie. And the piano player would be forgotten again.

Marie did not want to go back to her room again, except to sleep. She was only nineteen but she had been here for three years. She couldn't begin to count the number of men she had serviced, nor did she want to. She wanted to forget this part of her life—to think of it as a period of time she would later remember as an old *grandmaman* with a distant secret—but she had nothing to look forward to. It was better than taking in cleaning, or sewing in one of the big textile factories, or even worse, taking care of some rich old lady who would heap abuse on her. But because of her occupation, she had no prospects for marriage, or even of becoming a mistress to a wealthy gentleman. Besides, she wasn't pretty enough—not like Aimée and Héloïse, who constantly told of men who wanted to give them clothes and jewelry and even set them up in their own luxury flats. All for exclusive rights to call on them as the gentlemen chose. Marie didn't know if she believed them—why would you work in a whorehouse if you could live like a queen?—but she knew one thing for certain: No gentleman was going to make her such an offer.

She had noticed the tall dark figure standing at the bar when she returned from her encounter with the foolish young man who insisted that he was the son of the wealthiest tanner in Marseille. But what was that to her? She had probably been with the father a time or two. Besides, the idiot did not leave her a little extra—as was proper—on the top of the bureau, as her regulars did. But she had gotten her revenge. She had made him come by just guiding him into her a little too sensually, a caress here, a pull there. And it was over before she had to break a sweat.

She was tired but she was also afraid of Olivier, who had thrown more than one girl into the street for being less than enthusiastic. He was quite sweet and deferential to his customers but hard on the girls. Some of her coworkers suggested that he did not like women, even on a social level. They all knew he was a queer, that he often went to bed with one of his boys, but so what? Many of the whorehouse owners were that way.

She glanced toward the door and saw Gérard, who was helping a gentleman on with his coat. She saw him slip a franc note into his pocket with one hand as he dusted the man's collar with the other. He was at the door not only to greet and keep order, but also to keep an eye on the girls. One word from him and Marie would be walking the streets.

"Would you like to go with me, monsieur?"

The room was much smaller than Charging Elk had imagined. He had assumed, from the size of the parlor, that the bedrooms would be equally spacious. But there was barely room for a single bed, a bureau, a small armoire, and a washstand. And there was no window. The only light came from a small electric lamp with a beaded shade on the bureau. But it did cast a rosy warmth across the red bedspread. Except for the lamp and the bedspread, he thought this room was not much better than the stone room in the ironhouse. At least he had a window there, even if he could only see legs.

Charging Elk had already given the girl six francs, almost a week's rent, which she had handed to someone waiting just outside the door. The quick transaction made him a little wary, but then he heard footsteps walking away, down the dim hallway.

The girl took off her robe and hung it on a peg on the back of the door. She said something about his clothes and motioned toward a skeletal hall tree at the foot of the bed. A white mantle hung from one of the curved branches. Except for a small statue of the holy woman and an unadorned cross on the wall above the bed, it was the only sign of anything personal. Charging Elk wondered if this was her real room.

But he was beginning to understand what was about to happen, and the thought filled him with fear, excitement, and lust. He hadn't been with a woman in this way since the crazy woman out at the

Stronghold over four years ago. And she had been the only woman he had fucked. He felt a flush of shame come over him as he thought that the only two women he had been with had demanded payment of him. But he was now hard as he took off his clothes and hung them on the hall tree. He was as ready as he ever would be.

When he turned around the girl was looking at him, or rather at his cock. She seemed unperturbed as she leaned against the wash-stand. "Come over here," she said, as she slipped a wash mitt over her hand and plunged it into the water in the basin.

It took Charging Elk only two steps to cover the distance, but in that space, he had what seemed to be a hundred different emotions, including wonderment and fear. He looked at her hair as she rubbed the mitt with a bar of soap. Again he smelled the lavender and he became almost faint. He leaned farther forward and sniffed the top of her head, breathing deeply as though to keep the fra-grance in his nostrils forever, and then he felt the cold, soapy mitt on his cock. At first the touch was like the shock he felt when he used to flop naked in a runoff stream in Paha Sapa. It took his breath away and he almost withdrew himself from the mitt. But then the rubbing and squeezing of the hand inside the mitt, the slickness of the suds, the scent of lavender, excited him so much that he looked at the statue of the holy woman beyond the girl's hair to keep from embarrassing himself. He thought of many things, of the horse he had drawn for Chloé, of his own horse, High Runner, of the venomous snakes in the badlands, to take his mind off what was happening to him. He did not look down, for fear the sight of what she was doing to him would carry him over the precipice.

Finally the girl dried him with a thin towel and told him to lie on the bed. He glanced down at the narrow bed, then sat on the edge. A wave of nausea came over him and he felt dizzy and sick, as though he had drunk too much of the *mni wakan*. But the girl gen-tly pushed him back until he was lying, helplessly, weakly, drunkenly, on the hard mattress with his head wedged against the wall and his feet hanging over the other end. He watched the girl straddle him, and even in his weakened state, he was momentarily disappointed that she hadn't taken off the shift. He had wanted to see her breasts, perhaps even touch them. But that feeling disappeared into the ether when he felt her stubby hand grasp his cock, holding it upright, as she eased herself down. He felt her thick thighs on either side of his hips and he imagined the whiteness of them, like the thick cream Madeleine used to make sweet things. He was surprised by that thought, but by now his thoughts were jumping around like the green singers after a good rain. He had spent the past four years thinking without consequence and now his mind was running wild, images crowding one on top of another, as he felt the warmth of her sex pocket, slick and powerful, pulling and sucking his cock deeper inside of her.

He looked at her face, and at first she was looking down at him and he saw the depth of her large, brown eyes. It was the first time she had actually looked at him, looked into his own eyes. But soon she closed her eyes and moved her hips, first one way, then another, now fast, now slow, and she began to grunt, a series of grunts, a sound he had not heard before from a woman, and then he raised his hips off the bed and he felt his warm juice go out of him and into her, and she squalled abruptly, holding herself above him, then collapsed heavily on his lap, and he fell back and closed his eyes against the soft glow of the beaded lamp.

Marie Colet sat at the large table in the kitchen, listening but not really hearing the other young women talk about the men they had been with the night before. It was just past noon and she was still half asleep, as usual.

"Look at my arms. And here—" The girl across the table, Aimée, stood and lifted her robe. *"Voilà!"* she said, pointing to a bruise on the inside of her perfect thigh, her eyes dark with triumph.

"You should tell Olivier—or Gérard. These so-called gentlemen can't abuse us like this."

"Humph. That would be like telling a monkey you don't like his fleas. Fat chance."

"And now I have to go out and buy a new shift because he ruined my only good one. A judge, too. Can you believe it?"

"Pass the butter, Chantal. And do share those croissants. You're fat enough as it is."

Marie absentmindedly stirred her *café crème*, although it was cold by now. She was more tired than usual and she thought she might be coming down with something. She almost wished it were so, because she had to work tonight. It would hardly be worth it. Sunday nights were the quietest of all, as the good bourgeois took a light meal with their families and prepared for the week ahead. The only men who came in were those who were too shy or wished to hide their identities. And they usually went with one of the boys in the back parlor. Just as well. The way they slunk around made her feel ill at ease.

Marie thought again about the tall dark man in the shabby clothes. She couldn't believe that Gérard had let him in, and even more astonishing, that he had chosen her and that she had gone with him. But it was her duty and the consequences would be grave if she started refusing customers.

She couldn't remember the last time she had been truly afraid of a man, and she hadn't been afraid of this one until he turned from the hall tree, naked and erect. He seemed so big and full of lust. She had hidden her feelings, of course—one had to in this business. But the massive dark body had filled her with apprehension. She could tell he hadn't had much experience with a woman, and perhaps that was what scared her. She hardly ever made a man lie down first, unless he was so drunk that he needed working on. She could usually coax him up and then she could control him by being on top. But she was afraid of the dark uncertain mass of the man last night. One of the girls, just last year, had been found dead, and the rumor circulated among the others that her last customer had been a huge Levantine. Marie had thought this absurd, since Gérard did not allow them in. But now, she was not sure. The man last night was not a bourgeois.

But he had done something to her that almost none of the other gentlemen had—he had made her come. She smiled sheepishly to herself.

"What is it, Marie?"

"What is what?"

"I recognize that grin. You are holding a secret from us." Aimée was looking at her like a cat.

"Have you found a patron, Marie?" Laurence was the youngest of the girls, barely older than Marie herself when she had first started.

"Of course not. Don't be absurd, you silly thing."

As the girls went back to their complaints, Marie tried to figure out what about the dark man had excited her into an orgasm. He had done nothing really, except lie there like a statue with an erection, while she did all the work. She had done it hundreds of times over the past two and a half years and she had never succumbed to her own pleasure. She wouldn't allow herself. In that way, she could feel almost virginal—as though she were performing a duty, just as a scullery maid cleans up the kitchen or the factory girl sews women's dresses or men's shirts. She stirred the cold coffee and watched the thin film of cream swirl, then disappear into the caramel-colored liquid. It could be only one thing: her fear of him. Somehow that fear had at some point turned into an excitement she had not felt before.

But she was quite certain she would not see the man again. Just

CHAPTER ELEVEN

Charging Elk *still didn't know much about love, its complications,* heartaches, and rewards, but he had learned enough to make life almost unbearable and yet worth the waiting. Ever since he had left the Soulases' home it seemed that most of his waking hours had been consumed with desire. And now that the girl in the blue wrapper had satisfied his desire once, he wanted more. Just thinking about her, the way she rode on top of his loins, the scent of lavender in her hair, her small square hands washing him, aroused him to a point of sweet agony. He thought about her constantly, riding the omnibus to and from work, shoveling coal into the flat furnaces, eating his lunch of bread and cheese, soaping himself in the bathhouse—his last thought at night was of her as he lay in bed.

He spent half of his saved-up francs to order a tailored suit, buy two shirts, some collars, and a new pair of shoes. The only shoes the clerk could find that would fit him were brown and just a bit cruder than the ones the gentlemen wore around town. And in fact, the brown shoes looked somewhat awkward when he tried on his black suit a week later. Nevertheless, they were new and shiny and a vast improvement over his old ones, which he threw into the very alley in which he had found the dead baby. He thought that one of the vagabonds who often slept there might have a use for them.

Madeleine taught him how to tie a proper gentleman's tie that Sunday after dinner. René made several comments about his love life until Madeleine scolded him for being so rude and made him leave the room. Charging Elk enjoyed standing beside Madeleine in front of the mirror, both of them tying ties simultaneously, he just a step behind. After five or six attempts, Charging Elk tied a decent-looking knot, with both tails coming out just about even. Then Madeleine had him tie another knot all by himself. After a time, he did it just right. As he admired himself in the mirror, she asked, "Is it true? Have you found yourself a girl?"

Charging Elk felt his face go hot with shame. He hadn't expected that René and Madeleine would guess that he was dandifying himself for a woman. How could he tell them that the girl was a whore? Without turning around, he said, "Perhaps so, perhaps not. It is early yet."

He sneaked a quick glance at her in the mirror and saw a hint of a smile on her face. He liked her to smile—she rarely smiled more than she was doing now—but now he wasn't sure what the smile meant.

But then she said, "If so, you must bring her to dinner. Perhaps next Sunday. But you must ask her parents for permission."

Charging Elk thought about Madeleine's invitation for the next few days. He wondered if whores were allowed to leave their whorehouses, if they were allowed to go with men, if they had parents to ask permission of. Madeleine had inadvertently planted a seed in his mind, a seed which grew until he began to glance around his flat, imagining the girl sitting on the bench in front of the window or washing her face at the washstand or lying in her white shift—or even naked!—on his bed. He even imagined her cooking a big piece of meat on a kitchen stove like his mother's back at Pine Ridge while he sat at the small table paring potatoes, which he often did for Madeleine.

One night Charging Elk dreamed. He had wanted to dream of the girl, because in dreams many things happen that one desires. But this dream was not a happy one; nor was it about the girl in the blue robe. In his dream he was standing on one of the sheer cliffs of the Stronghold. Something was wrong and he was weeping. He wanted to jump off the cliff, but every time he tried, a big gust of wind blew him back. He tried four times, five times, ten times, but each time the wind pushed him back, until he was exhausted from his labors. But the next time he approached the cliff, too weak to even attempt to jump, he looked down and he saw his people lying in a heap at the bottom. They lay in all positions and directions— men, women, and children, even old ones. They lay like buffaloes that had been driven over the cliffs by hunters, and Charging Elk understood why he had been weeping. As he stood and looked down at his people, he heard the wind roar in his ears like a thousand running buffaloes, but in the roar, he heard a voice, a familiar voice, a Lakota voice, and it said, "You are my only son." And when he turned back to his village at the Stronghold, there was nothing there—no people, no horses or lodges, not even the rings of rock that held the lodge covers down—not even one smoldering fire pit. Everything was gone.

When the dream ended, Charging Elk found himself awake and staring up into the darkness of his room. It was as though the dream hadn't been a dream and he hadn't really awakened because he had not been asleep. And yet he had seen everything as though he had been there. Even now he could see himself leap over the edge of the cliff, only to be pushed back by the wind. He could see the people lying at the bottom. He could hear the rush of the wind, and the voice breathing into his ear. But whose voice was it? And why had it chosen him?

Charging Elk spent the rest of the night sitting on the little bench with his quilt around his shoulders, smoking cigarettes and looking at the dark sky beyond the window. There was no moon, no constellation of stars to remind him of home. But he didn't need any reminders. His heart was not here; nor was it there, at the Stronghold. It was somewhere he could not name just now, just as he could not name the familiar voice.

The dream haunted him for several days. It was not a question of understanding the dream but of not believing it. Bird Tail, the old *wicasa wakan* at the Stronghold, had interpreted dreams for Charging Elk, as well as for others. Often Strikes Plenty and he discussed these interpretations, and they discovered that there was a truth that the dreams told of. Now Charging Elk knew what Bird Tail would say of this dream, but he didn't want to believe it. Instead he put the dream away in a corner of his mind. He was tired of being troubled. He had been troubled ever since he had left the safety of the Stronghold over four years before.

But every once in a while, when he was least expecting it, when he was wiping the sweat from his face at the furnaces, while he stood in line waiting for his baguette, the dream would sneak out and he would hear the voice whispering above the roar of the wind and he would tremble with a dangerous knowledge.

The only way he could think of to combat the persistent dream was to crowd it out with thoughts of the girl in the blue robe. And so he became even more obsessed with her, even to the point of practicing things he would say to her when next they met. He stood before the small, smoky mirror and made sentences in the French tongue — "Where do you come from? I am François from America.

This night is very beautiful"—and he was pleasantly surprised that the words came out almost as he wished. Mathias and Chloé would be pleased with his attempts but perhaps not with the object of his desire.

Charging Elk now not only desired the girl sexually but wanted her for his own. She was the woman he had been wanting for the past four years. That she was a whore did not diminish this wanting; rather, it only added a complication. How could he get her to come with him? He knew next to nothing about courting a girl. There had been a few girls out at the Stronghold that he and Strikes Plenty had flirted with, but he mostly hung back and listened to the happy teasing. Later Strikes Plenty would admonish him: "She had big eyes for you, anybody could see that. You are going to become an old man and you will still be grabbing yourself." Now Charging Elk wished he had had the courage to ask René how one goes about getting a woman, but he would have had to endure the little fishmonger's questions and jokes.

On a Thursday, a week and a half after his first visit to Le Salon, Charging Elk walked purposefully along the Quai des Belges on his way to the whorehouse in Rue Sainte. He was wearing his new black suit, a starched white shirt with a neatly tied gray tie, and his new brown shoes and was carrying the duck's head walking stick. The shoes were softer than his old ones but still they bit into his heels. He had left his topcoat at home. It was far too shabby and ill-fitting. When he had put it on over the crisp suit, he knew how ridiculous he must have looked last time in such splendid company.

There was something of a festive atmosphere around the Old Port—a small band of horns and drums was playing songs of the Noël season; the juggler in the white face was throwing his burning sticks into the air and catching them in a kaleidoscope of flame; not far away, two acrobats in skimpy tights and singlets performed their feats of balance and strength. Several tables lined the quai, each displaying for sale the small figures that Charging Elk now knew were called *santons*. Lights strung from some of the ships' riggings turned the murky water a golden velvet. The day of the Noël was only two sleeps away, and for some reason, Charging Elk dreaded spending such a long day with the Soulas family. On the other hand, the shops and cafés would be closed and the streets all but deserted. He remembered that first Noël when he had wandered the streets of the city, lonely and desperate. He would need the comfort of René and Madeleine and the children.

Charging Elk thought for a moment of stopping at Le Royal and offering the old waiter a *Joyeux Noël*, a peculiar greeting that he had learned from the Soulases and their friends. It had to do with the birth of the holy child, who would later become the *wasichu* god's child and sit with him in a place called heaven. Charging Elk wondered why Wakan Tanka never took a real child into his home to keep him company, to become his own. He had wondered a good deal about Wakan Tanka lately—the only real contact he had had with the Great Spirit had been in his dream, and he had only sent the dream. Why would he send such a sad dream if he meant to help Charging Elk? And why were these people so happy with their god? Charging Elk couldn't bring himself to think the next thought.

He thought about the old waiter, who seemed to know so much without saying much. Somehow, he knew the old man would have the answers to his questions. But now the girl in the blue wrapper was waiting for him and so he quickened his pace. He would wish the waiter a *Joyeux Noël* tomorrow night.

But the girl wasn't there. Charging Elk stood at the bar for two hours, checking the large watch that fit so snugly into his vest pocket every five minutes. The little fat man was also absent. The woman with the yellow hair was not at her table surrounded by fancy men. In fact, the whole atmosphere of the whorehouse seemed strangely subdued. The girls went to the back rooms with men occasionally, but mostly they sat on the divans or wandered back and forth by themselves or in pairs.

Charging Elk thought of asking the short, broad man at the door why the girl in the blue wrapper wasn't there tonight, but he knew the man did not like him and would be curt, even hostile. Instead, he asked the bartender why it was quiet in the whorehouse.

"It is the season," he said, without looking up from his newspaper. "Our clients are very religious. They do not want *le péché* on their souls so close to Noël."

Le péché. Or as Sees Twice had called it, the sin. According to him, fornicating with the girls of Paris was a sin to the *wasichu*'s god. When Featherman had mentioned that fornication made one feel good, Sees Twice had said that was the devil's work. The devil wanted the Oglalas to have their pleasure with the white girls of Paris so he could claim their *nagis*. Although Charging Elk and some of the others had laughed at such an absurdity, none of the Indians went with the girls.

But now he was bitterly disappointed as he bade a sad good night to the unheeding bartender and walked slowly, aimlessly, back to his flat. Perhaps she was ill tonight or perhaps she didn't go with men on Thursdays. It was natural to take an evening off. But he was worried that she had gotten tired of fornicating with men and had quit. It was this possibility that he chose to believe. Charging Elk put his hand in his pants pocket and closed his fingers around the small brown velvet box. It contained a cameo that he had purchased in the flea market on Rue St.-Ferréol. He had meant to give it to her. He wanted to tie the blue velvet ribbon around her neck and watch her as she admired herself in the mirror over the dresser. He had not thought that he would end up walking home with it still in his pocket. He felt sad for himself.

By now the Old Port was nearly deserted—the juggler, the acrobats, the band, were gone. The tables filled with *santons* had been packed up and the lights on the big boats were extinguished. Le Royal was still lit, but he did not have the heart to wish the old waiter a *Joyeux Noël*. There was nothing merry or holy about this night. The waiter would take one look at him and see that.

The morning of Noël dawned crisp and clear and filled Charging Elk with a strong sense of nostalgia. The sharpness of the air and the sun that streamed into his window to make a bright patch of yellow on the cement floor reminded him of those mornings at the Stronghold during the Moon of the Falling Leaves when he would snuggle closer into his robe and bask in the airy light of the canvas tipi. It was always a contest to try to outwait Strikes Plenty to see who would build the fire. By the time the boys left their lodge, although they could still see their breath, the sun would already be warming the earth. Charging Elk could almost see the frosty buttes golden in the distance, could almost feel the dry grass crunch under his feet, could almost smell the frost turning to water and the toasty musk of High Runner as he bridled him for a day of hunting.

But now he heard the clanky sound of the bell of the small church in the next street and he was reminded of where he was and it was not unpleasant. He didn't have to work. That fact meant more to him than the significance of the holy day. In the four years he had been in this country he had had a holiday from work only on the holy day of Noël and the day before Pâques. Even on other holy days that some of the men took off, Charging Elk kept the fires glowing a bright orange beneath the cast-iron vats. He preferred work to the empty streets of holy days.

He glanced at the pocket watch on the stool beside his bed. Seven-thirty. He lifted himself onto an elbow and looked again. He had not slept this long in years. His first reaction was to jump out of bed, eat some soup and bread, then go for a long walk, perhaps out to the beach off the Corniche. It was always fascinating, and a little sad, to watch the fire boats going out to sea bound for other ports—America?—or the tiny fishing boats, drifting with the current like small pieces of flotsam in the silvery shine that hid their work. It would be nice and peaceful to do that, but this day he had another obligation, one that he looked forward to with less and less enthusiasm as the seasons passed.

From where he lay, he could see a patch of blue sky above the building across the street. Then he heard a child calling, and he thought this day would be like any other to them. They were North Africans, heathens, as René called them. Today, Charging Elk envied them. As he listened to another child calling back, he thought of the girl in Rue Sainte and he wondered how she would spend this holy day.

René's old widowed mother was at the Noël dinner, as were Madeleine's parents, who were not so old. Charging Elk liked Madame Soulas. A small, thin woman with a prominent nose, who always wore a shapeless black dress, with her white hair pinned up beneath a black cloth, she lived just around the corner from her son and his wife and came to dinner every Friday night. She had not been frightened or even apprehensive about Charging Elk. From the beginning, she had expressed a great interest in him and had talked to him as though he could understand her. When Madeleine pointed out that he was a savage and didn't understand the Occitan, and only a tiny bit of French, she resorted to a kind of sign language that Charging Elk seldom understood. When his eyes did light up with recognition—as they did once when she pointed at him and made a downward fork with her index and middle fingers, then made the same figures with both hands, her fingers dancing from left to right, until he understood that she was making a man on a horse—she laughed, a high, thin laugh that was nevertheless genuine, and she would repeat the gesture and laugh until her eyes grew wet. Then she would talk again, in the strange language that was not French but Provençal, as though they shared a good joke on the family.

Of course, Charging Elk didn't understand anything but the occasional figure, but he shared in a confused way her good humor. Madeleine's parents were another matter. They came much less frequently—Charging Elk had seen them less than a dozen times in the two years he had lived with the Soulases—and they sat stiffly on the sofa or at their places around the table. They spoke French only, like good citizens, although both of them came from the Midi. They were much attached to Mathias and Chloé, bringing them expensive gifts and reaching out to touch their heads awkwardly or hug their thin shoulders when they could catch them. They ignored Charging Elk as best they could, but they ignored René as well, a fact which did not seem to make René unhappy. Monsieur Daviel was a furniture maker who employed fifteen craftsmen and numerous apprentices. He often complained that his business was getting too large and that he would one day have to retire or go mad. It was clear that he considered himself and Madame Daviel bourgeois and pitied their daughter for marrying a common fishmonger after the education and upbringing they had provided.

Madeleine had prepared a large *rascasse*, hogfish as the locals called it, as well as a ham haunch with lentils and sweet yams. René had joked that they would be eating ham until Easter; then they would have to buy a new one and start all over. As usual Madeleine scolded him, asking if he preferred that she cook a small capon for her parents to nibble on. But dinner went well; even Madeleine's parents seemed to loosen up on the bottles of good wine (bought especially for them) and the high spirits of the children. Mathias in particular was happy; his grandparents had given him an expensive new spyglass, with which he could watch birds in the trees and shrubs of Parc Borely, and the ships under sail from the battlements of Fort St-Jean. Chloé was more subdued, but nevertheless intrigued with a magic lantern that showed all the prominent features of Paris, including the miraculous Eiffel Tower. Charging Elk had once drawn the iron tree for her, but it was a poor substitute for the illuminated picture.

In fact, Charging Elk's presents to the children were rather poor. He had spent a large part of his savings on clothes and drink. He bought himself bottles of wine to drink in his room for the first time. It was cheap wine, to be sure, nothing like tonight's wine, but each bottle cost nearly half a franc. And he had bought a new set of work clothes, for he was tired of wearing the same grimy clothes every day. Each purchase, except for his new suit and shoes, had seemed small enough; but taken together, they had severely diminished the contents of the purse at the foot of his duffel bag.

And so he had bought Chloé a crude imitation of a Spanish-style barrette, which she thanked him for, then left in the box buried in excelsior. The colored pencil set he gave Mathias was not even thoughtful—the boy had no interest in making pictures. Madeleine had exclaimed over the colorful tin of candied apricots stuffed with almonds, and René had admired the craftsmanship of the second-hand snuffbox, but Charging Elk could tell that they were surprised and let down by the gifts. Only last year he had given Madeleine a filigree brooch to hold her mantle in place and René a burly fisherman's sweater to replace his old one, which had holes in the elbows and had been patched many times.

Charging Elk felt ashamed in his new suit and shiny brown

shoes. He had learned from his Oglala people to share with others, whether it was the pain of the loss of a child or husband or an abundance of meat and berries. Somewhere along the way, he had lost that desire to share, replaced by an attention only to himself and his own desires. His shame deepened when he unwrapped the gift from Madame Soulas and held up the black holy beads with the small silver cross. He had brought nothing for her. The fact that she didn't mind at all, her eyes shining with the act of giving, only made him feel worse.

After dinner, he sat with René and Monsieur Daviel in the parlor, where they smoked cigars and drank plum brandy. The children helped Madeleine and Madame Soulas clear the table and wash dishes. Madame Daviel sat at the piano and played a lively song for the season. She sat primly but somehow managed to make swooping movements with her upper body as her fingers danced over the keys. Charging Elk was amazed at her ability to make the piano sing so richly, as though it had a voice of its own. By contrast, the piano sounded hollow and abrupt under Chloé's fingers, as though it had a will of its own. After listening to the music and conversation, which consisted mostly of Monsieur Daviel's complaints over the lack of good kiln-dried wood and exorbitant wages, Charging Elk felt a sudden need to get out into the fresh air. He had never left the Soulases' home on his own volition before, always waiting until René gave him permission, but now he stood and wished the two men good night. Then he walked into the kitchen and said his farewell to the rest of the family. Chloé hugged him and thanked him for the barrette; Mathias shook hands and said the colored pencils would come in handy for drawing maps. Madeleine kissed him on both cheeks and wished him a *Joyeux Noël*, pressing a package of parchment paper in his hand. It was heavy with ham. Finally he bent over and kissed Madame Soulas on one cheek, then the other. He had never done that before, but the old lady, her shabby black sleeves rolled up and her hands soapy with dishwater, laughed and made a gesture that looked disturbingly like the Lakota sign for fucking.

A week after Noël, Charging Elk walked through a heavy downpour toward Rue Sainte. His shoes were soaked and the bottoms of his suit pants were heavy with dampness. The umbrella at least kept his upper body dry, but sudden gusts of wind blew the rain sideways, and he held his coat tight around his neck to keep the new silk scarf that Madeleine and René had given him from getting wet. The guilt that had weighed on him all week was now replaced by anticipation of another encounter with the girl in the blue wrapper. On the other hand, he was ready for disappointment. He had made up his mind that if she wasn't there this time, it would be his last visit to Le Salon.

But she was there, sitting on the same red divan. It was Saturday night and the large room was buzzing with talk, music, and laughter. The yellow-haired woman was at her familiar table, again surrounded by men, young and old. The piano player in the far corner with his back to the room played the same songs as before. One of the whores led a man in evening clothes through the curtains to the back.

Charging Elk gave his coat and umbrella to the short, broad man, who had not greeted him, and walked toward the bar, but halfway there, he turned and walked across the floor to the red divan. He realized that he still had on the white scarf but it was too late to do anything about it.

"Bonsoir, mademoiselle," he said, half-bowing before her. "If you remember—I am François. How are you?"

"Well," she said, not really looking up at him. "And you, monsieur?"

"I am happy," he said.

"It is good for you, yes?"

"Yes. I have a new scarf. I have many friends."

This time Marie did look up at him. The dark face with the slanted eyes and high, hollow cheeks seemed on the verge of smiling. Yet there was something tight, almost impassive about it, almost like a mask.

Charging Elk couldn't believe his good fortune. First, to find her by herself; then, to be able to say the sentences that he had practiced. And she understood! "I would like to sit with you," he said, his voice suddenly trembling with a joy he had not felt since last time he saw her. But then, he had become almost sick with it.

And so he sat and spoke some more. Sometimes, she responded; other times, she looked at her clasped hands or toward the corner of the room where the piano was making music. A woman in a long black skirt and white blouse came with drinks on a silver tray, a stemmed glass filled with the sparkling wine for him, a tall glass full of amber liquid for her. Charging Elk was surprised that she had come without bidding, but he gave her the two francs, then lifted his glass and the girl did likewise. Neither spoke, but Charging Elk drank in the lavender smell of her along with the bubbly liquid. The combination made him unexpectedly light-headed, and he closed his eyes for just a moment. When he opened them and started to speak, he suddenly stopped. The girl was looking right at him.

Marie Colet sat on the edge of the bed and loosened the laces on her shoes. François would be the fifth man she had been with that night and there would probably be five or seven or eight more after him, including one or two who liked to top off an evening's drinking with a good screw. She hated that part. They would either slobber all over her or become frustrated and abusive when they couldn't perform. When the girls complained to Olivier and suggested that he throw these drunkards out, he would become furious and say that they came from the best families, what would become of his business without them, and the girls were free to walk Rue Sainte with the other common whores anytime. Gérard would help them pack up and escort them out the door. Goodbye. Good riddance.

Marie placed the shoes side by side between the dresser and the armoire and laid her stockings on top of them. She glanced over at François, who was hanging his damp pants on the hall tree. His square shoulders and long, sinewy arms sent just the smallest tremor of fear through her body. He was sober and polite, even shy, but so big! He didn't wear long underwear like most of the men, just a pair of briefs that covered his loins and nothing else. His dark skin made the white briefs almost luminescent in the dim light. Marie hesitated for just a second; then she pulled the shift over the top of her head, hoping that he wouldn't notice the fading bruise on her right breast, where only last week one of the drunkards had bitten down until she cried out.

She sat on the edge of the bed and waited for him, and when he turned he had something in his hand. He walked over to her, his penis only partially erect, a far cry from that first night. She looked at the brown velvet box in his hand, then up into his eyes, her own eyes questioning.

"For you, mademoiselle." Smiling, he added: "For your beauty."

Marie took the box and opened the hinged lid. There, on the satin lining, lay a cameo, white against a pale blue background. She lifted it from the box by the slightly darker ribbon and studied the profile of an elegant woman. Then she looked up at François again.

"But I can't accept this, monsieur. It is much too beautiful." She cradled the cameo in her palm, running her thumb over the raised profile. How could he know that she had always wanted one?

"Perhaps you had better give it to your wife." She almost added, with the slightest bitterness, "not your whore."

The man, François, laughed, a rumbling laugh from deep in his chest. Then he sat on the edge of the bed beside her and took the cameo, and she turned her back to him. The small piece of jewelry was cold against her skin as he tied the ribbon snugly around her neck. Then she turned toward him. "It is for a beautiful woman, I think," she said, not looking into his eyes.

"Look at yourself," he said, indicating the mirror above the dresser.

She stood and walked the couple of steps to the mirror. He followed her and stood behind her. The red-beaded lamp cast just enough light to illuminate the cameo and the blue ribbon that circled her neck. He watched her touch the cameo with tentative fingers. Then he looked down at her breasts, and the large dark nipples aroused him immediately. But he didn't touch her yet. There would be time for that. For now, he was content to look into the mirror at her dark eyes, which glistened with a kind of awed radiance.

Charging Elk had never felt such pride in all his life.

At three in the morning, Marie returned to her room for good. There was nobody downstairs, except for Olivier and Gérard and a couple of girls. The street outside was empty and dark, but the rain had let up and a few high, white stars glittered over the town.

Normally, Marie felt exhausted and sad at this time of night. Normally, she would collapse in the bed, not bothering to wash herself or change the bedding. She would be mildly depressed that her room was so small and airless. And she would envy Aimée her corner room with the large window that overlooked the small courtyard behind the building. And as she drifted off, she would see the endless white bodies of men and the stiff cocks they were so proud of.

But tonight Marie was not exhausted and her nose was offended by the smell of sex. After her first few weeks in the whorehouse, she had become used to the odor and thought nothing of it. It became as much a part of her ambience as the lavender body lotion or the smell of cigars and spirits. Now, she hated this part of her life, which had in fact become her whole life and which seemed to consist of nothing more than sitting in the parlor, engaging in the forced cheerfulness of sex talk, then taking a heavy breather to her room and steeling herself for yet another joyless encounter.

Marie lay on her bed in a flannel nightgown, a chenille robe, and wool slippers, necessities against the late-night chill, her head resting on a pillow propped against the wall. The small brown box lay on her stomach. She didn't want to open it just yet. Instead, she closed her eyes and saw herself standing before the mirror, admiring the cameo but stealing a glance at the dark, wild face behind her. The face seemed to float in the mirror, somewhere above her head, and the eyes were not so savage and the lips were parted in a real smile.

Marie stroked the velvet box and tried to understand her feelings for François. At the age of nineteen, she was too cynical to believe in love—at least as far as she was concerned. Laurence, who was sixteen, seemed to fall in love every night. Sometimes Marie let the young girl sleep with her and she would prattle on about one man or another who had promised to make her his own girl. It was true Laurence was cute and she had a ripe body for one of her age, but she would learn that the promises were empty and that working girls, even the beautiful Aimée, never left the houses until they became too old and lost their looks and their firmness. Then they became servants or took in washing (if they were lucky enough to find a place to live) or even beggars. Although Marie was young yet, she had been having dreams in which she found herself wandering in the streets of a town she almost recognized. She had nothing but the clothes on her back, and children teased her. The dream always ended with her standing on a dark street corner not knowing which direction to take. All four directions looked exactly the same—empty and bleak and familiar. And when she sat up, panicked by the darkness, not knowing where she was for an instant, she wanted to cry out for someone, anyone, to comfort her. But the only comfort she could find in her situation was that she could probably be a whore for at least ten more years. She would have a place and a job for at least that long. And her immediate future didn't look so bad after all.

But now she had been touched by the tall dark man, and in more ways than one. He was certainly a gentle giant, a welcome relief from her usual rutting customers, who seemed to think that smothering her would be a fine idea. He was quite shy and had been almost delicate in their coupling, his weight barely there, his smooth chest just brushing against her nipples. And although she didn't come this time—she was too preoccupied with the cameo tight and cool against her throat—she did feel a kind of tingling disappointment when he lifted himself off her. That surprised her more than the fact that he had made her come last time. She had seldom felt anything with a man, much less disappointment when he left her. That the man was a strange, dark foreigner confused her. She had always considered herself lucky that she worked in a house that did not allow foreigners, especially the dark ones. And now—what?

She sighed. Now nothing, she thought, and she was relieved to have regained her senses. He was a customer and nothing more. He had given her a present, he had fucked her, and now he was gone, probably home to his wife, feeling a little guilty but smug that he had gotten some fucking on the side. Marie knew that some men needed whores, and that was what she was there for. Their wives were too proper to allow their men to sweat and rut all over them. This one was just a bit more considerate.

Marie stood and shook off the robe, which she draped over the headboard. Then she knelt before the dresser and pulled out the bottom drawer. This was where she kept her small things—her mending kit, a stack of letters from her parents that had been written by a schoolmaster and that she couldn't read, a beaded purse that had belonged to her *grand-maman*, three small *santons* that she put on her dresser during the season, and her Bible with the white cover. She decided that she would not look at the cameo tonight. As she placed the velvet box in the drawer, she remembered that he had asked her name and she had told him. "Marie," he had said. Then he said it again, and yet again, as though to memorize it. She had never heard her name so reverently pronounced.

And she further remembered, as he stood in the doorway, about to leave, she had said, "François," and when he turned, she had said, "Thank you, François." That was another first. She had never thanked one of her customers for anything. Even when they left a tip on the dresser, she had preferred a demure silence.

Marie had tried to be cynical about François, but now she knew that he was a man who excited her in a puzzling way. As she turned out the light and crawled into bed, curling herself into a ball against the cold sheets, she wondered what his home was like, what it would be like to be there, perhaps to wake up in the morning next to him. She knew, in spite of her cynical ruminations, that he wasn't married. But what would it be like—to wake up next to him?

She closed her eyes and thought about the beautiful cameo. It was the first true gift she had received from a man that had no strings attached. But what did he want?

CHAPTER TWELVE

harging Elk had been seeing Marie once a week for the past three months. Now as he sat on the bench before the open window, buffing the brown shoes, which had never been the same since he had walked through the downpour, the leather stiffer, the toes slightly curled, he wished things were a little different. For one thing, he lived from payday to payday now, without a thought of saving any money. He bought wine, he ate out more often, he took his shirts to the laundry to be cleaned and pressed each week, he bought a few gifts for Marie, although none as expensive as the cameo. Consequently, he had nothing in the purse in the duffel bag. He hadn't even seen the purse for two months. As for his hope that one day he would get home to his land and his people, it became more and more a distant dream. He thought of his parents often enough, his mother beading or standing at her iron stove, his father sunning himself with the other men or perhaps riding High Runner for the pleasure of it; he thought of Strikes Plenty, now planting potatoes and surrounded by his own children—it was almost more than he could imagine, his *kola* married to a woman of his own kind, living in his own country, watching the same sun rise every day, the familiar animals, the distant but loyal Paha Sapa. He thought of these things and his people, but always the dream he had had would creep into his pleasant reverie and fill him with a cold fear.

Charging Elk knew that the dream should have made him anxious, even desperate, to go home. He should have wanted more than anything to see if the dream had been true. If it was true, it would be a catastrophe beyond belief. *You are my only son.* But whose voice? Bird Tail's? His father's? Lately, since he had dreamed one time of Crazy Horse, he had begun to believe that the war chief had contacted him from the real world. Charging Elk's own father, Scrub, had said Crazy Horse had lived in the world of dreams and vision even when he was alive. Perhaps the wind that held him back was from the real world. It would not let him join his people, his ancestors. *You are my only son.* Even now the voice and the wind sent chills through his body, as though to warn him away from his degraded life.

But Charging Elk always had an antidote to this fearful dream. He would force himself to think of Marie. He still knew almost nothing about her, only that she had worked in the whorehouse for three years and that she came from a village outside of Marseille. But he knew her body and he knew her eyes—the way they would light up when he walked into the whorehouse or brought her a gift, then go dark when she sat with him in the large parlor, watching the crowd of men surrounding the girls or singing around the piano. He knew she didn't like to be with them, even if it was her job. Charging Elk always left Le Salon after their time together, because he didn't want to see her misery. But as he walked back to Le Panier, he felt a burning frustration that became a confused anger by the time he reached his flat.

Why didn't she leave? He couldn't understand why she wouldn't just leave. But he was more angry with himself for not having the guts to ask her to go with him—home to his flat. And he felt ashamed for not even being able to ask her to go for a walk or to a café. He knew the words to ask her out of that place. He just didn't have the guts to utter them. He had become a coward since he left the Stronghold. It pained him to think that as a youth he had taunted the miners in the Black Hills, stolen from them, sneaked down to Pine Ridge at night to visit his parents even though he knew if the *wasicuns* caught him, they would send him away. He hadn't been afraid of anything in those days. He had lived as he imagined the old-time Oglalas lived, fearing nothing, risking everything for the sake of adventure. Now he was afraid of the smallest obstacle, the smallest pebble in the road.

Charging Elk laced up the brown shoes, stood, and shuffled into his freshly pressed suit coat. He checked his hair in the mirror. He had taken to wearing it in a bob in back, folding it under and tying it with a blue ribbon, much like the one on the cameo. Marie would take the cameo from her dresser and he would tie it around her neck. For some reason, the fact that both of them would be wearing blue ribbons excited them. It still stunned him when he thought of how she would wiggle and whisper beneath him, slapping his flanks with her thighs, until she began the now familiar grunting that led to a loud, startling keen that inflamed his ears and his cock at the same time and he would feel himself rushing into her with an agonizing grinding that left him almost senseless with pain and ecstasy.

Because it was too early yet for his appointment with Marie and because it was a warm evening in early April, the Moon of the Red Grass Appearing, Charging Elk decided to stop at Le Royal for an anisette. He hadn't been there for many moons—since the hot summer—and he wanted to see the old waiter. Or rather, have the old waiter see him in his suit and bobbed hair.

But a young waiter, with black hair slicked down from a central part and a thin mustache that curled up on the ends in the latest style, served him. The waiter seemed confused by the large, dark man in the fine suit and starched shirt and at first didn't understand what Charging Elk was asking. What did he mean?

Finally Charging Elk was able to say, "Your predecessor, the old waiter, my friend."

"Ah, you mean Lachaisse. Of course." The waiter set the anisette before Charging Elk. "But he is long gone."

"Where?"

"They say he went to live with a sister in Arles or Nîmes. Since last fall." The waiter tore off a piece of paper with a number on it and left it on the table. "Was he really a friend of yours?"

Charging Elk looked off toward the ships resting in the harbor. In the warmer weather, the smells of offal mixed with the brine were already sharp in his nostrils. He had never known the waiter's name, Lachaisse. "An old friend," he said, and he felt bad for having stopped coming to Le Royal.

At first, Breteuil was shocked more than anything else. Usually he never stood at the bar in Le Salon. He loathed the kind of men who came here. Ironically, they were the same kind of men who made his restaurant the most exclusive in Marseille. But Breteuil, arrogant as he was, considered himself apart from the *haute bourgeoisie* — inferior in his upbringing but superior in his refinement. These were the kind of men who drank too much wine and treated his food as though it were the meanest of peasant fare, meant to plug up that empty hole in their guts so they could swill more wine. Of course, he did have patrons who waited for a month or more to pay homage to his creativity. These were the ones he toasted as he emerged from the stifling kitchen, only slightly disheveled, and made his round of the tables. He barely acknowledged pigs like the ones that surrounded him now in Le Salon. He usually went through to the back parlor, to the beautiful Miguel, a young Spaniard, who eagerly accepted Breteuil's lavishments of affection. Today, he was waiting for a cutlery salesman from Paris, who insisted on meeting here so he could kill two birds with one stone.

But the tall dark one sitting with the dark-haired whore had intrigued him. Although he was very exotic, there was something familiar about him. Was he an entertainer of some sort? A strongman perhaps? An actor? He was very handsome in a crude, almost fearsome way. Breteuil had seen that face before—the slitted eyes, the high cheekbones, the thin lips that were now curled into a faint smile as the whore talked to him. But what was he doing in here? Breteuil looked around him. Except for a light-skinned redheaded man and the beautiful transvestite with the short blond hair, all the men looked pretty much alike—mustached or bearded, impeccably clothed, young or old, all alike. He even recognized a judge, an officious whippet, who often entertained large parties at the restaurant. And a marquis who had sold his title but still insisted on the appellation.

Breteuil took a sip of his champagne, then turned his back on the room, but he could still see the dark man in the bar mirror's reflection. Why would Olivier let such a strange creature into his establishment? Unless he was famous. Or rich.

He watched the man stand, then assist the whore to her feet. Such manners. And for a slut—not very pretty at that. The man looked even bigger now that he was on his feet. Breteuil turned and watched the two walk toward the back room, the whore in the lead. Such shoulders. Such a slender waist. The man turned slightly to slip between the red velvet drapes. He glanced back toward the bar, a casual glance, and Breteuil almost gagged on his champagne. He did spill a bit on his lapel but he didn't notice. He was shocked. Something in that backward glance, the eyes that did not seem to really see anything, had jolted Breteuil as though he had been struck with one of his own tenderizing mallets. He stared at the velvet drapes for a moment; then he beckoned to the bartender.

"That big, dark man—do you know him?"

The bartender looked around the room, his mouth open with curiosity.

"He just went back with one of the whores." Breteuil thought the man looked stupid, but surely he couldn't mistake whom he was talking about. There was, or had been, only one man of that description. "Come on, man."

The bartender lifted Breteuil's glass and wiped the bar. "You mean the big fellow with the squinty eyes. Don't know him. He comes in here every Saturday night about this time. Goes upstairs with the same girl. Marie. Kind of unusual-looking, eh? A Turkoman maybe. Don't know."

Breteuil didn't bother to answer. He knew who the man was, had in fact thought of him quite often. What was it—three, four years ago? He remembered the man's handshake, oddly limp for such a powerful hand. He remembered looking him up and down and thinking how dangerous—and desirable—he looked. He was the miserable little fishmonger's helper, the Peau-Rouge who had been in the Buffalo Bill Wild West show and had somehow been left behind. As the memories came back, Breteuil felt almost faint with excitement. The Peau-Rouge had helped the chef load his fish onto the cart. He had accepted a cigar. In an unguarded moment, he had looked right into Breteuil's eyes and made him look away. Breteuil had never looked away before—or since. He knew that he was quite beautiful and that men and women alike looked at him with admiration, often desire. He enjoyed staring their eyes away, so that they became confused and suddenly shy. He enjoyed his power to humiliate them, especially if they were with their friends. But this Peau-Rouge had looked into his eyes as though he could see the very soul of Armand Breteuil.

Breteuil pushed his champagne glass toward the bartender, who had been watching him. He too was impressed by the pale, slender man's fine looks. "Are you all right, monsieur?" He poured the glass full, let the bubbles die down, then poured again.

"Of course," Breteuil snapped, not looking up. "Leave me." He took off his spectacles and rubbed his eyes. Where was that damn cutlery salesman? He wanted to do business, then get out of there. Already some men were gathered around the piano player, singing a martial song.

Charging Elk. Soulas had pronounced the name so proudly. My new helper. Breteuil remembered with some satisfaction that he had almost stolen Soulas's new helper away that very first morning. And he might have done so, if he had known what to do with him. Charging Elk was so helpless then, so vulnerable. Breteuil was almost certain, given the right circumstances, he would have come with him. Like a lost puppy. Charging Elk. What could such a name mean?

Breteuil was so lost in his memories of that dark morning four years ago that he didn't notice the light touch of a hand on his back. He hooked his spectacles over his ears, glancing at himself in the mirror—he was afraid he had been noticeable in his uncharacteristic behavior—and he saw the plump face of Olivier gazing sideways at him. He had been noticed! Angrily, he said to the mirror, "What do you want, Olivier?"

Olivier stepped back half a step. "Just to say hello, Armand," he stammered. "To ask after your health, my friend."

"There is nothing wrong with my health, and it is not a particularly good evening, thank you."

"But what are you doing out here?" Olivier lifted his hand and swept the room with it. "Normally, you do not stop here, I think."

"Tonight is not normal. I am being stood up by a cutlery sales-man who wants to sell me knives and fuck your girls all at once. Can you imagine?" Breteuil meant being stood up.

But Olivier misunderstood. "One can sell and one can fuck — but not at the same time. There is a time and a place for everything, but one must use a little common sense."

Breteuil turned and glanced down at the pathetic little man in his ruffled shirt and expensive scent, his plastered-down thinning hair and slim mustache low on his lip. He couldn't believe that they had once been lovers. But he had been poor then and Olivier had been infatuated with him. Still was. This thought cheered him up a little, and he said, "And you, Olivier, are you prospering?"

"As you can see, Armand," Olivier said, turning to survey the room, "my girls are the loveliest in town." He smiled up at Breteuil, his narrow mustache twitching. "My boys are not so bad either, eh?"

Breteuil suddenly hated Olivier. Although they both liked their boys, Olivier was a common pederast, whereas he, Breteuil, was ca-pable of a purer, higher-minded kind of love, one more consistent with his artistic temperament. He considered the six francs he paid for Miguel more an expression of his largesse than a pimp's fee. He also knew that he had no time to make assignations on his own — he spent six days a week at his restaurant, all day, from buying the fish and meat and vegetables in the morning to cooking until eleven at night. Most nights he got only four or five hours of sleep. Still, it would be nice to have somebody he could spend all day Monday with. Even at that, he jealously guarded his day off from all intrud-ers, preferring to sleep, to walk, to read, to sleep some more. Even though his restaurant was a great success — the cutlery salesman had promised to bring an article from *Le Figaro* in Paris, which had listed La Petite Nani (named after his grandmother) the best restaurant in all of Provence—Breteuil was not a happy man. Lately he had been yelling at his sous-chef and his waiters, even his busboys. He controlled all aspects of his restaurant, and that is why it was the best. But he would have to slow down, to relax, or he would burst something inside of him. Already, for the past three weeks, he had been troubled by a gnawing in his gut, a burning sensation that made it difficult to even taste his own dishes.

Breteuil sighed, then smiled at Olivier. "I was noticing one of your girls—a bit chunky, dark hair, a blue wrapper, I think—she was with a man just a moment ago. She reminds me of someone."

Olivier looked back—there were at least twenty to thirty men and six or seven of his girls. He had twelve girls in all, and all of them were working on this Saturday night. Suddenly, his eyes brightened. He enjoyed doing favors for Breteuil. "Ah, you mean Marie. Yes. Not very elegant, but healthy. Some men like them that way."

"I suppose—I suppose the man she was with is even now enjoying her fruits. Such an unusual creature—not the type one usually finds in your house, Olivier."

Olivier laughed, a high pinched giggle that Breteuil knew too well. "He showed up one night some months ago. I don't know why, but I was taken with him. I thought maybe—but no, he likes his girls, especially Marie. Anyway, he does no harm, so I think why not?"

"And does he come often?"

"Every Saturday night. You can mark your calendar by his visits."

"Does he have a name?" Breteuil was reaching some.

Olivier glanced at him, eyes suddenly alert and suspicious. Jealous.

"Just asking. No matter really." Breteuil turned to the bar and took a sip of champagne. He had dismissed Olivier—or at least had given that impression.

Olivier hesitated for a moment, not sure what to do. The Spanish boy in the back parlor was one thing, but now—one of his customers? Olivier knew Breteuil and he knew that nothing good could come of such an interest. Still, he said, "His name is François. From the Orient, I think. Did you notice his eyes?"

Breteuil didn't respond. He lit one of his thin cigars and watched the smoke curl up and away to join the haze of all the other cigars and cigarettes. But yes, he had noticed the dark man's eyes. They were the same eyes that had stripped him bare that dark morning four years before on the Quai des Belges.

CHAPTER THIRTEEN

⸻

The leaves were already large and dark green on the heavily pruned plane trees on Cours St-Louis and the evening sky was a warm yellow as the sun set over the rooftops to the west. It was early May and Charging Elk was still full of wonder and hope, as he looked at the green awning over the flower kiosk. But it was the lettering in white that caught his eye and kept it: NAISSANCES MARIAGES FUNÉRAILLES. A woman was arranging a bouquet in a porcelain vase. The flowers came from the immense greenhouses just inland from the Côte d'Azur. They were mostly hothouse carnations this time of year, with a few bunches of irises and roses, even lavender, in cone-shaped containers secured in wire racks. A small white dog, which seemed to belong to the woman, sat for a while, then stood and scratched its belly before walking daintily among the passersby. It was completely at home on the busy thoroughfare.

Charging Elk was celebrating his new job at the soap factory. He sat at the small metal table in the warm air and watched the dog scatter a flock of pigeons, which flew up, circled, then came down five or six meters behind it. The dog went on to sniff the base of a plane tree before lifting its leg.

Just five sleeps ago, as Charging Elk was hanging up his coat, his boss had come to him and led him to another part of the factory, a large clean room with plenty of windows. The boss introduced him to another man, but the other man had heard of him. In spite of having the lowliest, dirtiest job in the factory, Charging Elk was well known as the Peau-Rouge from America. Even in a factory as large as Monsieur Deferre's, word gets around. Some of the men made jokes about him; others made what they thought were war whoops when he was out of hearing range; still others watched him with a wary awe, some with hatred because he was different. And except for Louis Granat, all had given him a wide berth. But they all had heard of him.

The other man, whose name was Monsieur Billedoux, said, "I hear you are ready to make soap, Charging Elk. We'll see. But first, this morning, you must watch and help out as I ask. It is hard work, but you'll find it much cleaner than shoveling coal." Charging Elk noticed that the man spoke slowly and clearly. He could understand most of the words and all of the gist. He was grateful, as he always was, for this small courtesy.

And so Charging Elk watched the vat of hot curd tipped out into heavy metal frames, a sea of almond-scented cream. And when it had set, men began to slice it into bars with wires. Other men shaped the settled soap, rounding off the crude corners with curious knives, while others threw the bars onto a moving table. Here the bars passed before two men, who sporadically tossed a flawed bar into a tub at their feet.

Billedoux led Charging Elk along the table following the progress of the bars, until they came to two other men who stamped the smooth soap on both sides with metal presses. Billedoux snatched one of the bars off the table and held it before Charging Elk. "You see?" he shouted over the patient chug of a steam engine. The lettering on the bar read "PRÉ DE PROVENCE." Below the writing, Charging Elk saw a perfect flying bird with a flowering twig in its beak. Billedoux turned the bar over. In an oval, letters said "SAVON DE MARSEILLE." Beneath, in smaller figures, "250 g." Billedoux dropped the bar into Charging Elk's hand. "It goes all over the world—even to your country!"

Charging Elk was startled by the man's statement. How had he known? He lifted the soap and smelled it. It smelled of almond oil, but to his nose the pleasant odor could not disguise the familiar lye that bubbled in vats above his coal furnaces. Would his own parents use this soap? He couldn't imagine it. But with the fire boats and the iron road, it was possible. René had said the soap of Marseille was famous the world over. But Pine Ridge was beyond the world of this soap.

At the end of the moving table, four men were taking the soap and putting them into boxes in neat rows. The boxes rested on a metal cart. They worked quickly but carefully.

"Come with me." Monsieur Billedoux was a lean man in his mid-thirties, with wavy brown hair and neatly trimmed goatee. He looked out of place in the factory, even in his blue smock and shapeless beret. Charging Elk thought he looked more like the gentlemen who came into Le Salon than he did the other workers. Maybe he was a big boss who dressed like a worker. There was something about him, his quick movements, his bright face, that seemed to suggest authority. And yet he was taking the time to explain all the steps in the mysterious process. Even though Charging Elk didn't understand much of it, he appreciated the fact that he was being talked to.

He still held the bar of soap as he walked faster than normal to keep up with Billedoux. In one of those quirks of the mind that pop up when one least expects it, he suddenly envied the soap. Perhaps it would cross the big water and end up at Pine Ridge. Perhaps in another moon, or two, his mother would be washing her face with it in the morning. Or his father would scrub his hands after planting potatoes.

Billedoux led him through a large stone arch into a bright room with wooden floors. Three long rows of tables stood in the center, several women standing around each. Charging Elk was surprised to see the women there, but he had seen them among the men in the mornings when they filed through the factory gates. He hadn't really thought what their jobs might be. They were just more women who were as unobtainable as the others on the streets of Marseille.

"This is the packing room. From here the crates go to the loading dock. But watch for a moment."

The two men stood at the end of one of the tables and watched the women wrap each bar in tissue, folding it neatly and quickly over each bar, then affixing a moistened seal on each. When they had ten or twelve wrapped, they stacked them neatly in a wooden crate at their feet, each layer cushioned with excelsior. Then they repeated the procedure.

Charging Elk had never seen such quick, practiced movements. Each of the many folds over the bar was perfect, so that all the edges came together under the seal. He had seen the bars of soap in pharmacies but had not thought of all the effort that went into each from the cutting and shaping to the wrapping. He now realized that he could have been shoveling coal in any factory in Marseille for all he knew about the process of making the smooth bars in their pretty wrappers.

Billedoux introduced him to Madame Braque, who was in charge of the wrapping room. She was a stout woman in her mid-forties with dyed red hair pinned up over her ears and a round pleasant face. In her white smock and white shoes, she reminded

Charging Elk of the nurses' helpers who had fed him soup in the sickhouse a lifetime ago.

"You must do as madame says. For now, she is your boss."

And so Charging Elk began his new job. He kept the women supplied with bars of soap from the moving table. He hammered the lids on each crate as they were filled and hauled them out to the loading dock, where a man put a big label on each and told him where to stack them. Sometimes he read the labels, but they meant nothing to him except for one batch: NEW YORK, ÉTAT DE NEW YORK L'ÉTATS-UNIS D'AMÉRIQUE. Charging Elk said to the man, "*Amérique*. I am from *Amérique*. Dakota."

The man glanced up at him, said something under his breath, then walked away. But Charging Elk didn't mind. He liked his new job. He was always moving, always carting, carrying, lifting, but when he left the factory at the end of the day, he was not covered with soot and coal dust, he was not drenched in greasy sweat, his hands were relatively clean. He was tired but not bone-weary. And he liked to be in the room where the women worked. They paid little attention to him after the first day, but they were good to look at and be around.

Charging Elk sipped the milky anisette and wondered about his life now. He couldn't recall how many times he had assessed his life in the past four years. But it seemed as though his life was changing so much so rapidly. Without knowing quite how, apart from Mathias and Chloé's early teaching, he had learned enough of the French tongue so that he could take instructions from Madame Braque as readily as anyone in the room. But to have a woman for a boss and to work in a room with women! It was too much to comprehend. He had never been around women like this. When he started his new job, he had felt vaguely ashamed of himself.

Although his job was different from theirs, he was afraid the other men in the factory, especially those who worked along the moving table, would think of his work as women's work. He had never worked with women, and he had never had a woman boss. All of his bosses—from the Wild West show, to René, to the boss of the furnace room—had been men. All of his fellow performers or workers had been men. And yet, for the first time in his four years in Marseille, he looked forward each morning to going to work.

Charging Elk watched the little white dog eating a scrap of something from the pavement. The woman, who had been arranging the bouquet, was now pulling the shutters down on her kiosk. He looked up at the awning again. MARIAGES. Somehow, this evening the idea didn't seem so farfetched to him.

Marie was speechless when the pale, handsome man sat down beside her. Of course, she had seen him before. Such a man stands out in any crowd. But he always went through the parlor to the lounge in back, to the boys. Through the kitchen gossip, she even knew which boy he liked—the young Spaniard named—Miguel? The boys didn't live in, so Marie never got to know them, but Miguel stood out for his dark beauty. If Marie had seen him on the street, she might have taken him for an artist or perhaps a musician. He had such a sensitivity. One of the girls said he was the son of a diplomat; another said his father was a nobleman; but Aimée said he was an illegal and if he was ever caught in the house, the whole business would be shut down by the gendarmes and they'd all be standing on street corners.

Marie did not look at the pale man's face, but she could smell his cologne, which seemed very complex, like perfume. It made her light-headed; at the same time, it was almost suffocating. She stared at the man's smooth but strong fingers, which were twined over one knee. The nails glistened in the light from the chandelier, as though they were lacquered.

The man sat for a moment, taking in the noise and activity of the room. Marie herself tore her eyes away from his fingers and looked off toward the group surrounding the piano player. He was playing a Provençal troubador song about the fighting bulls of the Camargue. It was an old song, one her father had sung to her and her brothers and sisters many times; and now, the three or four men around the piano were singing the familiar lyrics with the same bravado.

It was eleven o'clock on a Thursday night and not particularly busy. Marie had been upstairs with only two men so far, and until the pale man sat down beside her, she had begun to think that she could have an early evening. She didn't know if she should feel relieved or worried. She glanced down to the other end of the bar and she saw Olivier standing in his usual spot. He was looking at her, his face blank. Just the fact that he was looking at her surprised her. That his face was stripped of its normal ingratiating smile surprised her even more. And worried her. Had he noticed that she had had only two customers the whole evening?

In a sudden attack of desperation, she turned toward the pale gentleman and said, *"Bonsoir, monsieur."*

He took a pull on a long, thin cigar he had just lit and puffed the smoke up into the smoggy air. He seemed to be enjoying a leisure moment, and Marie instantly regretted her intrusion. But out of the corner of her eye she saw Olivier still watching her. What was she to do?

Just then, he turned and fixed her with a smile that made her skin suddenly turn cold. The pale blue eyes were set wide apart, almost too wide apart for the round spectacles. It was as though the eyes and the spectacles didn't quite match. He had long, blond lashes and perfectly arched eyebrows. His nose was thin but the nostrils flared dramatically. On any other face, this nose would have been an imperfection; even the eyes would have seemed curious. But on this man, these features were sensual. And the smile, the slightly opened lips, the small square teeth, made Marie's heart jump a little more than she would have liked. She had never looked into such a face.

"Hello, Marie."

Marie heard her name escape those lips but it didn't register just then.

"I've been watching you the past couple of weeks. You interest me."

"Me?"

"You are from country. I can tell. From the Vaucluse?"

"Yes," she said, surprised not only by this knowledge but by the fact that he knew her name, which had just dawned on her. "Cavaillon."

"Ah. And does your father raise the famous melons?"

"Everything—melons, asparagus, cherries, some apples—but very small."

"Vineyards?"

"No, monsieur. It is just a patch of land."

"And how long have you been here—in Marseille?"

Marie still couldn't believe that this man was interested in her. He liked the boys. She suddenly became even more shy than normal. And just a little frightened. What did he want?

"Did you not hear my question?" He held his head higher and his spectacles glinted beneath the chandelier and she couldn't see the eyes.

"Three years, monsieur."

"And have you always been a whore?"

Marie had been transfixed by the flaring nostrils, the long upper lip that arched delicately over the small teeth. But his question, the cruelty of it, made her look down quickly at her lap. She saw how square her hands were, how blunt the fingers were, and she felt heavy and awkward in his presence. A small flame kindled inside her—no, she hadn't always been a whore. She had been to Fontaine-de-Vaucluse, she had seen the mysterious water bubble up from the cave, she had been to school for three years, she had played with her sisters, picked melons and cherries, flirted with a boy from the next farm, crushed poppy seeds between her teeth, and dreamed of love, of a husband and children when she grew up, of a simple, happy life. More than anything, even now, she tried to dream of that simple, happy life, but all she got was the familiar dark, deserted streets and nowhere to go.

"Well?"

"*Oui, monsieur*. But not always."

The man laughed—a beautiful high, mirthless laugh, like the chimes that sometimes rang in the wind outside her room at night, the source of which she could never identify.

She glanced up at the pale face but the eyes were looking at something beyond her. She instinctively turned her gaze and she saw Olivier standing apart from the bar now, his hands crossed tightly over his belly, a strange, stormy look in his eyes.

"Well, Marie, shall we go up now—to your room?"

She suddenly wanted to run away—yes, to her room—to lock the door, to crawl under the covers by herself, to sleep without dreams. She had no idea what this man could want with her, but she had seen, beneath the beauty, the eyes grow cold and the mouth hard. It was as though his sensuality had been frozen into a mask. And yet, the perfume which had now surrounded her and entered her whole body seemed to cause her to lose her senses and she felt a wave of dizziness when she stood.

"*Oui, monsieur,*" she said. But the voice seemed very far away, as though it were an echo of another voice in another room. "*Oui, monsieur*, if it would please you."

⟶

Marie sat on the edge of her bed, still in her plain white shift, her black stockings, her high shoes. She stared at the small glassine envelope between her fingers. The man was gone, had been gone for twenty minutes, had in fact only stayed for fifteen minutes. When she started to remove her shift, he had said, "Don't bother. I don't want to see your body. I have come only to talk to you."

Marie had been horrified at the man's proposition. She had shaken her head and said, "No, no, monsieur, I cannot do this. You ask too much." Even when he dropped a ten-francs note on the bed she had refused just as vociferously. And when he dropped another ten, she had swept them off the bed onto the floor. "Take your money. I will not do it." And she had looked up at him with a rare defiance.

That's when he stepped forward quickly and slapped her on the cheek. It was not a hard blow. It barely stung. She had been hit harder by men in the throes of frustrated lust, when they were angry at that part of them that remained limp and took it out on her. She lowered her head and shook it again, almost violently, her dark hair swirling like the skirt of a dervish.

He called her a bitch, a slut, a cunt, and still she shook her head wordlessly. He told her she was not worth fucking, that she was a fat cow not fit to be mounted by the meanest, most disease-ridden bull of her pathetic Vaucluse.

Then he cajoled her. He was sorry, he had been angry at other things in his life. She was very attractive and he knew why men desired her so. What a nice room. And look—what a pretty little lamp.

But Marie responded to neither insult nor compliment. The insults did hurt her — they confirmed how she felt about herself in her worst moments, when she thought no decent man would ever want her. But now a decent man had come into her life and this pale villain wanted her to help him harm François. To what end, she didn't know, but the thought that she could be an agent of such harm horrified her.

She lay across her bed and listened to the almost cheerful voice go on about her Rubenesque figure, her lush hair, and she wanted to cry but couldn't. She just felt drained, as though the man had performed the one act on her she loathed but had to accept.

Then there was a moment of silence. She knew he was looking down at her, thinking of his next move, but she turned her head to the wall and kept her eyes closed. She heard him sigh and thought, with some joyless hope, that he had given up.

"Very well then. I can see that you do not want to do this. I accept that." She heard his footsteps as he walked toward the door. Then he paused. "I'm afraid I'll have to tell Olivier that you didn't please me. He will be very offended." Another pause, as though to give her a chance to respond. Then the voice said, "You see, he is in love with me, but I find him as attractive as a fat toad. I'm sure you do too. Nevertheless, you will have to answer to him. Perhaps you will go back to your family in the Vaucluse."

Marie heard the doorknob turn, and she sat up quickly. "Wait a moment, monsieur," she said. "I beg you — wait a moment."

Now, Marie knelt before the bureau and opened the bottom drawer. She stared at the few things in it. She opened the velvet box and ran her finger over the cool stone of the cameo, tracing the bust of a beautiful lady. Who was she? Had there really been such a lady? Marie closed the box and hooked the tiny brass latch. Then she opened her Bible to a place marked by a ribbon. Her eyes fell on a familiar passage underlined in ink. Although she couldn't read, she could hear the priest's voice reciting it a long time ago: "Why then hast thou not kept the oath of the Lord, and the commandment that I have charged thee with?" The commandment that I have charged thee with. The Lord would not condone this commandment. She placed the glassine envelope in the crease, along with the two ten-franc notes, and closed the Bible.

Perhaps she would go to Abbaye St-Victor tomorrow and pray to the Black Virgin for forgiveness for this thing she was obligated to do. Marie had stopped going to church, except for the holy days, since she had become a whore. Part of it was that it was too difficult to get up on Sunday morning after a long, busy Saturday night. The other part was that she felt unworthy to enter a church, ashamed to confess her sins, and afraid that she might incur the wrath of God. She had grown up with stories about an unforgiving, vengeful God, who would inflict punishment on those who didn't glorify him. It was too horrific to think about. She only went on holy days because some of the other whores went. Perhaps they all thought there was safety in numbers. Marie didn't question them. Religion was a private matter in a whorehouse.

Marie closed the drawer and stood and looked at her face in the mirror. She rouged her cheeks and painted her lips. She didn't look into the eyes. She dreaded going back downstairs. But it was only for a couple more hours. And she still had a job and a place. As for Saturday night, she would do it and François would be out of her life forever. She was sure of that. But he hadn't really been a part of a life that she wanted, only the dream of it.

Charging Elk was puzzled by the coolness between him and Marie. Even as they sat on the divan, virtually thigh to thigh, she seemed very far away. When he told her about his new job, and the extra three francs a week it brought him, she had barely acknowledged his good fortune. When he told her he was thinking of moving into a nicer flat, a larger one, one that might be big enough for two (although he didn't know how such a move was accomplished), she had looked away and said, "That will be nice for you, François."

It was then he realized she had not really looked at him since he had crossed the floor to sit beside her. Now she sat quite still, looking off toward the piano player. Something else was occupying her thoughts. Or perhaps she had no thoughts at all.

"Is your family fine?" he said. They had never discussed her family, but he could think of nothing else to say just then. He had decided earlier to tell her his real name tonight when they were alone. He would tell her all about Buffalo Bill and his people and his country. He had told her one night that he was American—but nothing else. He would explain, if he could, how he came to be in Marseille. But would she understand? Or would she think he was only a savage who had been deceiving her with his gifts and good manners?

"I don't think of them much." Her voice was dull, almost a mumble, unlike the shy but clear language she had come to use around him.

"I think you should leave here," he said too abruptly. This was what he had come to say tonight but the words sounded wrong in the big room. For six sleeps, ever since he started his new job, he had been practicing a speech that would end with a request that she come with him to a new flat. They could be married and have children. She could cook him good meals. He could buy her a nice dress and a hat. They could walk along the Corniche on Sundays and watch the fishing boats. He had imagined that her eyes would light up over these plans, that she would be happy to leave this place and the many men she had to fuck. He had imagined that she would be happy to be with only him for the rest of her life. But the words seemed too thin and inconsequential in the strangely festive atmosphere of the whorehouse.

Her lips thinned into a pained smile as she snorted a pale imitation of mirth. "And where would I go? Home? To pick cherries? To cart melons to the market?"

The bitterness in her voice startled Charging Elk, but he said, "You come with me. I have a good job. I have plenty of friends."

Marie almost looked at him then. Way down deep within her, she had expected that such a moment might happen. She had thought about it, in an offhand—almost dreamlike—manner when she sat in the kitchen with the other girls and had her *café crème*. She had listened to the other girls and thought how lucky she must be to have at least one good man in her life. And she had thought that such a moment as this just might occur. But now it was too late. Or was it?

Why couldn't she say yes, right now, and leave this unnatural life behind forever? She would probably never have this opportunity again. She didn't know if she loved François, but does one really need love? And couldn't she learn to love him over time? That happened. It had happened to her grandmother. One day when she was fifteen, as they were shelling peas in the kitchen, her grandmother had told her that love is better if it comes gradually. Marie had fallen for the boy at the next farm and wanted to be with him in a most desperate way. But her *grand-maman* told her to be patient, that she had married Marie's grandfather late and had to learn to love him. It took a few years but she had put her trust in God and it had worked out for the best. They had had seven children and were still in love. If she had married the first boy she fell in love with it would have been a disaster. The man was now a big wine producer but he was rumored to be a drunkard and a womanizer. So, you see?

Marie was beginning to think that such a thing was possible. She could learn to love François and together they could have seven children and live a gentle life, perhaps in the country, perhaps her

own. She could go back with him and they could live and work
with her family.

But then the air went out of her imaginings. Expecting her family, the people of the Vaucluse, to accept this dark giant was too
much. He would be a freak and she would be married to a freak.
And what if they stayed in Marseille? He now had a good job. He
was going to acquire a big flat. He was gentle and considerate, unlike her other customers. In his own way, he was striking if not
handsome. And he made her feel something that she never thought
possible when they fucked. She felt that they were actually making
love even if they were not real lovers.

But he was not French. He was not from Provence. He came
from America. What if, after they were married, he just decided to
disappear? He could do that. Or what if he decided to start drinking and to beat her? Perhaps these Americans were not as sane as
the French. But the thought that worried Marie the most was that
he could one day just disappear. Back to America. And where
would she be? Out of a job and a place. She could not come back
here. And perhaps by then she would be too old or too fat to be a
whore.

No, she could not take the chance. She would not. For all its un-
pleasantness—for the monotony of sitting down here, then taking
men upstairs, of drinking coffee with the girls when decent women
were shopping or taking their children for a stroll—this was her
life, a life she could count on for some time to come.

Marie almost moaned with disgust for herself as she turned to
the tall dark man, who was smiling expectantly. "Would you like to
go to my room, François?"

Charging Elk was surprised but pleased to see a bottle of wine and
two glasses on the top of the bureau. Had she known that he was

going to ask her to come live with him? Perhaps she had acted so distant downstairs because the other men—men who had probably gone upstairs with her—were watching them. He was used to being looked at, up and down, but Marie was not, at least not as a curiosity. She was always reserved when they sat downstairs. But in her room she came alive and for a few long moments they were as close as a man and woman can be. He still marveled at the act and in fact was becoming erect. But was this to be a celebration of something so fantastical that he could scarcely breathe at the thought of what might happen?

Charging Elk hung his jacket on the hall tree and loosened his tie and slipped it over his head. Then on a whim, he undid the blue ribbon that tied his hair up and felt the long, dark hair cascade down over his shoulders. He had his shirt unbuttoned when Marie called to him.

"Come, have a glass of wine with me, François." She held out a glass half full of the deep red wine. He noticed that the liquid trembled with little waves. But perhaps she was nervous.

He bowed slightly and said, "Beautiful wine for a beautiful woman." Then he drank and watched her take a sip. "Perfect for such a joyous moment," he said, pleased with his nice words.

Marie sat on the edge of the bed and looked up at him. She didn't know how long the drug took, so she patted the bed beside her. She felt his weight settle, drawing her a little nearer to him. She felt his arm behind her, then his fingers along her waist. By now she was trembling all over.

"Can you be cold? It is so warm in your room."

"No, no, it is nothing—only a thought."

Charging Elk took a sip of wine and it warmed him inside and out. He wanted her to say something that would tell him that he hadn't been mistaken about the celebration. But when she sat and said nothing, he finally said, "You will come with me?"

She looked at him, and he thought it was a strange look, as though she were searching in his eyes for something. He thought perhaps she was deciding, and his heart was high with anticipation. He could feel it beating against his chest and he could hear it in his ears. He felt warm and suddenly very lazy. She was still looking into his eyes but her own eyes were dark and watery. He heard his own voice but he couldn't make out the words. And then he felt himself lying back across the bed and he looked up and saw Marie very close, standing over him, and then she leaned closer still so that her face was a golden blur above his eyes and he felt her mouth on his. She had never kissed him on the lips before, and he thought how strange and pleasant it was. He closed his eyes and enjoyed the lavender scent of her hair, the light brush of her hand on his face . . .

Charging Elk looked up and saw a dark, ever-changing cloud. He had seen clouds like this on very cold days near the end of the Moon When the White Calves Grow Hair—large, dark clouds with silver-tinted edges. Sometimes the sun came between them and lit the earth with a fire that crossed one's head and shoulders and suddenly it grew warm and pleasant and he and Strikes Plenty lifted their faces to it. Charging Elk could see the plains between Pine Ridge and the badlands dappled with such sunstreaks, lighting the dark earth beneath the clouds with ragged patches of fire that almost hurt the eye. High Runner lifted his head and whickered, as though he too knew that Wakan Tanka was teasing the boys, that winter was not far off.

Charging Elk watched the cloud move and change shapes, and the realization came to him that it was a lone cloud, drifting all by itself against a gray sky. And then he noticed that there were jagged rents in the sky, as though it were filled with lightning all at once, crisscrossing the gray sky. And then the cloud ceased to drift and became something else. He studied the cloud and the lightning and then he realized he was in a room.

His head was tight against a hard wall. The cloud became a water stain and the lightning cracks in the plastered ceiling. His first thought was that he was back in the iron house. But it was too warm. Then he thought it was the sickhouse. He strained to move his head to see if the room was full of beds, of sleeping men. He tried to lift his head, his shoulders; he tried to get up on his elbows to look around; but his body would not obey him. It didn't hurt as it had in the sickhouse; in fact, it felt pleasant, as though the warmth came from him, a warmth that spread from his center to his whole body.

He quit trying to raise himself for a moment and enjoyed the tingling pleasure in his loins. And he recognized a plain wooden cross on the wall to his left. He was in Marie's room. He lay back and closed his eyes, relieved and full of joy, as he felt the pleasure that he now recognized as sex. Marie was doing something to him but he couldn't quite figure out what, only that it was causing his hips to move and his breathing to sharpen into quick gasps. He tried to raise himself again and this time he managed to get his elbows to support him.

And he saw hair. And ears. The tip of a nose. A head. And the head was moving between his naked thighs. It took him a time to recognize that the mouth was sliding up and down on the smooth shaft of his cock, and the sight filled him with excitement. Marie had not done this to him before. He remembered the vague blur of her face as her mouth kissed his. And he remembered the celebration, the wine. It was all too new, these things she was doing.

As he watched the bobbing head, moving faster now, it began to dawn on him that the hair was not Marie's. It was light and wavy, shorter than hers. The sharp scent that filled the room was not lavender.

Charging Elk's arms and shoulders grew weak, and he fell back on the bed and closed his eyes. His head was fuzzy and empty of thought and he felt both lazy and excited. Then he drifted off. And when he came back he felt the warm mouth on his cock and both mouth and cock seemed remote, as though he had left his body and was watching the act from a long way off. He saw the sandy hair, the ears, from his far-off corner; he saw the lips and the tip of the nose. Then he froze. And he was back inside his body.

His hand brushed against something and he turned his head. It was his pants bunched up on the bed beside him. His head was clearer now and he saw his hand move over the pants until it found a pocket. But there was nothing there, save for a few coins. He moved his hand again under the pants until he found the other pocket. Then he felt the long, slender knife and he held it before him. It was a beautiful knife, the handle silver at both ends with a strip of ebony between. He saw the small silver button and he pressed it and saw a blade as long as his forefinger magically appear with a small click.

As his eyes focused themselves on the gleaming blade, he knew what he must do. It was not so much a decision as a resolve. And he suddenly felt strong, as though he had awakened from a waking dream. He sat up slowly, deliberately, so as not to disturb the bobbing head. He looked at the slender back, the knobs of the spine and the indentations around the ribs. He saw the slope of the thin buttocks and the narrow cleft between them.

And he saw the knife, poised in the air for just a second in the dim room, suddenly strike the naked back, and he heard a harsh grunt and felt his fist thud against flesh almost simultaneously. He struck again and then again, each time burying the knife in the pale back. Then he grabbed a handful of the sandy hair and pulled the head back. He looked into the wide blue eyes as he set the blade against the side of the throat, and they looked familiar. He saw the pink froth bubbling from the delicate lips, which were moving but making no sound. And then he drew the blade across the throat, leaning into his work when it reached the windpipe. But the knife was sharp and he heard a sharp sucking sound and then he let go of the hair and the head fell forward, heavily, into his lap.

The whole incident had taken only a few seconds, but Charging Elk had seen the several movements clearly as though time had stood still. He sat for a moment, now exhausted from his labors, still not believing what had just happened even as his mind relived it over and over again.

Then he panicked. He had to get out of there. For an instant he wanted to be sick, but he had no time. He squirmed from beneath the head and saw that his thighs were covered with the pink bubbles and the dark blood. He almost tripped over the still-kneeling body in the cramped space as he edged his way to the washstand, where he poured water into the basin. He soaked a towel in the water, then began to scrub the blood from his thighs and groin. He looked around the room, trying to spot each piece of his clothing so that he could dress quickly. And he saw on the nightstand behind him something that made him stop scrubbing, made him stop breathing for an instant.

A pair of gold-rimmed spectacles, neatly folded, gleamed in the dim light which leaked from beneath the red-beaded lampshade.

Fortunately the large parlor was nearly deserted. Two men and one of the girls were huddled around a table against the far wall. Olivier and the bartender were conversing over the opened cash register, their backs to the room, and the surly doorman was not in sight. The door was a good fifteen to twenty meters away, and his mind flashed back to his escape through the great room of the sickhouse with its soft chairs and sofas four years ago, but this time Charging Elk walked deliberately, on the balls of his feet to keep his heels from striking the tile floor, the length of the room. He sang a song he had not sung for some time under his breath and he knew that he had become invisible. He walked quietly and confidently, and when he reached the door he held the the little bell ringer so that it remained silent when the door swung open.

Once outside he hurried along the now empty, dark street, not caring that his heels echoed over the cobblestones. He tried not to think but to make his escape as quickly as he could. And when he turned the corner in the direction of the Old Port, he allowed himself a long, almost gasping sigh, and he realized that he had been holding his breath since—he didn't know when. He had just stopped breathing some time ago.

He opened his pocket watch and glanced down at the white face: four-thirty. He and Marie had gone upstairs a little after eleven o'clock. What had happened to the time? Five and a half hours had passed since then. He felt his legs grow weak, and he stopped and leaned against a hitching post. In spite of the cool early-morning air, he felt icy needles of sweat trickle down his rib cage.

Marie. What had happened to Marie? What would happen to Marie? Charging Elk groaned with dismay. He should have moved the *siyoko*'s body. Why hadn't he thought of that? Surely there would have been another room empty. Charging Elk felt his legs give way as he envisioned Marie opening the door and seeing the dead *siyoko* kneeling over her bed, the black stains glistening on the sheet, on the floor, the keen smell of blood in the close room. He didn't even feel the hard cobblestones when his knees struck them.

He had to go back. But he fell onto his side and lay there, too weak to even focus his eyes on the shadows. What had happened to him? Why was he here? Where was his animal helper? Wakan Tanka? Why had he been left in this foreign town? Why him?

Charging Elk closed his eyes and felt almost a comfort in his despair. The cobblestones were solid and cool beneath him and he didn't want to move, perhaps ever again. He knew that he would die soon, that what had happened in Marie's room would start a chain of events that would lead to his end. Wicked men were always punished. Wakan Tanka saw to that. And Charging Elk welcomed it.

But now his head was swimming with images past and present. He saw Marie raise her glass of wine, he saw the gold-rimmed spectacles in the lamplight, and he saw his dream as though he were dreaming it again. He saw his people lying at the foot of the cliff and he heard the roaring wind and the voice that entered his ears: *You are my only son.* Now there will be no one left, he thought, and the idea did not frighten him. He would rather be dead with his people than alone in the world.

His lips were moving as he lay on the cobblestones and he realized that he was praying—in Lakota—to Wakan Tanka. He was laying down his life, and he begged the Great Spirit to now let him join his people in the real world. Perhaps it was the sound of his own language—he had neither prayed nor spoken in Lakota for some time—that gave him comfort. After these four years of not being able to really communicate, he felt almost intimate with the sound of his voice and the prayer it offered up. He felt renewed even as he waited to die.

But he had been hearing something far off without knowing it. Now his head was coming back and he heard a man shout and another one answer. He couldn't hear the words but the voices echoed through the narrow streets and he couldn't tell how near or far they were. He opened his eyes and waited.

CHAPTER FOURTEEN

Martin St-Cyr *felt a pang in his stomach that almost took his* breath away. He cursed himself for ordering oysters this time of year. Although it was only May, it was sweltering in Marseille and the oysters could go bad early. It only took one. And leave it to him to find the one without the pearl.

He took a sip of the *digestif* and read the article once again. It was only three column inches, but it was the most amazing thing. How could it happen again? At first when he read the article he thought it was a prime case of *déjà vu*. It happened to him all the time. Just last night, he had been with a woman who told him her secret desire was to help the North Africans find our savior, Jesus Christ. The daughter of English missionaries, she had grown up in the Sudan and now wanted to go to Algeria to work in a French mission or perhaps a hospital. Because he hadn't really thought of his former fiancée in well over three years, it took a second or two for the young woman's story to trigger the memory of Odile. But in those few seconds, his senses were overwhelmed with an unnamed familiarity.

Now it was happening again. Even before he saw the name, Charging Elk, he had the feeling that he had read this article before, perhaps even had something to do with it.

But this time Charging Elk had killed a man. This time he was in jail for a reason, not just because the Marseille authorities didn't know what to do with him. This time there was probably not much that could be done for him.

Still, St-Cyr was curious. And he felt slightly beholden to the Indian. His two stories on the injustice of Charging Elk's incarceration had landed him a job on *La Gazette du Midi*, first as a reporter, then as a columnist. It was a good fit. The *Gazette* was known for its socialist leaning, and St-Cyr could fight the good fight without the dangers he had experienced in Grenoble. After his tenure with the conservative *Le Petit Marseillais*, the *Gazette* was a breath of freedom for him. His two columns a week usually involved the exploitation of the workingman, the dockworkers, the draymen, the harassment of immigrants (although he didn't particularly like them), of the small tradespeople who were taxed beyond reason by the all-devouring state. He loved his job and he had become something of a celebrity, even a hero to the *prolétariat* and the *petite bourgeoisie*. Of course, he never sent any of his columns to his father, who, at the age of eighty, still mourned his betrayal by the silk workers in Lyon.

St-Cyr sat up straight in his chair and grimaced as another pang swept through his body. But they were coming less frequently now and he was in the process of concluding that it was only his dyspepsia, painful as it was, which seemed to go hand in hand with his outraged, muckraking sensibility. When the burning subsided, he picked up the telephone and hit the cradle a couple of times. Then he sat back.

"Hello! Get me the desk sergeant at the Préfecture, if you would."

St-Cyr listened to the grainy static on the telephone and wondered at this new invention, less at its novelty than at its efficacy. More often than not, especially during the day when it was most needed, the static made it almost impossible to communicate. But this time, he got lucky.

"Hello! Sergeant Vautrin here." The voice was clear and tinny, as though it spoke from the opposite end of a metal tube.

"Hello, sergeant. This is Martin St-Cyr of *La Gazette du Midi*. I understand you are holding a Peau-Rouge by the name of Charging Elk. Is it true?"

"Yes." Nothing more.

"It says here in my newspaper that he killed a man in Rue Sainte."

St-Cyr scribbled "Vautrin" in his notebook while he waited for the sergeant to confirm his statement. He was used to this waiting game from his two years as a police reporter. But then he had walked the beat of the precincts and gotten to know the desk sergeants. Now, on the telephone, he felt anonymous, even though he was fairly certain that the sergeant had heard of him, perhaps had read his columns. He took a sip of *digestif* and wished Borely were still on the job. They would be talking like the friendly adversaries they once were. Now Borely was the head of a special unit that scoured the waterfront for contraband. It was difficult to think of Borely as a real policeman, perhaps even in some danger from the gangs who worked the docks, but there it was.

"It says that the deceased was a prominent businessman."

The sergeant must have decided that he could answer this innocuous question. "That is true."

"And what was a prominent businessman doing in Rue Sainte at four-thirty in the morning?" But St-Cyr knew. There were four or five whorehouses down there, including the one he used to go to

until Fortune gave him a dose of the clap. He had taken sulfur pow-
ders for two weeks to relieve the terrible burning. The disease and
treatment had also cured him of the need to seek out the whores, at
least those in Rue Sainte. On the other hand, he missed his dark,
pillowy Fortune.

Again the silence. It was as though the man hadn't learned yet
that one could actually have a conversation on the telephone. "Is he
being held in the Préfecture? — Charging Elk, I mean. Surely you
can tell me that much."

This time the voice answered quickly. "You might want to try the
American Consulate, Monsieur St-Cyr. Their man was here all
morning."

St-Cyr hung up the receiver and looked at the face he had just
drawn. It was crude but it had some features that he remembered —
the prominent cheekbones, the narrow eyes, the even narrower
mouth, and the long black hair that hung past the shoulders from a
part in the middle of the head. What he couldn't depict was the aura
of death, the ashy smell that filled the small cell in the bowels of the
Préfecture. Even now he shuddered to think of it.

But Charging Elk had survived; moreover, he had apparently
lived in Marseille for the past four years. How was this possible?
Why hadn't he gone home to America? Or back to the Wild West
show, which had been somewhere on the continent when he was released that winter? Somehow there had been a dire mistake by
somebody. He was still here in Marseille. And now he had killed a
"prominent businessman" who frequented the whores in Rue Sainte.
St-Cyr almost licked his chops as he picked up the receiver again.

The several restaurants on Cours Estienne-d'Orves were filled
with the usual variety of people — shopgirls, butchers, officer
workers, financiers from the Bourse, military and navy people,

deckhands and dockworkers, mothers with children, husbands with mistresses, old ladies with tiny dogs, boulevardiers—and Franklin Bell. If he wasn't at some three-hour luncheon or another, he usually preferred the quiet of his own apartment and the simple salads or fish prepared by his housekeeper.

But today he sat in the shade of an umbrella at an outdoor table of Chez Louis, surrounded by happy, intense, loud eaters, sipping a mineral water and waiting for the notorious Martin St-Cyr. Even in such a gay atmosphere he felt a little soiled and obvious.

He glanced up at the sky and thought he would miss this Mediterranean climate. Even the heat wave of the past two weeks and the stench emanating from the Old Port had done nothing to diminish his almost sexual enjoyment of the city. But today was a perfect May day—warm but not hot, at least not yet, a hazy blue sky, and people enjoying a break from whatever labors guided them through the week.

He looked out to the open space of the *cours* and watched two young women in long slender dresses and straw hats with black velvet ribbons trailing over the back brim walking arm in arm, laughing as though they hadn't a care in the world. Normally he would have appraised them as possible partners, but today he just envied them their youth and innocence. They were completely at home in their world, unlike him, the perpetual outsider.

Just then he saw a slender man in his late twenties, dressed in a white suit, a starched blue shirt with a red cravat, and a straw boater with a candy-striped band around the crown, step around the girls and make his way through the tables of Chez Louis. Although he had never met St-Cyr, he recognized the delicate face, with its pencil mustache and neatly trimmed goatee, from the illustrated portrait at the head of his column in *La Gazette du Midi*. Bell stood up, astonished at how much younger the dandy St-Cyr looked in real life.

"Monsieur St-Cyr? Franklin Bell."

"*Enchanté*, Monsieur Bell. So good of you to agree to meet with me. And on such a lovely day."

Bell wasn't surprised that the hand was soft, but the way it was offered, arched with the palm down, like a lady's, took him aback. For an instant, he wondered if he should kiss it. Instead, he withdrew his own hand and indicated a chair opposite his. "Please sit," he said.

When the drinks came—another mineral water for Bell, a glass of Chardonnay for St-Cyr—the young columnist raised his glass and said, "To your health, Mr. Bell."

"You speak English then."

"Only a very little. I studied it at university but I'm afraid I have little use of it here in Marseille." He laughed. "My father said that I had better learn it, as the Americans were getting ready to take over the world."

Bell noticed that St-Cyr spoke with a decided British clip, which didn't surprise him. Many Brits taught English in the universities of France. Must be a blow to the national pride to have to learn English, Bell thought of saying but didn't. He didn't feel very chauvinistic today. He had been up since five-thirty dealing with the latest mess involving Charging Elk, and his nerves were very close to the skin. In fact, he was downright scared that he was about to lose his job. There was no doubt now in anybody's mind at the consulate that Charging Elk had been his responsibility four years ago and he had muffed it badly. It had been so easy then to lose the big Indian, to let him disappear into Marseille, to forget about him. But Bell had never really forgotten him, had thought about him almost daily, if only briefly. But what really fascinated Bell in a perverse way was the dreams he had had of Charging Elk. Whether because of a guilty conscience or fear of discovery of his blunder, he had dreamed several times that Charging Elk showed up at his door in the early morning, covered with blood, unable to speak, a toma-hawk clutched in a dangling hand, dripping blood on the Persian carpet in the hallway. Each time Bell would slam the door shut and scream as the blood seeped slowly beneath the door into the room. Then he would awaken and find himself sitting upright, pajamas soaked with sweat on the coldest night, not knowing if he had actually screamed but listening for a commotion outside his door.

Always the next day Bell would sit at his desk, ignoring the paperwork, and analyze the dream, looking for a reason for the nighttime visitations. But he knew the answer deep down: He had failed the Indian. He had neither gotten him home safely nor reunited him with the Wild West show. He had simply willed the Indian out of his life, and with the help of the Soulas family, it had happened. For four years now. But he knew that Charging Elk would come back to haunt him someday, in some way that bore resemblance to the dream. The dream was too strong and persistent.

So why was he taking lunch with the celebrated columnist of *La Gazette du Midi* on such a momentous day? Bell didn't even like what the man wrote about the institutions of commerce, of government. That socialist garbage only went so far. What would these supposed downtrodden citizens do without their leaders, the men who ran the country, the men who supplied the goods and services, the men who greased the wheels of industry, who gave them their jobs? It was absurd to blame them for every little injustice that occurred in the normal business of business. So what was he doing here with this foppish antithesis of everything he stood for?

He was having his last absurdly normal meal before he had to go back to the consulate and face the controlled (he hoped) rage of Atkinson, who would probably blame him for harming years of delicate negotiations between the two countries with this one act of immense stupidity and incompetence. Unfortunately, Bell would only be able to agree with the old man. The French were notoriously difficult to deal with. They seemed to look for incidents like this one to turn a cold shoulder in other matters. If he was fortunate he would have time to write a letter of resignation after lunch. It would be a token gesture, a small way of saving face. He knew he would never work for the foreign service again. And to think that he had thought he was just a few steps away from replacing Atkinson as consul general. Of course, he had thought that for four years now.

"I see that you are smiling, Mr. Bell. Perhaps you will share your amusement."

Bell was almost amused, in a dark way, to think that he had been smiling through the horror of it all. "Actually, nothing is amusing, Monsieur St-Cyr. I have spent all morning at the Préfecture, trying to appease your people—notably Chef de Police Vaugirard—to no avail. I have had nothing to say in defense of our Indian friend. I have been browbeaten, horsewhipped, keelhauled, and I have been able to say nothing. I'm afraid his ship is sunk." And mine too, he almost added.

"It is a grave matter, my friend, very grave indeed. But why would the vice-consul engage himself in such a matter? Surely, you have a legal attaché to handle such an unfortunate incident. Or perhaps you have a personal interest. . . ."

Bell listened to the voice trail away, and he wondered how much the columnist knew. He had read the articles in *Le Petit Marseillais* when Charging Elk had been kept in the jail of the Préfecture the first time. And he had grudgingly admitted that St-Cyr had done more with those two pieces of overheated journalism than he himself ever could, even with the weight of the United States government behind him. The weight had been surprisingly light and completely ignored by the Marseille authorities. St-Cyr had probably saved Charging Elk's life. The power of the press, thought Bell, in this case more powerful than two of the most powerful governments in the world.

The waiter came with a basket of bread, and both men ordered *salades niçoises*. St-Cyr insisted that they also order a bottle of wine, and Bell, tired physically and emotionally, put up no resistance.

When the waiter had gone, Bell said, "I'm sure there's a reason you asked me to lunch with you. And I'm quite sure I know the reason. We might as well have at it."

St-Cyr laughed, a surprisingly deep laugh for such a thin body, and said, "Ah, I am afraid you are too quick for me, Mr. Bell. It is supposed to be my job to initiate this interview." Then he leaned forward, his sudden burst of mirth behind him. "It is about the Indian, of course. I have not been able to acquire any information from our police about the case. I talked to the reporter who initially wrote the news article, but he knows nothing more." St-Cyr paused for just a moment, toying with a piece of the dry bread, as though he were hesitant to ask the big question. "I was hoping—could you give me an account of what happened in Rue Sainte?"

This time it was Bell's turn to hesitate. He glanced up at the buildings on the other side of the *cours*. Rue Sainte was just behind them. They were sitting, having lunch, less than two blocks away from where it happened. Tired as he was, Bell tried to estimate the pros and cons of speaking frankly with a journalist. Of course, he knew the whole incredibly sordid story, at least the story as told to him by the scolding Chef de Police Vaugirard. But how much could he divulge to a man who would undoubtedly twist it into something that would reflect badly on the American Consulate and probably Bell himself? Should he tell him anything at all? Wouldn't it be better, if rude, to just get up and walk away?

Bell tried to think of something positive that might come from such a revelation. He sat silently as the waiter poured the wine, then automatically lifted his glass to St-Cyr and drank. The wine was cool and tart to the tongue, just the way he liked it, and he was a little relieved that he could enjoy something so simple. He glanced across the table at St-Cyr, who had taken a notebook and pencil from his pocket and was poised with a slight smile. Bell suddenly felt too big, too shabby and unwashed, in the presence of the elegant journalist. But he had made up his mind.

The only positive thing Bell could think of was that *he* would tell the story. And he would tell it from the very beginning, from his first meeting with Charging Elk in the hospital, then again at the Préfecture. It was important that the journalist have all the facts so that he might understand why Charging Elk had done what he had. What he did with the facts—well, who knew? At least, Bell could walk away with a somewhat cleaner conscience. It wouldn't ease his burden any—he was a goner—but it might help Charging Elk in a way his muddy mind couldn't foresee just then. He simply knew that St-Cyr had a reputation for a sympathetic ear and voice for the downtrodden working classes and the misfits of society. Ironically, that's just what Bell wanted at the moment.

And so he told the journalist everything he knew about Charging Elk's history in Marseille. He told of the family (without mentioning the name) who had taken care of the Indian. He told of the crucial mistake the doctor had made in pronouncing Charging Elk dead instead of Featherman. Then the fake death certificate to justify his decision. Bell's own futile attempts to get Charging Elk documents so that he could rejoin the Wild West show. His frustration at every turn in dealing with the French authorities. And surprisingly—Bell hadn't meant to reveal this—his ultimate helplessness and subsequent surrender to the system. He had simply given up and purposely lost track of Charging Elk until today.

Bell took a sip of wine and watched the pencil scribbling furiously down the sheets, one after another, each one snapping back as the pencil missed not a beat. Bell noticed the salads, the lettuce wilted and the olive oil and vinegar separated, lying in glistening amber globs around the tuna. He looked around and noticed that the lunch crowd had pretty much dispersed. Only one other table at Chez Louis was occupied — by a young couple who were drinking *citrons pressés* between long soulful kisses. Right now he was too drained to envy them.

Finally St-Cyr put the pencil down, rubbed his eyes, and leaned his head back to ease the stiffness in his neck. Bell studied the slender neck, the slight protrusion of the Adam's apple, and the dark goatee, which was so thin he could see the chin clearly outlined, and he realized that he had not had time to shave. St-Cyr slowly leaned forward, murmuring, "Well, well, such a story, my friend."

"You can understand why I hesitated to tell you my role in this sorry mess. If I had been more dogged, perhaps Charging Elk would be back in America with his people — instead of . . ." Bell shrugged.

"Of course! But you mustn't blame yourself. The French are famous for their bureaucracy. Everything must be rubber-stamped three times, then three times more. Sometimes things get 'lost.' Always there is a petty bureaucrat in the way who does not get enough loving at home and takes it out on the people." St-Cyr caught himself and laughed. "Of course, that is not your case. You are the United States, but sometimes that is enough to make the bureaucrats even more recalcitrant. They feel threatened with a loss of power and so they do the one thing they do well — they obstruct until the aggrieved party, even the United States of America, finally gives up. It is natural, Mr. Bell, to give up at a certain point in this interminable process. But you are blameless. What else could you do?"

Although Bell was suspicious of the journalist's sympathetic response to his part in the Charging Elk affair — after all, he was a bureaucrat too — he felt a great deal lighter in spirit than he had just an hour ago. He knew that this interview was political suicide, but the unburdening of his story, of his very soul, after four years of carrying his load of guilt and bad dreams made up for his fear that St-Cyr would turn this story on its head.

St-Cyr was sharpening his pencil with a small silver penknife, carefully shaving the lead to a perfect point. Without looking up, he said, "But the story is only half finished, of course."

"Ah yes, the juicy part."

"Juicy?"

"Sorry. The sensational part."

"Voilà!" It is distasteful, I know, but you see the importance of my having all the details of this dreadful incident. If I am to help our friend."

"Of course." But again Bell hesitated, taking a sip of the Chardonnay, which was warm by now. He wanted an American coffee. But he wanted this interview to be over even more. He would go back to the consulate and face the music. Atkinson would relieve him of his duties and probably set up a debriefing session in the morning, at which time he would give up his documents and explain the status of his current projects. Then he would be free to pack his steamer trunk, his suitcases, and when he stepped on the ship bound for Philadelphia, he would be a private citizen. A fitting end to what had become an increasingly ineffectual career.

So Bell, because he could think of no reason not to, told St-Cyr the story of the murder as he had heard it from Chief Vaugirard. But unlike the chief's stern, animated manner, Bell's was flat and monotonous. He had never been a good storyteller—he always thought of the perfect phrase, the devastating punch line, the next day while shaving or eating dinner—but this time he did not care that he was boring. Nonetheless, St-Cyr muttered to himself as he wrote, sometimes exclaimed in disbelief and wrote faster. Only once did the pen stop moving.

"Breteuil? You mean Armand Breteuil? The chef?"

"Yes. He owns a restaurant called La Petite Nani over on Rue de la Croix."

"But I have eaten there. He is considered the best chef in all of Provence."

"So I've heard."

"Oh! This is dreadful, Mr. Bell."

Bell looked at the foppish journalist in astonishment. Was the death dreadful—the multiple knife wounds, the cut throat, the sea of blood—or the fact that St-Cyr couldn't eat Breteuil's fine food at La Petite Nani again?

"Of course, the whole incident is very tragic."

"Isn't it?" Bell said in a dry voice, but he finished the story as rapidly as he could manage. He was very tired, even a little sleepy from the wine, but he left out no detail. And when he had finished, he sat back in his chair and listened to the furious pencil while watching two sweepers, leaning on their long crescent-shaped brooms, smoke in the shade of a chestnut tree. He wondered, with just a little envy, what it would be like to be a simple street sweeper in a complex world.

"You said you had the chance to speak with the Peau-Rouge— Charging Elk. How did he seem?"

"They only gave me twenty minutes. Surprisingly calm. As though he didn't grasp the magnitude of his situation."

"And you said you thought he wanted to be caught."

"He was lying in the street. He put up no resistance."

"And the girl—the prostitute—in whose room this murder took place—you say she has also been arrested?"

Bell's eyes had begun to twitch from exhaustion. "Vaugirard said she is being held. He said nothing about charges against her."

"And does she have a name?"

"None that I heard." Bell fished out his watch. Five-thirty. My God, he thought. Twelve hours since I received the telephone call from the Préfecture. It had not been a long time, but it had been the longest twelve hours of his life. He stood. "I'm afraid I have to get back." In truth, he felt a great wave of relief that it was five-thirty. Atkinson would be gone for the day.

St-Cyr stood then and offered his hand in that peculiar way. "Thank you for your time, Mr. Bell. I know it's been a great strain on you."

"Yes." Bell took the hand and squeezed it. *"Adieu*, Monsieur St-Cyr."

"Adieu, Mr. Bell. And good fortune to you."

Bell turned and began to walk away, but he suddenly stopped and turned back. "I hope you will be kind to Charging Elk, Monsieur St-Cyr. I know what he did was unspeakable." Bell tried to think. "But it was a matter of honor, you see. I think he had to do what he did. He had no choice."

"Code of the savage, I suppose." The journalist did not look up. He was flipping pages in his notebook, which lay on the table.

"Something like that. He said Breteuil did something to him that men do not do to each other. He was quite firm on that point."

St-Cyr looked up. "He speaks French now?"

"A little. He was not very forthcoming, but he did ask about the prostitute. He was very concerned about her."

"Interesting." St-Cyr made a notation in his notebook, then closed it and tucked it into his pocket. "Again, I thank you for your time, Mr. Bell. And please assure yourself that I will be completely fair. You may rest easy on that point."

St-Cyr watched the vice-consul walk away down Cours Estienne-d'Orves. His shoulders slumped under the dark coat of the bureaucrat and his walk was the trudge of a man who wasn't going anywhere anymore. Even the straw hat seemed to sag under the

weight of the bright sunlight. From the back, one wouldn't know
that he was a big man, handsome in a rumpled way. But there were
too many lines in his forehead. His eyes were too old.

St-Cyr felt a small pity for the man. True, he didn't like the
Americans and more than once, in his column, had chastised them
for being arrogant and demanding. He did not like their ships in the
harbor, he did not like the sailors, and he did not like the trade del-
egations who demanded more and more and gave less than fair
value. They are the new Romans, he thought, who came to Massilia
with their big ships and demands for tribute.

Still, he felt a little sorry for Bell, who would surely lose his job
over this scandal. And he had given St-Cyr enough material to
make sure that this *would* be a full-blown scandal, with all the trim-
mings. It had been a strange afternoon. Never had St-Cyr watched
a man hang himself so willingly with his own rope.

He opened his watch. Five forty-five. Too late to go to the
Préfecture. Plenty of time, though—his column wasn't due until tomorrow evening. And too, he didn't know yet who was the villain
and who the victim. Can one feel sympathy for a savage who murders a pervert? Can one be outraged over the death of a man who
performs a sex act on a drugged, helpless savage? He took the notebook out of his pocket and flipped back to the beginning. Vautrin.
Sergeant Vautrin. Desk sergeant. On his salary he could probably
do with a box of good cigars, perhaps a bottle of Rémy-Martin.
Thank God not all the desk sergeants were as incorruptible as
Borely.

St-Cyr placed the boater on his head and stepped out from the
shade of the table umbrella. The heat of the day struck him, and he
realized that he had been in a cocoon of pure concentration the past
four hours. He hadn't noticed that the breeze had shifted from
north to south and the heat wave hadn't really broken. The morning coolness had been a deception. But as he walked down the *cours*

in the opposite direction from Bell, he felt light and lively, perhaps even giddy, the way he used to feel when he went to visit Fortune. In a way, he could understand Charging Elk's infatuation with the whore at Le Salon.

At the end of the *cours*, he caught a hansom cab back to the *La Gazette du Midi* offices. As he settled back in the black leather seat and listened to the sharp clip-clop of the horse's shoes on the cobblestones, he closed his eyes and wondered if Fortune was still doling out the clap. He missed her. Although they had gotten together only once in a while, two or three times a month, he hadn't been lonely then.

Then he suddenly knew what it was about Bell that had been playing around the edges of his mind all afternoon. He had no one to go home to. He had no one to talk to, to comfort him. That was why he had unburdened himself so completely. St-Cyr opened his eyes and stared at the gray horse's dappled rump. He now knew what he would do. He would make the Charging Elk affair a *cause célèbre* in the *Gazette*. He would cover the trial until its conclusion, however it came out. All of Marseille would come to know the exotic creature from America and his strange habits, his pathetic attempt to become a Frenchman, and the clash between his savage code and the laws of civilization.

St-Cyr almost kicked the dappled rump himself to make the horse go faster. He felt good about his life now, as though everything about it had been leading up to this moment. He pitied Bell, and he knew he would pity Charging Elk tomorrow when he interviewed him, but right now he was reaching for the top—and it was there for him to grasp.

CHAPTER FIFTEEN

The cell, because it was underground and stone, was almost cold, but Charging Elk lay on his cot clad only in his trousers. He had been looking at the ceiling, at first remembering the cracked, stained ceiling in Marie's room at Le Salon, but now wondering how the ceiling was made to stay up. There were no supports, only the walls of the cell. Even when he had watched the building going up along the omnibus route (it seemed so long ago, yet it was less than a year), he had not questioned the magic of the builders. Now he wondered why the massive stone building did not crash down on him, crushing the life juices from his body like an insect underfoot.

He would have welcomed it, for he had no pleasure left in his life. He would never go home. He knew that in spite of Brown Suit's reassurances that the Americans would help him get through this trouble. What could they do? Brown Suit hadn't helped him in the sickhouse or in the stone house the time before. What could he do now? No, this time the police would cut off his head with their big iron knife, and he didn't care. He didn't even wish to rejoin his people in the real world. How could he face them without his head? How would they know him? And how could he tell them that he was Charging Elk, son of Scrub, the shirtwearer, and Doubles Back Woman, grandson of Scabby Bull, the great band chief, and Goodkill, who had been in the shadowland for so long he only knew them by name. Even his brother and sister—lucky ones!— would not know him. And when Strikes Plenty came, he would laugh and make jokes about his old friend Charging Elk, not know- ing that he was talking to him. No, it was better to die and let his spirit wander, blind and mute, over a world he now knew it could never be part of.

Even so, two sleeps later, he still felt strong about killing the *siyoko*. It was simple enough—when one comes upon evil, one kills it. Evil is not a dangerous animal. One does not kill a bear or a big cat or a rattlesnake simply for the sake of killing. These things were put on earth by Wakan Tanka and one lived harmoniously with them—unless they threatened. Or were meant to provide food. Then one offered up prayers upon killing them, prayers that honored the spirit of the animals. And the world remained in balance—or did in the old days. Now the circle was broken and the people had been dying in flesh and spirit. Even the sacred Paha Sapa had been taken away from the people. The *wasichus* gouged holes in the holy hills, looking for the yellow stuff that made them crazy. They cut down the trees and built their villages. They changed the course of the streams with their wooden troughs and dams. They tried to kill the Lakotas who went there to pray and to have visions that would make them strong in life. These sacred hills that had begat the Lakotas were now lost to them for- ever. And the buffalo that had entered the cave in the hills, the buffalo in Bird Tail's dream, would never come back to this world.

The evil that the *wasichus* brought was everywhere.

But even though the *siyoko* was just one and there were many more out there just beyond the high window, to kill one was worth a hundred acts of counting coup on the enemies. He would die now with honor, even though he was a world away from his people. Wakan Tanka would know. And Charging Elk, in the past two sleeps, had come to his own special knowledge: All of the tests that the Great Mystery had sent his way these past four years had no promise of reward. They were simply tests of his courage and resolution, preparation for this one final test. When he slit the throat of the *siyoko*, he had, in that instant, fulfilled his time on earth.

Charging Elk sat up and swung his legs over the bed and felt the cool stones with his bare feet. His back was sore and stiff where one of the men who found him lying in the street had kicked him two or three times. He knew there would be ugly bruises there, but he hurt more inside. His piss had been red with blood since then. But it didn't matter. He would be dead soon. René had once told him that when the guillotine sliced off the head, the body would live for a little while, twitching and jerking. He said one headless man had gotten up and run twenty meters before the legs finally collapsed. He said one head spat out oaths and curses on all who watched and cheered. At the time, Charging Elk had been horrified, but now he smiled. He had killed birds and animals and had watched them twitch in their final moments. It was no cause for alarm. Bird Tail, the old *wicasa wakan*, had said it was just their spirits leaving their bodies, and if one made the right prayers all would be well. Charging Elk would make his own prayers when the time came. But his prayers would be of thanks for having lived on this earth, not for his *nagi*'s future.

Charging Elk idly reached for the chain of his pocket watch to look at the time, but when he found nothing, he remembered the jailer had taken it, along with his purse. He couldn't remember what had happened with his knife. Had he left it in the room? Or had the jailer taken that too?

Suddenly his sense of resigned serenity left him. Marie! It seemed that every few minutes he thought of her, always with that same alarm. Had the *siyoko* harmed her? Surely she would have been in the room helping Charging Elk if she had still been alive. She had touched his mouth with her own lips just before he went to sleep. He had seen lovers do that on the quais of the Old Port and in the cafés of Cours St-Louis. But had she said words to him? He could almost remember a humming in his ear, but was it from her lips? Charging Elk couldn't help but fear the worst. In their tenderest of moments, he had fallen into a black sleep and the *siyoko* must have killed her before performing his vile act on Charging Elk's cock, a cock meant for Marie alone and certainly forbidden to a man. Charging Elk had to remind himself, even as he thought with shame of the pleasure that had grown in his loins, that the *siyoko* was not a man but an evil spirit. It had simply taken over the pale, bespectacled one's body.

Charging Elk was confused in a funny way. He knew he had done a right thing in killing the evil spirit, but he also mourned the death of the woman who was to become his wife and give him children and happiness. Were the two events related? More important, was he to blame? If not for him, the *siyoko* would not have come there and Marie would be alive. But he had come only to ask Marie to be his wife.

Charging Elk fell back on the bed. His head had begun to ache. Ever since that night he had been having headaches. Before, he only had headaches when he drank too much of the *mni sha*. He had slept very little since coming to the stone house, just a couple of lapses of consciousness each night when his mind turned off and his eyes quit seeing. And when he came back, it was as if he had never stopped thinking. He simply carried on with the last thought he could remember.

Now he closed his eyes and felt a warm buzzing in his head. He saw yellow and black fuzzy stripes before his eyes and he watched them in a kind of peaceful surrender. Then they were gone and he was too. He slept long and deeply, and even though he would have welcomed a dream to give him direction, his mind retreated, like a gopher that has seen a hawk, into a deep hole of labyrinthian safety.

First he heard the heavy slide of the metal plate that opened and closed the small window in the door. A few seconds later, he heard the key turn and the door creaked open. He didn't open his eyes yet. He sniffed, expecting the sour smell of soup.

But the jailer said, "Wake up. You have a visitor."

Charging Elk sat up on his elbows, expecting to see Brown Suit again, but the man standing just inside the doorway was slender and sleekly dressed in a light creamy suit and straw hat with a wide, sloping brim that covered his head like an umbrella. His eyes were in the shade of the brim, but Charging Elk could see that he was pale and young, in spite of the hair on his chin.

"You have twenty minutes," said the jailer.

Charging Elk looked at the jailer. This was not the vile fat man of four years ago. He was younger and dark-skinned beneath a full dark beard. Except for the beard he could have been Lakota, but he was probably a Levantine, perhaps a Musulman. This was surprising, because all of the gendarmes and jailers Charging Elk had seen were French.

The pale man said, "Thank you, monsieur," then pressed a franc note into the man's hand.

Charging Elk watched the jailer ease his way out of the small cell, then close the door behind him. He sat up, on the edge of the bed.

The pale man took the small stool and moved it a little, then sat. If they had been sitting opposite each other their knees would have touched.

"So—Monsieur Charging Elk. How is it going for you? Are they treating you well?"

"Well enough."

"You look a little better than last time."

Charging Elk had been staring straight ahead at the stone wall, which had initials and other markings carved into it, but now he glanced at the man.

"You don't remember me, do you?" The man smiled. "Martin St-Cyr. I visited you some four years ago—in this very jail. You were in a different room, I think."

Charging Elk's expression didn't change but he was trying to remember the man.

"Back then you couldn't speak our language. Now I hear things are different. You have become a real Frenchman—even to the point of visiting one of our famous houses of pleasure."

Charging Elk didn't understand much of what the man said—only something about language and whorehouse. But his mind suddenly flashed on Marie's bloody room and his stomach grew sour with fear. Was this man an *akecita* boss who had come to take him to the guillotine already?

But the man reached into his coat pocket and drew out a packet of cigarettes and a box of matches. He pulled a cigarette out and handed it to Charging Elk. He put another between his lips, then struck a match and lit both, half rising from the stool to light Charging Elk's. "Forgive me. I think I speak too fast for you. I will try to say things slowly and clearly."

Charging Elk looked at him with his mouth open and his eyes wide. "Yellow Breast," he said in Lakota. "It is Yellow Breast, the *heyoka*." He had remembered that Yellow Breast had given him a half-empty packet of cigarettes last time. He remembered his little ceremony with the tobacco and his heart suddenly lightened. "You have come to help me," he said, again in Lakota.

This time it was St-Cyr's turn to be astonished. He couldn't believe the sound of the strange, rough language. Not one word made sense. He laughed. "Now you have me confused. Is that your Indian tongue? I was told you speak French."

"Ah, yes! I speak French. Only not so good."

St-Cyr threw the cigarettes and matches on the cot beside Charging Elk. "These are for you, my friend." He pulled out his notebook and said, "We don't have much time. Could you tell me what happened in the whorehouse?"

Charging Elk drew on the cigarette and looked up at the high mesh window. The word "whorehouse" did not frighten him this time, but he didn't want to remember.

"Why are you in jail?"

But what if this man had come to save him? Shouldn't he tell him everything? He would understand why he had done what he had done. "I killed an evil," he said.

"Why?"

Charging Elk drew on the cigarette and watched the smoke curl up toward the window. He suddenly felt naked in the presence of the pale man, so he shrugged into his shirt, noticing that the stiff collar was missing. He busied himself with the buttons.

"Why did you kill a man in this whorehouse? What was he to you?"

Charging Elk took the cigarette from between his lips and looked at St-Cyr. The man did not look like a gendarme, but he suspected a trick of some sort. But why would this man who had been kind to him before and was kind now seek to deceive him?

St-Cyr seemed to understand the Indian's reluctance to answer. He also felt uncomfortable for the first time under the frank stare. "Of course! I forgot to tell you—I am a journalist, *La Gazette ∂u*

Midi. Perhaps you know it?" When Charging Elk didn't answer, he said, slowly and clearly, "I write about injustice. If I am to help you, I must have answers to my questions."

"You are not gendarme?"

"I swear to the Black Virgin, I am nothing more than a humble reporter who wishes to help you if I can. All right?"

"All right then." Charging Elk threw his cigarette butt into the slop bucket at the foot of the cot. "That man that I killed was not a man like you and me but a *siyoko*."

St-Cyr had begun to write but he abruptly stopped. "Pardon me? A see—a seek . . ."

"*Siyoko*."

"Can you spell it?"

"No."

"But what does it mean?"

"An evilness."

"Like an evil spirit?"

"Evilness."

St-Cyr shook his head and wrote "evilness." Then he said, "And what made you kill him?"

"I killed it because it was evil. One always kills evil."

St-Cyr tapped his pencil on the pad. He had been told that this Indian spoke French, but nothing he said made sense. It was as if the savage's brain worked differently from ordinary men's. He decided to try another tack. "If I am to get you out of jail you must tell me everything—in every detail. Do you understand?"

"Of course. I will tell you everything, yes."

"Good. Let's start a little earlier. You were seeing one of the whores, one of the girls. Her name was—" He flipped back in his notebook. "Let's see. Ah. Marie Colet. Was she your girl?"

"Yes! Marie!" Charging Elk's heart jumped up, then just as suddenly fell. "But the *siyoko* killed her."

"No, no, monsieur. This—this evilness did not kill her. She is very much alive; in fact, she's here, at the Préfecture. I talked to her less than an hour ago."

Charging Elk again looked at the journalist, his eyes hardening into narrow slits. Now he knew the man was not to be trusted. "The *siyoko* killed her," he said, his voice barely audible in the high-ceilinged room.

St-Cyr had lowered his eyes to his notebook, not daring to look back into the savage's murderous eyes. He thought he should call to the guard, who he knew was standing just outside the door, listening to every word. His eyes fell upon his notes and he recited: "Dark hair, stout, nineteen years of age. From the country, from the Vaucluse. She's been at Le Salon for three years." He sneaked a look up and he noticed that the Indian's eyes had widened somewhat. "She said you came to her every Saturday night since December or January. She couldn't be sure."

"Then she is alive!"

"She said you once gave her a cameo—"

"Wakan Tanka has saved her!" He suddenly closed his eyes and spoke quietly, as though St-Cyr were not there. "Thank you, Tunkashila, thank you for her beating heart and her warm skin and her shining hair. I have walked with you for all the years of my life and now you have given me another gift. You are my good Grandfather who has shown me the red road and now I will die with you in my *wanagi* forever. Thank you, my Tunkashila, thank you for her beating heart. And thank you for Yellow Breast, whose heart also beats strong for your poor grandson."

St-Cyr listened to the strange, almost chanting language with fascination. He wished desperately that he could understand what was going on inside the *indien's* head. He knew that the real story lay somewhere behind that lean, coppery face, those obsidian eyes, those wide, thin lips that mouthed the incomprehensible

words. He was barely conscious that he was writing this description down.

"But what is she doing here?"

St-Cyr almost didn't recognize the crude locution, so engrossed
was he in his own ruefulness. He smiled sheepishly, in spite of the
circumstance of the stone room and its implications. "They are
holding her," he said.

"But why?"

"They suspect she . . ." St-Cyr suddenly stopped. A memory
flashed through his head and he saw this same Indian in a cell
identical to this one, looking drawn and defeated. He remembered
the limp handshake, the dull eyes, the look of death. And now,
Charging Elk was almost certain to lose his life. How could he tell
him that this girl he cared for—who might have been all he cared
for in his circumscribed life—had conspired with Breteuil to drug
him so that the invert could perform his infamous act? She had
told it all to St-Cyr only an hour ago. She felt very bad about her
role and she was frightened and concerned—but really only about
herself. What would become of her? She had expressed little concern over what might happen to Charging Elk. At the time, St-
Cyr had thought it a natural reaction. Why should she care what
happened to a customer? But now, the Indian seemed to think
that they were lovers. But that was natural too. It was natural for
a man to become infatuated with a particular whore. Oh, my
great, pillowy Fortune!

"Time's up, monsieur!"

"Only one moment, if you please." St-Cyr glanced down at his
notes. There was hardly anything there. Just a description and a
doodle. And a hesitant attempt to spell the strange word. *Siyoko*, he
had called it. Evilness. He closed up the notebook. He had plenty
of material from Bell and Marie Colet to write his first column. And
he had a pretty good angle on how to portray the Peau-Rouge, one

that surprised even him. But he would need much more before the trial began.

"Can I bring you something next time—besides some more cigarettes?"

Charging Elk had been leaning forward, elbows on knees, studying the initials on the wall. "No thank you," he said.

"Can I contact someone for you—perhaps where you work or where you live?" St-Cyr had been sincere in his offer, but when he saw the look of alarm come into the savage's eyes his journalist's instincts, which had abandoned him twenty minutes ago, suddenly returned. "Surely there is someone who cares about you, who would like to know that you are alive and well. If I could have a name, Charging Elk, perhaps I could reassure this person."

The jailer entered the small room. "You must leave now, monsieur. It is my neck if you are found here."

"You must let me help you. A name . . ."

"Come now, monsieur. I have three little mouths to feed." The jailer grasped St-Cyr by the upper arm and lifted him from the stool.

"René Soulas."

Both St-Cyr and the jailer froze for an instant, locked in their awkward pose. A smile flickered across Charging Elk's face, a twitch of the thin lips, as though he found the moment amusing. But his eyes did not participate in the amusement.

"Where does he live?" St-Cyr had recovered but so had the jailer, who was propelling the journalist out the door.

"11 Rue d'Aubagne. He is my friend. You must tell him not to worry."

But the door clanged shut, cutting this last sentence off. Charging Elk sat on the edge of the bed for a moment, looking at the initials without seeing them. He hadn't thought of the Soulas family at all in the past two sleeps. Even when he said René's name, it sounded strange on his tongue. He shook another cigarette out of the packet and looked at it, running his finger over the smooth paper cylinder. He felt his heart falling down. What would Madeleine think? She had thought he had a real girlfriend, one he might bring to Sunday dinner. Now she would know the truth. He looked toward the door but there was nothing but silence behind it. It was too late to tell Yellow Breast that he had changed his mind, that he mustn't contact René Soulas. Charging Elk felt a familiar throbbing in his temples. Soon he would have a full-blown headache that would make him lie back on the bed and shut his eyes tight against the brightness of the high window.

He dreaded the inevitable pain just as he dreaded the last few sleeps of his life. He wondered if they would come for him this night, or tomorrow, or the day after that. He didn't mind dying — and yet he didn't seek it as he did four years before when he sang his death song for three sleeps straight — but he didn't like the waiting. If they did come this night he would welcome them. He put the cigarette between his lips and struck a match and a thought occurred to him — Wakan Tanka had sent Yellow Breast to him twice now. Perhaps there was a plan after all. But what could Yellow Breast do? He was no magician who could make Charging Elk invisible or put his head back on his body after the big iron knife fell. And yet he had said he would help. Charging Elk stared at the small yellow flame and dared to hope just a little.

As he sucked in the smoke, Marie entered his mind and he wondered, just before the first hot wire of pain coursed through his brain, why she was still alive, why the *siyoko* hadn't killed her. He had meant to ask Yellow Breast but now it was too late. Now he would never know. Somehow he knew that.

CHAPTER SIXTEEN

The morning of August 16 of 1894 was typical for late summer in Marseille—hot, still, humid, cloudless—and relatively quiet at eleven o'clock after the early-morning markets as the citizens retreated into their homes or factories or stores. A few people sat in front of cafés under umbrellas, drinking small dark *cafés* or *citrons pressés*. Occasionally a hansom cab or delivery wagon rattled by, and even more occasionally a nearly empty omnibus made its slow way along La Canebière or Rue de la République, the dark-sweated horses stopping automatically at each corner.

This morning René Soulas and his wife, Madeleine, standing on the corner of La Canebière and Cours St-Louis, pulled themselves up on the rear platform and found a seat just inside the coach. René had put in his full shift in the fish stall but had left François to clean up by himself. He had hurried home, washed himself, and put on his best suit. Madeleine was already dressed in her dark blue Provençal dress with the lace collar and sleeves, and her black straw hat with the artificial berries on the front of the crown. They had been quiet all morning, dreading this morning and the several mornings which would follow.

René had read the small article in *La Gazette du Midi* during a quiet time at the market. He had been so shocked he hadn't told Madeleine or François about it. Instead, he had gone through the motions of selling fish until the market ended. Then he removed his apron and washed his hands—thank God Madeleine had already left for home to prepare lunch—and half walked, half ran all the way down to the Préfecture, and when he arrived, he had to lean against a column in the foyer to catch his breath.

He had been doubly shocked: because Charging Elk had murdered a man, of course, but also because it had happened in Rue Sainte. And he had felt doubly betrayed: Charging Elk had wanted to leave the Soulas home almost three years ago, and after all of René's preaching about the evil temptations that Marseille offered, Charging Elk had ended up in a whorehouse in one of the most godforsaken parts of town.

René had leaned against the cool marble column, catching his breath, cooling down, and alternating between anger and fright. He was angry at Charging Elk for having gotten himself in such trouble, and he was angry at himself for having allowed it. He could have been more forceful about the evils of the waterfront. And he was frightened because the young Indian would surely face the guillotine. He had to do something. He had to see Charging Elk. He made up his mind to lay aside his anger, to concentrate on whatever comfort for the Indian he could muster.

But the desk sergeant said that the prisoner was allowed no visitors. When René explained that the prisoner had lived with his family for two years, that he was like a father to the young man, that Charging Elk had nobody else, the desk sergeant simply said, "No visitors, monsieur—period."

René didn't tell Madeleine about the article and he knew she wouldn't come across it herself. She didn't read the newspaper. None of it had to do with her, she always said, better to wrap fish or chestnuts in it than to read it. René was unusually hearty at dinner, but he didn't sleep that night, and the next morning, after market, he went back down to the Préfecture. This time he managed to get an interview with a captain, who seemed quite sympathetic, taking down names and notes, but in the end, he told him what the desk sergeant had. He did give René a reason, of sorts—that the examining magistrate had to conduct his interviews with the prisoner in a private and unsullied manner. Only in this way could he determine if a crime had been committed and a trial before the full tribunal was in order. This was the course of justice. Surely Monsieur Soulas could understand that.

But René couldn't understand that. What harm could come of comforting a poor wretch when he had fallen? Was it not God's will that we do all we can for one another? Didn't the Bible say "Do unto others as we would have them do unto us"? Surely the captain could understand that.

The captain could understand that, but God's law wasn't the only law, as unfortunate as it might be. But cheer up, monsieur, he said, perhaps the examining magistrate will find nothing to charge your Peau-Rouge with. Perhaps it is all an unfortunate mistake.

René had walked home, as downcast as he had ever been. And he felt an overwhelming guilt for having convinced the American— Monsieur Bell—that Charging Elk would be fine in his care. He passed the fortune-teller's window, with the red drapes, the candles burning at midday and the big eye painted on the glass, in La Canebière and thought for an instant of entering. He had never been to a fortune-teller, had never even considered it until then. But then he shuddered at the thought of what he might learn and hurried home to the unsuspecting Madeleine and the nice lunch she would have set out.

But he had been surprised to find a stranger in his flat, and a very striking one at that. The stranger sat on the divan, one leg crossed over the other, a cup of coffee balanced on his knee. He wore a dark blue silk smock and a poet's tie made of the same material. His cream-colored trousers came to a knife-edge crease, echoing the pointed toes of the rich brown boots. René looked at Madeleine, as if to assure himself that he was in the right flat, and he saw a look on her face that was somewhere between pale horror and anxious pleasure.

"This is Monsieur St-Cyr. He is a famous journalist." Then she turned toward the man. "And this is my husband, René."

The man stood and offered his hand. *"Enchanté,* Monsieur Soulas. This is indeed a pleasure." As René took the hand and pumped it, the man said, "Of course, the circumstances are unfortunate."

"Yes, of course." René glanced quickly at Madeleine and he knew she knew. He had wanted to tell her in his own good time, but perhaps it was better that she know from the beginning. The next few weeks or months would be hard on her. But she deserved to know.

"I read your column faithfully, Monsieur St-Cyr. It is an honor to have such a famous journalist in our home." Then he added, "But your picture doesn't do you justice," and wished he hadn't.

But St-Cyr laughed. He was used to this kind of reaction. Even at the *Gazette,* his fellow reporters teased him about his flamboyant costumes, which seemed to get more outlandish as the years passed. But then so had his columns, and the people loved it.

"Please sit, monsieur. Would you like some more coffee? Madeleine—" But she had already gone into the kitchen. René watched St-Cyr settle his thin frame back in the cushions of the divan and he marveled at the delicacy with which one leg swung over the other. The journalist slouched on the divan as though he owned it, as though he were at ease anywhere he was in the world. In spite of the "unfortunate circumstances." René was thrilled to see such a celebrated journalist at ease in his home. "Would you like a cigar?" he said.

"No, no, monsieur. Thank you. I have my own cigarettes." St-Cyr tapped one out of the packet. René noticed that he had been using Madeleine's silver salver, which was full of potpourri, for an ashtray. There were two butts in it. The journalist lit his cigarette and dropped the match in the dish. Even though René was worried that the potpourri would catch on fire, it would be awkward to get him a proper ashtray.

St-Cyr leaned forward and said in a low voice, "I'm terribly sorry about your wife. I thought she knew. I'm afraid it was quite a shock to her."

"She would have to know eventually. I was going to tell her myself, perhaps today." But René wanted to see Charging Elk, to have some words with him, before he broke the sad news to Madeleine. He said as much to St-Cyr.

"Perhaps I can help. Perhaps I can arrange a visitation. Even tomorrow."

That had been two and a half months ago, and René had yet to see Charging Elk. He had read St-Cyr's column two days later and was more than impressed with the journalist's ability to make such a spellbinding story out of a bit of knowledge of Charging Elk. He still remembered snatches of the column, including the way it began: "M. Charging Elk, child of nature or born killer? That is the question that confronts us. . . ." But he had been completely shocked to read the name of the dead man—Armand Breteuil.

According to the article they were unknown to each other until Breteuil and the whore, one Marie Colet, hatched their dastardly plot, but René remembered that dark morning on the Quai des Belges when he had introduced him to Charging Elk and Breteuil had later enlisted the *indien* to help him load his fish. René had been worried then, but he thought his warning to stay away from perverts like Breteuil had been forceful enough. So René had been shocked by the whole business, start to finish, but he also wondered if the incident in the whorehouse was really the only time the two men had come together since the introduction on the Quai des Belges. He had wanted to tell St-Cyr about the incident on the quai, but he thought it could only do more harm than good. In a far corner of his mind, one that he barely acknowledged for fear of what he would find out, he wondered about Charging Elk's sex life.

René and Madeleine got off the omnibus a block from the Palais de Justice. They stood for a moment, watching the lumbering wagon turn into Cours Pierre Puget. A worker in a blue peasant's uniform was washing windows on the shady side of the street. He had a wet rag tied around his neck and he worked fast. The windows dried almost immediately in the close heat. But René envied him—a simple man performing a simple task. He would probably grumble to his wife tonight about his menial lot in life, but right now it didn't seem so bad. He took Madeleine's elbow and urged her toward their destination. Both of them were tight-lipped and awkward, as though they were the accused and were showing up for their own trial.

Between the Palais de Justice and another building, René could see, on the high hill, Notre Dame de la Garde and the golden Virgin surmounting the steeple, and he remembered having prayed just last night, as he did every night, to the Virgin for succor for his young friend. But he had no sign that she heard him. Now he couldn't look at her, for she cast a dazzling light beneath the late-morning sun.

René showed the letter of summons to a young man behind a desk in the tall, gloomy foyer of the Palais de Justice. He gave them directions and they ascended a wide staircase and walked to the end of a windowless hall, their footsteps echoing sharply on the marble floor. Another young man, this one in the dark tunic and blue trousers with the red stripe of the gendarmes, looked over the letter, then glanced pointedly at each of them before leading them into courtroom B.

René was surprised that they were in a long balcony that arched around the large courtroom. There were three rows of benches, each stepped down to the railing. And he was surprised that the benches were nearly filled. He had never been in a courtroom and at first he thought these must be the officials. But there were so many of them. How would justice ever get done?

The floor below was nearly deserted by comparison. A few men in black robes sat at each of several dark wooden tables, chatting among themselves. On one side, sitting in two rows in a box, were a group of men, all staring straight ahead, as though they were waiting for a theatrical performance to begin, but their faces were as grim as infantrymen waiting for the order to charge into the teeth of the Huns.

The gendarme brought them to a special roped-off section of the balcony. He unfastened a brass hook from a stanchion and said, "Here we are." René almost bowed to the young gendarme, as though he were a monsignor or a *grand bourgeois*. "Thank you," he whispered as he sat hesitantly on the hard bench. He could not remember being this intimidated ever before. He pulled his handkerchief from a pocket and wiped the sweat from his forehead and upper lip. He glanced back toward the door they had come in, which was now closed. And he felt trapped in the large, airless room.

He suddenly felt Madeleine's hand on his own. "Are you all right, René?"

"It's just a little warm. That's all."

"But your hand is trembling."

"I didn't realize it would be this big. And the people . . ." Just then he spotted a small oval platform, like a pulpit, just below them. It had a picket balustrade around it and a single chair in the middle. René suddenly forgot his discomfort and gazed lovingly at the man sitting on the chair. "Madeleine," he whispered, as though in a daze, and she looked at him, then followed his eyes to the man in the chair.

"Good Lord," she said. "He is so young still."

They sat in silence for a moment, looking at the long, dark hair, the deep copper face, the narrow eyes, and the shadowy cheeks beneath the ridge of bone. They were no more than seven meters away from Charging Elk.

"He looks so handsome," Madeleine said.

René leaned forward over the balcony rail and whispered as loudly as he dared, "Charging Elk. Sssst. My friend."

Charging Elk glanced around him but he didn't look up.

"Sssst. Here, my friend."

But a gendarme suddenly appeared from beneath the bacony and René ducked back.

Just then a man beside a door in the front of the room announced that the people should all rise, and the murmuring and shifting ceased as the people obeyed. They watched in silence as three older men in red robes, white bibs, and caps of office filed up to the ornate bench beneath the seal of the French Republic. Each carried a portfolio, and as they settled into the tall red velvet chairs, the one in the center turned in one direction, then the other. The other magistrates nodded, and the one in the middle, a spare man with spectacles and a blunt white beard, announced that the Cour d'Assises de la République was now in session. He cautioned the spectators to refrain from disruptive behavior. He urged both the *procureur général* and the advocate for the accused to be "to the point." He pointed out that he himself would ask questions not only of the accused, but of his advocate and of the *procureur général*. He also addressed the jury, cautioning them to use good judgment, to refrain from speaking of the proceedings outside the courtroom, and to remember that they were to make their decision of guilt or innocence based solely on the evidence they were to hear. Then he nodded to the *procureur*, who was conferring with one of his associates. The *procureur*, a tall, ruddy man with white muttonchops and a prominent stomach that caused his robe to stick out over the tips of his glossy shoes, stood, and with a slight bow to the magistrates, commenced his opening argument.

René and Madeleine were tight-lipped but spellbound by the *procureur général's* oratory as he accused Charging Elk of the most heinous crime he had come across in his nineteen years of public service. He pounded the railing in front of the jurors and pointed at the accused and said he was not only an illegal immigrant but a savage who could never comprehend the necessary rules and obligations of a civilized society. He cited poets and painters, composers and sculptors, politicians and priests, the great chefs of France, one of whom had been brutally, coldheartedly murdered by a villain who would not know a leg of mutton from a *noisette de veau*. "Why," the prosecutor sputtered, "he lives in Le Panier, that notorious district of cutpurses and murderers and drug-runners. He is not a simple vagabond or a poor child of nature, as some would have us believe. He is a part of that den of iniquity, that black wound in the breast of decent Marseille society. If I were ten years younger, I would go up there and clean it out myself. You can mark my words."

Even though they had been forewarned by Charging Elk's advocate, René was startled by the exaggerations and outright lies and Madeleine was outraged. She gripped his knee harder and harder and puffed and snorted. René glanced around and he noticed that some in the balcony were looking at them. He squeezed his wife's hand and attempted a comforting smile, but she would not look at him.

Charging Elk either did not understand what the prosecutor was saying about him or chose to accept the outrageous accusations as part of this strange proceeding. He sat calmly but alertly, his legs crossed, his long, brown hands nestled in his lap. Réne had seen this pose hundreds of times, when he dragged Charging Elk to a café to drink anisette with his friends, or when one of the children, when they were younger, told him about the day's adventures. Even if he didn't understand the words, the expression of friendly alertness never left his face.

That was the Charging Elk that René knew, the Charging Elk who had eventually won over Madeleine with his patience and goodwill, so that now she was seething with every word the unlucky prosecutor uttered.

"Can't they stop his filthy lies?" she suddenly whispered in a fierce voice that carried far enough to make René cast a nervous glance toward the chief magistrate.

"It is his job, my dear wife," he whispered, without looking at her. "This is the way they do it. Next it will be Charging Elk's advocate's turn to defend him. When he interviewed me, he said not to worry. It is the prosecutor's job to make our friend look bad. It's the way things are done."

"But it's not fair to have to listen to all these lies. What if the magistrates believe him?"

"They take it all with a grain of salt. They are experienced men, men of honor." René glanced over at the two rows of men in the oblong box. They are the ones we have to worry about, he thought.

The advocate had said that the jurors held Charging Elk's fate in their hands. They might be honorable men but they were not experienced. Even now, they sat expressionless, but with eyes and ears wide open to the prosecutor and his venomous accusations. René remembered the dazzling gold virgin atop Notre Dame de la Garde and said a small, halting prayer to her. He was beginning to have that hopeless feeling again.

"He looks like a boiled pig," said Madeleine, thrusting her chin toward the prosecutor.

Charging Elk sat on the plain wooden chair in the prisoner's dock, looking at his brown shoes, which were now scuffed and dull. He was wearing his dark suit, the one the tailor had made for him in a happier time. The man who was on his side and who would speak up for him had sent it to the cleaners and had gotten him a couple of clean shirts and a tie. He said Charging Elk had to look like a respectable gentleman. But Charging Elk was disappointed in the scuffed brown shoes. He had been only too happy to dress up after the many sleeps in the gray prisoner's clothes. And when he pointed out to the man who would speak for him the sad state of the brown shoes, the man said not to worry, nobody would see them. But Charging Elk could see them and he was disappointed.

He sat on a level between the balcony and the floor where all the important ones sat and sometimes stood. All were silent except for the man who accused him of many bad things. His advocate had said that the other man was his enemy and would try to convince the jury and the magistrates that Charging Elk was a bad man. And although Charging Elk could make out only a little of what the accusing one said, he knew that he was in trouble. He understood the words "savage" and "murderer" and "evil heart." He could see that the men in the box were listening with big ears.

Charging Elk had heard somebody whisper his name, but when he looked around he saw only strangers. Some of them had been looking at him, especially those in the balcony, as though he were some sort of wild animal on display, like the big cats and wolves in the Wild West show. For the first time in a long time, he was annoyed by this prurience and wanted to show them his teeth, but the one who spoke for him had told him it was important to act the gentleman. So he ignored them and focused his attention on the bad-mouthed one and the jurymen who watched him. And his heart grew heavy to think that these people did not understand the ways of the *siyokos* and the necessity to kill them.

He understood from his advocate that the situation did not look good, that perhaps the most the advocate could do would be to save him from the guillotine. Even that would be a great triumph. But if he could show that Charging Elk had been a good citizen up to this event, perhaps the court would show mercy. He wanted the names of all the people who knew Charging Elk, every one of them, friend or enemy; he would sort them out. And so Charging Elk gave him the names of all who had been friendly toward him—the Soulas family, Brown Suit, Yellow Breast, his bosses at the soap factory, Monsieur Billedoux and Madame Braque, the little fat man at Le Salon, Olivier. Then, after a few moments of thought, he included Marie.

But the advocate had said she was already coming to the stand "in another capacity." Charging Elk had not understood this language and was pleased that he would be able to see her again, even if only from a distance. In fact, the thought that he would be able to look at her and that she might look at him was what had sustained him the past three weeks. He had been questioned repeatedly the previous two and a half weeks by the special magistrate, who seemed to want him to say that he had killed the good chef with a cold heart, as a country butcher cuts the neck of a lamb and throws it into the brambles to bleed out. And he wouldn't listen to the simple explanation that Charging Elk did it for all of the people, including the special magistrate. It was his obligation.

Now Charging Elk glanced around the courtroom, the prosecutor's words just a meaningless recitation in his ears. It occurred to him that Marie might be here now—perhaps in the balcony, perhaps seated at one of the tables beneath the balcony. There were a few women there, but none of them was Marie. Of course he couldn't see into the balcony just over his head, but he imagined that she might be there. And it occurred to him that he had never seen her in going-out clothes, and the idea of her in a long, perhaps satiny dress and a beautiful hat made of feathers excited him almost visibly. He leaned forward to get a better look at the tables beneath the balcony, but they were filled with men, all of them writing in little notebooks. But there at the front right-hand corner of the long table in the middle sat Yellow Breast, head down, pencil moving furiously across and down the page.

Charging Elk had seen him only once more after that initial meeting. He brought cigarettes, candy, and greetings from Réne and Madeleine. He also brought a copy of the article he had written about Charging Elk. He had been excited about the reaction the article had brought, but when Charging Elk simply looked at it, he paused. "You can't read," he said. Then he told Charging Elk what it said, leaving out some parts that he thought might upset the *indien*. He said that many people were angry that an innocent savage could be seduced by a voracious predator like Breteuil. They were even angrier that the justice system could not see that the crime had actually been committed by the perverted chef. Many of the comments on the street included the declaration "I would have done the same thing myself."

But that had been four or five weeks ago and Charging Elk had heard nothing since; nor had he seen Yellow Breast again until now. He had begun to think that the journalist had forgotten all about him—after all, Marseille was a big town and there were many things for a journalist to write about. So when Yellow Breast, during a pause while the prosecutor drank a glass of water, glanced up and winked, the *indien* smiled. He had not seen a friendly face other than Yellow Breast's since before the incident in Le Salon. He was suddenly filled with hope that Yellow Breast could make these citizens see the truth of what he had done.

During the next nine days of trial, excepting the weekend, many witnesses were brought to the stand to testify. The prosecutor's witnesses were mostly officials—gendarmes, including the one who had arrested him the first time in front of the Basilique St-Victor for vagabondage; a doctor who affirmed that he had left the hospital without being discharged; another doctor who claimed that Charging Elk did not have the mental capacity to understand the rules of a civilized society; yet another doctor whose specialty was phrenology and who stated that in the scientific community it was common knowledge that savages' brains were smaller on average and therefore less developed, less capable of making sound decisions; and a government official who testified that the defendant had no legal status in the Republic, that he was in fact an illegal immigrant who should have been deported long ago but had somehow fallen through the cracks of the immigration service.

Finally, the prosecutor called his last witness. And Charging Elk was beside himself with joy. He watched, his bottom barely touching the chair, as Marie walked with her eyes down to the witness stand. She was not only alive but she was flesh and blood—the same sturdy body, the clean, round face that he had looked into so often. But she was different. She was wearing a dress—a long, gray dress, not silky but crisp and neat. And a gray straw hat with her hair tucked underneath. As she walked up the aisle, he could hear the swish of her dress, of the things under it, and he was awed by this new Marie.

The advocate, in preparing his case, had questioned Charging Elk again and again about his relationship with Marie and what had taken place between them on the night in question. What was she like that night? Happy? Angry? Aloof? Secretive? Had he seen her pour a powder or liquid into his wine? Did they have any sexual contact? Did he see her talking with the chef before he passed out? Charging Elk had resented these questions because they made her look as if she was in league with the *siyoko*. In fact, he was surprised to find himself feeling a twinge of jealousy at such a thought. But he had recovered and told the advocate that he didn't want to talk about her anymore. He never told the advocate that he had asked her to come live with him, to marry him. After his long days and nights in his cell, he had come to feel embarrassed that he might have thought he had such a chance for happiness.

And now here she was, standing in the small enclosure, swearing to God that she would be truthful. Her hands, small but square in black net gloves, held the railing tightly, as if she would collapse without its support. And when the prosecutor asked the first question, she answered in the small, reluctant voice that Charging Elk knew so well. And although he had to lean forward and listen with great intensity, he understood most of what she said, including the fact that she was still working at Le Salon.

The prosecutor spent most of his time asking her about her relationship with the defendant. When did she first meet him? How often did he come to Le Salon? Would they always have sex? Was he an abusive lover? Did he demand of her acts that were beyond the bounds of propriety? Finally he questioned her about that night. Where was she during the time the two men were together in her room? And finally, what did she find upon returning to her room?

Marie almost collapsed at this last question, swaying, leaning on the railing for support, and sobbing as the sight of the slain man came back to her. At the prosecutor's gentle prodding, she described, between sobs, the thin, naked body still hunched over the edge of the bed, the dark stain on the bedspread, the blood which was still dripping from his wounds on the floor, the smell which almost made her faint and did make her vomit.

When the prosecutor thanked her in a soft voice and walked back to his desk, the whole courtroom was deathly quiet. Even Charging Elk held his breath as he listened to Marie's diminishing sobs and remembered the room that night. He had understood enough to remember washing his groin and thighs at the washstand, tucking the blood-spattered shirt into his trousers, spying the spectacles on the small table beside the bed, and leaving the room with a curiously mixed feeling of fear and triumph. And the smell of blood, as vivid in his nostrils now as it had been that night. But now he felt the horror that had haunted him since—the horror of imagining Marie opening her door and taking in the carnage. As he watched her on the stand, head down, still sobbing into a handkerchief, he knew that the horror that had visited him again and again had been only too accurate.

The president of the tribunal, the chief magistrate, gave Marie a few moments to collect herself; then he asked the defendant's advocate to proceed. The advocate stood but did not leave his desk, some six or seven meters from the witness stand. He was a cadaverous man whose white bib was a couple of sizes too big for his neck and whose robe hung from his shoulders like a shroud. A pair of spectacles perched above a curving nose that seemed almost a caricature of a hawk's beak. He studied his notes for a short time, then asked in a surprisingly loud voice, "Had you met the deceased, Armand Breteuil, before the night of May 17th, Mademoiselle Colet?"

"No, monsieur."

"Excuse me?"

"No," she said, a little louder this time.

"Are you certain about that?" The advocate's voice rose to a quizzical pitch, with just a note of sarcasm, as he glanced at the jurors.

"Yes, monsieur."

The advocate looked down at his notes, pretending to study them. "Well, we'll come back to this issue, mademoiselle. But let me proceed. Had you ever *seen* him before the night of May 17th?"

"No. Yes. Once in a while."

"And what were the circumstances of these occasional sightings?"

"He came into Le Salon sometimes."

"Ah. To visit the girls, no doubt."

Marie looked up at the advocate for the first time, a puzzled look on her face.

"He came to enjoy the fruits of young womanhood—is that not correct, mademoiselle?"

"No. He always went into the back parlor."

"I don't understand," the advocate said, staring at the jury.

"That's where the boys are."

"The boys? Again, I'm afraid I don't understand."

Marie glanced up at the advocate, but he was looking at the group of men in the long box. "He came to visit the boys," she said.

"You mean, to have sex with the boys?"

"Just one. Just the Spaniard—Miguel." Marie was surprised to hear rustling and murmuring in the balcony. She looked up and saw the several spectators—some fanning themselves with heavy paper fans, others with hats, still others mopping their faces against the stuffy heat—and saw that all were looking at her, all silent now, expectant. She began to feel faint again and rocked unsteadily against the balustrade.

"So he was a practicing homosexual, would you say, mademoiselle?"

"Yes, monsieur."

"Thank you." He came out from behind the desk and stood between it and the jury box, tapping his spectacles against his thumbnail. He seemed lost in thought, and Marie could hear the tap, tap, tap clearly in the hushed room. She glanced quickly at the magistrates, who were seated less than two meters above her and to the side. They too were watching the advocate, perhaps a little disdainfully, perhaps impatiently.

"We must come back to my first question, Mademoiselle Colet. And I feel I must inform you that you have sworn an oath to God that you would be truthful in your testimony. You do understand that you have an obligation to be truthful and that the consequences of perjury are quite grave, do you not?"

"Yes, monsieur," she said in a small, wary voice.

"Good. Now then—had you met Armand Breteuil before the night of the incident in question?"

Marie did something then that she had sworn to herself that she would not do—she glanced over to the prisoner's dock. She glanced at Charging Elk and saw that he was watching her in a way that seemed curiously detached from the proceedings. She felt his eyes encompass her in a way that seemed too intimate for the time and place. She had seen that look only in her small room and she had felt a stirring then that seemed to lift her out of her drab, unhappy nights in Le Salon.

"The witness will answer the advocate's question," came a voice from above.

"Yes," she said. "Yes."

"And when did this meeting take place?"

"Three, four days before . . ."

"And what was the nature of this meeting?"

"Pardon?"

"What did you and the deceased talk about?"

Marie felt sick and faint. She shouldn't have looked at him. It made it all too difficult. "Please, monsieur," she said. "Have pity."

"It's a simple question."

"But I can't . . ." And with that, she buried her face in her hands and cried.

The chief magistrate called for silence, then said, "Perhaps the mademoiselle would like a short break."

Marie actually looked up at the magistrates, dabbing at her eyes with the handkerchief. She felt grateful for this small kindness, but as she looked at them, she knew that there was no chance to put an end to this cruelty. She looked back at the advocate, who was leaning against his desk, wiping his spectacles on the corner of his black robe. No, there was no way out but to answer his questions truly. Only then would they stop.

"He wanted me to . . ."

"Breteuil."

"He wanted me to arrange a meeting with François."

"François?"

"Charging Elk." Marie could barely say the name. She had learned it only when the journalist came to see her in the Préfecture five weeks before. She remembered feeling a little angry then at the big man's deception, but now she felt only a desire to finish her story and get away from the voracious eyes in the balcony.

"A meeting! To what purpose?"

"He wanted to have sex with . . . with Charging Elk." It was peculiar how saying the strange name made their relationship seem distant and impersonal. She was glad he was not François anymore.

"I see. And did the defendant"—he waved his hand toward the prisoner's dock—"also desire sex with the deceased?"

"He didn't know . . . no."

"Then how in the world could Monsieur Breteuil have sex with an unwilling partner, a man who didn't even know him?"

Marie looked down at her gloved hands and remembered how heavy and awkward she had felt with the beautiful man. Even now, in the august chamber with the magistrates and the other officials finely dressed in their red robes and black robes, she felt more like the farm girl from the Vaucluse than a whore in the big port city. At the same time, she felt a sort of serenity that comes from being emotionally drained.

"He gave me some powder that would put François—Charging Elk—to sleep. I was to put it in the wine . . ."

Once again she heard a commotion from the balcony—even a few whistles of derision—but she didn't look up. They were not important.

The advocate, looking at the jurymen, said, "In essence, you drugged the defendant, Monsieur Charging Elk, so that Breteuil could have sex with him. Is that correct?"

"Yes."

"And were you paid for this—this favor?"

"Yes."

"How much?"

"Twenty francs." Marie looked at the jury for the first time. "But I didn't want it. I wanted nothing to do with it, as God is my witness. He threatened—"

"That will be enough, mademoiselle." The sharp voice of the chief magistrate startled Marie. "We do not tolerate such outbursts in this courtroom. As for God, you may have cause to invoke his forgiveness whenever you think upon your part in this."

"If it pleases the court, I will conclude my interview with just a couple of questions." The advocate glanced down at a piece of paper an assistant offered. "So you and the deceased plotted to drug Monsieur Charging Elk, who, I might add, was completely innocent of your scheme, as he is innocent of most things in our so-called civilized society. But did you actually see the fruits of your labor—for which you were paid the grand sum of twenty francs—the sex act being performed by the deviant?"

With an abrupt scraping of his chair, the procureur stood. "I must object to this inflammatory term, your honors. While we all, as God-fearing men, frown upon the nature of the homosexual act, in some quarters, indeed in the deceased's milieu, it is considered quite normal. Much like the young lady's chosen profession." He smiled toward the jury, his ruddy face now genial with camaraderie. "Besides which, I believe my worthy but desperate friend is trying to shift the onus of responsibility for this remarkably heinous crime away from his client."

The chief magistrate agreed that the prosecutor's objection was justified and warned the advocate against any like insinuations. He ordered that the advocate's last remark be deleted from the record.

"Forgive me, your honors," the advocate said with a slight bow and a slight smile. "Just one more question, if it pleases the court." He left his desk and walked toward the witness stand, removing his spectacles along the way. He glanced up at the magistrates, as if expecting them to stop him from invading this neutral space. Finally, he stopped little more than a meter from the witness stand and folded his arms. He turned slowly, deliberately, three-quarters of a turn to his left, until he was looking toward the prisoner's dock. "Take a good look, Mademoiselle Colet. That is the man accused of the murder of Monsieur Armand Breteuil. Even now, he understands imperfectly the nature of these proceedings. See how he looks at you? I would wager all of my meager salary that he is remembering the many Saturday nights he came to see you, exclusively you, because he found in you someone he could trust—and yes, in his own way, love." He turned back and looked into her eyes. "Can you find it in your heart to say that this man is guilty of anything more than defending himself from an assault on his dignity and pride? Can you say you feel nothing for this man? Surely you must regret your complicity in the wicked act perpetrated by the pervert Breteuil—"

"I object! This is beyond the bounds of propriety! For shame!"

But before the chief magistrate could admonish him, the advocate held up his hands and said, "I am finished with this witness. Thank you."

René was surprisingly cheerful on the witness stand. After being scolded for waving at Charging Elk, he told of a normal, happy family, an honest family, and how the defendant had fit right in, had in fact become a second son to the little fishmonger. He worked hard in the fish stall, he only took a little wine with his meals, and he taught Réne's daughter how to draw a horse. In turn, his daughter and son gave the defendant lessons in proper French, not Provençal, as the government so ordered. Even after Charging Elk left the Soulases' home, he came every Sunday and every holiday to dinner. He was a very generous man who brought them all presents. And as anyone could see, he had become a proper gentleman. "But you should have seen him as I first saw him in Buffalo Bill's Wild West show—a whooping, naked savage who scared the children half to death." René laughed and lifted his arm toward Charging Elk, but remembered the scolding and snatched it back. "Forgive me, your graces," he said.

Some in the balcony laughed, and the advocate sat down, satisfied with the personable little fishmonger's portrayal of his client's character. The prosecutor then stood and blotted his forehead with a handkerchief. He smiled at René, a broad smile, as though he shared in the good humor that had broken the monotonous tension of the courtroom.

"You make me wish I had seen this Wild West show, monsieur. It would surely be preferable to sitting in a stuffy courtroom, bent on a sad duty." The prosecutor wiped his upper lip with the handkerchief. His ruddy face had become splotchy in the heat. "And let me add that I respect your noble profession. To offer our citizens the fruits of the sea—I'm sure at very little profit to yourself—is certainly a high calling."

"Thank you, your honor."

The prosecutor laughed. "You give me too much authority, monsieur. I am a simple prosecutor, not worthy of such an appellation." He glanced up at the magistrates, one of whom was actually smiling. "I appreciate your honesty in describing your family life. It is rare these days that such a generous family exists, what with all the trouble with the immigrants and socialists. To take in a total stranger—especially a savage given to war whoops and nakedness—is truly commendable."

"Thank you."

"You say that the defendant lived with you for two years—two idyllic years, if I understand correctly."

"Yes."

"And he was happy with your little family, he ate madame's excellent cooking, he played with the children, he enjoyed working in the fish stall and taking a little wine with his meals . . ."

"Oh yes. He was quite happy in our home. He never took too much wine."

"Then why do you suppose this happy—savage—insisted on moving out after only two years?"

René thought a moment. He didn't want to say the wrong thing.

"To a neighborhood that can only be termed a hellhole of North Africans and Turks, of thieves and cutthroats? To a shabby, dingy one-room flat in the worst neighborhood in all of Marseille?"

"I ask myself that, monsieur! I say, Why Le Panier? But

Charging Elk—he is very happy here. He says the people remind him of his own."

"Ah! He finds the true Frenchmen, the God-fearing natives of this soil, not to his liking?" The prosecutor had directed his question to the jury. There was not a dark face among them.

The hawk-faced advocate objected, and the chief magistrate agreed that the question was inflammatory. The prosecutor explained that he was merely trying to establish a pattern of behavior that began when the defendant left a fine French family and went to live in an area of the city where the morals of the inhabitants left much to be desired. The magistrate relented but warned the prosecutor to establish his pattern a little more objectively.

The solicitor thanked the court and went on. "Monsieur Soulas, you say the defendant—after he moved out—came to your house every Sunday to enjoy a pleasant dinner and a romp with the children. Is that correct?"

"Yes, of course. Although the children were a little too old to romp with. You understand how it is with children. They grow up." René laughed, but it was a tentative laugh. "He especially enjoyed my dear wife's dinners—he always ate two helpings of everything—and we would have a nice talk and often a stroll."

"Never missed a Sunday?"

René again thought for a moment. He didn't want to answer. He was under oath to God, an oath he took very seriously.

"Isn't it true that he stopped coming to Sunday dinner some two months before the incident he is being tried for?"

"Because of his job. To work in a soap factory is very taxing. Often he was too tired."

"I understand, monsieur. So he quit coming to Sunday dinner because his job made him tired."

"Yes."

"But not too tired to satisfy himself with the young prostitute every Saturday night. Doesn't that strike you as an insult to your hospitality, Monsieur Soulas?"

René looked up to the balcony. He could just see Madeleine's shoulders and head above the balustrade. She sat rigidly with little expression, and René realized then that their lives would not be the same again. They would never again be so trusting.

"He is a man," he said glumly.

CHAPTER SEVENTEEN

artin St-Cyr's column, "La Vie de Marseille," normally came out twice weekly, on Tuesdays and Fridays, but since the trial began it had appeared every day, under such headings as "A Strange Justice," "The Forgotten Flag," and "Innocent in the Dock?" He railed against a justice system that seemed to have been imported from Paris and had little to do with the values and traditions of the Marseillais. He wrote of the shameless trampling of the *tricolore* that had been proudly raised over the Bastille by bloody but unbowed peasants and workers. He accused politicians of failing in their duty to protect the citizenry by appointing to office mediocre men whose sole attribute was slavery to a corrupt system.

But he was at his most deadly in portraying Charging Elk as a victim of not only the district court but of the American and French governments. He noted that the only American to testify was an obscure solicitor who toiled in the bowels of the consulate and seemed not to have seen the light of day around the Old Port. He professed to know nothing of the Charging Elk affair, except that the American government was investigating. Meanwhile, the only official who knew anything about the affair, former vice-consul Franklin Bell, had been sent packing to America, far beyond the reach of the court.

As for the French government, it had become so enmeshed in its medieval bureaucracy that it had done absolutely nothing to help the poor savage find his way home four long years ago. This was a crime that needn't have been committed; indeed, should never have occurred in anyone's wildest imaginings. The savage, Charging Elk, should long have been back in America "riding gaily across the plains of his beloved Dakota, hunting and fishing with his comrades, or perhaps married to a comely squaw and settled into a productive life of raising papooses and corn. Who is to blame for the murder of Breteuil, the master planner of his own fate? And who is to blame for the inevitable execution of the savage? Consider, citizens of Marseille! Raise your voices!"

Charging Elk sat in the black police wagon, which was carrying him back to the jail in the Préfecture, and listened to the voices in the street. He had made this journey for three weeks now and it always depressed him. He would have to give up his suit for the gray prisoner's uniform. He would be locked away in the small cell with the high window. And he would be fed the sour soup with the stringy green things and the dry bread which disintegrated into hard crumbs when he bit into it.

He knew the end was near. He could hear it in the voices in the courtroom; he could tell by the harshness in the red-robed judge's voice as he constantly interrupted Charging Elk's advocate to scold him for one thing or another. During a break, his advocate climbed

the small curving stairs to the prisoner's dock to ask Charging Elk
if he could think of anything to say that might be of help. He had a
right to speak and would be asked to speak shortly. The advocate's
narrow face gleamed with a pasty glaze of sweat, and his eyes were
hollow with frustration. Charging Elk could almost see through the
skin to the bony structure of the advocate's skull, and it discon-
certed him. He felt as though he were looking into the face of his
own impending death. He answered in a voice that was at once
calm and unfamiliar. "I would like to say something to the big men,"
he said, gesturing with his head to the front of the courtroom.

That had been the day before, but so far he hadn't been asked to
speak. Now he leaned forward and looked out one of the windows.
There was one on each side of the wagon and they were barely
twenty centimeters square. The first week of the trial, he had
looked forward to the ride through the streets of Marseille. He saw
familiar buildings, a few men and women in the streets, shop windows full of suits and dresses and cooking pans and maritime
equipment, dogs, wagons and carriages, horses of all types, from
smart matched sets of blacks or whites to lumbering beasts who
pulled their burdens with their heads down and eyes closed. At
first, these sights had excited him, but now he mostly dozed in the
hot, nearly airless confinement of the rolling box.

Perhaps it was the voices that had entered his consciousness —
he had almost never heard voices before, certainly none this loud
and insistent — but he leaned forward to look out the window. And
he saw several people lining the street. Some were well dressed but
most seemed to be workers and even immigrants in shirtsleeves and
suspenders, the women in shabby dresses and soiled aprons. Many
of them carried umbrellas against the burning sun; most wore hats
or bonnets; some were bareheaded. The voices seemed to be shouting the same thing, a kind of angry chant that he couldn't make out.
But he almost grasped what was happening. He had seen demon-

strations several times before, and he thought the police wagon had been caught in the middle of a protest against higher taxes or low wages or some new restriction. But then he saw a placard raised above the heads of a knot of protesters, and his jaw dropped. He kneeled on the bench to get a better look, and there it was—his name, just as Mathias had taught him to draw it: CHARGING ELK LIBRE! He crossed the short distance to the other window, grazing his head on the low ceiling, but he didn't notice. There were even more people on this side of the street, as it was in the shade. And he saw more placards, some with his name, others with other words that he did not know.

A young man in a collarless shirt and bright yellow straw cap broke loose from the crowd and ran alongside the wagon. He pointed at Charging Elk's face, or that portion of his face that was visible, and shouted back at the crowd. Suddenly they too pointed and clapped and shouted his name and *"Vive!"* and *"Libre!"* The placards bobbed above their heads, and Charging Elk grew dizzy from trying to see so much through the little window. He lurched to the back when the wagon abruptly picked up speed, and by the time he got back to the window, there were only a few people in the street and no placards. And when the wagon turned into the service entrance to the Prefecture, he heard only a slight buzzing in his head and he knew he was in danger of passing out from the heat. Still, he had heard them—*Vive! Libre! Charging Elk!*—and he tried to think what it all might mean.

Martin St-Cyr had watched the demonstration with a great deal of satisfaction. Although there were only a few gendarmes present and no threat of violence, the anger and self-righteousness reminded him of his student days in Grenoble. The daily rallies and marches that took the students and workers from the university to

Place St-André, to the Palais de Justice, came back to him with a fuzzy warmth that obscured the fear and panic he felt when the gendarmes waded into the crowd with their truncheons swinging. But he did remember looking out from the safety of the Palais and seeing his fellows stagger away, their hands holding their bloodied heads, or lying in the street, moaning and twitching. He was confident this demonstration (or, he hoped, series of demonstrations) wouldn't come to that, but one could never be certain. The riots in Grenoble had started out with such boisterous but peaceable intentions.

St-Cyr's columns had created a sensation in the streets. Everywhere he went, people were talking about the trial, and it was true that the great majority had the opinion that the Peau-Rouge was being tried for a crime that was not rightfully his own. The crime happened before the killing when the invert performed his nefarious act. And the girl, this Marie What's-her-name, should be locked up for her role in the deception. Too bad the savage hadn't done her in too.

Although St-Cyr had been pleased at this reaction, nothing much was happening. The people stood in markets or sat in cafés and restaurants and talked about the scandal as though it were too exotic to be a part of their lives. He heard time and time again a man or a woman, with a knowing shrug, say, "But that is what happens down there," meaning the waterfront with all of its foreigners and thugs and whorehouses and American bars, which was not the same Marseille they lived in.

Three days before the first demonstration, St-Cyr had decided to get involved in more than a journalistic way. The time was ripe to organize something that would shake the city fathers to their well-polished boots. Some months earlier he had interviewed three students from the Faculté des Sciences et Techniques who had led a series of demonstrations against the Centre Universitaire for firing

a professor for his socialist views. The students' fervor and his own
column had not dissuaded the university from its intent, but St-Cyr
had been impressed with the young anarchists. So he had tracked
them down. They had been expelled from university for the rest of
the year but they were popular troublemakers and still met at the
Café Belfleur on Rue de Crimée, where he had interviewed them
before. And they were more than interested in the cause of the savage, Charging Elk. They had led small demonstrations protesting
the exploitation of the Algerians, but the persecution of "the vanishing American" (as St-Cyr himself termed the plight of the
American Indian) was more than they could bear. They began immediately to make plans, to suggest names of the union leaders, the
socialists, the radical Catholics, their university comrades, even immigrant leaders, who could use the rally to protest the treatment of
immigrants in France. By the time St-Cyr caught a hansom cab
back downtown, he was full of high hopes and more than a little impressed with his own behind-the-scene machinations.

And the protests had come off. The crowd increased day by day,
from less than a hundred to six to eight hundred, which completely
filled Place Montyon beside the Palais de Justice. The leaders took
turns making speeches, not all of them protesting the injustice done
to Charging Elk, but all containing the same object of protest: government. The French government, the American government, the
government of Marseille and the Midi. Most speeches blasted the
corrupt politicians who looked the other way or actually facilitated
the exploitation of the workers and immigrants by business interests.

Songs were sung—Provençal songs about bravery, loyalty, and
independence. At least twice a day "La Marseillaise" was sung in
the proper fighting spirit of the Revolution. Even the great poet
Frédéric Mistral gave a speech about the pride of the Provençal
people and the necessity to speak their native tongue to ensure the

survival of their culture. He ignored the plight of Charging Elk and the other immigrants. And in fact, while the crowd listened with patience and even awe, the small, white-haired poet seemed strangely out of place among the protesters. Nevertheless, St-Cyr made him the hero of his next day's column, portraying him as the fiery patron saint of the Félibrige, a movement to preserve the Provençal language and traditions against a "cold, grasping French government, which had on more than one occasion threatened him with silence . . . and still he sings the songs of the people, undaunted, fearless in the face of the puppet-politicians who would still the tongue of Provence's—and yes, France's—greatest poet by any desperate means possible."

St-Cyr was not satisfied with this column. He had tried to associate the poet with the Indian, but it was next to impossible. The man sounded more like an academician than an activist. He apparently had no interest in the cause at hand and certainly no interest in playing to the crowd. But the crowd was there, and that was the important thing. With a few deft strokes of the pen, St-Cyr had made it seem that the poet was as outraged at the proceedings inside the courtroom as all the citizens of Marseille.

But things were not going well for Charging Elk and his advocate. After the first demonstration the chief magistrate had ordered the windows closed and the drapes drawn. And while the sounds were not completely muffled—for instance, "La Marseillaise" almost raised the spectators to their feet—the rest became a dull background noise, interrupted briefly by shouts and applause.

Of course, everybody in the courtroom knew what was going on. Except for the jurors, they read the newspapers every day. And when court adjourned for the day, the spectators rushed outside to stand among the demonstrators as they waited for the black police wagon to begin its journey back to the Préfecture. And when they saw it, they cheered as loudly as anyone. The jurors themselves were kept informed by the bailiff, who swore them to secrecy.

But the protests only seemed to make the magistrates irritable and seemingly anxious to get to the closing arguments. Charging Elk did get a chance to speak, but he made a poor job of it—at least in French. The advocate had coached him in the ready room, appealing to him to admit his guilt but explain that it was an impulsive act in response to the terrible act being committed on him. Above all, he said, ask for the court's mercy.

And so Charging Elk began, "I am Charging Elk, son of Scrub and Doubles Back Woman, grandson of Scabby Bull and Goodkill. I am of the Lakota tribe. I come from America with Buffalo Bill and my Lakota friends. But they are gone now and I am alone. For four years I have lived among you but you do not know me and I do not know you. Even the white birds that fly among your fire boats and fishing boats I do not know. The fish that you bring from the big waters are not tasty to me. Even the meat of your animals is not filling to one who has tasted the flesh of the buffalo. I do not know of this room full of laws or that man"—he pointed to the prosecutor—"who tells you that Charging Elk is a bad man. I see these men in the long box listen to him with big ears and I know they are with him. And yet I have only done what any of my people would do when they come upon a *siyoko*—" Charging Elk stopped suddenly and ran his hand over his nose and mouth. He hadn't thought about it before, but now he realized that he did not have the French words to explain about evil. It could only be explained in the Lakota tongue. He stood for a moment, confused, feeling a helplessness that hadn't visited him for some time. But slowly his thoughts swirled and gathered themselves in his head, as a bird builds a nest out of all those bits of things that lie on the ground and in the trees and are of no use to men. Then, in Lakota, he explained about evil, how the *siyokos* were there among them even now, how the spirits wandered about searching for an opportunity to perform their evil, how the bespectacled one, Breteuil as he was called, had the misfortune to be susceptible to evil. And yet there he was in Marie's room that night, with the *siyoko* within, doing the evil's bidding. And so Charging Elk had had to kill him to get rid of the evil.

Charging Elk kept his eyes on the magistrates as he spoke but he knew, by the silence, that all of the people gathered in the courtroom were listening. Even the dull noise outside the room seemed to have stopped. Many times in the past four years Wakan Tanka had made him invisible to the people in this land, but now he wanted them to see him, to hear him. And in some way, the Great Mystery had opened their ears to his words. And so he thanked Wakan Tanka for giving him the good words that opened the hearts of these people and allowed them to see into his own.

After he finished speaking, Charging Elk remained standing, hands lightly gripping the railing of the prisoner's dock, and looked around at all the people in the courtroom—the jurors, the prosecutor and his helpers, his own advocate, the tables of reporters, and the people in the balcony. They were all looking at him, even the reporters, who had written nothing during his speech. But he was especially interested in the balcony. Marie was not there, but he didn't expect her to be. But René was there, not far from him. If the dock had been a little closer to the balcony, René could have leaned down and shaken his hand.

The fishmonger had a sad smile on his face, but Charging Elk saw him as he first saw him in the office of the police captain—the slicked-back black hair almost gone on top, the missing lower front teeth, the kind eyes—and he was sorry for the shame he had brought on the home of the family that had cared for him when he probably would have died on his own. He wanted to thank him—

and Madeleine. But she wasn't there. Charging Elk knew that she had little patience for things that went on outside her home, and the many sleeps of the trial had bored even him. Still, he was disappointed that he wouldn't see her again.

The chief magistrate finally cleared his throat and all eyes swung from Charging Elk to him. "I hope the jurors understood the accused's statement better than I did," he said, and the whole courtroom burst into laughter.

The next day it rained. Overnight the tramontane had kicked up, blowing in a long, continuous slide of gray clouds from the northwest. It wasn't a hard rain but it was steady. It rained all day, cooling the pavement and the brick and stone buildings, bringing in a fresh damp smell that made the town seem almost young. Suddenly the streets were filled with people, some with umbrellas, some without. It didn't seem to matter whether one got wet or not. The people walked with more bounce in their steps and more purpose. They went into shops and came out with their baskets brimming with good cheese, fresh fish, perhaps a new pair of stockings or some colored candles. Some men loitered on corners, smoking and laughing. It was already near the end of August and the rain was the first rain of summer.

Perhaps the demonstrators had decided to join their more unconcerned fellow citizens in enjoying the coolness that the rain brought, but the turnout at the Palais de Justice was remarkably sparse. Less than fifty people milled about Place Montyon, and they seemed hesitant, rudderless. The only speaker among them was an old man in an oilskin cape and sandals who warned them about the wages of sin and the wrath of God. It was unclear whether he was referring to the particular sins being discussed in the court of law or those vague sins that are committed every day in an offhand way. Finally, he demanded a cigarette from one of the demonstrators and ambled off down the street, smoking and growling. And the demonstrators, singly, in pairs, in small knots, began to drift away in all directions. They did not seem particularly angry today, or even reluctant to leave Place Montyon. And why should they? The rain had made Marseille young again.

The jurors were out for only two hours, and when they filed back into the jury box, their expressions were much as they were on the very first day of the trial—expectant, somber—but now battle-weary. The only difference was that each now had a recognizable face after the long days of trial—and presumably a family, or a lover, or an aging mother, a life that he was anxious to get home to. Many of them had worn the same dark suits since the trial began and were ready to put them away for a long time. Many of their families had suffered financially. All these things may have contributed to the brief deliberation—or they may have found that there was very little to discuss, that in the end the decision was remarkably simple.

"Will the defendant please rise." It was not a question. Charging Elk got to his feet and stood tall, hands clasped in front of him. He had been used to hearing small sounds in the room—a chair squeak, a low whisper, a cough or the rattle of paper. Now it was silent. "How finds the jury?"

The foreman stood, and Charging Elk was surprised to see that he was the youngest of the men. His thin, almost frail body reminded Charging Elk of Mathias. But his voice was strong and clear. "We find the defendant guilty, as charged, of the act of murder, your honor."

The abrupt reaction in the balcony made Charging Elk look around. There were whistles of disapproval and loud groans amid a buzz of rapid conversation. Then he heard the familiar sound of the magistrate's wooden hammer banging on the desk.

"That will be enough!" he shouted. "We will have order in this court!" When the buzz died away, he said, "Let me remind you, this is a very serious procedure. If I hear another word, I will have the entire balcony cleared. You may mark my words."

The chief magistrate stared into the balcony for a full minute until there was again not a sound in the room, except for the scratching of the journalists' pencils. Satisfied, he turned to the jurors and thanked them for their patience and good judgment. Then he conferred with his fellow magistrates for a moment before speaking again. "After discussing the matter, the court finds that the act was committed with provocation and without premeditation. While murder is never justified in a civilized society, we do believe that the two conditions constitute mitigating circumstances under which the crime was committed.

"Before passing sentence I feel compelled to point out that the man who now stands convicted of murder is not of a civilized race of people. It is clear that he does not hold the same beliefs and principles that contribute to an orderly, law-abiding society. We may deduce from the gibberish we heard yesterday that passes for language among his people and from the pattern of his behavior leading up to the crime, as the *procureur-général* so ably laid out, that he simply cannot conform to even the most elementary code of conduct—and therefore will always remain a threat to society." The chief magistrate paused and removed his spectacles. His pale eyes searched out the prisoner's dock. "It is the judgment of this court that the convicted felon be removed to a highly secured place of detention where he will spend the rest of his natural life contemplating this most heinous crime." He put the spectacles on and picked up his portfolio. "This court stands adjourned."

St-Cyr sat for a moment and watched Charging Elk stand patiently as the two gendarmes fitted him with handcuffs and ankle bracelets. The heavy chain between them clanked and clattered on the floor with a din of finality that sent shivers up his back. So this is how it ends, he thought. This is the reality—the harsh sound of iron in the sudden serenity of the gloomy wood-paneled room. The room itself seemed cavernous now and almost unbearably empty as the last of the officials and spectators filed out.

St-Cyr didn't know how he felt, and that surprised him. He had been ready to rush out with the other journalists to write his column, which was due in the next day's *Gazette*, but his legs were curiously weak and he just felt empty of thought or emotion. Should he have felt good? His columns had transformed the trial from a mere scandal into a *cause célèbre*—all the people in the markets and cafés, on the quais of the Old Port, even in the salons of the *haute bourgeoisie*, were talking about the case. And he had been able to organize an outcry in the streets, in a somewhat devious but effective manner. And most important of all, Charging Elk had escaped the guillotine, which was a minor miracle—perhaps a major miracle in his case. St-Cyr, in spite of his background as a crime reporter, then a columnist, had attended only one other trial—that of an elderly woman accused of poisoning her husband—but he had been in Marseille long enough to know that a case such as this almost always ended with a severed head. The crimes were harsh in the port city but the punishment was even harsher. But the court had been lenient, perhaps in part because of his columns and the public outcry they engendered. So he should have felt good, if not ecstatic, about Charging Elk's fate. But did he?

St-Cyr heard the scraping of chains on the wooden floor and he looked up and saw the gendarmes leading Charging Elk from the room. Without thinking he called out, *"Adieu, mon ami! Bonne chance!"* But when the tall Indian hesitated for a moment to look down at him, St-Cyr knew why he didn't feel good. It was the eyes. The same eyes he had looked into when he first met Charging Elk in the cell of the Préfecture four years before. They had already gone dead.

St-Cyr sat at the long table until he no longer heard the scrape of the chains. His small triumphs had been as hollow and empty as he now felt. He had betrayed Charging Elk. The court had betrayed Charging Elk. St-Cyr sighed, but it came out more like a rueful gasp. Then he picked up his pencil and wrote: *I'm afraid the court has done the poor savage no favor by giving him life in prison over death. I looked into his eyes as he was being led away in chains and I saw a living death. May his God forgive us all.*

CHAPTER EIGHTEEN

L a Tombe was located in the extreme southwest of France, in the dry hills behind Carcassonne, not far from Montségur, which the Crusaders of Louis IX laid siege to, capturing the Cathars and burning them alive in a great bonfire. This was in 1244.

La Tombe itself had been a Crusader fortress. It had long fallen into ruin by 1866. At that time, the French government decided it needed a high-security prison to supplement Devil's Island, the penal colony off the coast of French Guiana. And so they built the prison on the foundation of the ancient fortress. The walls, made of stone, were three meters thick at the base, tapering to one meter thirty centimeters at the top. The walls ran 300 meters one way and 250 the other. Watchtowers stood at the corners of the walls, each with a small open window that looked down into the caked-earth yard. In the yard itself stood three identical long buildings connected at each end and in the middle by enclosed walkways. Tucked away in the corner by the gate was a smaller building with two white columns supporting a triangular stone pediment, the only architectural feature within the walls that wasn't built on the square. Outside the walls, terraced vegetable gardens led down the hill to the small village of St-Paul-de-Fenouillet. But the inmates once they entered the prison would never see the gardens or the village again. They would not see anything but the blue sky, the sun, the clouds, and the rare bird.

La Tombe accepted only the worst criminals in France—serial killers, men who had murdered and dismembered their mistresses, a doctor who had poisoned five wives, a *chocolatier* who had disemboweled several boys in Nantes, a young vintner who had burned his father- and mother-in-law alive by dousing them in cognac and setting it afire—and of course the usual array of unrepentant cutthroats and thugs who had somehow managed to escape the guillotine. Unlike Devil's Island, La Tombe held no political prisoners to speak of—just a handful of men who preferred to think of their crimes as a particularly vicious form of anarchy.

The prison was officially named Samatan Prison but was nicknamed La Tombe for the obvious reason that nobody would leave there alive. Although it had been in existence for only twenty-seven years, by 1894 215 inmates had died within its walls, only forty-eight by natural causes.

It was to this prison that Charging Elk was bound on the night train from Marseille to Perpignan. He sat in a private compartment along with two guards from the Préfecture de Police and looked out the window into the darkness while the guards played cards. As he watched for occasional lighted farms and villages, he thought of the night train from Lyon or Vienne—he couldn't remember which—to Marseille. He remembered how Featherman exclaimed each time they saw a village or a chateau in the moonlight, how his own heart had jumped up when he saw a horse that looked like High Runner. And he remembered even further back to when the train pulled out of the station in Gordon, Nebraska. His parents along with the others on the platform had sung their braveheart song to the young Indians. He had sat for a long time with his father's breastplate on his lap—young, apprehensive, even fearful of what lay ahead. But he had been excited by the prospect of traveling far and seeing much. Although he didn't know exactly how it would happen, he looked forward to riding a horse, chasing buffalo, pretending to fight the soldiers before a large audience of *wasichus*. Best of all, he knew that he would return to Pine Ridge in two years with many of the American frogskins in his purse. He could get married and acquire many horses, a thought that had seemed so impossible on those winter nights out at the Stronghold.

One of guards exclaimed and slapped a handful of cards down. The other groaned. And Charging Elk searched for lights in the pitch-black landscape outside the rumbling wagon as it made its way along the Mediterranean coastline bound for Perpignan and, finally, La Tombe.

Charging Elk spent his first week in an underground cave secured by iron bars. The cave was one of a series dug out by the Crusaders to store their wine and grains and dried fish. They butchered animals in the caves and hung the carcasses to cure and keep in the cool, dry air. Now the prison utilized the caves as a kind of reception area. All new prisoners had to undergo this trial by claustrophobia and light deprivation. The only lights were gas lamps on the walls of a central corridor. Charging Elk shared his cave with three others, all of whom seemed to choose to suffer in silence. In fact, there was very little in the way of noise down there. He learned to recognize the squeaking wheels of the trolley that brought the soup and bread. He could hear a murmur of voices from the guard's station at the head of the corridor once in a while.

One night he heard a roar coming from a cell across the way, followed by a silence. Then another roar, and another; then it was quiet. Charging Elk had gotten up and walked to the bars and looked around. He was almost certain there was some kind of wild beast in one of the caves. But he could see nothing. And he never heard another roar.

When the week was up, he was led aboveground and across the dazzling yellow earth of the yard to one of the long buildings. Although his eyes were squinted almost shut against the harsh light and he could barely see the back of the guard in front of him, he felt the warm tears leaking down onto his cheeks. Then he was in the building and his eyes didn't hurt so much.

He was led into a small room, where he was ordered to strip and wash himself. Then he was deloused and given a pair of thin gray trousers and a blouse made of the same material. Both garments had vertical stripes, which had once been black but now were just a darker shade of gray. He was given a folded blanket, a slop bucket, and a battered tin cup. Then he was led through a walkway into another building by the two guards. They climbed a set of iron stairs up to the second level, then walked down a wide corridor flanked by cells on both sides. The cells all had floor-to-ceiling iron bars, unlike his cell back in the Préfecture, so the inmates within could see clearly into the corridor. But there were no windows looking outside.

Charging Elk was surprised, after the silence of the caves, to hear the inmates talking with each other across the corridor or in their cells. Although he looked straight ahead, he could see out of the corners of his eyes that the cells had two beds and two inmates in each. He wasn't surprised that the conversations stopped when he walked by. He could feel the eyes of all the men in the cells watching him.

Finally the lead guard stopped and inserted a key into one of the

cells near the end of the corridor. He swung the door open and motioned for Charging Elk to enter. Only when he locked the door behind Charging Elk did he speak: "This is your home now. Keep it
clean." Then he and the other guard walked off.

"Insufferable bastards."

Charging Elk turned just as a clean-shaven man jumped off his
sleeping platform and walked up to him with the quick, fluid movement of a dancer or an acrobat. Charging Elk took a step backward, but the man extended his hand.

"Marcus Aurelius Causeret—and I too am innocent."

Charging Elk took the hand. "I am Charging Elk."

The man laughed. "Just as I thought. When I first laid eyes on
you just one moment ago I said to myself, 'Believe it or not, that is
an American Indian.' Well, Monsieur Charging Elk, welcome to
our suite."

"But how could you tell?"

"How could I not tell? Did I not go to the Wild West show every
night when it was in Paris? Did I not wander through your village
of tipis every chance I got?"

Charging Elk was still holding the blanket, the slop bucket, and the
tin cup. This was the first time anybody, except René, had mentioned
the show in such a way. He was stunned. "Did you see me?" he said.

The man's eyes grew wide and a grin lit up his face. "You were
there? At the Exposition Universelle?"

"Yes. I performed every afternoon and every evening. I played
poker in the village and saw many famous sights in Paris."

"Small world!" The man laughed. "I'm certain I saw you, but no,
I don't recognize you. I just recognize the physiognomy. The
American Indian is very striking, but there is a similarity among
them. To an untrained eye like mine, you all looked alike—no offense intended, my friend."

"No, no." Charging Elk smiled. He couldn't believe his luck in finding a man who had seen him perform in Paris, whether this Causeret knew it or not. "The people of Marseille—except for the immigrants—all looked alike to me."

"Ah, Marseille. We French call it the armpit of France. We look down our long noses at this foul, flyblown dark hole of—what?— pestilence! See? We don't even know what. That's what." Causeret held his head back so that he did actually look down his nose at Charging Elk. He had to lean back a way because he was a head shorter.

"What are you here for?" Charging Elk set the slop bucket down and threw the blanket on the unoccupied bed. He didn't know what to do with the tin cup.

"Right to the point. I like that." Causeret climbed back onto his cot and sat with his legs crossed beneath him. "They say I murdered my wife and her lover. They say I found them in bed together—my marriage bed, incidentally—and cut both their throats. They say it was a particularly gruesome affair. They say I actually laughed when I described the murders to the police. The newspapers called me a heartless fiend. No remorse. They say if I had shown just a bit of remorse I might have gotten off—crime of passion, you see, the wronged husband."

Charging Elk sat down tentatively on his cot and looked at the lithe, clean-shaven man. At first glance, he had looked almost frail, but now Charging Elk could see that Causeret's shoulders were wide, his arms longer than usual, and his waist small. There was an energy, a quickness, about him. Even his speech was fast—but clear. Charging Elk could understand much of what he said, especially the part about cutting the throats of his wife and her lover.

"But you are innocent," he said.

Causeret laughed again. "Of course, my friend. You will find that we are all innocent in here." He suddenly shouted, "Dax! Are you innocent?"

A lazy voice from across the corridor answered, "It goes without saying."

"You see? I'll bet you're innocent too."

Charging Elk was still looking across the corridor. He hadn't really thought of himself as innocent or guilty—except in the eyes of the courtroom. He had done what he had to do. It was that simple.

"And what did you do that you're innocent of?"

"Killed a—a man."

Causeret leaned forward with his hands on his knees and an almost gentle smile. "Did he need killing?"

"He—he was evil."

Causeret slapped both knees and laughed. "Good enough for me! 'He was evil.' I hadn't thought of that one." He suddenly flopped back and stretched out on the cot. He lay perfectly still, looking up at the ceiling.

Charging Elk waited, but when the man said nothing, he took off his shoes—the brown dress shoes which by now were dull and scuffed beyond hope—and lay back on his own cot. He closed his eyes and felt his whole body melt. He hadn't realized how tense he had been for the past several months. It had become his natural state ever since he had killed Breteuil. But now that he was here—and would remain here until he died—he felt it all, all the days of jail and the trial, the train ride, his past, let go and he didn't care if he ever moved again.

"Buckwheat and horsehair—that's what these pads are stuffed with. You'll get used to it." The man spoke without moving. When Charging Elk didn't respond, Causeret said, "You want to know what I did on the outside?" After a pause, he said, "I was a juggler. I juggled at flea markets, outside theaters, velodromes, fairs, you name it. Did lots of fairs, all over. Batons, torches, balls—I could juggle watermelons. Think of it. Big, fat watermelons. I could balance a watermelon on a stick on my chin. I could balance a chair on

one leg on my chin. Crazy, isn't it? I'm probably the only man you'll
ever meet with a callus on his chin." Another long silence. "That's
how I came to be at the Wild West show in Paris. I performed outside the gate before the show. And when the show began, I went inside. I'm sure I saw you." Causeret lay quietly for several minutes.
Then he said, "Itinerant juggler. That's what they called me, because I performed all over — Lyon, Orléans, Tours, Besançon,
Bordeaux. Never got to Marseille. Pity. Can you imagine? They
call me itinerant because I go where the work is. How can I be itinerant when I have a wife and a home, I tell them. So the magistrate
says, Well, you don't have a wife and home anymore. You killed
your wife and you are in jail. If you can find the justice in that,
please enlighten me, monsieur."

But Charging Elk had fallen into a deep sleep, one beyond voices
or thoughts or even dreams. He had never slept this deeply before,
not even as a child on the Little Bighorn River, nor as a young man
out at the Stronghold, nor as a bone-weary performer in Paris, not
even after an exhausting day of shoveling coal into the furnaces of
the soap factory. If he could have caught himself on a limb on his
way down into the black hole of unconsciousness, he would have
gladly let go, for he would never again in his life come as close to
joining his ancestors as he did that late afternoon in La Tombe. The
sleep of death, he would later think ruefully, but not the real thing.

Charging Elk and Causeret were cellmates for three years, and
they became very close. Even out in the yard, during their one hour
a day of fresh air, they would wander the perimeter together,
Charging Elk for the exercise, Causeret looking for a means of escape. He had no doubt that he could scale the stone walls — that
was the easy part. But what would he do on the outside? He had
plans to go to America, but he didn't want to leave without

Charging Elk. Together they could make their way to Charging Elk's homeland and hide out in the hills. He was especially interested in the gold miners in Paha Sapa. Where did they find the gold? How much did they find? Where did they sell it? Charging Elk, of course, cared nothing about the gold, but to placate the juggler, he said the miners picked the gold up from the ground, big chunks of it. Once he had stubbed his toe on a piece of gold as big around as a watermelon. Causeret would become silent, almost sullen, at such news and Charging Elk would regret feeding the juggler's dreams.

But for the most part, Causeret was a good companion. He had a job in the kitchen and so twice a day, at four-thirty in the morning and again at three-thirty in the afternoon, he would be gone for three or four hours. Because he helped prepare food for the administrators and the guards, he would sometimes smuggle back a treat—a croissant in the morning, a sausage or chicken thigh in the afternoon. Once, a few days after Charging Elk had lamented that he would never see a piece of real meat again, he came back with a chunk of beef the size of his fist. As he watched Charging Elk tear into it, he said, "Good Lord, you have the jaws of a wolf."

Near the end of his third year, Charging Elk was summoned to the warden's office in the administration building in the corner of the yard near the heavy iron gates. As he was led into the small anteroom, he almost stopped in astonishment. Behind a desk of dark wood sat a woman who looked to be in her mid-thirties. She wasn't particularly attractive—her hair was pulled up into a tight bun, she wore no rouge or lipstick, her blouse was a stark white, and her long skirt, what he could see of it above her shoe tops, was black and slightly frayed at the edge. But she was a woman and he hadn't seen one in three years. He bowed awkwardly when the guard announced him.

The woman got up without a word and knocked on a door behind her. Charging Elk looked her up and down, from her small feet to her narrow waist to her small shoulders and slender neck. He immediately thought of Marie, but then another young woman came into his mind—the one who had given him the holy picture, which he now knew was Jesus Christ, the man who died for these people's sins. He remembered the pleasant, hopeful afternoon beside the lake in Paris. He tried to think of her name but couldn't.

The woman opened the door and stepped aside and said they could go in now. The guard pushed him gently in the back and Charging Elk said, "Sandrine," but no one seemed to hear.

The warden was block of a man, as wide in the waist and hips as in the shoulders, which pulled his suit coat taut to the point of catastrophe. His shiny bald head was jammed into a neck that was too short and thick for the stiff collar of his shirt. He had been writing something but now he stopped, placed the pen in a tray, and rolled a blotter over the wet ink. Then he looked up. His eyes were small and dark in the round, red face and his nose was incongruously long and thin. He looked like a strange bird that Charging Elk had once seen in a tabloid, a bird that couldn't fly.

"Ah, Monsieur Charging Elk. How goes it? All right?"

"Yes sir. Just fine."

"Very good." The warden picked up a wrinkled, damp handkerchief and mopped his forehead. "They tell me you are a good prisoner, you don't make trouble for us. Is that correct?"

"Yes sir."

"We like that and we are going to give you a little reward, a little more freedom. You would like that, wouldn't you?"

"Yes sir."

"We are going to move you to another unit. We think you will like the company there a little better. And you will have a few priv-

ileges that are currently denied you—more time outside your cell—
for legitimate purposes, of course—access to our library, such as it
is, and most important, a job. Now you can't complain about that,
can you?"

"No sir. Thank you."

"All right then. That's about it. Oh, one other thing—you will be
able to send and receive one letter each month, no funny business,
keep in mind that we read everything. And you may have up to two
visitors once every three months." The warden picked up his pen
and dipped it into an inkwell. That seemed to be an end to the interview, and the guard touched Charging Elk's elbow.

But the warden looked up again and the guard stepped back.
The warden smiled. It was a crooked smile as wide as his mouth
was long. Charging Elk tried to remember the name of the bird.
Somebody—Mathias?—had said the name.

"You must tell me sometime about your wild west. I hope to go
to America someday and I would like to see this country—the cowboys and the Indians and Buffalo Bill. Someday you will tell me
everything so that I may prepare for my journey. Yes?"

The next morning a guard arrived at Charging Elk's cell in another building, which was identical to the one he had just left. It
was five-thirty, an hour before breakfast time. He waited while
Charging Elk dressed, then led him down to the mess hall.

About thirty men were seated at one of the long tables. The
guard motioned for Charging Elk to sit at the far end. Then he went
away.

Charging Elk glanced up the table, taking in the faces, but not
one looked familiar. He had been a little surprised at the variety of
faces in the prison. Except for the immigrants, the men of Marseille
were of a certain type. There were variations, but for the most part,

they were shorter, darker, and thicker than most of the men in prison. But Causeret had told Charging Elk that the inmates came from all over France—some were even foreign. Charging Elk had already met an Englishman and a Dutchman, two of Causeret's friends. They had been in La Tombe long enough to have learned passable French.

Soon a small group of men in white aprons began to set bowls of mush, baskets of bread, and pitchers of water on the table. Some of the inmates groaned and protested but the men in the aprons paid no attention. And soon the malcontents were eating as fast as the others. Then the servers cleared off the food and bowls and set cups before each man. Pitchers of coffee and hot milk were passed down the table, and now the malcontents were yelling for sugar and complaining about the weakness of the coffee.

Charging Elk had just filled his cup when one of the guards banged his baton against a pan at the serving table and the men began to get up. He gulped the lukewarm liquid and stood along with them.

As they departed in various directions, a large, dark-skinned man ambled over to Charging Elk. He was a *wasichu* but he looked as if he had been baked in the sun for all the years of his life.

"You are this Charging Elk, yes?" He stood as tall as Charging Elk and ten kilos heavier. His heavy beard was streaked with white on his chin, otherwise coal-black. "Can you do a day's work?"

"I will do my best, monsieur."

"Come along, then."

Charging Elk and four others followed the big man out of the mess hall. They crossed the packed-earth yard toward the administration building. But instead of going in, they stopped before the main gates. A guard unlocked a small door in one of the gates and opened it. The big man stepped through and the others followed, Charging Elk bringing up the rear. He had to duck his head, and when he straightened up, he was overcome by the sight before him.

The first things that caught his eye were the green trees at the bottom of the hill. In the hazy morning light, they seemed to float above the valley floor, like round green balloons. Then he saw the little village of St-Paul-de-Fenouillet. Although the houses were all alike, with their whitewashed walls and orange roofs, to Charging Elk, who had become so accustomed to the dull yellow stone of the prison, they looked as exotic as circus tents. Beyond the valley, the hills were fuzzy with pine forests and stone outcroppings and meadows full of grazing sheep.

Charging Elk had never seen a more beautiful sight. Not even the smoky-black Paha Sapa could compare with such colors and lushness. Taking in the scene all at once, he realized that he had not really seen a country landscape in all his time in France. He had performed in cities, and when the show traveled, it was always at night after the last performance. And he had not been outside of Marseille in the four years he lived there.

One of the guards who had accompanied the men outside nudged him in the back. "Over there. To the toolshed."

Charging Elk followed the men to a low, ramshackle building with a thatched roof. Once inside, the big man handed Charging Elk a floppy straw hat. "Put it on. You'll need it." Then he grabbed a hoe, which had been hanging from a peg on the wall, and thrust it at the newcomer. "Come with me."

Charging Elk, in his almost mesmerized state of a few moments ago, had not really noticed the terraces of plants that grew down the hillside.

"Have you ever gardened before?"

"No, monsieur." The hat was too small for his head, and the stiff breeze that blew up the hill threatened to take it off.

"Do you know your plants?"

"Some," he said, thinking of Réne's flowers. "I know geraniums and lavender—and wild poppies."

The big man grunted in disgust as he led Charging Elk down a path through the terraces. He stopped at a series of long rows of thin, limp stalks. "These are onions. And over there, garlic." They walked down to another terrace. "And these are leeks. And those bushy ones just below us are tomatoes. Come."

Charging Elk followed the big man down to the rows of tomato plants. He noticed that there were five or six terraces of plants below them. Two of the men were down on one of the terraces taking things out of the ground and throwing them into a wheelbarrow.

"New potatoes," the man said. He had noticed the newcomer's eyes on the men. "And here we are." The man took the hoe from Charging Elk. "I plant my tomatoes in neat rows, as you see. Everything you see between the rows is a weed. I hate weeds. They are my enemies. At night I dream of weeds and always they are big and wild and threaten to strangle my vegetables. Here." He walked a couple of steps into the rows of tomatoes. He struck down with the hoe and chipped a clod of earth away, which he picked up. "You see? Bindweed. The very worst. Just one bindweed can strangle three of my tomatoes. This is a small one, but in one week it would begin its evil task." He handed the hoe back to Charging Elk. "Now it is up to you to save my beautiful tomatoes. You walk between the rows and every green thing that doesn't belong, you take out. And make sure you get all the roots. Do you understand?"

And so Charging Elk began the job that would fill his days for the rest of his time at La Tombe. Eight months a year, from early March to the end of October, he spent his days in the terraced gardens or in the apple and almond orchards at the bottom of the hill.

In the spring, he pushed a wheeled plow to break up the hardened soil, spread manure, mixed it in, and raked it smooth. He planted radishes and onions, leeks and peas and tomatoes. Then he tended them through the growing season, watering the plants, weeding and watching for pests. From mid to late summer he harvested vegetables, picked apples, and shook down the olives and almonds. In the fall, after the first frost, he pulled the spent plants, pruned the trees, and cleaned up debris. He repaired tools, sharpened hoes and shovels, straightened up the toolroom and the greenhouse. Then he walked through the prison gates for the last time each season, cold and tired, feeling a peculiar mixture of satisfaction and sadness.

And for the first few weeks, as the weather turned wintery, he would sit in his cell, wrapped in his blanket against the draft, and try not to think that he was there for the rest of his life. In the gardens, it was easy to forget. All the hard work beneath a blazing sun or a chilling rain blocked out any despair that he would remain in La Tombe until they carried him out for burial in the plot not far to the north of the garden. And when he rested, looking out over the valley or at the orange roofs of the small town, he knew that the work was necessary to his survival. He had heard too often of inmates who hung themselves in the laundry or the latrine when no one was around, or late at night in their cells while the others slept. He had heard of, and twice seen, inmates stabbing other inmates with a sharpened piece of metal from the blacksmith's shop or a knife stolen from the kitchen. He had seen guards take troublesome inmates away in chains—never to be seen again. But out in the fields, Charging Elk could forget about all that went on within the walls of La Tombe.

Although they were never close, the big man who ran the gardens, Gustave Boucq, was pleased not only with Charging Elk's work but with his constancy. The others came and went, but Charging Elk was always there. Sometimes Boucq would come and watch the Indian hoe weeds or pick corn. He would wait until Charging Elk stopped to wipe his brow or pull up his trousers (he lost five to ten kilos every summer), then ask, "How goes it? Not too hot?" When Charging Elk would assure him that he was fine, Boucq would kick the crumbly earth or look away toward the far side of the valley and say, "Well, you'd better drink some water," or "Those tomatoes need pinching off when you're done here—but take a break. Don't want to be responsible for killing you off." Then he would mutter some words that passed for appreciation and walk off to his own job. These moments under the hot sun were as close as the two men ever got.

Charging Elk never received a letter in all those years he spent in prison and certainly not a visitor. La Tombe was a long way from Marseille, and while René had remained loyal and supportive during the trial, he had to sell fish every day to support his family. And there was no one else on the outside.

Causeret remained a good friend. Although they were in different units now, they did see each other in the yard and the mess hall. If he was serving the line of inmates, he would put an extra potato or sausage link on Charging Elk's plate. But after a few years, the juggler smiled and laughed less often. When they walked the yard during those cold months Charging Elk didn't work, he no longer talked of scaling the wall and going to America to look for gold. Instead he spoke of a wasted life of going from town to town, to fairs and markets, performing his meager art for people who considered him, rightly, a mere sideshow. And when Charging Elk reminded him that he had made people happy, he laughed. But it was not the laugh of old, the laugh that had raised Charging Elk's own heart; it was a weak laugh of regret that trailed off into a cold wind. Eventually, Causeret quit walking. Charging Elk would walk the perimeter of the yard by himself, and when he came back, he would find the once-vigorous, acrobatic little man shivering in the lee of the wall, holding his thin jacket closed, waiting to return to his cell.

One day Causeret did not show up in the yard. Charging Elk was puzzled, but he went through his routine of walking to ward off the chill. But the next day, when his friend didn't show again, he asked the Englishman whose cell was just across the corridor from the juggler's what was going on. And the Englishman said he thought Causeret was sick. He hadn't gone to work the past two days — he just lay on his cot and stared at the ceiling. The next day, the Englishman said that two orderlies from the dispensary had wheeled the juggler away in the dead of night. Two days later, he said a guard had come to Causeret's cell and removed his bedding and small effects. Charging Elk had stared at the Englishman for a moment, then turned and began to walk the perimeter as always.

It rained most of that winter, and sometimes Charging Elk would find himself virtually alone in the yard. But he walked because he had to. If he didn't walk every day, he knew he would think about his friend's death and the fact that he too would die someday in La Tombe, perhaps soon, unexpectedly, like Causeret. But quite often, at the very moment Charging Elk's despair was at its apex, the snow would fall. And he would lift his head and feel the downy flakes settle on his face and melt and he would be transported, as if by magic, as if Wakan Tanka had sent the snow to remind him, back to the Stronghold and the winters he had spent with Kills Plenty. The memories that rushed through his mind — High Runner snorting out a greeting just outside the lodge in the morning, Kills Plenty pretending to be asleep so that Charging Elk would have to build the fire, hunting all day only to return with a long-legged rabbit — took him a long way from La Tombe and sustained him for a few days. But then the thought of dying would return and he would lie on his cot wrapped in his blanket and wonder when. Many times in his life in this country he had wanted to die.

He should have wanted to die now more than ever—but he didn't. Not even when it rained every day.

In the early spring of his tenth year, on the 12th of March of 1904, a guard unlocked Charging Elk's cell and told him to come along. Charging Elk had been waiting for this moment, and he felt his heart beat high in his chest. He put on his jacket and watch cap and followed the guard out into the yard and toward the gate. It was a raw, windy day, but he was anxious to get out into the terraces, to work hard, to put another bleak winter behind him.

But the guard instead led him into the administration building. Charging Elk became alarmed at this detour and tried to think of what he might have done wrong. Just three days before he had gone to the library for the first time but had only picked up a book about horses and thumbed through it to look at the pictures. Had the man at the desk reported him for some violation? He tried to think of what he might have done that was wrong. He was panicked at the thought that he wouldn't be able to work in the gardens anymore.

A different woman, much older and heavier than the first one, let him into the warden's office. She smiled at him but he was too frightened to notice.

"Ah, here is our man." The warden actually stood and stepped from behind his desk. Charging Elk glanced into his round, red face, at the long nose, and remembered thinking that he looked like a strange bird. But that had been many years ago and now he no longer looked like that bird. With his stumpy legs and his shiny head growing out of his collar, he looked like the sightless creature that burrows into the earth. "Good day, Charging Elk."

"Good day, monsieur." Charging Elk shook the warden's hand,

but he was already glancing toward the other two people in the room, who were rising to their feet.

The warden kept Charging Elk's hand in his own as he turned to the two people. "Allow me to introduce you to Monsieur Murat of the Department of Corrections in Paris, and Madame Loiseau of the Catholic Relief Society of Marseille. They have both come a long way to see you." The warden laughed, and Charging Elk could detect a nervous deference in the laughter. "You must be an important man."

As he shook hands with the two visitors, he couldn't help but notice a difference in their demeanor toward him. The man was stiff and perfunctory, while the woman smiled in a kindly way and gripped his hand with both of hers. Charging Elk noticed that her pearl-colored gloves were smooth and soft, like velvet. He hadn't touched such fine fabric for many years.

"To be brief, Monsieur Charging Elk"—the man picked up a thin leather portfolio and pulled a piece of heavy paper from it— "you have been reclassified as a political prisoner and herewith have been granted a pardon by the Republic of France." The man handed the piece of paper to Charging Elk.

Charging Elk had heard his name pronounced as the Americans did, as Brown Suit did. He thought the man must be an American, but he spoke French like a Frenchman.

Charging Elk studied the piece of paper, and he saw his name in heavy black ink in the center and the date in the upper right-hand corner. In the lower left-hand corner he saw a gold seal with two short red ribbons. The rest was written in perfect script that he didn't understand. He said, "Thank you very much, monsieur." Then he looked at the madame, not knowing what else to do. She was smiling, an expectant look in her eyes. "Thank you, madame."

There was a brief silence. Then Madame Loiseau said, "Of

course!" She laughed and tapped the paper in his hand. "This means you are free. A pardon means that the government excuses you for your transgression—or, as in this case, admits that it made a mistake. It seems you were tried as a citizen of the United States of America. As it turns out, by treaty, your tribe is its own separate nation and therefore not subject to the legal agreements between the United States and France. Thus the reclassification from common criminal to political prisoner. You have been held illegally all these years." Madame Loiseau glanced toward Monsieur Murat and smiled triumphantly. "You are at liberty to come with us, Charging Elk."

He looked at her. She was not tall but imposing nonetheless. She wore a black dress with a high collar and long narrow cuffs with a row of buttons running up each cuff. Her waist was pinched but her bosom stood out like the naked figures on some of the ships in the Old Port. Her gray hair was tucked up under a black felt hat with a narrow turned-up brim. Although her dress was stark, almost stern, she continued to smile with a warmth that Charging Elk had not felt since Causeret was alive and in good spirits. He decided he liked her and trusted her.

"It's true, my friend. I have some papers here." The warden dipped a pen into an inkwell, handed it to Charging Elk, and showed him where to sign. He drew the letters of his name slowly, carefully, but he couldn't keep his hand from shaking. He had not drawn his name since the trial, and it was not as clear as he would have wished. But the shaking came from suddenly realizing that he was going to leave La Tombe. Then he panicked again. Unless this all was a trick. René had told him not to sign anything until he knew what it said. He almost asked madame to read the papers to him.

But the warden said, "That's it. You're a free man, Charging Elk. You may get your belongings. And may God go with you."

As Charging Elk crossed the yard behind the guard, he glanced toward the gate. He wondered if Gustave Boucq was waiting for him. He wanted to say goodbye to someone, but with Causeret dead and the big bearded man probably in his toolshed, examining the hoes and spades, he didn't know of anybody else who might like to wish him well. He glanced around at the looming walls, the empty yard, and the gray sky above, and he thought that it would be best to slip out quietly.

And he suddenly wondered where he would go. He had been so stunned by the news he had forgotten to ask. But he knew madame would take care of him. He felt his whole face open up into a wide grin, and when the guard held the door for him into his unit, Charging Elk saw a look of astonishment on the guard's face.

The guard had been at La Tombe for all of Charging Elk's years and he had never seen such a look on the Indian. The grin on the usually passive face was almost frightening. It was as though the savage had been sleepwalking for the past ten years.

CHAPTER NINETEEN

athalie Gazier stood on the stone platform of the railway station and looked across the tracks in the direction of the Garonne. She could see the orderly row of plane trees beside the wide cinder path with just a glint of the river on the far side of a taller row of oaks. A kiosk that sold flowers in the summer was shuttered and covered with posters and flyers advertising musical events, soccer games, lectures, political speeches, and a theater schedule. Just yesterday, Sunday, an unusually warm day for March, she had been walking along the path arm in arm with her girlfriend Catherine, who was a year older and already going with a young *fusilier* from the military post on the road to Bordeaux. As they watched a group of men playing boules, Catherine had informed her that Thierry, her lover (as she referred to him), had stuck his tongue in her mouth last week. Nathalie had squealed in horror, but a moment later, as they were watching two sculls race along the Garonne, the oarsmen gliding smoothly back and forth as the big oars creased the water, curiosity got the best of her.

"What did it feel like?" she had said.

"How would you imagine it felt like?"

"Like a slimy, raw sausage."

"That's how much you know, little girl. You don't have a lover."

"Well, what did it feel like then?"

Catherine had laughed, but then she said, "I don't know. He said that's how the girls in Bordeaux kiss, but it made me dizzy. I almost fainted in his arms."

Now Nathalie wondered what would happen to her if a man kissed her that way. The idea still disgusted her, but men put something else into a woman and it was fine as long as you were married. Although she was only sixteen, she knew several girls her age who were already engaged, some even married.

Nathalie looked up the tracks, which curved to the right and disappeared behind the wall of the lycée. When she was younger, she had wanted to go to the lycée in a most desperate way because one of the boys in her school had bragged that he would go there someday and then become a scientist. She had had a crush on him even in the third grade, her last year of school. She hadn't seen him since. But now she wondered if he had become the type of young man who put his tongue in girls' mouths. The idea still revolted her. How could it make one dizzy? She would probably just get sick.

Maybe that was what was the matter with her. She wasn't compliant like Catherine. She didn't have Catherine's easy manner around men. Whatever was the matter, the fact was she didn't have a boyfriend or even the prospect of a boyfriend, if you didn't count Alain, the boy from the next farm. They had kissed four or five times in the orchards, but she had felt exactly nothing. He was not a handsome young *fusilier*—not even a strong farmhand, like the one who worked for Alain's father. Nathalie often watched him prune trees or pitch hay. In the heat of the day, he would strip down to his undershirt and she would secretly spy on him, transfixed by his strong, glistening shoulders and taut arms and his narrow waist. She had never spoken to him but she just knew he would prefer a girl like Catherine or one of the faster girls who sat in the cafés and smoked and flirted shamelessly. What chance did a gawky farm girl have?

A gust of wind blew up and Nathalie pressed her bonnet to her head, squinting against the dust cloud. Then she heard a whistle and she became excited again. She wondered what the stranger would look like. She had never seen an American savage before. And he was a convict! Just like the other two who had lived with them for a while. But they were just farm boys who had found themselves on the wrong side of the law, as her father liked to say. Nothing that a little hard work wouldn't cure. Nathalie hadn't fallen in love with either one, though she tried a little with the boy from Souillac. But they were homely, dull-witted boys whose only real crime had been thinking that they were smart enough to get away with something. Her father liked to say that to his friends, who would disapprove but laugh knowingly, then get on with their complaints about the drought or the endless rain and the poor price for prunes or artichokes.

Nathalie suddenly felt a little faint. She had been up all night and had had only two hours of sleep this morning. Her stomach felt hollow and bitter, even though she had eaten a piece of bread on the way to the train station. She tried not to think about Catherine's lover's fat tongue which almost made her friend faint; instead she concentrated on the moment at hand and the stranger who would come to live with them for the next few months. She was nervous about having a savage around, not because she was afraid of him—her father had been assured that he was not dangerous—but because she was afraid of what the neighbors might think. She did have her reputation to think of. In spite of her lack of success with boys, she was becoming a woman. There were certain parts of her that were filling out while other parts were diminishing. When she looked into the mirror these days she saw actual cheekbones and a nose that didn't quite look like a pudgy button. Such knowledge made her feel secretly superior, as though she were becoming the swan she always knew she would be.

Vincent Gazier stood beside his daughter with his arms crossed, a thin cigar in one hand, a scowl on his gaunt face. The stiff March wind blew from the west, picking up the chill from the Atlantic, and this troubled him. Usually it was this very wind that kept his trees safe from freezing, but last night the breeze had blown away the clouds and he and his wife and daughter had had to build fires among the trees and tend them until early morning. This night promised to be just as clear and cold. Even now he should be gathering more wood from the forest to the east of Agen. And the train was late.

Gazier's family had raised plums just outside Agen for countless generations. Most of the time it was a pleasant occupation, but hardly one that would make a man rich. Still, in a normal year, if God granted him just an average harvest, he could keep his family clothed and fed until the next year. And that was all he had come to ask for. That was all any of the generations of Gaziers had ever asked for. But too often a late frost would kill off the buds or the setting fruit, or a year without rain would make the plums small and hard, or a couple of days of rain late in the season would split the ripening plums and all the year's work would wither on the trees or go to the hogs. Fortunately, last year had been a good one; his family had harvested a heavy crop and delivered it to the processing plant for a decent sum of money.

But it only takes one bad year, thought Gazier, and then you have to humiliate yourself in front of the bankers to borrow enough to see you through the winter. This could be one of those seasons. He pulled out his watch. One-thirty. Twenty minutes late. He was already having second and third thoughts about what he had let himself and his family in for.

He had received the letter from Madame Loiseau of the Catholic Relief Society two weeks before. He had read it to himself, then to his wife and daughter, leaving out the portion that described the crime. After the obligatory familiarities, it had gotten down to the meat of the matter.

By now you may have guessed that I am about to avail myself of your kind offices and more than generous offer to help the Society in any way we might see fit. Well, you may feel inclined, and indeed justified, to rescind your generosity, because I am going to ask of you an enormous favor. And I only ask it because twice in the past you have extended your hospitality to our Prisoner Rehabilitation Project subjects. I do believe that both endeavors proved successful and came to a happy ending. We hear that both young men are engaged in honest labors and go to mass regularly.

Now to the heart of this letter: We have taken up, as part of our project, the case of a prisoner to be released in two weeks — if all goes well. This is a most unusual case, and after you hear the particulars, you may find that he is an unsuitable candidate to take in. You may rest assured that we will be in absolute accordance with your decision.

The subject's name is Charging Elk and he is an American Indian, thirty-seven years of age. He came to this country in 1889 as part of the Wild West show of Buffalo Bill. Perhaps you have heard of this show. It performed in Paris during the Exposition of that year, then moved on to tour Europe. One of its first stops was here in Marseille, where he met with an accident during a performance and entered hospital. For some reason the show moved on without him without making any provisions for his well-being. At the time he couldn't speak our language, and so he found himself in the hands of the authorities, who had no idea of what to do with him. Fortunately, a good family took him in— the man is a hardworking fishmonger—and he lived with them for the next two years. After that, he lived on his own, working in a soap factory, accustoming himself to our way of life. From all reports he was doing very well when—alas!—he found himself in a compromising situation with a despicable man—please don't ask me to go into it—and ended up killing the man. Many thought, as the trial brought the whole matter into the light, that Charging Elk was justified in his actions. In fact, the trial became quite the *cause célèbre*. The magistrates agreed, to a degree, with the public—that indeed there were extenuating circumstances— and sentenced him to life imprisonment, instead of the expected death penalty.

Now for the good part, Monsieur Gazier. Charging Elk served nine and a half years in Samatan Prison and by every account was a model prisoner. He had not a single disciplinary report in that whole time (and you may be assured that he was virtually alone in that respect—I'm sure you are aware of the reputation of "La Tombe"). Moreover, he worked every day possible during the last seven years of his imprisonment in the gardens and orchards.

This latter fact made us here at the Relief Society think of you, my dear fellow. We thought you, as an orchardist, might have some interest in taking on this hardworking, experienced hand.

I'm sure you could use some help now that spring and summer approach. Of course, we will compensate you for Charging Elk's room and board to the tune of twenty francs per month. And we won't ask you to keep him one minute longer than you choose. But we are hoping that you will keep him on through the growing and harvesting seasons.

By now I am sure you are asking yourself, Why Agen, why me, why not Marseille? And those would be fair questions. The answer to all is simply this: We feel that after almost a decade in prison he is not ready for the faster-paced life of this seaport, with all of its distractions and, yes, temptations. We feel that Agen and environs would be perfectly suited for his reentry into society. The strong Catholic presence in your part of the country would do him a world of good. As for you, we know of no one better to set our poor stranger on the straight and narrow path of hard work and piety.

I neglected to mention earlier that Charging Elk is due to be pardoned, a fact which might make your decision a little easier. Let me add that he is a very gentle man who wants nothing more than an opportunity to better himself as a human being so that he may more easily adapt to our modern society. He is most deserving to benefit from your tutelage and guidance.

Yours in Christ,
Mme. Sophie A. Loiseau

Gazier heard the whistle over the blowing wind and thought he must have been mad to agree to take on this ex-prisoner. The other two that he had taken in were just farm boys — one was only nineteen, the other twenty-one. They were still malleable. But this one was thirty-seven years old, and he had spent the last ten of those years in Samatan, the worst prison in France. Moreover, he was a

Peau-Rouge from America. How could he possibly "adapt to our modern society"? Gazier threw his cigar down onto the tracks and thought how complicated his life, and that of his family, had become. He glanced at Nathalie, but she had her back to him, watching the locomotive steam up to the platform. Poor Nathalie, he thought, she is just a girl and now she will have to adjust to however this endeavor turns out. Thank God she is strong and healthy, unlike her mother. Lucienne would be in bed all day after her labors of the night before. But she had insisted on helping with the fires. Oh Lord, he prayed, please give me the strength to get through these next few days. Give all of us the strength.

Charging Elk stepped down from the car and looked at all the people on the platform. He wore the suit he had owned for eleven winters now, and it was shapeless and baggy. His new collarless white shirt was too small, even though it was the largest Madame Loiseau had been able to find in Toulouse. She had also bought him some toiletries, underclothing, work clothes, a duffel bag, and a beret. She couldn't find any shoes to fit him, so he still wore the prison-issue canvas shoes with the hemp soles. In the past, he would have been disappointed, but now he was resigned to the fact that he was different not only physically but also in that he had spent the last nine and a half years in prison. He was sure the people in Toulouse knew it, and so he kept to the edge of the sidewalks and he said very little in response to Madame Loiseau and the store clerks' queries. The truth was, he was frightened by the movement of the people, the carriages and wagons, the clanging bells of the omnibuses, even the horses. Once, while Madame Loiseau was in a shop, he had walked over to the curb where a carriage horse was dozing and smelled it. He filled his nostrils with the musky odor, and it smelled familiar and good. But when the horse abruptly raised its head and and jangled the metalwork of its traces, he had stepped back in alarm.

They had spent the night in a small hotel near the railway station, and this morning she had put him on the train to Agen before catching one back to Marseille. Just before they parted, she had written his name on a piece of paper and pinned it to his lapel. Then she said, "They are a good Christian family and they will look out for you. You must always remember that you are as good as anybody, Charging Elk. May God go with you." Now as he surveyed the people on the platform, he was somewhat comforted by the fact that most of them seemed to be simple people, as simply dressed as himself. Still, this was a different town in a different part of the country, and he was apprehensive as he stepped aside to let some people on the train. He almost wished he were back at La Tombe, getting the ground ready for another planting. He thought more fondly of Gustave Boucq now than he ever had. The big, taciturn man was probably spreading manure, perhaps even breaking in a new man to take Charging Elk's place. As he looked at the faces, many of which were now staring at him, he began to wish more fervently that he was back at the prison. They knew as well as he that he belonged there.

"Monsieur Charging Elk?"

A slender man in a dark suit and a beret had approached him from the side. A young woman trailed behind him, her eyes looking at Charging Elk's feet.

"I am Vincent Gazier, and this is my daughter, Nathalie. We have been expecting you."

Charging Elk took the man's hand. *"Enchanté, monsieur."* He bowed slightly to the young woman, who was now looking at the piece of paper on his lapel. "Madame Loiseau said I would work for you. I am a good worker."

"So the madame says. That's excellent, because we have much to do right now." Gazier glanced down at the duffel. "Is that all you've got?"

Just then the conductor blew his whistle and they heard a hiss of steam, then the heavy clank of the couplings as the train began to grind ahead.

"Come. We will get you situated in your new home. Then I'm afraid we have some heavy work ahead of us." Gazier turned and walked off at a rapid pace, and Charging Elk noticed he had a limp. "You will earn your keep tonight, monsieur."

After that first frantic night of hauling wood, setting fires and keeping them stoked and burning until daybreak, Charging Elk's life at the farm settled into a predictable, almost easy routine of work, eat, smoke, and sleep. He had his own room, which opened up into the courtyard. Although it was part of the main house, it was one of many additions the generations of Gaziers had built onto the house for various reasons. It had been a storage room, filled with old furniture and small pieces of broken equipment, tack that had become stiff and brittle with age—things that somehow never got thrown away or fixed. Gazier and his daughter had spent two days clearing the room, moving the objects to other rooms in other buildings around the courtyard. They had managed to salvage an iron bed, a bureau, a small table, and a chair from the debris. And although it had an earthen floor and only one small window beside the oak door, it was quite comfortable until the heat of summer days stayed in the room until well after dark. Charging Elk didn't mind. He took his chair outside and smoked in the twilight, content to be alone and free. After his years in the cell blocks of La Tombe, he luxuriated in his evening thoughts as he watched the shadows lengthen, then disappear. He listened to the buzz of insects in the dark, the snuffling of a hog in its sleep or the shudder of one of the two draft horses, the gabbling of a goose that might have heard a distant bark, and he felt a part of the world around him. He imagined the Gaziers, already asleep in the dark house, and he imagined he would come to feel a part of their world, with time. Just as with the Soulas family.

The summer came and stayed for a long time. The farm was on the side of a sloping hill to the north and east of Agen, just out of the river valley. Below the compound of buildings, the Gaziers had a large vegetable garden, which Nathalie, and sometimes her mother, when she felt well enough, kept weeded and watered. Sometimes Charging Elk would help them out, turning water into the rows from a ditch that originated at the base of a spring in the hillside above the farm, or breaking ground for melons or squash. His job also consisted, in part, of taking care of the hogs, turning them out into the orchards to root for things that he couldn't even see, keeping an eye on the geese, or rather an eye out for weasels and foxes, which occasionally prowled the farm at night. But mostly he worked in the orchards, helping Vincent Gazier spray the trees for bugs or prune out blight-stricken or dead limbs. He painstakingly thinned the small, green prunes, moving from tree to tree with his ladder, pinching off the hard fruit that even the hogs found distasteful. Every couple of weeks he hitched the horses to a cultivator and weeded and aerated the earth between the rows of trees. After his summers in the prison gardens and orchards, the work came easily for him. The trees offered shade and he was left alone to work at his own pace. Some days he had to make work for himself, but he always managed to find something to do, from oiling the tack to sharpening pruning shears and saws to whitewashing the stucco horse shed.

At least once a week he rode into Agen with Gazier. Sometimes Nathalie came with them, sitting on a sack of onions or new potatoes or an overturned bucket in the back of the wagon. In town, she would disappear for a half hour or so and come back with some cloth for her mother or a bottle of olive oil and a bag of coffee beans. Meanwhile, her father and Charging Elk would unload whatever produce they had in the wagon at a local market, perhaps buy a sack of feed or poison for whatever insect happened to be harassing the trees; then Charging Elk would buy some tobacco and papers while Vincent talked with one merchant or another, or another orchardist or farmer who also was running errands. His wife, Lucienne, never came with them.

Charging Elk felt sorry for Vincent's wife, for although she was always gracious, even cheerful at times, there was something wrong with her. She was given to long coughing fits that would leave her slumped in a chair or leaning against a wall, gasping for breath. She could work in the garden for only about an hour in the morning before she would have to walk slowly back up to the house. Once she collapsed while she was picking peas and both Charging Elk and Nathalie ran to her. Nathalie reached her first and held her in her arms, cradling her as one cradles a sleepy but unhappy child. Her face had turned as white as the flesh of the onions Charging Elk was harvesting, and he became frightened for her. But slowly, as Nathalie fanned her mother with her bonnet, her color returned and she blinked her eyes and noticed him looking down at her.

"It's all right, you two. I am a foolish woman to work so hard today. It's the sun, you see."

Charging Elk took his morning and evening meals with the family, and usually it was a happy occasion. Nathalie would talk about a dress she had seen in town, or something about her friend who was engaged to a soldier, and her mother and father would listen and tease or scold her, always with affection. But sometimes Lucienne would be absent, even though she had cooked the meal, and both Vincent and Nathalie would eat quietly, without the usual repartee. On these occasions, Charging Elk would excuse himself after coffee and sit and smoke in the cool evening air outside his room.

One day, as they were preparing a poison for borers, Vincent Gazier straightened up and walked to the shed doorway. He stood for a long moment, surveying the wild hill above the orange tile roofs of the old buildings, while Charging Elk stirred the liquid, dissolving the poison crystals.

"She has the consumption, you know. Her lungs are rotten with it."

Charging Elk stopped stirring and glanced at the thin back, the long, sunburned neck, and the narrow head beneath the beret. There was a natural list to Gazier's shoulders, because of the bad leg that made him limp. But it seemed more pronounced just then.

"I don't know how long she will be with us—not long, I'm sure. Maybe a month, maybe six. Who knows?"

Charging Elk stirred the liquid slowly, quietly. He didn't know what to say. He had heard of consumption. He had heard that there was a unit in La Tombe where they kept the consumptive prisoners away from the population.

"I don't know. Sometimes I think she wants to die, to make things easier for Nathalie and me. Do you understand that?"

Charging Elk laid the stirring stick on a small board. The poison was strong and filled the room with an unnatural smell. He thought of all the times he had wanted to die since he came to this country. But the woman, Lucienne, had much to live for. She had a fine husband and a handsome daughter. "I will pray for your wife," he said. He wanted to comfort the man but he could think of nothing else to say. He suddenly felt the immense poverty of his experience. He didn't know how to comfort another human being anymore.

But Gazier turned and looked at him. The eyes were large and moist in the gaunt face. "Will you?"

Charging Elk had to look away. He had not seen such desperation for a small ray of sunshine. "I will pray to Wakan Tanka. He is the Great Spirit who can accomplish all things. Sometimes he hears the words of his poor grandson." Charging Elk wanted to add, But sometimes he doesn't think his grandson's selfish prayers are worthy of attention. He glanced back at Vincent Gazier and saw a small, weary, hopeful smile.

"Thank you, Charging Elk. That is all I ask. Perhaps your Great Spirit . . ." The gaunt man suddenly stopped. He had almost committed a sacrilege. He crossed himself and asked his God for forgiveness. Still, he felt a little lighter. Perhaps it was just the talk he needed. "Well, let's get after those trees, shall we?"

In late August the prunes were ripe. In a small ritual that the Gazier family had practiced for generations, Vincent, Lucienne, and Nathalie, along with Charging Elk, walked out to the orchards and stood under a large old tree that had been a bellwether for at least five generations of Gaziers. They each picked a prune, smelled it, squeezed it until the juice ran out the stem end, then bit into it, tasting the sweet flesh. Vincent pronounced the fruit to be at the firm edge of perfection. He said a prayer to God for once again giving them a good crop and he prayed for a successful harvest. Even Charging Elk said "Amen," although he didn't cross himself. Nor did he look at Lucienne, who by now was matchstick-thin and dark around the eyes.

Vincent hired three boys from Agen to help with the harvest. They had to work quickly while the fruit was still firm, and so the workdays began at daybreak and ended with nightfall. Still, it took ten days to pick the four hectares of orchards.

Nathalie spent part of her time in the orchards and part taking care of her mother. She carried water out to the men in canvas bags, managed to cook a midday meal every day with the direction of her mother, and joined in the picking later in the afternoon. At the end of five days, she was near the point of physical and emotional exhaustion. It pained her to watch her mother become so helpless so quickly. For most of the days, all she could think about was the fact that soon her mother would be gone. What would happen then?

Lucienne's doctor from Agen had come out one evening halfway through the harvest, examined her, then held a conference with Vincent. He gave him a tonic to give to her and told him to make sure she got an hour of sun every morning before the heat of the day. Otherwise, she must stay in bed. Vincent had listened to the doctor somewhat impatiently, then asked bluntly, "How much longer does she have?"

The doctor, who had first diagnosed the disease some twelve years before and had come to believe that the consumption was in a latent state and would remain so for many years to come if not forever, shook his head as he snapped his bag closed. "It is in her upper and lower lungs. The infection has spread rapidly in the last month." He shook his head again as he picked up his bag. "It's remarkable."

"How much longer?"

"If I said less than a week, it would be a lie. If I said six months, nine months—that too would be a lie. The only true thing I know is that she will not recover, barring a miracle from God. You would do well to pray for her soul now, Vincent."

By four o'clock in the afternoon of the tenth day, Charging Elk and one of the boys from Agen hoisted the last box full of prunes up onto the wagon. Then the three boys climbed into the wagon and Vincent snapped the reins and the horses started for Agen. Although the processing plant was only three kilometers away, the horses had made the trip twice and sometimes three times a day during the harvest and they were just a little reluctant. Vincent snapped the reins again and whistled, and the wagon slowly creaked down the hill toward Agen.

Charging Elk stood among the trees and watched the heavy wagon lumber along the main road that led past the farm and into the valley. He looked beyond the valley to the wooded hills and the patches of farmland. A tall thin spire stood above the trees, shining white and distinct amid the jumble of greenery. He had often thought about this spire. In fact, he could see it when he sat out in the evening. It was always the last thing the sunlight found as the valley began to darken. He always thought of it as a beacon—like Notre Dame de la Garde in Marseille—a shining beacon that one could see from a long way off that might offer guidance to lost souls like himself.

The next day Charging Elk and Nathalie were in the garden, she picking the last of the tomatoes and beans and he pulling up the spent plants and vines and turning over the earth. The garden had existed for many years, and the soil, beneath the crusty surface, was as soft as powder under his spade. They worked separately and quietly for an hour or so, until they suddenly found themselves within two meters of each other.

Although Nathalie was open, even loquacious, around her parents, she and Charging Elk had never spoken directly to each other, except for the usual greetings or small exchanges that were necessary to the day's activities. He always felt uncomfortable around her because he had been in prison and she was still as innocent as a young deer. She felt uncomfortable around him for the same reason.

But today she said, "What is it like in America, Charging Elk?" She said this without looking up at him, but she had stopped picking the beans.

Charging Elk noticed this and he was surprised. Usually she addressed him while she was doing something else, in an offhand sort of way. And he could not remember her ever saying his name. "It is very big, very beautiful," he said, although after fifteen years he could not really remember all the country he had seen on the way to New York. Somewhere after Omaha the land had turned green and the cities were plentiful. "Like France," he said.

"And where do you come from—in America?"

Charging Elk remembered the big ball of the earth that Mathias had shown him in the stationery shop. "Dakota," he said. "It is dry and not so many trees. The sun takes many hours to cross the sky. One can see it all day."

Nathalie now looked up at him, squinting a little against the sun. "Are there cities in Dakota?"

"Not so much. Little towns along the iron road. Not like Marseille or Agen."

"But Agen is small. I took the train once to Bordeaux with my parents. Now, that's a big city." She smiled. "I have an aunt and uncle there. He owns a *cave* and sells only the best of wines—or so my aunt says. But I prefer to live here where there are not so many people. Don't you?"

Charging Elk was surprised by the question. He hadn't really considered this farm, this town, as a place to live. He was only here for the growing season. Madame Loiseau had said so. She said he could go back to Marseille after that, after the news of his release had died down.

Now he looked around—down into the valley, toward Agen and the slow-moving Garonne; up at the orchards behind the house; at the spire across the valley. Then he looked down at Nathalie. She was wearing a large straw hat, which covered her face when she worked. But now she was looking up at him, an expectant smile on her face, as though she knew the answer to her question.

Charging Elk had not looked at her like this before. Her face was still that of a girl of sixteen winters—clean, unlined, with just a hint of summer tan because of the hat she always wore. But in the five moons he had been there she had changed. Now when he saw her walking across the yard, he saw a different person. If her face was hidden, he would take the figure to be that of a slender young woman. She had lost the gawkiness of childhood, almost without his noticing it. It was only in the face that he recognized the girl who had greeted him so shyly at the railway station.

He squatted down, ran his fingers through the soft loam, and said, "I like it here because you are here. You make me feel good."

As she went about her chores for the next few weeks, Nathalie thought about what Charging Elk had said. Did he mean just her? Or her and her family? What did he mean by "feel good"? And the way he said it was just as confusing. He had looked at her, and the penetrating look in his eyes had made her fearful that he would try to touch her. But he hadn't. He had carried her basket of tomatoes to the stone cellar beside the toolroom. She had followed with her beans, and in the cool darkness of the cellar, she had shivered in a way that had nothing to do with coolness. She had dumped her basket of beans into a wooden box on the earthen floor, then left, almost running out into the hot sun.

She had been confused then, less by Charging Elk's words than by her own feelings. She had actually felt faint. Later that night, as she lay in bed, listening to her mother's ragged breathing in the next room, she thought of Catherine and her soldier and she tried to believe that the faintness she had felt had something to do with a man and a woman together. She tried to believe that she was falling in love against her will.

Vincent had been spending more of his time in the house with his wife than in the orchards or the farmyard. Since there was not much work at that particular time of the year, Charging Elk and Nathalie were able to handle all that needed to be done. Vincent took dinner with them, eating very little, but much of the time he could be found standing outside the house, or limping slowly down the road toward Agen, only to turn around and walk back to the house. In the evenings, when Charging Elk sat outside his room, he could see a glow from Vincent's cigar, then an orange arc, and the door would open, letting out a soft warmth into the night, and then close with a click of the latch.

On September 22, Lucienne went to sleep and didn't wake up again. Charging Elk went to breakfast the next morning, but neither Vincent nor Nathalie was around. His place had been set and there was bread and confiture and melon on the table, along with lukewarm pots of coffee and milk. Across the table, he noticed a half-drunk *café au lait*. He took his coffee and a piece of bread back to his room and sat inside, looking out the open doorway. He knew that Lucienne was dead.

Charging Elk drank his *café au lait* and thought of death. Back at the Stronghold, death was a frequent visitor. He had been a child during the summer of the big fight on the Greasy Grass and had seen much death. That winter, he had seen many of his people starve to death or die of disease. His own brother and sister had died from the coughing sickness after the Oglalas surrendered. He himself had been near death in the hospital in Marseille.

Other than his own experience, he had not been much involved with death in his fifteen years in France. He had seen it in La Tombe, but he had not been close to the dead ones, except for Causeret. Death was expected in La Tombe and was not a cause for mourning. There were no loved ones there to mourn.

Lucienne's death was different. Although he had never become close to her as he had to Madeleine—probably because she was already preoccupied with dying when he had first looked at her—he had come to like Vincent and Nathalie and he worried about what would become of them now. Surely they would stay here and continue on, but there would be a big hole in their lives.

Charging Elk walked outside into the sunshine and offered up a prayer to Wakan Tanka. He closed his eyes and faced the sun. And he prayed not only for Lucienne's *nagi*, but for Nathalie's and Vincent's as well. And he prayed for himself, for he knew that his time here was almost over. Soon he would be back in Marseille, and the thought both frightened and excited him. He tried not to think of the Soulas family, because he was certain they would not welcome him back, not after his disgrace. And Marie—he had thought of her often during the cold winter months in La Tombe and at night he had dreamed of a life with her. But he knew that she would not care for him now. Still, Marseille was the only place in this country he knew.

Vincent Gazier sat on the bed and caressed his daughter's shoulders, which shook uncontrollably beneath his hand. He himself had no tears in him. He had mourned his wife long before she was gone and now he felt that his body was as dry as the dust on the road to Agen. If anything, he felt relieved that his dear wife's suffering was now over. But he was also saddened that his daughter's was just beginning. True, Nathalie had suffered much in the past few months with the knowledge that there was no hope for her mother, but she was strong and had worked hard during the illness. Now she would wake up in the mornings to come and realize that her mother would not be there—ever. And she would mourn all over again.

Vincent himself could scarcely believe that now there would just be the two of them. And Charging Elk. But soon he would be gone.

Surprisingly, Nathalie came out of her room later that morning and heated some water on the stove, even though she knew the act was unnecessary. She poured the water into a ceramic pitcher and took it into her parents' room. There she washed her mother's body, just as she had for the past few weeks, and with her father's help, dressed her in the white summer dress she had worn to town and to mass when she was healthy. Nathalie almost broke down again when she saw how loosely the dress fit her mother's wasted body, but she took a deep, shuddering breath to steady herself, then applied rouge to the sunken cheeks and the pale lips. She took a little comfort in seeing how peaceful and beautiful her mother looked, even younger, as though she had fallen asleep on her wedding night.

The funeral took place two days later in a little church near the central *place* of Agen. At dinner the night before, Vincent had asked Charging Elk to come with them, and when he looked a little reluctant, Nathalie said, "Please come. My mother liked you and would wish you to be there." So he sat in the back of the church and listened to the strange words and songs of the holy man and looked around at the statues and smelled the holy smoke. It was the first time he had ever been in a *wasichu* church, and it didn't seem to be a bad place. He thought of the times he had gotten angry with his parents and the other Lakotas for going to the white man's church and he shook his head in a kind of stupefied wonderment. Those days were a long time past and in another life altogether.

Charging Elk spent the next four months with Vincent and Nathalie, and during that time several things happened that would change all their lives considerably. When he later looked back on

this part of his life, Charging Elk would stop whatever he was doing and try to understand the succession of events that led to his
happiness.

And it would always come out something like this: First, Vincent
asked him to stay on to help with the pruning when the sap went
out of the limbs. Although he was getting restless and was anxious
to go back to Marseille, he knew he could not refuse to help the
family that had taken him in. And so he had stayed on, doing little
chores until pruning time. He even took up horsehair braiding, a
craft he had learned from a Hunkpapa out at the Stronghold. It had
helped him pass the winter moons until the grass greened and High
Runner became impatient for adventure. He spent his evenings in
his room at the Gaziers' farm braiding a belt with Lakota designs.
It was a clumsy attempt, but it was a belt, one that Nathalie marveled at one day when she came to fetch him to lift something for her.

As the clouds thickened into a monotonous gray and a bitter
wind off the ocean to the west came more frequently, Charging Elk
spent more time in the main house. He did his chores and came in
for coffee in the afternoon. He arrived an hour earlier for dinner
and stayed an hour later. He and Vincent always drank an *eau-de-
vie* after dinner and talked of plans for the next spring, almost as
though Charging Elk would be there. Nathalie, after washing the
dishes, would often sit with them and sew or look through an old
magazine that showed what the fashionable women wore in Paris.
She enjoyed the talking and the closeness of the kitchen. Often she
would look at Charging Elk, and she would see a man not much
younger than her father, but she would remember the Indian's
words in the garden and her own reaction that night in bed. Now
she felt a warmth toward him, almost a dependence on his presence
in the chair opposite her father. She could not imagine what life at
the farm would be like if he were not there. Both she and her father
needed him.

One night in late November, Charging Elk sat at the table in his room, working on the belt. The small oil lamp gave off a warm glow in the cold room and just enough light for him to attempt his intricate designs. He used red and white and gray horsetail for the designs and black for the border. He was getting better but he knew it would not pass muster at the Stronghold. The Hunkpapa had been a patient teacher but he would have had a good joke over this one.

Charging Elk's eyes were beginning to sting with the strain of braiding the fine horsehair and he was just about ready to quit when he heard a light rapping on his door. Because nobody had ever come to his room after dark, he was startled and filled with a sense of foreboding. He stood and crossed the room in two quick paces and flung open the door, expecting the worst.

But it was Nathalie and she smiled at him. She wore a gray cloak with a hood, and he could see that the hood and shoulders were dark. He looked up and saw water dripping off the eave. "It's raining," he said. "Come in." When she crossed the threshold and threw back the hood, he felt his heart jump up, but a knot of apprehension tightened in his stomach at the same time. He hadn't been alone with a woman—or a girl—since Marie.

Nathalie shook her head and patted her long dark curls into place. She smiled again, not really looking at him, and he saw the calm, beautiful smile of a woman. It was the kind of smile he had seen on the faces of women in the streets and the cafés of Marseille. It was the smile of young women who looked into the eyes of their men. Charging Elk couldn't believe this moment. He had walked the streets of Marseille in his fine clothes; he had sat in cafés drinking wine; he had watched the women, looking for just such smiles. And he had gone home alone, only to dream of a young woman who might give him such a smile. A young woman like Marie.

But Nathalie now spotted the half-finished belt and the smile became a youthful grin. "Can I watch you work?"

Charging Elk looked at the belt, and all he could see was the poor designs at the beginning. "It is not so good. I was just quitting for the night."

"Please, Charging Elk. Do just a little more for me."

When he heard her say his name, so carefully, his heart rose even higher. But he knew he shouldn't feel this way about her, so he walked back to the table and sat down. He began to braid, trying to ignore the fact that her face was just above his head. His eyes felt better from the break and his fingers did not tremble as he wove the twisted strands of horsehair into the design.

He began to concentrate even harder on his work and soon got into his usual painstaking rhythm. Then he suddenly felt a slight pressure on his shoulder. Out of the corner of his eye he could see her pale fingers against the rough fabric of his wool coat. It was a friendly gesture, but too close, and he knew he should somehow ask her to leave, but he couldn't think of a polite way. So he tried to ignore the hand.

"It's so lovely," she said, and he felt her hand stroking his long hair. He kept it cut to just down to his shoulder blades now. He usually wore it in a ponytail but tonight, in his room, it was loose. As she stroked his hair, he became light-headed, almost sleepy, and he watched his fingers twist and braid the horsehair. Then his fingers became clumsy and then they stopped. He sat for a moment, in a kind of blissful torpor, feeling the fingers weave their way through his hair.

He didn't know how long he sat there with his eyes closed, but he suddenly smelled a sweetness close to him and he felt her lips brush his cheek very near his mouth. He heard three or four light steps, then the door open and close, and he was alone in his room, suddenly, helplessly, in love.

～～～

Nathalie came often after that first night. At first, Charging Elk was worried that Vincent would find out and disapprove, but he knew that Vincent always retired after their *eau-de-vie* after dinner. Since his wife died, he seemed to have lost much of the energy that allowed him to work hard day after day, then make plans and tease Nathalie in the evening. Although he sometimes became animated when he talked with Charging Elk, for the most part he was quiet and thoughtful, and sometimes he just gave out and sighed and slumped in his chair, like an old man. Then he went to bed.

Charging Elk was puzzled by Nathalie's personality—sometimes she was the young girl who teased him, tickled him, and giggled at odd moments; at others, she was a demure young woman who blushed at his compliments or spoke of a life away from the farm now that her mother was gone. Whoever she was at any given time, she liked to run her fingers through his hair, place his arms around her, and kiss him, an act Charging Elk found pleasurable but was not experienced at. Once she told him to put his tongue in her mouth, and when he did, she giggled and fell back on his bed and said, *"Oh là là!"*

But soon that became her favorite way of kissing, and Charging Elk could feel a change in her body as she went from the young girl to the young woman. Her breath came in gasps and she allowed him to touch her breasts and her hips, but never her center. "That is for later," she would say as she moved his hand.

Charging Elk endured the girl's teasing, which was not disagreeable, for she made him feel young again and more alive than he had ever been since he left the Stronghold fifteen years before, while he waited for her to become the young woman that he could excite into such passion. At first, Charging Elk had tried not to become aroused for fear that it might frighten Nathalie. But it was hopeless. And she was fascinated. Sometimes she would run her fingers along his pants, feeling the rigidity of his cock. The first time, she had asked if it hurt to stretch himself like this, and he had burst out in a laugh so loud she had clamped her hand on his mouth in alarm. "Do you want to wake up my father, you fool?" But the laugh had felt good to him and he hugged her in gratitude.

Nathalie, in their quieter moments, wanted to know all about his life before he came to France. And so he told her about his childhood out on the plains, about living in a tipi, and galloping his horse, about the battle with the soldiers and coming in to Fort Robinson. His French was good enough now to even tell some of the details, although he left out the violent parts, like the time he and his friends had cut off the dead soldier's finger to get his ring. He enjoyed talking about his life, for he really hadn't had the opportunity since coming to France. He had told Causeret a little about his life at the Stronghold, but the juggler had become obsessed with the gold in Paha Sapa and only wanted to hear about that.

Nathalie listened to the stories, and often she would look at him in disbelief. Part of that disbelief came from the fact that she had an Indian for a lover. Never in her wildest dreams could she have imagined this. And the more he told of his life, the more she realized that she knew nothing about this kind of a man and the kind of life he came from. She had seen illustrations of Indians in magazines, but they had feather headdresses and painted faces and carried hatchets or guns. More often than not, the faces were cruel, even inhuman. But Charging Elk was not cruel or inhuman. He didn't carry a weapon or paint his face. He was gentle, even pliable. He never did anything until she let him. Sometimes when she was apart from him, Nathalie wondered what would happen if they walked along the promenade beside the Garonne in Agen. What would people think? What would Catherine think?

Of course, the very idea was impossible. People would point at them, men and women would disapprove, young people would laugh behind their backs—even Catherine would tease her about not being able to do better than a savage. In her darker moments, Nathalie herself wondered if she couldn't do better—find a young man of her own kind, perhaps a farmer or, what, a druggist, a carpenter?

Nathalie had never seen a dark person until Charging Elk. She had never seen a black African, or a Musulman, or a Levantine. There were only French people in Agen and the countryside, and they were suspicious of, even hostile toward, anyone who was of a different color.

Charging Elk *was* different. But he was good, strong and gentle at the same time. Shouldn't that be enough for her? When she was with him in his little room, it was enough. But when they rode into town in the wagon with her father, she saw how the people looked at him and she became embarrassed, even ashamed of sitting next to him. She made it a point not to sit too close to him or talk with him while people were watching. Back at the farm she became ashamed of herself for her hateful actions and showered him with even more affection. She resolved that next time it would be different—she would laugh with him, look into his eyes, touch him, perhaps even walk along the promenade with him. Who cared what other people thought?

One morning in mid-December, just after breakfast, Vincent asked Charging Elk to harness the horses and hook them up to the wagon. He and Nathalie were going to visit his younger brother, who lived on the other side of the Garonne, a few kilometers to the south of Agen.

It had rained lightly but steadily for several days, and this morning, while not rainy, was damp, with large pockets of fog hiding the Garonne. The farmyard was muddy and quiet, with only the flock of geese waddling among the puddles, making their strange conversation. The pigs were already up in the orchards. Charging Elk held the horses as Vincent and Nathalie climbed up into the wagon. Nathalie wore her next-to-best dress under her cloak, and a real hat had replaced the usual white bonnet. She looked somber and sat stiffly on the seat beside her father.

Charging Elk watched the wagon creak slowly out of the compound and down the road toward Agen. He watched until the road curved behind an abandoned outbuilding and the wagon disappeared. Something was going on. He could see it in Nathalie's eyes, in the tense slump of Vincent's shoulders. He didn't know what it was, but he knew that things were not good. He felt empty and alone as he stood in the damp courtyard, watching for another glimpse of the wagon, of Nathalie, but he didn't see her again, and his thoughts became as gloomy as the fog-shrouded river bottom. Something was happening.

He spent most of the day in the orchards above the farm buildings. He pruned trees, stacked the prunings into neat piles among the trees. When the earth dried, he would come up in the wagon and haul the limbs and shoots to the pile behind the hog pen to season for firewood and fencing.

Around four o'clock he came back down, wet and cold, and made a fire in the kitchen stove. He sat at the table, drinking a cup of warmed-over coffee, until it began to get dark. He lit an oil lamp, put more wood in the firebox, damped it down, then walked outside to his room. He lit his lamp, looked down at the belt, which was just about finished, then lay down on his bed. He tried not to think of the many things that could be wrong, but his mind ran through every possibility, from Nathalie's not coming back to another death in Vincent's family that would change everything. When he ran out of possibilities, he dozed off. He slept fitfully for the next three hours, waking often to rain ticking off the tile roof or the touch of a draft on his face.

Around eight o'clock, he heard a light rapping on his door and sat up, head clear and his heart suddenly high. He crossed the room and opened the door, ready to pull Nathalie into the room and hug her to him. But it was Vincent.

"Good evening, Charging Elk. We have returned." In the dim light of the small lamp, his face looked thin and rough-edged, his large, round eyes deep-set and glittering in their sockets. "Will you put the horses away—give them some grain—then come up to the house. Nathalie is putting something together, nothing much, but you must be starved."

Twenty minutes later, Charging Elk walked into the kitchen. He had been so anxious to see Nathalie that he had forgotten to change out of his muddy work clothes. Vincent sat at the table, a glass of wine before him.

"Come in. Take off your coat and have a glass with me."

Charging Elk hung his coat on a peg beside the door and glanced around the room. A pot of soup simmered on the stove, its warm smell making his empty stomach growl. A loaf of bread, a crock of butter, a bowl of olives, and a sausage lay untouched in the middle of the table. One of Vincent's long, thin cigars burned in an ashtray. He watched Vincent pour the wine, then said as calmly as he could manage: "But where is Nathalie? Didn't she come home?"

"Went to bed. She's not too happy, I think." Vincent handed him the wine, and they clicked glasses without a word, as was their habit. "It's been a long, troubling day for her. It's easy to understand."

Charging Elk wanted to ask a hundred questions but he knew that Vincent would talk only when he was ready. So they sat across from each other and sipped their wine. Charging Elk was very hungry, but he couldn't have eaten the best cut of beef just then. He sat and looked everywhere in the room but at the haggard man across the table.

He heard a long sigh and he waited for something, but when it came, it was not one of the possibilities he had considered.

"You might as well know, Charging Elk — I've decided to sell out to my younger brother, Raymond. He doesn't really have anything but a good wife and six children, one just born. He grows artichokes and a few grapes and he works in an abattoir on the other side of Agen. But the work is unsteady and artichokes brought a poor price this year." Vincent paused and looked down into his wineglass. "I just can't think of those children going without."

"But what about you? What about Nathalie? This is her home."

"It will be hard on her. It already has been. But she is a strong girl, a good girl. She will find her happiness. You know how young people are — one minute the roof is falling in, the next they're on to something else like nothing happened. It will take a while...." Vincent leaned forward and smiled wearily. "Besides, she is of an age when she should start thinking of marriage. She will turn seventeen next month. Her mother was only fifteen when we got married."

Charging Elk suddenly felt the weariness of the day in the orchards. His shoulders and upper arms ached from reaching for the high branches and his legs ached from standing on the ladder all day. He was hungry, but the act of eating now seemed inconsequential next to his hunger for Nathalie. He realized that he was tired not from his work in the orchards but from a life of almost constant disappointment. It seemed that just when something was in his grasp it slipped away like water between his fingers. He knew he didn't deserve more than what was given him, but he thought that he and Nathalie would somehow become something; at least they would have the opportunity to be together here on her father's farm. Maybe not forever, but who could think that far ahead?

Vincent relit his cigar, which had gone out in the ashtray. He blew the smoke in the air above their heads and leaned back. "I am only forty-three and yet I feel like an old man. My leg is getting worse—you see me limp. In the wintertime, sometimes I can hardly stand on it. Since I was twelve, since I fell out of a tree right here, it hasn't been right." Vincent slapped his hand down on the table and muttered something but Charging Elk didn't hear. "Anyway, this farm is too much for me now. With Lucienne gone, all I want is for Nathalie to have a good chance at a decent life."

"What will you do?"

Vincent pulled a letter from his coat pocket. The envelope was crumpled around the edges and Charging Elk could see that the ink was smeared. "I have another brother in Bordeaux—Paul. We are nearly the same age, but he's the smart one." Vincent said this last with a hint of anger. "He has offered me a chance to come work for him. He owns a large *cave*—very successful. He even imports wine from Bourgogne, Côte d'Or, Alsace, you name it. Whatever the *haute bourgeoisie* asks for. Very successful."

"And what will Nathalie do?"

Vincent looked at him with a quizzical expression, as though he didn't understand Charging Elk's interest in his daughter. "She'll find something—or someone, the good Lord willing. Bordeaux is a big city."

Charging Elk remembered the first real conversation he had had with Nathalie that day in the garden. ". . . I prefer to live here where there are not so many people. Don't you?" How could he tell Vincent that she was happy on the farm—with him? Why didn't he already know that? As he thought about this, another memory came to him, this one from a long time ago, in another life—his dear *kola*, Strikes Plenty, saying, "What good is this life we now lead?

One day we will be old men and we will have nothing but memories of bad winters and no meat and no woman. I do not want this."

Now Charging Elk's chance to be happy had been dashed. He knew Vincent was right. She would find someone else. In a few moons she would have forgotten all about him and she would be a young woman with someone else, stroking his hair, feeling his hot hands on her body. And Charging Elk would grow old and have nothing but memories. He almost moaned with self-pity.

"I will write to Madame Loiseau tomorrow and tell her you are ready to return to Marseille." Vincent stood and walked over to the simmering soup. "You have been a good worker, Charging Elk. I don't know how we would have gotten through this season without you." He lifted the cover and sniffed. "But my brother has sons— unlike me. He has a strong wife. He will have all the help he needs." Vincent turned and looked at Charging Elk. "These orchards have been good to my family for generations. Now it is time for my brother's sons. You understand, my friend."

CHAPTER TWENTY

Vincent Gazier *stood beneath the tree Charging Elk was pruning.*
He had heard what Charging Elk had said, but now all he
heard was the noise of his own blood pulsing through his
head. This was not possible; yet he had heard it.

Charging Elk climbed down from the ladder and examined the
saw he had sharpened just that morning. Small bits of the sweet
blond wood hung from its teeth. "I wish to take your daughter to be
my wife," he said, now looking up. "It would be an honor to me."

Vincent looked into Charging Elk's face. He didn't know where
to begin. He wasn't angry; he was too dumbfounded to be angry.
He just saw the impossibility of such a request. There was no reason in the world to make such a request, much less grant it. Surely
the savage would understand that. But in the back of his mind
Vincent wondered if the Indians of America just decided to take a
wife, no matter who or why.

"You must see the impossibility of your request, my friend. It is not done so lightly in France. It is true that marriages are arranged sometimes, but it is done so within families." Vincent smiled. He had regained his composure. "You and Nathalie have become friends, but that is all. And soon she'll be gone and you will be back in Marseille. There are plenty of good women down there, I am sure." But Vincent wasn't sure. He had heard of the reputation of Marseille women from young men who had been on the ships.

"None for me but Nathalie, Monsieur Gazier. We are different, but everyone is different from me in your country. She is interested in my life, in the country of my ancestors, in who my parents are — she is the first woman who seeks to know me and I would like her to be with me. She is my first real woman."

"But don't you see — this is the purest selfishness. She is only a girl. You are nearly as old as I am. You have nothing in common." Vincent was beginning to be nervous. Charging Elk was a savage! The idea of the two of them together was absurd. She was only a girl. And a devout Catholic. Her life would be ruined — and so would his. "You must forget this, Charging Elk. Do you hear me? She is my little girl and I won't give her away until she is ready." Vincent's large cavernous eyes narrowed until the sockets looked like dark plums with just a glitter of morning dew on the skin. "Until I determine she is ready. Now there's the end of it."

Nathalie, in spite of her unhappiness at the prospect of leaving the farm and Agen, had hung dried fruit garlands in the windows and a bay leaf wreath over the doorway between the parlor and the kitchen. She had gotten the family crèche from the attic, and now it stood between the fireplace and the upholstered chair where her mother had sat during the cold winter nights when times were happier. Noël was only three days away and she was determined to make it seem normal. She had even remembered her mother's plum pudding recipe and tonight she would ask Charging Elk to kill and hang a goose the next day—just as her mother would have done.

As Nathalie prepared a white bean soup with chunks of pork fat and sausage, it occurred to her that Charging Elk had never been in the parlor. He had never been invited into any part of the house but the kitchen. It further occurred to her that she was now the mistress of the household, if for only a short time until her uncle and his family moved in and she and her father moved out. The thought made her heart sink as it always did, but tonight she was determined to be the mistress. She would invite Charging Elk into the parlor after dinner to sit beside a proper fire, to take his *eau-de-vie* and admire the crèche.

But he didn't come to dinner. When she asked her father where he was, he shrugged and said maybe he was tired from pruning all day. And when she started for the door to fetch Charging Elk, her father said, "Let him be." That was all. But the tautness of those simple words made Nathalie catch her breath.

After her father went to bed, she hurried down to Charging Elk's room with a bowl of warm soup and a chunk of bread. It was a cold, clear night and the moon was nearly full, casting clean shadows from the buildings and the bare trees. When she was a small child, Nathalie used to thrill upon such a night with Noël drawing near. She would imagine that the Christ Child and the Virgin were up there, somewhere beyond the moon, looking down on her with great love and understanding for all her shortcomings. On such nights she would pray fervently that her family would always be whole and happy. But tonight she was anxious.

And when she saw no light in the small window, she feared the worst. She knocked and waited for a few seconds. Then she tried the door and it swung inward.

"Charging Elk? My dear?"

The window cast a small square of moonlight on the bed. The

covers were undisturbed. She looked at the table. The unfinished belt lay across it like the dark shadow of a rope.

Nathalie walked slowly into the room and sat down on the bed, still holding the bowl and the bread. The soup steamed in the chill air. Now everything was gone from her, she thought, first her mother, then her home, now her lover. She had been so resolute and determined before dinner—the mistress who would welcome Charging Elk like a member of the family, perhaps even pretend for an evening that he was her husband sitting before the fire—and now she felt like a little girl again, the little girl who had not experienced the love of a man. She set the soup and the bread on the floor and sank back on the bed. Then she cried and she did become the little girl—and the woman in love she had always wanted to be.

And when she awoke, the first thing she noticed was the light from the oil lamp, the soft glow that seemed to warm the cold room. And she saw Charging Elk sitting in his chair beside the bed, looking down at her. Without a thought, she held out her arms, almost like a child wanting to be picked up. Instead, he stretched out beside her and pulled her close into his open coat. They lay quietly for several moments, her chin tucked into his shoulder, his arms circling her in a warmth that made her almost cry again. Then he whispered in her ear and she said yes, yes.

The next morning Charging Elk wore his suit to breakfast. By now it was eleven years old and very much out of style, even by the standards of provincial Agen. More than that, the pants were baggy in the seat and in the knees and there was not even a suggestion of a crease. The coat looked like those worn by the peasants on town days, the pockets empty but retaining a vestigial bulge from long-forgotten cargo. Nevertheless, Charging Elk wore the suit with dignity, and the nearly clean white shirt, which had been packed away since his arrival in Agen, gave him an almost priestly look. Only the hair which flowed down his back to his shoulder blades was a reminder of his days at the Stronghold and later the Wild West show.

Charging Elk sat down in his usual place across from Vincent. Vincent toyed with his spoon, twirling it around and around. Nathalie had her back to the two men, stirring the porridge on the stove. Her brown hair, which she usually let fall loosely around her shoulders, was pinned up so that it formed a neat bun. She wore her usual dress and apron but her shoulders seemed a little higher and her back straighter. She left off her stirring and poured coffee and hot milk into a large bowl and set it before Charging Elk. He glanced up at her almost without recognition. He had his mind on another thing.

"Again I ask for your daughter's hand in marriage, Monsieur Gazier," he said, as though he were simply carrying on the conversation they had had in the orchard. He was looking at his own hands, which were folded together and resting on the oilcloth covering the table.

Vincent toyed with his spoon for a moment, tapping it against the table. Then he glanced toward his daughter, who had quit stirring the porridge and stood erect but motionless. There was much about her, now that she was filling out, that reminded him of Lucienne. Even the way she wore her hair in a loose bun today.

"And what does my daughter say to this?" he said to her back.

Nathalie didn't turn around right away. With her apron she moved the steaming pot of porridge to a cooler place on the stove. She wiped her hands, a practiced but unnecessary gesture. Only then did she turn, but instead of facing her father she looked toward Charging Elk.

"I would be very happy to become his wife," she said. Her

voice sounded weak to her, unused, but she added, "We are in love."

Vincent frowned. "So you two have discussed this—without telling me?"

For a moment neither of them answered. Perhaps they were deciding how much to tell him. Perhaps they were both remembering last night. Finally Charging Elk said, "Yes. Nathalie has agreed to become my wife. With your permission, monsieur."

"We love each other, father. We will be happy together."

"And if this marriage were to take place, would you move with him to Marseille?" But Vincent didn't wait for an answer. He stood stiffly and walked around the table and out the door, closing it behind him.

At any other time, Vincent would have marveled at such a beautiful morning. A thin fog hung in the courtyard, golden beneath the rising sun. Soon the fog would burn off and the sky would become the clean blue of a rare late-December day when the earth would warm just enough to remind him that the orchards were only sleeping, that in three months' time the tiny buds would begin to appear on the plum trees and the growing season would begin again, just as it had for the many generations that the Gaziers had owned this land. At any other time, Vincent would have given thanks to the Lord for allowing his family to enjoy the bounty of such a paradise. And Vincent would have considered himself a very lucky man on such a rare day.

But in truth, he was a dispirited man and had been so for the past several months. Perhaps he could have gotten over Lucienne's death. He had watched it coming for a long time, and when it came, in spite of his grief, he had felt relieved and almost was able to think of a new life for his daughter. He knew that eventually she would marry and go off to start her own family. But he could have lived with that, as long as she was happy. And who knew—perhaps her husband would end up working alongside Vincent in the orchards. Then they would all be together. He had always dreamed of grand-children playing in this very courtyard. In his best moments, he thought that life could be tolerable again for him. Even without Lucienne.

But Vincent's own health had taken a turn for the worse. His leg ached constantly now, no longer a matter of mere annoyance, and was actually growing thinner, weaker. He knew that even if Charging Elk managed to complete the pruning by himself, his leg would not allow him to endure the rigors of the growing and har-vesting seasons—and of taking care of the pigs and geese and do-ing the dozens of other chores around the farm. Even if Nathalie decided to stay with him, if they could somehow stay on the farm, she would become a slave to the garden, to the orchards, to a life of constant labor. He had seen it happen before—young women who became little more than beasts of burden, who became bitter and resentful, old before their time, and finally as unresponsive as the dumb oxen who pulled the millstones in circles.

No, he couldn't allow this to happen to his daughter. But to marry a savage! What would Lucienne think of such an ungodly union? Where was God in all this?

Later that day, Vincent composed a letter to Madame Loiseau. His hand was slow and deliberate but the words and letters were very readable, thanks to his mother, who had taught in a country school only a few kilometers to the south before she had married his father. Even as he wrote the words that he hoped would put an end to this insanity, he regretted never having insisted that Nathalie learn to read and write. Although she had gone to school for three years, she had been an indifferent pupil whose only concern seemed to be measuring up to her friends, and when her schooling had ended, so too ended any desire to read and write. She had been con-tent to learn the skills of the house and farm with the idea that such skills would serve her better as a farm wife. What good is it to learn to read and write when I have nothing to read and nobody to write to, she would say to his entreaties.

As Vincent folded up the letter, he felt a stabbing ache in his leg from having sat in one position too long. And when he stood, he couldn't feel any sensation in his foot. My God, he thought, it gets worse by the day now. He hadn't been to a doctor for many years, at least twenty, since the time he almost lost a finger splitting kindling. He had been embarrassed then at such a stupid accident, but this was serious. He sat down again and massaged the leg with both hands. Even as he felt the burden of his miseries seemingly mount by the hour, he tucked the folded letter into a cubbyhole of the writing desk, then closed the top. He suddenly was frightened for himself and for Nathalie. Dear, sweet Lucienne, what should I do?

Nothing more was said of the proposed marriage that day or the next. Vincent ate his breakfast in near silence, and at dinnertime, he retired early, even though Nathalie would light the fire in the parlor. He spent the days either inside or wandering among the buildings of the farm, rearranging tack, cleaning the goose pen, although that was Nathalie's job, or just standing in the horse shed, not really knowing why he was there.

Charging Elk spent the days pruning in the orchards. He had not pushed Vincent again because he sensed that the man was thinking, that he was not just ignoring the proposal. And so he pruned the trees, sometimes with a great burst of joy at what might be, other times with a numbing despondency at what would probably happen. In the evening, he and Nathalie would sit in the parlor and watch the fire and look at the crèche. They sat apart from each other, glancing at each other from time to time in an almost searching way, then he would swallow the last of his *eau-de-vie*, say his good night, and go to his room.

On the eve of Noël, Charging Elk hitched the horses to the wagon. He had not wanted to go to the *wasichu* church again but Vincent had insisted. This puzzled Charging Elk; nevertheless, he waited outside in the cold night air for Vincent and Nathalie.

Vincent sat between them during the service. Charging Elk was pleasantly overcome by the holy smoke and the songs of the priest and the choir, but he noticed that Vincent slumped when he knelt, half sitting against the bench, his forehead resting on his folded hands.

When Vincent slumped like this, Charging Elk had a clear view of Nathalie out of the corner of his eye. He had never seen a more beautiful woman, and in her finest dress and felt hat with a netting that half-hid her face, she was truly a woman. But even as he was thrilled at the sight of her, he almost felt that he didn't know this young woman, that she might have been a stranger that he admired from afar. And he suddenly felt unworthy—a savage that didn't deserve such beauty. Although he knew that this was not a holy place for him, he closed his eyes, breathed in the smoke which reminded him of burning sweetgrass, and asked Wakan Tanka for kindness and pity just this once.

After a late dinner of fish soup, a dish that Lucienne had always prepared on the eve of Noël, Nathalie cleared the table while the men sat and talked of the pruning. Nathalie listened with a feeling of annoyance and disbelief that such a mundane subject should occupy the two men. She had prepared the soup that afternoon, almost without thinking because her mind was on so many things—this was the first Noël without her mother, the first with Charging Elk, the last on the farm, and perhaps the last with her father.

She had made up her mind to run away with Charging Elk

rather than go to Bordeaux. She didn't know how they would get to Marseille, what they would do for money, and the thought of such a far, strange city filled with a different kind of people frightened her. But since the night he had opened up his coat for her she had come to feel that he would protect her no matter what they did, no matter where their fortunes took them.

Vincent insisted that she bring an extra glass when she brought the *eau-de-vie*, and she felt her heart leap. It could only mean one thing. But when they lifted their glasses, he said, "To your dear mother and my dear wife, may she be in heaven where all earthly woes are forgotten. *Adieu*, dear one."

Nathalie sipped and felt the liquor sear her throat. But the flush in her cheeks came not from liquor but from the guilt and anger she suddenly felt. Her disappointment in the toast seemed monstrous to her—her mother had been dead for only a few months—yet real enough. But it was unfair that her father did not consider her happiness. She was young and alive. She deserved to be happy with the man of her choice. She felt a welling behind her eyes and looked away, but not before a tear ran down her cheek.

"There now, my daughter, it is not so bad. I'm sure she looks down upon us this holy night and gives her consent to the toast I now propose. She was a wise and generous woman, your mother. And I have talked to her often these past few days." With that he raised his glass again. "To you and Charging Elk—may you be happy together." As he swallowed the drink, he thought, And may God and my dear wife forgive me.

Three weeks later, Nathalie and Charging Elk were married in a civil ceremony at the Hôtel de Ville in Agen. It was a simple proceeding and took less than fifteen minutes. Vincent's younger brother stood up for Charging Elk and his wife stood beside Nathalie.

Charging Elk's pardon, which declared his rights and duties as a citizen of the Republic of France, served as his official papers. And so, by quirk of fate, he finally acquired his citizenship, as well as a bride.

But his bride's happiness was mitigated by a crushing disappointment that she could not be married in the church. Vincent would not allow it, and even if he had, the priest would not have. Charging Elk was an unbaptized heathen in the eyes of the church, Vincent had explained. And so Nathalie had found herself in a quandary—wait for the long conversion process, even if he did want to convert, and he had been unresponsive to the idea, a reaction that she found strange; or forgo her dream of a real wedding, with a new white wedding dress and beaming family and a celebration afterward. Since she was a little girl she had always envisioned a real wedding where all the people loved her. In her daydreams she was a shy, humble bride but the people nevertheless remarked on her beauty. And her new groom, whoever he might be, gazed upon her with pure adoration, dumbstruck by his good fortune.

Perhaps even more than such worldly approval, Nathalie wanted the blessings of the priest, therefore of God, with the Virgin and Jesus and all the saints smiling in acquiescence. Only then would she feel truly wed. And forgiven for her wickedness in fornicating with the man now standing beside her.

But here she was, in a cold, high-ceilinged chamber, with a tall, balding man in an ill-fitting suit reciting the marriage contract in the most perfunctory way. Even her dress, which her mother had made a year and a half ago and which was already tight in the hips and bust, was not white or even lacy. Because of the season, her bouquet was a spray of dried flowers that Vincent had bought in a kiosk in the central *place*. And instead of a large audience of family and friends only her aunt and uncle and father were present.

When the man pronounced them man and wife, Nathalie and Charging Elk kissed for the first time in public. She kept her lips pressed tight, for she was afraid he would try to put his tongue in her mouth. But he didn't. He was as shy and awkward as she.

Vincent had destroyed the hateful letter he had written to Madame Loiseau some weeks ago and had written another telling her of Charging Elk's imminent arrival in Marseille. Almost as an afterthought, he mentioned that his daughter, Nathalie, who was engaged to become Madame Charging Elk, would accompany him and therefore they would probably need larger living quarters. He had received a reply from Madame Loiseau: "You can't imagine how surprised and pleased we all are here at the Relief Society. Surely his marriage to your chaste daughter will do much to ensure Charging Elk's future happiness. You must be very proud." She asked him to wire her when the newlyweds were ready to leave so that someone could meet them at the Gare St-Charles.

Now Vincent stood beside Nathalie and watched Charging Elk unload their possessions from the wagon. Nathalie had a steamer trunk, a smaller case, and a cloth valise. Charging Elk had the duffel bag and valise he had come with ten months ago. Vincent had presented him with a small leather pouch containing 250 francs, just about the sum that Madame Loiseau had sent for Charging Elk's keep. He had earned that much and more, but it was all Vincent could afford.

He had been worried sick ever since the evening he had given the two lovers his blessing. But now, seeing them walking together, Charging Elk wheeling a cart with their worldly goods, he suddenly saw them as they really were. True, Vincent had grown used to seeing them together the past few weeks, but still they made a handsome, even striking, couple. Nathalie even seemed taller, more dignified, more a woman. Since Lucienne's death, he had worried about his daughter's future. But now he felt an unfamiliar trust deep inside and he knew that Charging Elk would treat her well. And instead of the quiet but burning resentment he had felt toward the Indian for taking his daughter from him, he experienced a strange new pride in trailing after the couple and he tried to ignore his bad leg and walk with as much dignity as they possessed.

But an hour later, when he drove the team into the barnyard, he looked around and saw how shabby the buildings were. Several tiles were broken or missing on the roof of the horse shed. The pig-pen was a ramshackle affair of old branches and woven wire. Even the main house had three or four patches where the dirty white stucco had fallen out, exposing the red brick structure. Vincent had noticed these defects before, but always one at a time—a casual glance in passing at things that needed repair when he had time. Now he saw the entirety of the compound, and the sight depressed him. Even the trees on the hillside above, although neatly pruned, were old and would need replacing over the next few years, a sec-tion at a time.

Vincent now saw the farm with the perfect clarity of a man truly alone. It was hard to believe just now that he had had a happy life here, with a loving wife and a lively, lovely daughter. Now they were both gone. And soon he would be gone too. But the farm would remain in the family. His brother, Raymond, had promised to pay him 750 francs after every harvest season, but Vincent knew that he would never be able to do it. He had too many mouths to feed.

He climbed down from the wagon and unhitched the horses. He took them up to the spring on the hillside behind the house. As he watched them drink, he tried to imagine Nathalie and Charging Elk in their coach. They would probably be eating their lunch by now, looking out the window at the Garonne or the bare grape vines that ran so perfectly up the hillsides. They would probably be holding hands, perhaps a little frightened at their new adventure—at least Nathalie would be. Vincent listened to the old black horse shudder and he patted its shoulder and he was grateful for the warmth of the beast.

Later, he sat at the table in the kitchen, drinking a cup of coffee, listening for a footstep overhead, for the clank of pots on the stove, for the rasp of a pruning saw being filed in the toolshed, but he heard nothing. He had not dreamed that silence could be so complete in this world of his. He cleared his throat. Then he struck a match and lit a cigar and looked at the strange belt on the table. He ran his fingers over the tight, nubbly texture of the designs. He would miss Charging Elk. But he would ache in his heart for his daughter. She was all he had left and now she was gone.

CHAPTER TWENTY-ONE

harging Elk stood on the corner of Rue d'Aubagne and looked up the narrow cobblestone street toward the *place*, the square where three alleys came together, where all the market activity was going on. Women passed him on either side, singly, purposefully, some coming away from the market with spring vegetables and cheeses and fish or cuts of meat, others hurrying toward the market with empty baskets and coin purses. The only men seemed to be the sellers and a few old-timers who walked stiffly beside their wives.

He was surprised how small the market was. He had remembered it as huge, full of hundreds of people and dozens of stalls. He had remembered many men in suits, wandering among the women, looking them up and down or admiring the fish in René's stall. He had remembered the smell of tobacco mixed in with the earthy odor of produce and the pungent smell of aged cheese. The one thing that proved true to his memory was the street cries of the mongers, the loud shouts, the mocking, the teasing, the occasional angry voice rising above the rest.

The voices all sounded familiar to him, almost as though he could recognize them, but more than twelve years had passed since he had worked in the Soulases' fish stand and he knew that many of the voices would be silenced forever; others would have failed or moved on. Still, it was a small neighborhood, the people would have lived there for generations, so it was not impossible that he would know them.

Charging Elk was nervous, almost frightened at being discovered. He was still an oddity, a big man with dark skin and long black hair who looked as if he belonged in an immigrant neighborhood. Strangely, he had not felt so out of place since he had left Marseille, not in the prison, where there were many varieties of men, not in Agen, where he was different enough to feel unique but not a freak. Now the people looked at him with that same suspicion he had felt when he first walked these streets. It had been a puzzling hostility then, but now he was afraid someone would recognize him as the notorious killer of the famous chef.

He had enjoyed a quiet anonymity for four moons since arriving from Agen. He went to work on the quais every day but Sunday, loading and unloading the big ships; he stayed home at nights with Nathalie; they walked along the Corniche on Sundays. It was a quiet life and he treasured it. He had taken up drawing again and drew from memory his life on the plains of Dakota. Nathalie would watch him over her sewing or knitting until she couldn't stand the suspense and would beg him to show her his current effort. But he made her wait until he had finished each sketch. Then he would point out every detail and explain it to her. She was always enthusiastic and urged him to start selling them. There were always artists around the Old Port who sold worse pictures than his. He would laugh at her enthusiasm, but when he was heaving around the heavy crates or casks or walking home from work, he wondered if that was possible. He had never considered himself an artist, but what if she was right? He began to envy the real artists who sold their pictures on the quais and along the Corniche. And Nathalie was right—his pictures were better than many of those who seemed to draw or paint the same scene over and over. But the idea of selling sketches was a fleeting one, and by the time he walked up the stairs to their flat it was gone.

Charging Elk had not worked for six days, and he was restless and worried. He and Nathalie had only enough francs for food for another week. He went to the quais every morning, but he would be turned back by some of the men he worked with. His union had struck the shipping companies and several of the workers paced the quais, carrying placards and clubs. They wanted shorter hours—from ten hours a day to eight—and Saturday afternoons off to be with their families more. They were tired of being treated like West African slaves. Charging Elk agreed with his fellow workers, but what good would it do if they could not put food on the table or pay the rent in the meantime? What if the companies took their jobs from them and gave them away to others? There were always men hanging around the quais looking for work.

Charging Elk took a deep breath and put these thoughts out of mind. Today he needed to be clear of head, and he had stood there long enough. He would have to walk up the street or walk away. He wouldn't have very far to go to see René's stall. It was on the near edge of the *place*, under a familiar green awning that he could almost make out from here. It would say POISSONS COQUILLAGES FRUITS DE MER. He could almost envision the wooden trays filled with shaved ice, the separate displays of sardines, anchovies, and tuna, the langoustines, the *poulpe* and the *rascasse*, the hogfish, its big jaws propped open in a frightening display. Even now he thought he could smell the dull, clean odor of fresh fish, the metallic tinge of the oysters.

He rolled a cigarette, lit it, and took a few tentative steps toward the market. He had used part of the money Vincent had given him to buy a new suit. This one was made of a cheaper material, coarser, scratchier, but it was still fresh and draped smoothly over his long frame. He was happy with the suit and the wool cap, but he was especially proud of the way Nathalie looked on Sundays in her new silky gray dress with the lace sleeves and collar. Sometimes he sat in church and just watched her as she went through the gestures of her worship.

Charging Elk had worried all the way down from Agen about how Nathalie would take to Marseille. For him the city by the sea would be familiar, even welcome, after the cloistered valley of the Garonne. He had a few moments of doubt on his own account, but Madame Loiseau had assured him, in a letter to Vincent, that his previous notoriety had been all but forgotten. But Nathalie would not be accustomed to the variousness and energy of the big seaport. The French that people here spoke was different from that of Agen. Often it was not French at all but the strange language that René and Madeleine spoke to each other. He had tried to prepare her on the long trip by pointing out the differences in tongue and custom, but he only succeeded in spoiling the trip for her. She went from excitement over all the things they were seeing from the train window to a set-jaw apprehension when they reached the coast and turned east. And when they were met at the Gare St-Charles by a man from Madame Loiseau's office, Nathalie was visibly timid and frightened of all the trains and people in the large, glass-covered station.

Even as he remembered their dismal arrival, Charging Elk felt his heart jump up. When they walked into their flat, which had three rooms, a real bathroom, and a large three-sided window overlooking the dark street, her eyes had lit up again. And when the man left, she had pulled him down on the bed and said many wonderful things to him, punctuated with giggles and sighs. In spite of his dire warnings, she had managed to cheer up both herself and him. He had never been so grateful for her youth as that first night in their new flat.

Now Charging Elk could see the green awning with the big white letters. Just below the letters, in smaller print that he couldn't read but knew was there, were the words "M. Soulas, Poissonnier."

Charging Elk approached slowly, stopping to look into shop windows, then at tables filled with nuts, olives, radishes, lettuce, and all the other early-season riches of the market, until he was at the meat stall, looking at the large cuts of red meat. As he looked at them, he remembered how he had stood in the fish stall looking longingly at the meat. Later when he learned that it was horse meat, that the golden horse head was the insignia of all markets that sold horse meat, he had almost gotten sick. He had eaten the flesh of *ʃunka wakan* before, during the bad winter after the fight on the Greasy Grass, when the people were hungry all the time, but he hadn't eaten it since. Now he looked at the meat and he thought of all the horses the Oglalas had owned before they came in to Fort Robinson. None of the people were happy to eat their horses that winter but they had saved many from starvation.

He glanced over at the fish stall, his stomach turning a little from the smell of the meat and the apprehension he suddenly felt. At first he couldn't see the mongers through the crowd of women, who all seemed to be pointing at the fish at once, talking, shouting, arguing in those familiar voices. Then he heard a man's voice scolding one of the women and he recognized it at once. And when the woman walked off with her fish wrapped in newsprint, Charging Elk saw his old friend.

The few thin strands of hair that used to be plastered over the top of the shiny head were gone now. But from the distance of the width of the narrow street, everything else about René looked the same. The same open smile which showed the gap of missing lower teeth, the same small, bright eyes, the stocky little frame. Charging Elk felt his throat tighten and he looked between the heads of the women for Madeleine. In some way that he did not fully understand, he had come to see her. He had never forgotten the shame he had felt when she said that he must bring his girlfriend to dinner one Sunday. And his further shame when she had learned during the trial that his girlfriend was a whore. And when she had quit coming to the trial, when she chose not to see him anymore, he felt his shame was complete. But now why did he want to see her so much? To tell her that he was now a different man? That he had a wife who was young and virtuous, who went to church every Sunday? That he went to church too? What was it he wanted from Madeleine?

Another customer left the stall, and he saw a tall, thin young man in a soiled oilskin apron. It wasn't François. So René had a new helper. The young man was heaping more shrimps onto the ice from a box at his feet. Although it was a warm spring morning with the sun just now entering the narrow street, the young man wore a high-necked sweater beneath the apron. His long pale fingers scooped up mounds of shrimps and laid them on the ice. Even from across the street Charging Elk could see the red knuckles that seemed to be the lot of the fishmonger from day after day of the slimy moisture. But it was the hair of the new helper that held his gaze. It was brown and bushy, seeming to stand up from every angle. And when the young man looked up, right at him, Charging Elk turned quickly back to the red meat. He held his breath, waiting for the young man to call out, but he heard nothing except the haggling around him. He eased his way back toward the way he came, and when he was clear of the market, he walked quickly down Rue d'Aubagne in the direction of La Canebière.

Charging Elk never went back to the market after that. Although he hadn't seen Madeleine, for many days afterward he imagined her there and that she had looked at him with forgiveness in her eyes. He imagined that she beckoned to him and spoke his name. But he couldn't imagine anything beyond that. When he thought of that day, he only saw the large brown eyes of Mathias looking at him without a hint of expression.

The strike lasted for three weeks, and when it was settled, the dockworkers got their Saturday afternoons off and extra pay if they worked them. They did not get shorter hours for the other days of the week, but Charging Elk was happy to be back at work. The last of the 250 francs that Vincent had given him managed to get him and Nathalie through the three weeks, but they had ended up eating out of the same pot of soup for several days.

One afternoon, Charging Elk returned to the flat to find Nathalie slumped over the kitchen table in tears. She was barefoot and wore only a white cotton chemise. He immediately thought of Vincent. Something had happened to him. But when he hurried over to comfort her, she looked up at him with a small, scared smile that stopped him in his tracks.

"But what is it, Nathalie? Why are you crying? Is it your father?"

Nathalie dabbed at her eyes with a small cloth. Her face had grown leaner, shaplier, in the past several months—she had become a very attractive woman at eighteen—but now her eyes sparkled with tears. Her cheeks were red and her lips trembled almost imperceptibly.

Charging Elk knelt before her, suddenly frightened. "What is is? Are you all right?"

She nodded. "It is nothing. I'm just foolish to worry—" A single sob, like a hiccup, racked her body and the tears flowed again.

"You must tell me—what troubles you? Please."

"I can't tell you." She looked down at the table, but the small smile had returned. "You won't like it." Then she made a small sound which seemed to come from her bosom. It seemed to be a suppressed sob, but when it came again it sounded more like a giggle.

Charging Elk sat back on his heels, puzzled. "Please," he said in a low voice. "You can tell me. I'm your husband."

"I think you are part of the problem, my husband."

"What have I done?" Again he became frightened.

"It's what we have both done." She wound the damp cloth around her finger and stared intently at it. "We have created a baby perhaps."

"A baby!"

Nathalie looked at him. "Are you not happy? All day I was afraid you wouldn't be. Now I see it in your eyes. You are not happy."

"Yes. No. Of course I am happy, Nathalie. But how . . . ?"

Nathalie smiled and her cheeks reddened. "What do you mean, 'how'? Like anybody else—when they lie together as often as we do."

This time Charging Elk blushed. "But how do you know?"

Nathalie looked out the window, her young face suddenly serene. "A woman knows these things. It is not difficult to tell."

Charging Elk put his hand on her thigh, feeling the firmness of it through her thin chemise. He studied his dark hand against the cotton. As he did so often, he marveled at his good fortune that he had a woman of his own—and that his woman was Nathalie. And when he felt her small hand, so white and delicate, on his own, he couldn't imagine that he had ever been unhappy. "A baby," he whispered. "Our own baby."

Nathalie ran her fingers through his long hair, then pulled his head into her bosom. She stroked his hair, all the time staring out the window at the sooty stone building across the narrow street. But in her mind she was seeing the old farmhouse, its sunny courtyard and the lovely plum orchards of her childhood. The novelty of Marseille—its size, its shops, its different colors of people, the Old Port, the sea—was beginning to wear off, and at this moment she wished with all her heart that she and Charging Elk could return to Agen and her home. But that was impossible now. It was no longer her home. This strange, sweaty city was home.

The fall was nearly perfect that year and lasted well into October. Although the leaves around town had turned a dull yellow or soft pink, they hung on the trees like crisp paper ornaments. The mornings were fresh, and when Charging Elk walked down to the quais at dawn, he could see his breath in the glow of the streetlamps and feel the chill work its way through his wool jacket, but by midday the sun warmed the quais and he worked in his undershirt. He worked hard so the time would pass quickly; then he would hurry home to Nathalie, who was always there waiting for him.

One evening, after he had washed himself and put on a clean shirt, she held his hand against her swollen belly. "This is your son, I think," she said, her eyes wide, as though she were listening for something.

He felt a small movement and jerked his hand back.

Nathalie laughed. "You should see your face," she said. Then she placed his hand on her stomach again. "Now just hold it there, sissy."

And he felt what seemed to be a little thump, followed by another. As he felt the sporadic kicks he thought that he had never been this intimate with a woman, not even when he and Marie—

and later, Nathalie—made love. There was a part of him within Nathalie's flesh, a part that he could feel through her gingham dress. Of course, he knew all about birth; he had watched horses, dogs, even an ape in the Paris zoo during the months of the Exposition; he had seen women out at the Stronghold big with child, and later, holding babies in the sun outside their lodges. But he had never felt anything like this before. This was his wife and his child. And soon that child would come out and look around and the first thing it would see would be its mother and father.

"You do want a boy, don't you?"

"Yes," he said without hesitation, for he had been thinking of walking with his own son along the quais of the Old Port, showing him the sea from the parapet of Fort St-Jean, buying him a *glace* from one of the vendors on Cours Belsunce—just as he had seen other fathers do. He hadn't known until just this moment that he had envied them.

"What if it's a girl?" Nathalie's voice was almost hesitant. "It could just as easily be a girl. Would you like her as much?"

He thought for just a couple of seconds. "If she looks like you and not me," he said.

Nathalie laughed.

Toward the middle of October, the first real mistral blew down the valley of the Rhône, shaking the papery leaves off the trees, blowing the smoke sideways from the chimney pots on buildings, rocking even the steamships moored in the port. Instead of walking leisurely along La Canebière, people hurried from building to building, shop to shop, bundled up in their winter clothes. Horses trotted along the streets, as though the icy wind had given them new energy, or at least a desire to quickly reach whatever destination the driver chose, preferably in the lee of a building. The out-

door cafés moved indoors, leaving the chairs and tables stacked under awnings. Almost overnight, far too early, Marseille had been
transformed into a winter city.

But the dockworkers continued to load the ships, as though the
cold weather were a small inconvenience, a minor discomfort to be
endured. These were tough men, men who had carried clubs as well
as placards during the strike. Some had been anxious to get the police involved, to "crack a few heads" just to show them they were
serious. But when it came to work, they did their jobs efficiently, if
not enthusiastically. And they accepted Charging Elk as one of
them, a member of the union, in a way that he hadn't been used
to—not in the market when he had worked for René; not in the
soap factory; not even in prison. And he felt, for the first time since
he had left the Stronghold, that he was a part of a group of men
who looked out for each other. And he liked it.

As far as he could tell, in spite of his singular appearance, none
of his fellow workers knew who he was—except for the union boss,
Picard, a big-chested man with curly black hair and a drooping
mustache, who wore loud plaid suits and a chocolate-colored
bowler. As unlikely as it seemed, he was an acquaintance of
Madame Loiseau's and had taken on the Indian as a favor to her
and her organization. The boss sometimes winked at Charging Elk,
but that was all the contact between them.

On the 17th of October, a day that he would never forget,
Charging Elk took a few minutes of his midday break to walk down
toward the Quai des Belges to buy some tobacco. Although the
mistral had blown itself out, the day was cold and the sky was a flat
pewter over the port. The hills to the north of the town were completely invisible; to the south, the sea and the sky blended in a gray
seam that defied distinction and distance.

Charging Elk had been watching two men put up a poster along
a wall beside the tobacco shop as he walked along. The wall had the

remnants of many posters, some of them still readable, others faded or partially peeled away. The men stood on a platform and with long-handled brushes smoothed the wet poster into place. Charging Elk had often looked at the posters on his way home from work, and although he couldn't read the words, he could tell the subject of most—bicycle races, circuses, theater events. The posters changed often, sometimes between the time he went to work and the time he came home.

Now he was close enough to the tobacco shop to see the sign in detail as the men smoothed the last corners into place. And he stopped. He didn't believe what he was seeing. The last thing he ever expected to see again was the image of Buffalo Bill, with his white hat and goatee, surrounded by smaller images of cowboys, soldiers—and Indians. He walked slowly, hesitantly, closer, until he was just a few feet away from the men, who were now taking down their scaffolding. He looked at the three Indian portraits. They seemed realistic, like real faces, but he didn't recognize any of them. The headdresses and beaded tunics looked like they could have been Lakota. He looked at the words, but the only ones he could recognize were "Buffalo Bill," "Indiens," "Wild West," and the dates: November 1–12.

Charging Elk shuddered against the bite of a cold breeze that crawled up his backbone, but there was no wind that day.

⟡

Nathalie had noticed a distance in her husband for the past several days. Even when he helped her with the dishes or brought her a cup of tea in the evening, his eyes seemed not to focus on her or on the small chore. Of course, he was obliging in his ways and even more solicitous since she had announced her pregnancy. But when he sat down at the kitchen table to work on one of his sketches, she would see him sometimes staring at the paper or the shuttered window. And when she looked again, he would be looking at his hands or his teacup.

Although this behavior worried her, Nathalie hadn't inquired about the source of his distraction. She had problems of her own. It seemed that every morning she was sick, and when she wasn't sick, she was hungry, But nothing seemed to satisfy her. If she ate one thing, she would crave another; then another. And she could feel her body changing, growing heavier. Sometimes she felt at peace, even exhilarated on occasion, but at other times, she felt a great dread come over her. She knew nobody in Marseille that she could call a friend. There was no one to talk to, no one to help her when the time came. Except for Dr. Ventoux, whose office was just around the corner on Place des Capucins, and Madame Robichon, the midwife he introduced her to. But both of them were too professional to take a personal interest in her and her uneasiness. She did have a passing acquaintanceship with the woman in the fabric shop, where she bought cotton cloth to sew the tiny gowns and yarn to knit caps and socks. And there was the young mother she had met on the landing just below her flat. The woman had noticed Nathalie's stomach, and so they had a brief conversation about birth and motherhood. She invited Nathalie to tea sometime soon but she hadn't set a time. Nathalie tramped up and down the stairs more often than was necessary, running one errand, then another, on the chance that she might "run into" the young mother. She was tired of being alone all day. She wanted a friend.

But more than anything she missed her mother. She needed her now in a way that she never had. She needed someone to trust. How does one have a child? How does one raise it? On some days, when Charging Elk was at work, Nathalie would imagine conversations with her mother. She would imagine her mother there in the flat in Marseille, fluffing pillows, cooking a big pot of soup, dusting the sparse furnishings, sitting beside her daughter with her knitting—"There, there, babies happen all the time, nothing to worry about, you have good hips, Nathalie, easy as falling off a wagon." Nathalie took great comfort in these snippets of conversation, but when the daydream ended, she was alone, in a small flat, in a city far from Agen, and her mother couldn't help her.

Charging Elk knew none of this, and he was always surprised when she would run to him when he walked in the door and hug him tightly before he even got his coat and cap off. He would hold her, feeling her round belly against his lower abdomen, and kiss her on top of the head, smelling the clean scent of her. He would hold her, stroke her hair, whisper in her ear, but even then his mind would drift away.

Charging Elk told Nathalie about the return of the Wild West show two nights before it was to open at Rond Point du Prado. She became excited and wanted to know all about it.

"Will there be Indians?"

"Yes."

"Like you?"

"Yes."

"And Buffalo Bill—he is a big man?"

"Very big man."

"Will the Indians kill a bison?"

"Not really. They will only pretend." But he wondered if there were any buffalo left. He thought of Bird Tail's dream of the buffalo entering the cave in Paha Sapa. He had never heard of the buffalo returning. All he ever heard about America—well, he heard almost nothing. Because he couldn't read, he didn't know what the journals said about his homeland. Sometimes he unloaded ships from America. Sometimes he heard his fellow workers curse America for being greedy and arrogant. President Roosevelt had attacked the small country of Cuba for no reason. Now they were in the Philippines. The rabblerousers among the dockworkers often talked of refusing to unload American goods. Charging Elk didn't understand their anger and didn't know enough about America to come to its defense—even if he wanted to.

But now he would have his chance. He would be able to talk with the Lakotas in the Wild West show. He would see how it was in Dakota. He would learn how his parents were, how all of the Lakota people were. If they were still there. He hadn't forgotten his dream and the strange voice above the roaring wind: *You are my only son.* He had tried to put the voice out of his mind, and had succeeded for the most part in the winters he was in La Tombe. But during his several moons with the Gaziers, when he contemplated his freedom and the possibility of going home, the voice had come back, on rare and unexpected occasions—when he was picking plums or working on the horsehair belt—sometimes accompanied by the terrible vision of the broken bodies lying on the rocks below the cliff. And he would remember trying to join them and the terrifying hopelessness as the wind with the roaring voice pushed him back from the cliff time after time, until he lay in the grass and wept with frustration.

But the dream, as terrifying as it still was, was not the reason Charging Elk had become so distant from Nathalie, from his fellow workers, from this world. He was tormented inside, as though some animal were clawing at his guts. And the almost physical pain came because he was certain that he could have the one thing that he had wanted so desperately over the past sixteen years—and he didn't want to want it so much now.

On the Saturday evening that they were to go to the Wild West show, Nathalie had become ill. She had been feverish and tired all day, a condition that she thought was due to her advanced pregnancy—she was less than six weeks away and she often felt heavy and run-down. Just before supper she threw up, but when she sat down at the table, she looked a little better and actually ate some of the fish soup and a crust of bread. Charging Elk urged her to drink a glass of wine to settle her stomach, but when she touched the glass to her lips her eyes grew wide and she hurried into the bathroom. He listened to her retching and coughing and decided that they could not possibly go the performance. In one way he was disappointed almost to the point of dismay; in another way, he felt a great weight being lifted from his shoulders. And he couldn't tell which feeling was the stronger.

When Nathalie came back, he was startled and concerned by how pale and fragile she looked. Her dark hair, which she had pinned up so carefully, was coming loose and her eyes were flat and wet.

"You must come to bed," he said, holding her hand and leading her into the small bedroom. "You must rest. The show will wait."

"But tomorrow is the last day, my husband. If I am ill tomorrow, I will spoil everything for you."

"It is of no concern to me." He sat her on the edge of the bed and knelt to unlace her shoes. He helped her out of her good dress and into her flannel nightgown. Then he tucked her in bed and spread an extra quilt over her.

Nathalie had been quiet during these preparations, but now she said, "You must go, Charging Elk. I know how much you have been looking forward to this." She managed a weak smile. "I'll be all right. I swear."

Charging Elk sat on the bed and looked down at her. He remembered the time in the garden she had called him by his name, how she had said it in a way that sent a warmth into his heart. He remembered the morning sun and the fine earth, the musky smell of the spent tomato plants. And he remembered saying what was in his heart, and he said it again: "You make me feel good."

She smiled again and reached for his hand. She caressed the back of it with her thumb, her eyes focused on his carefully knotted tie. "You are very handsome this evening, my love." The smile faded and she was silent for a long moment. Then she looked into his eyes, her own eyes suddenly bright and intense. "I have seen how sometimes lately you stare off into the distance, as though you are seeing something that is not here, not now. It has troubled me because I think sometimes that you are not with me in such a momentous time. I do not want to feel alone. . . ." Her eyes grew wet and she wiped them with the sleeve of her nightgown. Then she laughed. "It is foolish, I know. . . ."

Charging Elk kissed her on the forehead. "I am here," he said. "Now you must rest, Nathalie. I will be here when you wake up." He stood and began to loosen his tie.

"No, please. This is important to you. They are your people. Please. I want you to go."

Charging Elk looked down at her. She smiled. "I will be here when you get back. I will feel better. I promise."

"I won't stay long," he said, cinching the knot again. "Just for the show."

"You must stay as long as you like. Promise me."

"Okay," he said. "But I won't stay long."

Charging Elk walked through Place des Capucins on his way to Rue de Rome. The square was filled with Saturday-night shoppers and diners, young people talking and laughing behind the glass of cafés. Although it was cold enough to see his breath, he felt a kind of exuberance that he recognized from the old days in Marseille. Saturday nights in La Tombe were just like any other night, just a quiet conversation with Causeret, perhaps a bit more melancholy as they reminisced about the good times on the outside. At the Gaziers' farm, he might stay an extra hour after dinner, have another *eau-de-vie*, one of Vincent's cigars. Nothing special.

But Marseille! How many Saturday nights had he walked these streets in his fine clothes, sat in cafés, visited Marie? For two years he had felt a sense of freedom that he hadn't known since his years at the Stronghold. But even the Stronghold was not exciting, only the things he and Strikes Plenty did when he was there. And now he thought of all those winter evenings he and his friend had sat in their lodge, nowhere to go and nothing to do. Charging Elk quickened his stride as he thought of the show and the possibility of seeing old friends. Surely he wouldn't know anybody anymore, not after sixteen years. But who knew? Maybe Broncho Billy would still be with the show.

Charging Elk boarded the trolley car on Rue de Rome. It was filled to overflowing with people—families, friends, lovers—all on their way to Rond Point du Prado. As he squeezed in between two men on the lower step, he thought briefly of Nathalie and a wave of guilt washed over him. Usually the trolley cars were quiet—all one heard was the crackling of the wires overhead and the flat clanging of the bell as the passengers ignored each other and rode silently, staring out the window or straight ahead—but tonight there was the sound of many voices, much shouting and laughter, as the crowd anticipated the thrills of the Wild West show. Charging Elk himself quickly overcame his guilt as the trolley started with a slight jerk, then lumbered along the smooth rails in the street. He remembered the first time he and Nathalie had dared to board one of these trolleys, the mixture of fear and excitement as they climbed aboard. And when the trolley started, they held each other's hand like children, listening to the frightful crackle of electricity above them, marveling at the ability of the car to move all by itself without the big engine. That had been ten or eleven moons ago but he still felt the wonder at such a miracle. And tonight he might find another miracle. He smiled at a man who was looking up at him, almost as though he recognized Charging Elk. But the man may have noticed the long hair flowing from beneath the wool cap, the slanting eyes and prominent cheekbones. There were now posters all over town.

Charging Elk was almost overcome by the familiarity of the scene around him: the large dirt arena surrounded by bleachers under the white peaked awnings that always looked to him from a distance like a snowy mountain range; the scenery painted on the canvas backdrop that spanned the entirety of the back of the arena; the many spotlights on the poles that lit up the whole area like daylight; and the distant hum of the portable generators. Even the settlers' cabin in the far corner looked exactly like the one when he had been in the show. And the tipi, with its drymeat racks and the small fire burning in front of it, in the other corner! An Indian woman with a baby on her back was stirring something in a pot hanging from a tripod over the fire. Suddenly his mind raced back to those days when he was a small child, an Oglala with Crazy Horse's band, living out on the buffalo ranges when times were good. Living with his mother and father and his sister and brother. Living with his people in a village of such tipis. Playing with his friends, eating real meat, listening to the stories of the elders. The lights on the poles began to twinkle, and when he looked at them he saw indistinct silver rays in all directions and he realized that his eyes were filled with tears.

Then he heard the music he had heard hundreds of times before, and a section of the backdrop swung open and the Cowboy Band came out on their white horses, playing their instruments, their horses obediently marching in formation until they reached the far side of the backdrop. That music, announcing the grand entry, had always filled his heart with excitement.

And he recognized the high notes of a bugle over the music, an urgent call, and suddenly a rider on a large white horse galloped into the arena, circled it at full speed, then came to a stop before the center of the grandstand. The horse bowed and the rider took off his hat and held it in the air. Charging Elk felt his throat tighten as he looked at the familiar figure of Pahuska, the long hair, now snow-white and thinning on top, the white goatee and mustache, the fringed and beaded buckskin tunic, the thigh boots. The face, once so chiseled and noble, was now gaunt and lined, but Pahuska held his head high as he trotted back and forth before the shouting, clapping audience.

Then the music changed to a sort of drumming beat, the horns imitating a Lakota song that Charging Elk knew well. And the gate swung open again and a file of Indians on horseback fanned out against the backdrop, in three rows, then moved forward in unison. Many of them wore headdresses spread out over the horses' rumps; some carried lances and feathered coupsticks, others guns and bows. Some of the young men, in spite of the chill, were shirtless, wearing only leggings, feathers in their hair, face paint, and brass bands around their biceps.

Charging Elk almost became sick with the familiarity of the moment. It was a sight he thought he would never see again, and he almost saw himself among the young men. How many times had he ridden in the grand entry in just their place? He knew the pride the young men felt as they trotted forward, faces immobile, but excited to be performing before the large audience. He also knew they would be looking for attractive women in the crowd, so they could focus their performance on them even though they would never acknowledge them. And he could almost feel the warm bodies of the ponies between their legs.

Then another thought came to him, a thought which surprised him because it hadn't come to him until just this moment: It was exactly sixteen winters ago, less a moon, that he had become ill and fallen from his horse in this very arena. That simple, lone accident had changed his life forever.

Charging Elk slumped back in stunned silence as he watched the other riders—the cowboys, the soldiers, the vaqueros, and other men in uniforms he didn't recognize—form up to join the Indians and Buffalo Bill. Then he watched two riders, an Indian and a soldier, circle the arena around the assembled entourage with just enough pace so that the American and French flags snapped out fully over their heads. Finally they came to a halt on either side of Buffalo Bill. All of the people around him stood, and so he stood. He laced his hand over his heart but he barely heard the Cowboy Band play the anthems of the two countries.

The Indian acts were familiar to Charging Elk—the attack on the settlers' cabin, the attempted attack on the Pony Express rider, the chasing of the Deadwood stage, the hunting of the buffalo, and finally the killing of Custer and his men. Only the last act was new to Charging Elk—Pahuska played a scout for the army and ended up going into a patch of fake trees and brush, where he was ambushed by an Indian. After hand-to-hand combat, Buffalo Bill drew his knife and ran it through the Indian's heart. Then he knelt over the prone Indian, and after much busywork in the bushes, held up the bloody scalp of the Indian. The announcer said, in French, "The first scalp for Custer!" And the audience cheered and stamped their feet, a rhythmic drumming that shook the stands. Charging Elk remembered the real fight with Custer on the Greasy Grass, the terror that ran through the village as the soldiers attacked. He had been a boy of ten winters then and had hidden with his mother and brother and sister in the cottonwoods along the creek, listening to the popping of the rifles and watching the big cloud of dust kicked up by the hundreds of horses drift over the village. Even now he could see that cloud of dust that blotted out the sun.

Charging Elk had been looking for Indians that were about his age, but there were very few. Most were far too young to have been in the show in 1889. Even though the acts were familiar, the riders were not. The announcer had said that the chief of the Indians was Queue de Fer, but he had not heard of an Iron Tail among any of the Lakota bands in his previous life.

Charging Elk watched the other acts — Buffalo Bill shooting glass balls out of the air, the trick riding of the cowboys, the elaborate synchronized maneuvers of the various military groups, a young woman who held a mirror before her eyes and shot a cigarette out of the mouth of a man behind her, and the vaquero in the shiny suit and big, decorated hat who performed lasso tricks. And when the entire company took the arena for the grand finale, he again watched the Indians trot their ponies by the grandstand, this time close enough so that he could see each face distinctly. But out of the whole troupe, the only person he recognized was Buffalo Bill.

And as he watched the old man lead the troupe out of the arena, a thought came to him: Would Pahuska recognize him? He had been hoping all along that some of the Lakotas would recognize him, but he hadn't thought of Buffalo Bill. He remembered the night in Paris that Black Elk had come to the Indian village behind the arena, how he was welcomed and feted, how Buffalo Bill had tried to get him to join the show again. Charging Elk, in spite of his exhaustion from the intensity with which he had watched the show, felt his heart suddenly beat strong again. Buffalo Bill had recognized him once before, on a train platform somewhere between here and Paris. He had complimented Charging Elk for being a "wild" Indian. Would Pahuska recognize him now? He was certainly not that wild Indian from the Stronghold anymore. He was no longer young and reckless. He had not seen any of his people for many years — except in his bad dream. The fleeting memory of the dream triggered another thought: Most of the Indians he had watched were Lakotas—Oglalas, Hunkpapas, Brulés—and they were alive. He had seen them. His dream had been wrong.

Since that dream, he had not really thought of going home because there would be no one there. The dream had shown them sprawled among the rocks under the cliff, pitiful and lifeless. And the words above the wind—*You are my only son*—meant something else. But what? Charging Elk realized now that his isolation had been more complete than he had ever imagined. If he had been at the Stronghold, Bird Tail, the old *wicasa wakan*, would have listened to him, smoked awhile, then told him what the dream meant. Even more—and the thought struck him like a lightning bolt—Wakan Tanka was not here in this land, had never been here! All those times he had prayed to the Great Mystery had been futile. He might as well have been praying to a stone or the silver timepiece in his breast pocket.

Charging Elk was so lost in these thoughts that he didn't notice that the grandstand, except for a few stragglers, was now empty. But even such discoveries—instead of causing his heart to fall down in despair—gave him a kind of hope, and that hope blackened his heart with the wickedness of it.

Charging Elk paid fifty centimes to wander around the avenue of sideshows. He wanted to give the Indians time to put away their horses, to change into warmer clothes, to settle down for a smoke or a card game. He knew how tiring the day-after-day, night-after-night performances could be. He knew that if you were injured—spraining an ankle from jumping off a horse, hurting your back from a fall or breaking a rib—it would take days, even weeks, to fully recover. But because they were proud, the young men would ride with these injuries. Charging Elk himself rode when he could barely get on his horse because of the flu, and that had been his downfall. He could have taken the night or even a couple of days off, but pride had won out over judgment. And where had it gotten him?

Charging Elk walked unseeing by the various tents of the sideshows. The barkers were enticing the crowds to come in and see the performers, the freaks. On a small stage, a female contortionist was walking around on her hands, her ankles locked behind her neck. On another, a giant in a white singlet and tights was holding a tiny woman in a sequined top and tutu. She had a pretty, round face framed by tight auburn curls. A man dressed only in shorts stood watching them, shivering in the cold November night. His head was shaved and his body, from top to bottom, was a bright shade of blue. But Charging Elk, even though he glanced at them, did not see. The images in his mind, the Indians in the show, his homeland, the Stronghold, his lonely nights of wandering around Marseille, Marie and Breteuil, the years in prison, were all that occupied him. He had been a stranger all along in this country and had paid the price for his ignorance. Even now he walked on the edge of the crowds, as solitary as he had always been.

Then he found himself at the far end of the avenue of sideshows. He walked out the gate and stood and rolled a cigarette. In the distance, he could see the bulk of Notre Dame de la Garde on its high, craggy hill. It was lit with electric spotlights.

Charging Elk called out a greeting before the first lodge he found that was lit from within.

"All my relatives!" he called in Lakota. "I am Charging Elk and I come to talk with you!"

After a minute, a head appeared, fingers holding the flap closed around it.

"I am Lakota. Oglala. But I have been gone a long time."

The head was that of a young man. He looked Charging Elk up and down, then said, "What do you want?"

Charging Elk was taken aback by the English tongue. "Are you Lakota?"

The young face looked at him blankly, neither friendly nor un-friendly.

"Lakota?"

The young man stepped out of the lodge. He was almost as tall as Charging Elk, but thinner. He pointed to a group of tipis across the circle. "Lakota," he said.

Charging Elk thanked him, but the youth had ducked back into the lodge without a word. He heard other voices inside and guessed that he had interrupted a card game.

He walked across the circle and announced himself before one of the larger tipis, taking in the layout of the village as he waited. It could have been the village of sixteen years ago. Several *wasichus* were wandering around but not like the crowds that came after the afternoon performances. He didn't see any Indians.

The flap opened and a man stepped out. He was dressed in wool pants and a canvas shirt. He had a blanket over his shoulders. His face was narrow, with wide cheekbones and a mouth that arced up at the corners, which gave his face an almost leering quality. He looked to be just short of thirty winters.

"*Hoka hey!* I am Charging Elk, son of Scrub, the shirtwearer, and Doubles Back Woman. Oglala people. I have been gone a long time."

The man looked at him a little longer than was necessary. Charging Elk could tell he was seeing the dark suit, the high, white collar, the necktie, the topcoat. The eyes seemed both confused and suspicious.

"I came to this country with the show in 1889." Charging Elk wondered if the man understood the *wasichu* way of counting win-ters. It didn't occur to him that he had given the date in French. But he had left Pine Ridge before the winter count could be made for

1889, so he didn't know the Lakota year. "Sixteen winters ago I came. With Pahuska and Rocky Bear."

"Ah," the man said. "I am Andrew Little Ring. Come in." And he stood aside with a disbelieving look to let the big dark man pass.

Charging Elk took off his cap and entered the lodge, and it was warm. A small stove sat in the middle where the fire pit would be. A stack of coal was piled beside it. He greeted a woman who was nursing a baby. And a young man, who was lying against a back-rest, smoking a cigarette. He was still wearing the leggings and moccasins from the show and was bare-chested beneath the blan-ket over his shoulders. A small leather pouch hung from his neck.

Little Ring indicated a stool near the young man's feet. Then he went around the stove to sit beside the woman. "This is my wife, Sarah. And that one"—he indicated the young man—"is my nephew, Joseph."

Charging Elk smiled at each, then sat down on the stool and un-buttoned his topcoat. "Do you know my father and mother?" he said. He knew it was impolite to begin in such a way, and he hadn't planned to, but he had been anxious to know the fate of his parents for many years. The question just came out.

The woman set the infant on a doubled-up quilt, pulled her blouse down, and poured a cup of coffee from a pot that rested on the stove. She walked around and handed the cup to Charging Elk. He thanked her and took a sip. He would have liked some sugar but he didn't see any.

Andrew Little Ring sat with the peculiar grin creasing the lower half of his face. He was looking at Charging Elk as though trying to remember him or deciding whether to trust him. Finally, he said, "Double Strike Woman still lives at Pine Ridge Agency. She has her little cabin. She is well." Then he was silent again.

Charging Elk suddenly felt his whole body go limp. He set down the coffee cup and fixed his eyes on the black stove. He wished it were an open fire. He wanted to look into an open fire, as he had so often so many years ago. "My father?"

The man looked at his wife, who looked down at the infant. "He died three winters ago. Influenza. I didn't know him well, but there was a big ceremony at the church, then at the community hall. Everybody went."

Charging Elk sat, looking at the smoke curling up toward the smoke hole from the short pipe of the stove. He was trying to see his father's face.

"He was an important man, your father—a shirtwearer." This time it was the young man, Joseph, who spoke. "You should have been home for him."

Charging Elk looked at him for a moment, until the young man looked away. "You are right, Joseph," he said. "I failed him—and my mother. For a long time I have thought only of myself."

"Your mother is still there. She lives alone, but many people look in on her. I'll bet she would like to see you there."

"How is it you have been away from the reservation all this time, Charging Elk? What did you do all these years? I can see you are still one of us, yet you are different."

Charging Elk looked back at Andrew Little Ring. He looked at the Lakota face, the dark skin, the eyes so like his own. He looked at the woman, Sarah. She wore her hair in long braids, in a way that he hadn't seen for a long time. Her face was round and smooth and the color of pecans. He looked at her and realized how much he had missed being with his own people.

"Do you live here in this town?"

The voice brought him back, and he felt the warmth of the stove, the small draft on his backside. "Yes. For sixteen years. I work here, loading and unloading the big boats."

"But why would you stay here? Why stay here now? Why not go home?"

Charging Elk laughed at the innocence of such a question. In the old days it was a question he would have asked of a stranger a long time gone from home. But now he didn't know how to answer. He would have to tell the whole story or nothing. So he lied: "I was curious to see how the *wasichus* lived over here—so I stayed. I have many friends here. They take me into their lodges and give me good things to eat and drink. They are very strong for me."

"Do you speak the Frenchmen's tongue?"

"Yes. We talk of many things—Teddy Roosevelt, New York." Charging Elk spoke fast, but he was uncomfortable with his lies. "And do you speak American?"

"Yes. We have all been to school, even Sarah. Young Joseph here went away to school. Everybody goes away to school now."

Charging Elk smiled at Joseph, who was sitting on a rug close to him. "Did they teach you to be smart like your grandfathers?"

Joseph looked up at Charging Elk, his eyes suddenly cold. "They taught me many things—how to cut off my hair, how to wear clothes just like them, how to use my knife and fork properly, how to say 'Yes, sir, yes, ma'am.' Oh yes, they taught me many things so that I could be smart—just like them." He snorted loudly, a sound of disgust that made Charging Elk aware of his own *wasichu* clothes.

"You see—they treated Joseph and the other children very badly. They were forbidden to speak Lakota, even to each other. If they made a prayer to Wakan Tanka at night, they were put in a dark room by themselves. If they sang one of our songs, they were beaten." Andrew Little Ring sighed. "Joseph went to the boarding school for eight years. Every summer we had to catch him up on Lakota—then his last two years they wouldn't let him come home. They said he was still stuck in the old ways."

"It is the same at home." Sarah was now rocking the infant in her arms. She spoke softly but bluntly. "We are forbidden to speak our language. We are forbidden to practice our ceremonies. If we do, they threaten to cut off our rations. Many people who didn't believe them now go hungry. There are many hungry people who beg at the agency."

"Are things so bad for our people?" Charging Elk couldn't believe what he was hearing. He remembered the white teacher who had torn up his picture of the dead soldier on the Greasy Grass, who wouldn't allow the children to speak Lakota. But to forbid the grown-ups to speak Lakota, to perform the ceremonies—it was unthinkable. It was all they had left even when he was there. But even then things were changing. "I remember, many people went to the white church when I was there. But I didn't like it, so I ran away even though I was just a boy. I went out to the Stronghold with my *kola*, Strikes Plenty, where there were still some Oglalas who preferred to live like the old times. But it was hard to live that way. The winters were hard and there was never enough to eat. And now I wonder what became of them, of Strikes Plenty."

Joseph had been rolling a cigarette, but now he looked up with wide eyes. "You were a ghost dancer?"

All three of them were looking at him intently. "I don't know about this ghost dancer," he said. "You must tell me."

Andrew Little Ring looked confused. "You were at the Stronghold. That's where the Ghost Dance took place."

"Fifteen years ago, three of our men went out west to meet a prophet who said that if we performed the Ghost Dance all the white people would go away. He told them the buffalo would return and we could live in the old way—as though the *wasichus* had never existed, as though our misery was just a dream." Joseph lit the cigarette he had been stroking into a cylinder with his fingers.

"What happened?" Charging Elk held his breath. He was remembering.

Joseph blew some smoke into the air above the stove. "It ended in sadness. They killed Sitting Bull, the Hunkpapa chief, up north. Then they killed a whole band of Minneconjous on Wounded Knee Creek. What was it, Uncle—how many were killed?"

But it was Sarah who answered. "Nearly two hundred—men, women, and children. Those people were sick and starving. They were dressed in rags. Now they are all buried in one grave overlooking Wounded Knee Creek. The government didn't have the decency to let their relatives have them, to give them proper burials."

Charging Elk looked away from Sarah. In the dim light of an oil lantern hanging from a lodgepole, he had seen a tear running down her cheek. Andrew held her hand, looking down at it. Joseph pulled his blanket higher over his naked shoulders, his cigarette dangling from his lips. The lodge was quiet enough to hear some voices speaking French outside. The language that he had finally learned sounded strange to his ears.

"I have seen all this in two dreams," Charging Elk said softly, breaking the glum silence. "In one dream I saw people heading up to the Stronghold. Some were riding horses, others were in travois, and many more were walking. I was coming back from somewhere, so I rode up among them. On top I first heard drumming and singing that was unfamiliar to me. And when I looked I saw many people and they were dancing hard, as though their feet were on fire. Some just jumped in one place, up and down. They were singing and crying, some women wailed. Then they began to fall down. I didn't recognize any of this, but now I see they were performing this Ghost Dance. It made me uneasy to see such a display. But now I see it for what it was.

"In my other dream, I saw people lying at the bottom of a cliff among the boulders. Their bodies were bent and broken, but I could see that they were Lakotas. I cried for them. I was afraid that all my people were dead, so I tried to join them. I tried to jump off the cliff, but the wind pushed me back. Many times I tried to jump and many times the wind prevented me. And I heard a voice enter my head and it said, 'You are my only son.' And when I went back to my camp at the Stronghold there was nothing there — no people, no horses, no dogs, no lodges. There were no tipi rings, no fire pits, just the long grass that covered everything. It was as though the Lakota people had vanished from the earth."

Charging Elk smiled at Joseph. "But now I see I was wrong. I had no one to interpret my dreams for me. You are here. I saw many Lakotas in the arena tonight. And you tell me that we have survived, pitiful and powerless as we are. But it doesn't have to al-ways be this way. You three young ones fill my heart with your strength. And I see the little one asleep in Sarah's arms. We will go on because we are strong people, we Lakotas."

Joseph smiled for the first time, uncertainly but perhaps a little hopefully. "I don't know — maybe."

Charging Elk squeezed his shoulder, then stood up, smoothing his topcoat into place, buttoning it. Joseph too got to his feet and stood face to face with the big man. Although he was slender, his shoulders were wide and his bare chest was almost a man's. His long arms with the brass bands around his biceps held the blanket in place. He was as tall as Charging Elk, and his loose hair fell to the small of his back.

"Where are you going?"

"Home," said Charging Elk. He walked around the stove and knelt before Sarah. "What is the infant's name?"

"Rose."

He held out his hand and the baby wrapped her tiny brown fin-gers over one of his. She looked up at him. Her brown eyes were alert and curious.

"That's a good name, one that will always bring you happiness when you say it."

He stood and walked to the entrance. Andrew and Joseph were

standing just to the side. Charging Elk clasped hands with Andrew. "Thank you for the warmth of your lodge. You have made a poor stranger feel as though a part of him which had been missing for many years has come home."

Andrew touched Charging Elk's arm lightly. The leering grin was there but his eyes were warm and dark. "You are not a stranger. You are Lakota, wherever you might go. You are one of us always."

Charging Elk turned to Joseph, but the young man said, "I will walk you to the edge of camp."

The two men walked side by side in silence through the quiet camp. Most of the lights in the lodges had been extinguished, but the sky above was lit by a three-quarter moon, throwing shadows before the men. Charging Elk looked around, wanting to remember what the camp looked like—the dozen lodges, the big fire pit in the middle of the circle. There were no drymeat racks, no dogs, no horses, no people walking about, but in his mind he was a boy of ten winters and the camp was pitched on the banks of the Greasy Grass. And although the soldiers were already looking for them, it had been a joyful camp, relatives coming together, friends meeting friends. It had been the last joyful camp of the Lakotas and of his youth. The Oglalas had come in to Fort Robinson less than a year later.

Joseph stopped him just before they reached the path that led to the show grounds. "I have been thinking—that voice, the one in your dream—" He hesitated, the way a youth does before telling of an important thing. "That voice belonged to your mother. She is alone now." He hesitated again, not looking at Charging Elk but at the base of a knobby plane tree flanking the path. "She was telling you to come home. She needs you now."

Charging Elk also looked away. He had come for this moment, but now that it had, he felt his heart sink. "I can't," he said.

Suddenly Joseph looked at him, and his eyes were bright in the moonlight. "You can come with us. Tomorrow is the last show of the season. We're going home for the winter. Come with us!"

"It isn't so easy. . . ."

"Come back tomorrow. We can talk with Buffalo Bill. He will be glad to see you. He always treats us well."

Charging Elk turned toward the path.

"But what about your mother? She cries for you."

Charging Elk stopped. He could almost hear Joseph's heart beating in his own chest. He saw his mother in the kitchen, cooking meat for him and Strikes Plenty. He saw her on the travois horse, the tears, as they waited to descend into the valley of Fort Robinson. Then he heard the singing, all of the people singing. "She will be all right," he said. "She will be better off without me. By now, she thinks I am dead for sixteen years. Let her remember me with a loving heart."

"But she would be happy. . . ."

Charging Elk turned on the path in the shadow of the plane tree. "This is my home now, Joseph. I have a wife. Soon I will have a child, the Moon of Frost in the Tipi." Charging Elk stopped as he realized how improbable this must have sounded to Joseph. Then he said, in a wistful voice, "I am not the young man who came to this country so long ago. I was just about your age and I thought of it all as a great adventure. But now here I am, a man of thirty-seven winters. I load and unload ships. I speak the language of these people. My wife is one of them and my heart is her heart. She is my life now and soon we will have another life and the same heart will sing in all of us." Charging Elk walked the few paces back to where Joseph stood. He hugged him, feeling the strength in the youthful body. Then he stepped back, suddenly shy at such a gesture.

Joseph said, "Wait," and he reached behind his head and his fingers became busy. Then he was holding the pouch that had hung around his neck in his hand. "It is only a stone. But it came from Paha Sapa. Perhaps one day it will bring you back to us." He put the pouch in Charging Elk's hand and turned back to his lodge.

Charging Elk watched him. Then he called out. "Joseph!"

The young man stopped.

"My father—did he ride a fine horse—before he became ill?"

The silence that followed was so long Charging Elk wondered if Joseph had heard him. Then he heard the words that filled his heart.

"He rode a tall red horse with a good mouth and eyes that looked far ahead. None of the horses in this show could compare with him."

Charging Elk turned and walked up the path. He walked past the sideshows, dark now, and the empty arena. The white, many-pointed awnings over the bleachers looked like distant mountains. He walked away from the show grounds. It was late now and the trolleys wouldn't be running, but he didn't mind. He needed to walk and the Moon of the Falling Leaves would light his way.

ACKNOWLEDGMENTS

From Montana to Marseille is a long jump and I never would have made it without the generosity and encouragement of a large number of people, both in this country and in France.

I would like to thank my longtime editor and friend, Gerry Howard, for encouraging me to write this story and for steering me back on course when I started listing. And I would like to thank my dear agent, Elaine Markson, for her perceptive reading, suggestions and, perhaps more importantly, faith and belief. I would also like to thank Sally Wofford-Girand and Elizabeth Clementson, Elaine's associates, for all their help and encouragement. And thanks to Mary Kling and Maggie Doyle, my French agents, for their help and hospitality at more than a few lunches over the years.

Thanks also to Liliane de Kermadec, and Thierry and Patricia Mouthiez for providing me with information on the court and prison systems of turn-of-the-century France. I also thank Nelcya

Delanoë and Joelle Rostkowski for their writings and conversations concerning Indians in France.

Thanks to my translator and friend, Michel Lederer, for providing prize-winning translations of my novels. And many thanks to Hélène Fournier and Jacqueline Lederer, dear friends, for their warm generosity and hospitality to my wife, Lois, and me. And thanks and love to Ripley Hugo, for her perspicacious reading of this novel in manuscript form, as well as the others I have written.

I would especially like to thank my editor at Albin Michel, Francis Geffard, for believing that my books could find an audience in France. He has done more to publish and promote the writings of American Indians and western Americans than any other soul in France. He is a treasure and a good friend. And thanks to his boss, Tony Cartano, for giving him the green light.

Thanks doesn't seem quite adequate when it comes to my wife, Lois. She has not only stood beside me, offering encouragement and consolation by turn, but she has taken a very active role in my writing, from reading chapters, to providing me with research books, to translating. A night on the town will have to do.

And finally, I would like to thank Pierre Falaise, without whom this book would not have been written. He not only gave me the germ of the story one hot afternoon over beers after a book-signing, but he was of great assistance during subsequent research trips to Marseille—from introducing Lois and me to other Marseillais who had interesting stories to tell, to taking us around to pertinent locations, to xeroxing newspaper articles about the Wild West shows of 1889 and 1905, to providing me with the official French program of the show and Featherman's death certificate. I have taken liberties, dear friend, but I hope you will find this book true to the spirit.

James Welch